THE GHOST OF CANDICE FREEMAN

DAVE GARTY

This book is a work of fiction. Names, characters, places and incidents are creations of the author's imagination or have been used fictitiously. Any resemblance to persons, whether living or dead, is coincidental.

Copyright © 2018 Dave Garty

All rights reserved

Cover photograph by Katalinks © 123RF
Cover design by Dave Garty
My thanks to Caroline Eagle for formatting the cover artwork

For Lee and Katie

Author's note

The character Candice Freeman appeared in a novel I wrote in 2015 called *The Ghost of Harry Black*. In the first edition of that book her profession was an author. After publication it came to my attention there were similarities with a character devised by an author in a novel published a number of years before. I made the decision to alter my character and changed her profession to that of an actress. I also changed the names of two of the supporting characters, thus Martha Braithwaite became Emily Braithwaite and Emily Blunt became Prudence Blunt. The plot and storyline remained largely unaffected and an updated version of *The Ghost of Harry Black* was published as a second edition. I mention this because in the story that follows there are references to Candice's past life as an actress which may have left you scratching your head if you knew her as an author. Whether you read the first book or not I hope you enjoy this one.

Dave Garty.

Death isn't the end. It's the beginning.

One

It had rained heavily overnight. Three days of hot, humid weather had made it a pleasant spring bank holiday weekend but when darkness fell on the Monday it led to a thunderstorm of biblical proportions.

The troubled night gave way to a peaceful morning in the village of Cloverdale St Mary. The sun had taken up residence in a clear blue sky and pools of water yet to dry provided the only evidence of a storm that had disturbed the sleep of many. The lightening that accompanied it had been quite a spectacle but at 4:00 a.m. it wasn't appreciated by those who had to get up early for work.

Harry Black had watched the storm throughout. He liked violent weather, especially at night. It appealed to his sense of the dramatic. Now, gazing through the lounge window of Meadow Cottage, he turned his thoughts to the aftermath and raised a concern he had raised a number of times before. "That grass needs cutting."

"What?" a disinterested voice came from behind him.

"Samantha is letting the grass get too long. It's meant to be a lawn. What we have out there could be mistaken for a jungle."

Candice Freeman turned another page of her TV guide. Unlike Harry she wasn't concerned about the lawn and answered without raising her head. "Sam isn't the kind of girl to let the grass grow beneath her feet."

"It isn't growing beneath her feet. It's growing in my front garden," Harry protested.

"Sam's front garden. Meadow Cottage belongs to her now."

"Allow me to correct you. It belongs to Emily who rents it to Samantha on the understanding that she looks after the place and breaks out the lawnmower every now and then. That grass hasn't been cut since your funeral nearly a year ago."

"That's an exaggeration. It was cut last week."

"She got a barber to do it with a pair of scissors, did she? Whoever it was they didn't take much off the top."

Candice sighed and turned another page of her TV guide. Harry Black in complaining mode was hard work and she didn't feel inclined to engage in a debate about gardens and barbers who cut lawns as a sideline.

"One of my films is on TV tonight," she said, changing the subject.

"Which one?"

"Killing Asia."

This gave Harry something else to moan about.

"Not again? That film is always on."

"It's become a modern-day classic," Candice said proudly.

"It's all right if you like that sort of thing."

She noted his unenthusiastic response and defended what critics and film-goers considered to be her finest work. There had been many before it and more would have followed had it not been for her untimely death in a plane crash in 2016. Since then, it was fair to say, work for one of the best known and highest paid actresses in the world had dried up but Candice Freeman remained an A-list celebrity even in death and her films would be shown for years to come.

"It won me a fourth Oscar," she told Harry.

"Which was awarded posthumously."

"Maybe so but they all count."

"I prefer The Diamond Cutter."

"Why?" Candice asked, already knowing the answer.

"You take your clothes off a lot in that one."

She rolled her eyes and turned her attention back to the TV guide. "You missed your vocation, Harry. You should have been a reviewer."

"I should have been a locksmith. I assume most of that film was a closed set."

"There wasn't that much nudity."

"You came down with a cold for three weeks afterwards."

Candice joined him at the window in the hope of veering him away from a film that saw the leading actors strip so often even the cameramen were down to their socks. "That grass is a bit long, isn't it?"

Harry harrumphed in reply. The truth was he didn't feel as comfortable as Candice did about Samantha Copeland renting what had once been his cottage.

Following his death in 2009 it was sold several times but Harry regarded each new owner as a trespasser and saw them off like a hungry lion chasing antelope across the African Serengeti. There was no telling what might have happened if he had caught one. His haunting with malice days came to an end when Candice bought the cottage. She refused to be intimidated by the ghost of Harry Black and he allowed her to stay, although in all honesty he had little choice in the matter.

Candice was a woman accustomed to living life in the fast lane but big cities that suffocated in noise and traffic fumes had lost their appeal so she moved to the countryside in a bid to put down roots and live at a more sedate pace. Her career continued to take her all over the world but she needed a home, somewhere she felt comfortable, somewhere she felt she belonged. She found what she was looking for in Cloverdale St Mary, a quiet, unassuming village in Kent, but when she met Harry Black she found something she hadn't expected. She found someone to love and cherish, a spirit who loved her in return and would provide companionship for life and the rest of eternity.

The life should have been long and eternity the forever time that came after it but Candice died at the age of thirty-five and eternity became the here and now. The village was devastated by her death. In the short time she lived there she made many friends and was accepted by all. For them their loss was personal. The world mourned the passing of a great star but they had lost someone close to them.

Candice too found it difficult to adjust. The outpouring of grief made her want to announce her continued presence to people she loved and knew well but that could never be. There were rules for that sort of thing and as a ghost she was bound by them. All she could do was watch them mourn in the knowledge that the passage of time would make their loss easier to bear. They had family and friends to help them through the worst of it and Candice had Harry, the love of her life and her reason for not moving on.

"Are we going down the pub tonight?" he asked from nowhere.

"I wasn't planning to."

"Ron and Maggie are back from their holiday. I want to know if they left Greece of their own accord or were deported like last time."

Candice smiled. Reports of Ron and Maggie Jones being deported from Spain the previous August had been grossly exaggerated. Yes, they were involved in an altercation with a taxi driver who took them to the airport and tried to over-charge them but it wasn't the international incident that Harry liked to make it out to be.

"I'm sure nothing bad happened. We would have heard about it on the six o'clock news if it had," she said.

"The Government hush things up. When World War II started it was three months before anyone got to hear about it."

"I thought we were gonna watch my movie?"

"I've seen it."

"You can see it again."

"Killing Asia loses its shine after five thousand viewings."

Candice ignored him and drifted away for a moment. She had grown accustomed to being dead, it allowed her to view life from a different perspective, but she missed the razzmatazz of show business and of the acting profession in particular. "It was a shame I couldn't attend the Oscars. I had a great speech worked out."

"If you had attended the Oscars you would have been talking to yourself. The audience would have run screaming from the building."

"I scrub up pretty well you know," she said, misunderstanding his response.

"I meant you were a ghost by then."

"Oh. Yeah, I guess it would have come as a shock."

"Not half as much as the shock I'll get if Sam ever mows that lawn."

Candice found herself in a place commonly referred to as square one and returned to the sofa and her TV guide. "I'm not going to the pub."

*

The car drove slowly along the high street. The two occupants eyed neat rows of thatched cottages to their left and right without drawing attention to themselves. Their leisurely pace didn't subtract a glance from passers-by. No one hurried through Cloverdale St Mary. It wasn't that sort of village. It turned off the main road and disappeared from view.

Emily Braithwaite was on her way to the butchers. A friend had taken her to Falworth earlier that morning to collect her pension and she planned to spend some of it on lamb chops for her evening meal. Emily didn't drive and was reliant on others to make the journey into town now the bus service had been cut.

After her shopping trip she was going to visit Harry and Candice. Emily was one of three people to know of their existence, Samantha Copeland and the Reverend Ian Dawson being the other two.

When Candice left Meadow Cottage to Emily what to do with it became the problem. She had her own cottage and didn't want to give it up, she loved it there and had no intention of moving, but a house with no one living in it would fall into disrepair so a plan of action was required. Four months after Candice died it was offered to Samantha on a rental basis. The timing couldn't have been better.

Samantha lived with her parents and was looking for a place of her own. She warmed to the idea the moment Emily put it to her but if she was to move into Meadow Cottage she would have to know about the other occupants. She was unaware that Candice was still there and mourned her passing like everyone else. Emily was worried about how she would react but her concerns proved to be unfounded.

Samantha was shocked to see Candice again but wasn't afraid. She had no reason to be. Candice was her friend and when shock gave way to acceptance she relished the prospect of continuing their friendship. Harry took a little getting used to but that came as no surprise to anyone.

What Samantha found difficult was keeping their existence a secret from her stepsister. Melanie Copeland thought the world of Candice and took her death harder than most. At the age of nine it was the first time she had experienced death and she struggled to come to terms with it. How could the pain of bereavement have been explained to someone so young? She still found it hard to accept that she would never see her again. Candice was the only real friend she had. It tore chunks out of Samantha that she couldn't tell her but there was no other way.

That aside it was the perfect arrangement. Part of the money Emily received in rent each month went towards the maintenance of the cottage and what was left was donated to a charity of Candice's choice. It suited everyone - or it would have if Samantha had mowed the lawn from time to time.

On the other side of the street a removals van was in the process of being unloaded and Emily stopped for a moment to watch. Someone unknown to them had moved to the village. The new owner of Brook Cottage was a man but that was all the locals knew. His arrival and everything about him was a mystery. Emily hoped to snatch a glimpse of him but only saw the removal men who were carrying a sofa that looked more expensive than all her furniture combined. Whoever the newcomer was he had an eye for the luxurious.

"Good morning, Emily. How are you today?" a familiar voice enquired.

"Oh, hello, Ian. I'm very well thank you."

The vicar nodded towards the van. "Have you met the new arrival?"

"No. Have you?"

"Not yet. I might pop over later. You know, offer a friendly hello and drum up some business for my services. The attendance figures have dropped recently."

"Yes, I noticed that. You must be losing your touch."

Ian grinned. "I'm not sure I had one to begin with. Ron and Maggie have returned from Greece. They got back this morning," he said, changing the subject.

Emily recalled a past conversation with Harry, similar to the one endured by Candice. "They weren't escorted to the airport by armed police then?"

"Not on this occasion," Ian replied.

Their attention turned to a man who appeared in the doorway of Brook Cottage. He was a short, rounded fellow in his mid sixties. A well-fitting tweed jacket and half-rimmed silver framed spectacles gave the appearance of an academic, a professor of economics or something equally highbrow. Emily wondered about him as she watched the new resident direct the removal men from the doorstep.

"That needs to go in the study. Please be careful, it's very delicate," she heard him say.

The removal men frowned at the unintentional implication that they were not to be trusted with fragile objects and carried a long wooden crate over the threshold. The man nodded at Emily and Ian and followed them inside.

"I wonder what that is," Emily said.

"It's long enough to be a coffin," Ian remarked.

They looked at one another nonplussed.

"Well, I should be getting on," the vicar finally said.

"Yes. Me too."

They parted company, both casting a nervous glance at the cottage. Ian's remark had been casual and made in fun but the more they thought about it the more unsettled they became.

As Emily walked to the butchers the car returned to the high street. It stopped outside the Coaching Inn. The occupants didn't get out. They studied the pub at length before driving on.

*

"A wooden crate you say?"

Emily felt herself shudder and shifted uncomfortably on the sofa in Meadow Cottage. "Yes. Ian said it resembled a coffin. Just thinking about it gives me the creeps."

Samantha was at work but Emily had a spare key and was free to come and go as she pleased. She often stopped by for afternoon tea with Harry and Candice. She always phoned Samantha first to make sure it was all right, it was her home and she didn't want to intrude, but Samantha had no objections to her going there. If she wanted privacy she wouldn't have lived with two ghosts.

"I think this warrants investigation," Harry said in his best Sherlock Holmes voice.

Candice rolled her eyes. "You guys are letting your imaginations run away with you. The man is moving house. He's gonna have boxes and crates."

"You didn't have a wooden crate as long as a coffin when you moved to the village," Emily said.

"A wooden crate with a dead body inside it," Harry

was quick to add.

"He told the removal men to be careful because it was delicate," Emily pointed out.

"That proves there is nothing to worry about," Candice replied. "Dead bodies aren't delicate, they can take a lot of rough treatment. I speak from personal experience. The coroner who carried out my post mortem should have been wearing boxing gloves."

Harry wasn't listening. He had been busy considering other possibilities. "There could be two bodies inside. They might be midgets."

Candice shook her head.

"You have to admit it's very strange," Emily said.

"Yeah. Who's gonna put stuff in a wooden crate when they move house?" Candice was forced to agree. "This has got murder written all over it."

"I think you should take this seriously," Emily replied, frowning at her.

"I am taking it seriously. It's you two I've got problems with."

"He could have three in there. Two midgets and one in body parts," Harry surmised.

"I rest my case," Candice said to Emily.

"Harry, you're not exactly helping," Emily told him.

"Two midgets, assorted body parts and a bloodstained axe," came a thoughtful response.

"You don't even know his name and you've got him down as a serial killer," Candice said, edging towards exasperation.

"I bet he's got a hacksaw in there too."

Candice felt a change of subject was called for and looked at Emily eagerly. "Are you watching my movie on TV tonight?"

"What film is it?"

"*Killing Asia.*"

"Again? It was on last week."

"It's a modern-day classic," Candice told her.

Emily didn't appear keen but took the positives out of it. "Well, at least you didn't come down with a cold afterwards."

Candice elected not to comment.

"Here's what we'll do," Harry said to Emily, having formed a plan of action regarding mass murderers recently moved to the village. "You break in after dark and I'll meet you there. We'll head straight for the study and open that crate."

"I'm not breaking into his cottage," Emily replied, horrified at the thought.

"He must be brought to justice," Harry insisted.

"Guys, he hasn't done anything wrong. His only crime is that he owns a wooden crate," Candice told them.

"With lots of dead midgets inside it," Harry replied.

"Harry, listen to yourself. You know I love you to bits but it must be said that on occasion what comes out of your mouth is total garbage."

"I resent that!"

"Maybe garbage isn't the right word," Candice said, giving it some thought. "Crap. That's a better one."

"If we don't do something about this everyone will be in wooden crates by the end of the week," he insisted.

"I wouldn't like that," Emily said.

Candice gave up. She saw no point in protesting the new arrival's innocence with Emily erring on the side of caution and Harry marching him off to the gallows. "It may not be so bad. He might put you in one with a golden retriever and a gerbil."

"Where do they come into it?" Harry asked.

"Why not? You've got him killing everything he can lay his hands on."

They heard the front door open. Samantha was home from work.

"Goodness, is that the time?" said Emily, looking at her watch. "I must be going."

"Thanks for stopping by, Em. It was crate to see you," Candice said.

"You may mock but the residents of this village are in danger," Harry retorted.

"Danger?" Samantha asked, entering the lounge.

"Yes," Harry replied. "How tall are you?"

"Five foot eight."

"You might last a couple of days then. Anything shorter and you wouldn't have made it to supper time."

Emily drained her teacup and stood up. Lunch was a faded memory and dinner hadn't been started yet. If she was destined to meet her maker she would rather have done so on a full stomach. "Well, I must be on my way. Those lamb chops won't cook themselves."

"If you're in a hurry I can drive you home," Samantha offered.

"No, that's all right, my dear. It's only a short walk."

"Don't walk past Brook Cottage," Harry warned her. "Someone your size wouldn't make it to seven o'clock."

Samantha was puzzled. She got the impression she had interrupted an important discussion that may have had serious repercussions for many. "Is there something going on that I should know about?"

"Yeah, a serial killer has moved to the village," Candice told her. "We know he's a murderer because he instructed the removal men to be careful with his belongings."

"Okay," Samantha said slowly. She wished she hadn't asked.

Emily picked up her bag and Samantha showed her out.

"How was your day?" Candice asked on her return.

"Yeah, it was good. You know, the usual."

"One of my films is on TV tonight."

"Which one?"

"*Killing Asia.*"

"Oh, nice."

There was a distinct lack of enthusiasm in Samantha's reply.

Candice resolved to phone the TV company in the morning to ensure it would never be shown again.

"I won't be able to watch it I'm afraid. I have a date," Samantha said with a smile.

"A date, huh? Anyone we know?" Candice asked.

"No. His name is Lewis. I met him in the Millstream last week. We've had lunch a couple of times and tonight he's taking me out to dinner."

"So technically this is the third date," Candice replied, grinning. "Do Harry and I have to make ourselves scarce when you come home?"

Harry wasn't grinning. He didn't like the idea of being forced out of his own cottage.

"I know I can rely on you for privacy," Samantha said.

Candice thought it best not to tell her that in the past Harry had been found wanting in that respect. The first time Samantha took a man home he would have spent the night standing at the foot of her bed watching if Candice hadn't dragged him away. At one point he had a

Thermos flask and sandwiches.

That the entire village would be wiped out within the next forty-eight hours left his thoughts and he looked at Samantha kindly.

"I have a question for you. What has four wheels, a blade and goes phut, phut, phut when you switch it on?"

"I have no idea," Samantha replied.

"I didn't think you did. Come with me to the garden shed. I'd like to introduce you to the lawnmower."

Candice shook her head again and picked up her TV guide.

Two

Maggie Jones handed a glass of sherry to Prudence Blunt in the Coaching Inn and shot her husband a sideways glance. Ron was trying to keep a low profile. It was best to in light of what had happened.

"Everything was going fine until he got involved," Maggie said.

"How long were you at the police station?" Miss Blunt asked her.

"Seven hours. That's why we came back a day late. We missed our flight because of it."

Miss Blunt looked at the landlord skulking at the end of the bar. He had the appearance of a man banished to Siberia at the time of the Tsars. He never thought his home would have turned into a Gulag.

"It was good of him to try to help. Many people would have walked away from someone in need," she said.

A glimmer of a smile crept across Ron's face in gratitude of Miss Blunt's comments.

"Punching a would-be thief is not something I would recommend however," she added.

The smile disappeared like a pleasant dream from which he was reluctant to wake.

"That's what the police said," Maggie replied. "They didn't charge him with assault but took their time over reaching their decision. I felt like a criminal myself being held at that police station." She looked at him again and scowled. "Berk."

"I was being a good Samaritan," Ron offered weakly. "I saw someone steal a man's wallet. The decent thing to do was to stop it from happening."

"By punching him," Maggie retorted. "A good Samaritan doesn't go in with all guns blazing. He says *'careful, mate, someone is stealing your wallet'* and leaves it to them."

"I stand by what I did," Ron said proudly.

"What did he do?" Emily asked, approaching the bar.

"He beat someone up before we left Corfu," Maggie told her. "Wine?"

"Yes please. Who did you beat up?"

"I didn't beat up anyone. I saw a pick-pocket steal a man's wallet at the airport and gave him a gentle tap on the chin to stop him," Ron said in his defence.

"A gentle tap that resulted in the pick-pocket losing two teeth and saw us detained at a police station for seven hours," Maggie said for the prosecution.

"Can't you leave any country quietly?" Emily asked him.

"Someone has to fight the injustice in this world," Ron replied.

"My hero," Maggie said falsely. She even fluttered her eyelashes. Then the scowl returned with a vengeance. "Berk."

She gave Emily a glass of wine, a Russian brand made in Minsk.

It was a throwback to the days when Candice lived in the village. She bought several boxes for her house warming party but Emily was the only person who liked it. Candice gave a box to her and donated what was left to Maggie and Ron to sell in the pub. When it was gone they ordered more just for Emily. She was a valued customer and nothing was too much trouble for her. Aside from that, as friends of Candice Freeman they received a healthy discount.

Emily was a gentle soul, a pleasant and kind-hearted woman who was loved by everyone and held in the highest regard. She never had a bad word to say about others and always saw the good in people. Candice warmed to her immediately but the same couldn't be said for her friend, Prudence Blunt.

Miss Blunt was the complete opposite. She was harsh and volatile, quick to judge and even quicker to condemn. She was a woman of impeccable moral values and expected everyone to meet the high standards she set. She and Candice got off to a terrible start. Miss Blunt regarded her as a brash, attention-seeking American, a super-rich megastar who had no right to live in a respectable village like Cloverdale St Mary. The two of them almost came to blows over it but in time Miss Blunt mellowed and they became close friends.

The depth of their friendship became clear to everyone when Candice died. Miss Blunt was greatly affected by her passing. Candice had brought out the best in her and people saw a more tolerant Prudence Blunt as a result but after her death she reverted to her former self. She was the Terror of Cloverdale St Mary again, the interfering busy-body who meddled in things that didn't concern her and made few friends because of it, the no-nonsense firebrand who insisted on having everything her own way.

One concession she made while Candice was alive that existed to the present day regarded the Coaching Inn. For a long time she refused to enter the building let alone drink there. Public houses were to be avoided. They were places of drunkenness and rowdy behaviour, a modern-day Sodom and Gomorrah that led people down the path of irresponsibility and over-indulgence. As a respected member of the community and champion of everything decent Miss Blunt refused to be a part of it but

Candice had other ideas. Within five months of arriving in the village she had her boozing with everyone else.

These days Miss Blunt popped in for the occasional sherry but nothing more than that. She made polite conversation with the locals but never stayed long. She felt uncomfortable there and made no attempt to disguise the look of disapproval that lived under her nose like an unpleasant smell.

No one knew that even now she cried herself to sleep every night, that the face she wore in public was different to the one she wore in private. They didn't know Prudence Blunt was angry because a woman who had come to mean so much to her had been snatched away suddenly and for no reason.

She and Emily moved to their usual table by the fireplace and Miss Blunt turned her thoughts to a busy day tomorrow.

"I am seeing Norman Grantley tomorrow morning," she said. "Do you want to come with me?"

"Who is Norman Grantley?" Emily asked, bemused.

Miss Blunt sighed. "The man who moved into Brook Cottage today. I do wish you would keep abreast with local events."

"How do you know his name?"

"I asked him."

"When?"

"When he arrived this morning. I saw his car and the removal van so I knocked on his door to arrange a formal meeting." Miss Blunt felt it was unnecessary to state the obvious and frowned to illustrate her dissatisfaction at having to. "It is no more than anyone else would have done."

Emily grinned. It was certainly no more than Prudence Blunt would have done. The poor man was in the process of moving in. He had boxes to unpack, a house to put in order, dead bodies to dispose of, yet there was Miss Blunt standing on his doorstep demanding an audience with him.

She remembered the last person she had vetted on their arrival in the village: one Candice Freeman. Emily had been present on that occasion and witnessed what was, essentially, the outbreak of World War III. Knowing that Prudence Mk II had reverted back to Prudence Mk 1 didn't fill her with confidence for a pleasant chat over tea and biscuits with Mr Grantley.

"You won't be too personal, will you?" she said.

"What is that supposed to mean?" Miss Blunt asked, raising her eyebrow.

"You've been known to get a bit carried away in the past."

"Carried away? I do not know what you are inferring by that remark."

"You accused Candice of being a drug addict."

"I did no such thing!"

What Miss Blunt didn't know was that Candice was sitting at the table with them. Harry too having gotten his way over going to the pub.

"Yeah you did. You hit me with everything you had, you bitch," she said grinning. Candice was able to smile about it now but at the time it was Armageddon.

"And you responded in kind," Harry said.

Emily knew they were present and grinned too.

"You can wipe that smirk off your face," Miss Blunt snapped.

"What time are you meeting him?" Emily asked.

"Nine o'clock sharp."

That came as no surprise. Miss Blunt always vetted

new arrivals at nine o'clock sharp. It was one of the reasons her meeting with Candice didn't go well. She forgot they were coming and hadn't even dressed when the doorbell rang. She opened the door to Miss Blunt barefoot and wearing a T-shirt that was just long enough to spare her blushes. She dressed soon after but it was too late. The damage had been done.

"Are you coming with me?" Miss Blunt asked again.

"I think you should," Harry said. "We need to get that crate open so we'll have evidence to take to the police."

"Yes, I'll come with you," Emily replied. "We can go to the police station afterwards."

"Why do we need to go to the police station?" Miss Blunt asked.

Emily realised her mistake and tried to repair. "Did I say police station? What I meant was we can go into Falworth to do a little shopping."

"I will not have time for shopping. I need to be at the riding school for eleven. Samantha and I are meeting the building contractor to discuss the stables extension."

Candice smiled. She was glad the Cross Drummond Equestrian Centre was doing well. This, more than anything, was what turned a hostile relationship with Miss Blunt into a friendly one.

"I will call for you at ten to nine," she told Emily. "Do try to be ready. You have developed an unerring talent for being late."

"Ten to nine. Yes, Prudence."

"And for God's sake make sure you're dressed," Candice said.

Emily couldn't help herself. She laughed.

"What is amusing you?" Miss Blunt asked.

"Nothing."

"People who laugh to themselves in public for no apparent reason run the risk of being put away," she was told.

Miss Blunt finished her sherry and rose from the table. "I will see you tomorrow. Have a pleasant evening."

"You too, Prudence."

Harry watched her go and clasped his hands under his chin. This was a time for action and the troops had to be rallied. "Right, here's what we'll do. Candice and I will get to Grantley's cottage for 8:45 and give it the once over. When you and Prudence arrive at nine manoeuvre the conversation to the dead midgets in the crate. If everything goes according to plan the police will be there by 9:15 and the village will be saved."

"I'm not gonna snoop around someone's home," Candice protested.

"You'll be acting in the best interests of the village."

"It's an evasion of privacy."

"Think of the lives you'll be saving," Harry insisted.

"Mouth, open, crap," was Candice's reply.

"We can't stand by and allow Grantley to murder everyone in their beds," Harry said.

Emily kept her voice down to ensure she wouldn't be overheard. Laughing to yourself in public was one thing, engaging in a full-blown conversation was another. "How am I supposed to manoeuvre the conversation to the crate?" she asked, not at all convinced about this.

"Tell him you want to see his dead midgets."

"I can't say that."

"Would you rather be murdered in your sleep?"

"If you ask me the whole thing is ridiculous," Candice said. "Okay, the guy has a wooden crate. Where's the harm in that? It doesn't make him a killer. He's just an ordinary guy with a wooden crate."

Harry wasn't listening. He had moved on to stage two of the plan and wanted to be sure it ran smoothly. "Have you got a gun?" he asked Emily. "You might need to protect yourself while you're waiting for the police to arrive."

"I have a pair of scissors that I keep in my sewing box."

"Take them."

Candice let out a heavy sigh. By the time they left the Coaching Inn at half past ten Harry had connected Grantley to the assassination of JFK, the St Valentine's Day Massacre and the sinking of the Titanic.

*

It didn't take Candice and Harry long to get home. They simply faded from Emily's view in the pub and reappeared a second later in the attic room they shared in Meadow Cottage. Most times they walked like everyone else but tonight they couldn't be bothered and took advantage of their ability to spirit themselves to wherever they wanted to go. It was a quick and easy way to get from A to B and saved on bus fares.

No sooner had they got there a knock came at the door and Samantha entered the room.

"I'm sorry to bother you but I need your help," she said.

She appeared anxious and on edge.

"What's wrong?" Candice asked.

"It's my date, Lewis. He's downstairs in the lounge."

Candice grinned. "I wouldn't have thought you'd need our help with that."

"No, you don't understand. He's turned weird on me. He produced a set of handcuffs and asked if I have any whipped cream."

"Whipped cream?" Harry asked.

"Or chocolate mousse. He doesn't have a preference. As long as it's dairy. I wondered if you could get rid of him. I've asked him to leave but he won't."

"He's refusing to go?" Candice asked her.

"Not exactly, he's putting it off. He just says *'let's have another drink'* while twirling the handcuffs around his finger. I think he's a bit kinky."

"You think?" Candice said alarmed. "Harry, go downstairs and dispatch him."

"I'm more than happy to assist but in return I want you to mow the lawn."

"I'm not mowing the lawn," Candice replied.

"I was talking to Sam."

"At this time of night?" Samantha asked.

"Tomorrow will do."

"Harry, that's blackmail. Sam is in a fix and needs our help," Candice said.

"That lawn won't mow itself," Harry persisted.

Candice narrowed her eyes at him. There was a time and place for gardening and this wasn't it. "I'm sure Sam will mow the lawn when she's good and ready. Go downstairs and see the weirdo off the premises."

Harry conceded and raised his hands in a calming gesture. The truth was he liked to scare people but Candice took a dim view of it and he couldn't indulge as much as he used to. To be given permission to let himself loose on an unsuspecting public was music to his ears. "Okay, consider it done. I won't be long."

He left the room.

Candice looked at the clock on the wall and began to count down. "Three, two, one..."

A loud piercing scream tore through the cottage.

"There it is," Candice said.

A moment later they heard the front door cannon off the wall and Samantha's unwelcome guest was gone.

Harry returned to the room looking very pleased with himself. "You never lose it," he proudly boasted.

"Did he take the handcuffs with him?" Candice asked.

"Yes, but he left his underpants. I said we would post them on."

"Thank you, Mr Black," Samantha said.

She always addressed him by his surname. He had told her not to many times but she did so out of respect.

"Would you like some company for a while?" Candice asked.

"No, I'll be all right. I think I'll go to bed. I should have spent a quiet evening in and watched your film."

"It is a modern-day classic," Harry said.

Candice pulled a face at him in fun.

"Well, thanks again. Goodnight."

"Goodnight, Sam."

"I'll look out the instruction manual for the lawnmower," Harry called after her as she walked along the landing to her room.

He joined Candice on the sofa and met her smile unexpectedly. "What are you grinning about?"

"You never cease to amaze me, Harry. What you did for Sam was really nice."

"I don't think Lewis enjoyed it."

"What guise did you use from your vast repertoire?"

"Number twelve."

Candice was hesitant and looked concerned. "Is that the one where you..."

"Yeah."

She winced. "He'll need counselling after that."

"I love you."

"Where did that come from?" she asked, surprised.

"I can tell you I love you, can't I?"

"Yeah, but I always took it as a given."

They were silent for a moment.

"This is where you say you love me," Harry prompted.

"Is it?"

"Yes."

Another passage of silence followed.

"Well go on then."

"Oh, you want me to say it now?"

Harry sighed. He wished he hadn't started this. Romance had never been his strongest point. "If it's not too much trouble."

Candice shrugged her shoulders. "Okay. Love 'ya."

"Is that it?" he asked.

"I would have referred to you by name but I've forgotten what it is."

"Charming," he snorted, looking hurt.

Candice smiled and gazed into his eyes. Eternity lived there, love and trust, everything she had wanted during a life that exceeded all expectations but never realised its true potential until she met him. Death wasn't the end. It was the beginning. "I'm goofing around. I've never loved anyone the way I love you, Steve."

*

Norman Grantley stared at the wooden crate resting on two decorating trestles in his study. It was a temporary measure. Tomorrow he would move it to its final resting place; the basement that lay dark and silent beneath Brook Cottage. It was the main reason he bought the property. A basement was important to his work.

It was late and he was tired. Moving house was a test of endurance and he was ready for bed. He could have done without the early morning visit of Prudence Blunt but on the positive side there were things he needed to know about the village and she would have proved a useful tool for extracting information.

He walked to the door and looked at the crate again before switching off the light.

Three

Janet Copeland, wife of Martin and stepmother of Samantha, was sat at the kitchen table of her house located on the outskirts of Cloverdale St Mary. She was crying. Melanie had left for school and now Janet had the house to herself she could let go of her emotions.

A cup of tea stood on the table before her and in it she saw images of a life gone wrong. She deserved better. They all did. What gave the Spectre of Doom the right to crash open their door and wreck everything inside? Why did it happen to her? To them? To a family that knew only happiness but would soon be torn apart.

Head bowed, she cried like she had never cried before, the crumpled letter held tightly in her right hand.

She deserved better. They all did.

*

"I don't feel comfortable with this."

"You're a ghost. You can't feel anything," Harry said, urging Candice to follow him into the study of Brook Cottage. He saw the crate in front of them and pointed at it. "There it is. He's probably got hundreds of dead midgets in there."

Candice drew beside him and looked around the room anxiously. Where romance wasn't Harry's strongest point trespassing wasn't hers and she would rather have been anywhere than in Norman Grantley's home. "What if we're discovered?"

"Why are you whispering?"

"We're not meant to be here."

"How is he going to know? He might feel a drop in temperature but unless we formerly introduce ourselves he'll be none the wiser. Help me to prize the lid off."

"What!"

"We have to see what's inside."

"I thought Emily was doing that?"

"She'll be holding him at bay with her scissors until the police arrive. Didn't you listen to my plan at all?"

"You told her to manoeuvre the conversation towards the crate."

"To get a confession, not to see what's inside. That's our job."

"Couldn't we forget this and go to Florida?"

A ringing doorbell stopped him from answering.

"Good day, Mr Grantley. Thank you for receiving us," they heard Miss Blunt say as they returned to the hallway.

"Not at all. You're very welcome," Grantley replied, extending his hand in greeting.

"This is my friend, Emily Braithwaite."

"Delighted to meet you," he said, shaking her hand too. "Please, come in."

Emily cast a nervous glance at Candice and Harry and followed their host to the lounge.

"Take a seat," Grantley said, gesturing to the leather sofa Emily had admired the previous day. "Would you care for something to drink? Tea? Coffee?"

"Tea would be very nice. Thank you," Miss Blunt replied.

"Would you like a butterfly bun?"

Miss Blunt smiled. "You have done your homework,

Mr Grantley."

"I popped down to the village shop this morning and took the liberty of asking what they thought your preference would be. Mr Pearce told me you have a liking for butterfly buns. It is Mr Pearce, isn't it?"

"Yes, that is correct. William and Susan Pearce."

Candice clicked her fingers as a past mistake came to mind. "That's where I went wrong. I didn't do my homework."

"The chocolate digestives you slapped on a plate looked appetising," Harry replied.

Candice smiled and allowed herself to slip away for a moment. Almost everything enjoyed in life was denied to the dead but her passion for chocolate was her biggest loss. It was on a par with asking a drunk to forgo their last drink or expecting a fish to live out of water. "I liked chocolate digestives. They were my favourite." Her smile faded into wishful thought and she sighed. "I miss them."

"I know you do but we're here to unmask a murderer. Pay attention."

Grantley left the lounge to prepare the tea. He passed within two feet of Candice and Harry without realising it.

"He has some very nice things, doesn't he?" Emily said to Miss Blunt.

"He is clearly a man of taste," she replied, suitably impressed. Truth be told, she had formed a good impression of him the moment they met.

"I had taste too," Candice complained to Harry. "My framed print of the Twin Towers was the finest you could get but Pru hated it."

"Is this your way of paying attention?" he asked.

"I bet my tea pot is better than his," she muttered,

sounding child-like.

Grantley returned with the refreshments carried on a silver tray. The tea pot wouldn't have looked out of place in Buckingham Palace.

"You were saying?" Harry said.

Candice sulked in silence.

"Yours was made of tin."

Still she said nothing.

"And it had a dent in it."

"Oh, shut the hell up."

"I was just saying to Prudence. You have some very nice things, Mr Grantley," Emily said, watching him pour the tea.

"Please, call me Norman. It's kind of you to say so, Emily. The fruits of a long and enjoyable career. Sugar?"

Candice raised her eyebrow. "Did he just call her sugar?"

"He was asking if she wanted some," Harry said.

"Oh."

"May I ask what your chosen field was?" Miss Blunt enquired.

"Certainly. I was a doctor. I had a practice in Harley Street for many years. Milk or cream?"

"He's asking if they want milk or cream," Harry clarified for Candice.

"I know."

"I'm just making sure you're still paying attention. Emily, get that tea down your neck and manoeuvre him towards the crate with the dead midgets in it."

Emily glanced at him anxiously.

"I also have a degree in chemistry, although that's more of a side-line," Grantley went on. He chuckled to himself as if privy to a closely-guarded secret. "Nothing more than a hobby really, albeit a very rewarding one."

Harry was mortified. "Emily, don't drink that tea. You'll be dead in ten seconds."

"What?" Candice asked.

"He has a degree in chemistry. That tea could be laced with poison. It's probably how he kills his victims."

"You said you *were* a doctor. Would I be correct in my assumption that you have retired?" Miss Blunt asked.

"Yes. It was time to hand over to a younger man. I retired six months ago." Grantley smiled and paid his guests the sort of compliment that came naturally to him. "You ladies are clearly in excellent health but if anything is worrying you at any time please feel free to come and see me. I'm no longer registered as a general practitioner so I would be unable to treat you but I can diagnose ailments and advise on the best course of action to take. If nothing else I can offer peace of mind."

"What made you decide to re-locate to Cloverdale St Mary?"

"To be honest, Prudence... may I be permitted to call you Prudence?"

"By all means."

She actually blushed.

"To be honest I hadn't heard of the village until the untimely death of Candice Freeman. Such a sad, tragic event. You must miss her very much."

"Yes, we do," Miss Blunt replied.

Her thoughts slipped away for a moment.

"It was, of course, headline news all over the world. When I saw Cloverdale St Mary on TV I was struck by its charm and beauty. It looked a very welcoming village. The perfect place to spend one's retirement."

"Harley Street's loss is Cloverdale St Mary's gain,

Norman," Miss Blunt cooed sweetly.

"Has he got another tea pot?" Candice asked Harry. "I need something to puke in."

"Is there a Mrs Grantley?" Miss Blunt asked.

"There was, but my wife passed away."

"Oh. I am very sorry."

"There is no need to be. You know what they say about the passage of time. I'm over it now."

"When did you lose her?" Emily asked.

"Three weeks ago."

The passage of time had hardly passed at all. It was barely long enough to have put the kettle on.

Neither Emily or Miss Blunt knew how to respond and the room fell silent.

Harry looked at Emily impatiently and tapped his watch. "Manoeuvre, manoeuvre."

She wasn't sure how to proceed and plunged awkwardly. "Um, I saw the removal men carry in a large wooden crate yesterday. You told them it was delicate. Did it have your chemistry set inside?"

Harry winced. "Oh, she could have done better than that."

Emily heard what he said and scowled at him.

"No, it contains a body," Grantley replied.

No one expected to hear that, least of all Candice. She actually stole a step backwards.

"Did you say a body?" Miss Blunt asked.

"Yes. Would you like to see it?"

"That would be lovely," Emily heard herself say.

"It's in the study. Follow me."

They rose from the sofa and followed Grantley out of the room.

"This is it," Harry said, stealing a march on them.

"Any moment now and we'll be knee-deep in dead midgets."

Candice didn't comment as she left the lounge too.

"I hope you have strong stomachs," Grantley said, poised over the crate.

Miss Blunt was astonished by what was taking place. Candice too as she lurked in the background.

"Get your scissors ready, Emily," Harry said.

It was all she could do to stop herself from fainting.

Grantley smiled and put his guests at ease. "Don't worry, I was just having some fun at your expense. Do forgive me."

He lifted the lid of the crate to reveal a skeleton. It was machine-made for educational purposes.

"Allow me to introduce Roland. I acquired him at medical school. I wouldn't have graduated if it hadn't been for this chap."

"That's why you told the removal men to be careful with it," Emily said, breathing a sigh of relief.

"Yes. Roland is a reproduction of an actual skeleton, held together by pins and screws. It would have taken me weeks to put him together again had they damaged it in any way. It's not a task I enjoy performing."

Candice felt vindicated and allowed an air of smugness to enter her voice. "It doesn't look like a dead midget to me," she said to Harry.

Even now he wasn't convinced.

"How do we know that's not a real skeleton? He might have soaked his victim in an acid bath. That would strip the flesh off it pretty quick."

"Harry, let it go. He's not a murderer, he's a retired doctor who has a plastic skeleton called Roland. There is nothing sinister about this man at all."

Harry was loathed to admit it but Candice was right.

"Florida?" he asked, shrugging his shoulders.

"Florida. I'll race you. Bye, Em."

Emily watched them fade from view. *Oh dear*, she thought. *What am I meant to do with my scissors now?*

Norman Grantley escorted his guests back to the lounge where they chatted for another hour.

Now she knew he wasn't a murderer Emily found herself liking him. He was pleasant and courteous, spoke well, and listened with genuine interest when others spoke. They asked about his practice in London and he asked about the village. He showed a desire to learn as much about Cloverdale St Mary as possible which went a long way to impressing Miss Blunt. He was the type of person she wanted to see living there and as such Grantley met her approval and was officially accepted as a resident.

When they left he went to the basement. He had risen early that morning. He had been up since five o'clock and got a lot done. All he had to do now was attach the restraints to the wall and mix the chemicals. Then he would be ready.

He looked at what had really been inside the crate and considered his work to come. It was his goal. His mission in life. The obsession that had driven him for almost twenty years.

"Soon, Candice Freeman," he said to himself. "I won't keep you waiting much longer."

*

Maggie looked at the police car parked off the village square and saw Ian walk towards her. He wore a pained expression.

"Hello, Ian. What are the police doing here?"

"Haven't you heard? Ted was burgled last night," the vicar replied.

"Burgled?"

"Yes. He wasn't there at the time. He was staying with his son in Chalborough."

Maggie cast the car another glance and hugged her arms. Crime was non-existent in Cloverdale St Mary. To hear news of this nature sent a chill down her spine. "Poor Ted. Did they take much?"

"Cleaned him out by all accounts. The police are making enquiries around the village. I was just on my way to his cottage to see if there is anything I can do."

"I'll get Ron to put together a selection of his favourite malts. I know it's not much but I'd like to do something."

"On the contrary, Maggie, that's very kind of you. I'll let him know."

"Why was he staying with his son?"

"Alan had an accident at work. It happened last week while you were on holiday. He was on a shout, it was a fire in a warehouse. A stairway he was on collapsed and he fell fifteen feet to the ground. He broke both legs."

"That's terrible."

"The doctors say he'll be all right. Ted was helping him out at home and in the meantime this happens."

"It makes you wonder how people can sleep at night," Maggie said.

"It certainly does. Anyway, I'd better be going. The police have already spoken to me. They came to the church earlier. I expect they'll talk to you and Ron too. They want to know if we've seen anyone acting suspiciously around the village."

"I can't say I have. We only got back yesterday."

"Well, keep your eyes open just in case."

"I will."

They said goodbye to each other and Maggie returned to the Coaching Inn.

"Why are the police here?" Emily asked, following her inside.

"Ted has been burgled. Make sure you lock your doors and windows at night."

"Goodness me. Did they take much?"

"Ian said they took practically everything. The house was empty at the time. Ted was staying with his son."

"The poor man. He must be devastated."

"Yeah, but we'll all pull together for him. It's what we do, isn't it?"

Maggie was right. Small communities stood as one in times of crisis, people rallied around. In a matter of hours a collection would be under way and Ted Cooper would be swamped with well-wishers determined to help. He wouldn't be without the comforts of home for long. The residents of Cloverdale St Mary simply wouldn't stand for it.

Maggie walked behind the bar and changed the subject with a tongue-in-cheek grin. Not for the first time she wished she had been a fly on the wall earlier that day. "How did you get on with the new arrival this morning? I hear he was due to undergo the vetting process at nine o'clock sharp."

Emily grinned too. Maggie and Ron had been subjected to the 'vetting process' when they moved to the village from Manchester almost eleven years previously. Ron had nightmares about it to this day.

"It went well. Mr Grantley is a nice man. Have you met him yet?"

"No. I hope he's not a teetotaller. We need the business. Are you staying for lunch or were you just being nosy about the police?"

"I was just being nosy."

"Ah, Emily. Nice to see you again," a voice came from behind her.

Speak of the Devil.

"Hello, Mr Grantley," she said, turning around.

"What do I have to do to get you to call me Norman?"

"Sorry, Norman. Have you come to sample the delights of our local watering hole?"

Maggie wasn't sure if she liked that description of her pub. Ron hadn't watered the drinks down since Trading Standards told him he couldn't do it anymore and the Coaching Inn was far from a hole.

"I thought I would pop in for lunch," Grantley replied. "Would you care to join me?"

"I was just passing," Emily said.

"Oh, please, don't rush away. You can tell me what's good on the menu."

Maggie detected a spark between them that she found nice but surprising. Emily was a widow, she had been all the time Maggie had known her, and seeing her pursued by the new arrival was unexpected.

"Everything on the menu is good. We send out. I'm Maggie Jones. I run this place with my husband, Ron," she said, shaking Grantley's hand.

"I'm delighted to make your acquaintance, Maggie. I look forward to becoming a regular here."

Maggie turned and fist-pumped the air. "Yes! There is a God." Her moment of silliness past, she looked at

Emily again. "Allow me to repeat my question. Are you staying for lunch or were you just being nosy about the police?"

"Well, lunch would be nice," Emily hedged, reconsidering.

"I noticed the police car outside. Is everything all right?" Grantley asked.

Maggie opened her mouth to answer but Emily beat her to it.

"I'm afraid there's been a burglary in the village, a man called Ted Cooper. That sort of thing never happens here. It's come as quite a shock."

"How awful for him. Is there anything I can do?"

Emily opened her mouth to answer but Maggie beat her to it.

"We'll be making a collection but as you don't know him you don't have to contribute."

"Not at all. Let me know when the hat goes around. Communities must stick together at times like these."

Maggie and Emily opened their mouths to answer but Ron beat them to it.

"You must be the new man," he said, appearing from nowhere.

"How do you do that?" Maggie asked him.

"Stealth. I can move as lightly as a cat."

"Pity you dance like an elephant."

"I didn't step on your toes that many times in Greece."

"I walked with a limp for two days. No one does that by choice. This is my husband, Ron," Maggie said, introducing him to Grantley.

"It's nice to meet you," he replied, shaking his hand.

"Are you staying in the village long?" Ron asked.

"He just moved in yesterday," Maggie said.

"Yeah, but he's been in conversation with you two. That usually sees a newcomer off pretty quickly."

Grantley laughed. "I don't know about that, Ron. How can anyone fail to feel at home in the company of two such enchanting ladies?"

Emily and Maggie were taken by his charm but Ron was made of harder stuff and wasn't so easily impressed. He had little time for the gallant *allow me to spread my cloak over this puddle* brigade. Ron was a man who relocated the teeth of pick-pockets whether there was a puddle present or not.

"Why is there a ventriloquists dummy at the end of the bar?" Grantley asked.

"That's Edmund. He belongs to Ron," Maggie said.

"In the absence of a teddy-bear?"

This endeared him to Ron all the more.

"He belonged to my father," he replied. "He was a children's entertainer. He left him to me when he died."

"What a nice gesture."

"I thought so."

"I didn't. I can't stand him," Maggie said. "We should have chopped it up for firewood years ago."

Grantley gestured to a table and he and Emily sat down.

"He seems pleasant enough, doesn't he?" Maggie said to Ron.

"If you like that sort of thing."

"You could try to inject a bit more enthusiasm into that."

Ron watched him peruse the menu with Emily. The publican was the sort of man who made friends easily and took to strangers well, it came naturally in his profession, but Grantley had left him feeling unsure. It went without saying that he wanted to create a good impression but it was almost as if he was trying too hard to be accepted.

"I don't know," Ron said, shrugging his shoulders. "There's something about him I can't put my finger on. He's too goody-goody."

"Would you rather he walked around insulting everyone?" Maggie asked.

"Yeah, I think I would."

Ron cast him a parting glance and returned to the kitchen.

Four

"What happened then?" Samantha asked, engrossed in the story Candice was telling her.

"He refused to surrender the gun so the cop shot him."

"Six times in the chest," Harry added, standing by the lounge window in Meadow Cottage. "I would have thought once would have sufficed but he shot him six times. I'm not going to Florida again. It's too dangerous."

"It was a volatile situation. The cop had to be sure," Candice said.

"There's erring on the side of caution and there's overkill. I call shooting someone six times a tad over the top," Harry persisted.

"I agree with Mr Black. It does seem excessive," Samantha said.

Harry was glad of her support. He knew he could rely on Samantha for a civilized approach to law enforcement.

"The lawn looks nice," he told her, turning his attention to the front garden.

That was Harry's subtle way of asking why it hadn't been mowed yet.

"I've just got home from work."

"There are still a few hours of daylight left," he said, lifting his eyes skyward.

Samantha's day had been tiring. The meeting with the building contractor had taken longer than expected and three members of staff had phoned in ill. That meant all hands to the deck and a lot of hard work for everyone.

She didn't have the energy to do the garden. Aside from that she didn't have time.

"I can't do it this evening, mum's coming over. She phoned me today. I'll do it on Saturday. Promise."

Harry tutted without comment.

Candice grinned. "Why is Jan coming over?"

"She probably wants some gardening tips," Harry muttered.

Samantha allowed the remark to go unchallenged. She had learnt from Candice that Harry in complaining mode was better ignored. "I don't know. She said she wanted to talk to me about something. She didn't sound her usual self. She was hesitant, you know, reluctant to go into details. I hope everything is okay."

"I'm sure it is," Candice said.

Samantha leaned forward and took the morning paper from the coffee table. Candice and Harry had been busy interrogating murder suspects and watching executions for much of the day. She assumed they hadn't seen it.

"Have you read the paper?"

"No," Candice replied.

"Cloverdale St Mary is in the news. Strange lights have been spotted in the sky over the village. The headline says we're being invaded by aliens."

"You're kidding?" Candice said smiling.

"They've been seen for the past four nights."

"It's the first I've heard of it," Harry said.

"The story only broke today," Samantha told him.

"I mean no one in the village has mentioned it. Who reported these sightings?"

Samantha read part of the story to refresh her memory. "It was a couple from East Anglia on a camping holiday. They were out in the fields past Cross Drummond."

"And they saw strange lights in the sky," Candice said, refusing to take it seriously. "The only thing they would have seen was the lightening that came with that storm if they were out there on Monday."

"Yes," Harry agreed, amused by the thought of them getting drenched at the same time. He didn't like camping and failed to understand why people did it. Why leave a perfectly good house to live in a tent for two weeks?

"What time is Jan coming over?" Candice asked Samantha.

"Right now," Harry answered on her behalf, looking out of the window. "She's walking down the path."

Candice stood up and went to the door. "Harry and I will leave you to it. I would ask you to say hi for us but that would be giving the game away."

Samantha smiled.

"Come on, Harry. It's time we were someplace else."

"Why do I have to vacate the area every time Sam has visitors?"

"Because what Jan has to say might be private and none of our business. To the attic."

"A fine how do you do this is, being forced to leave my own lounge," he mumbled, following Candice out of the room.

Samantha went to the hallway to let her mother in.

"Hello, Sam."

There was no hint of the smile that normally accompanied her arrival.

"Hi, mum. Come through. Would you like a cup of tea?" Samantha asked, closing the door after her.

"Not for me."

Janet walked through to the lounge.

Samantha followed her guardedly. It was clear Janet was troubled by something. Samantha had never seen her so sombre. Alarm bells rang in her mind as she sat beside her on the sofa. "What is it? What's wrong?"

Janet began to cry.

"Hey, it's all right," Samantha said, holding her hand.

"I'm sorry. I told myself I wouldn't do this."

"It's okay."

Janet took a handkerchief from her pocket and dabbed her eyes. She had bright, vibrant eyes. Now they were shallow and dull like the life had been drained from them, leaving pools of sadness and regret in a face normally cheerful and confident.

Samantha waited patiently. She had no intention of rushing her. Her mother needed to compose herself and find her own pace. It was obvious the news would be bad and she prepared for it as best she could.

Finally Janet spoke.

"Martin had an affair. It was a woman he works with."

Samantha was stunned. She couldn't believe what she was hearing. "An affair?"

"He ended it. The woman didn't want it to end and reacted badly, angrily. She wrote me a letter telling me about it. That's how I found out."

"When did she write to you?"

"I got the letter on Saturday."

"Have you spoken to dad?"

Janet nodded. "That afternoon. Mel was in the garden. He said he was sorry. It was a mistake and he regretted it. He cheated on me, Sam, and he called it a mistake, like forgetting to pay a bill or something..." She began to cry again. "How could he do that to me? How could he do it to us?"

Samantha responded instinctively. The woman she had come to regard as her real mother was in pieces and she embraced her. She was appalled that her father could have done such a thing. Martin Copeland knew what it was like to be cheated. His first wife left him for another man when Samantha was six years old but that hadn't stopped him from inflicting the same pain and misery on Janet. Why did he do it? What the hell was he thinking? What did anyone think when the bed of another was so enticing?

Janet composed herself a second time and stared into empty space, a space as vast as the gulf that now existed between her and her husband. "I told him to go. I can't bear to be near him at the moment."

"Where is he?"

"He's renting a room in Falworth. He was going to take one at the Coaching Inn but I didn't want him to stay in the village. I want him to be as far away from me as possible." Janet realised what she had said and apologized. Samantha was his daughter and love and loyalty were strong emotions. "I'm sorry. That's not what you want to hear."

"It's okay. I think it's the right decision."

Both women were silent.

"Does Mel know?" Samantha finally asked.

Janet shook her head. "I told her he had been called back to work and would be away from home for a while. I said he had to go to Scotland. I didn't know what else to say. How do you explain something like this to a ten year-old? I wouldn't know where to start."

"She's a bright kid, mum. She'll work it out."

"I can't tell her... not yet."

Janet stopped before more tears came to destroy her.

Samantha realised her mistake. It was wrong to compound the problem, to challenge a decision her mother had been forced to make on the spur of the moment when all she could see was betrayal and a broken marriage. It was a time for patience and understanding, not telling a devastated woman what she *should* have done.

"There's no need to rush into anything, take as long as you need. I'll help in any way I can. I'll support you."

"I don't want anyone to take sides, Sam."

"It won't be like that but I won't let you deal with this on your own. You're my mum and I love you."

"I thought Martin... loved me too..."

It was too much to bear and Janet broke down.

*

Candice and Harry didn't stay in the attic room. Harry was as slippery as an eel and would have been back in the lounge eavesdropping on Samantha and Janet's conversation before Candice knew which way was up so she forced him out of the house altogether. As a return to Florida was out of the question she took him somewhere closer to home. Candice had a vested interest in the Cross Drummond Equestrian Centre and decided to pay it a visit.

Cross Drummond stood to the north of Cloverdale St Mary. It was a vast woodland area that was wild and overgrown when Candice arrived in the village. It was home to Cross Drummond House, a school Miss Blunt had been headmistress of until its closure forced her into early retirement in 2006. Within a short time the 300 year-old building had fallen into disrepair.

It began life as a monastery but times changed and it became many things to many people. During the two world wars it was used as a hospital for wounded servicemen. Later it was turned into a retirement home, then the school that served the local community until its solid oak doors closed for the last time, trapping all those memories inside.

Cross Drummond House was an empty shell when Candice moved to Cloverdale St Mary. Once an integral part of village life, it had out-served its usefulness and stood derelict and forgotten, a tribute to the past that no one cared about. The only exception was Miss Blunt. She often went there to be alone with her thoughts, to remember days long ago when she and the grand old house had a role to play in a world that had left them behind. She longed for new life to be breathed into it, for the building to be something again, but when that day came it wasn't what she expected.

There were a lot of horse owners in the area and many stabled their mounts at a place called Beckley Point. When it closed soon after Candice arrived they were faced with the unenviable prospect of stabling their horses at Greybank, a larger and better equipped stables forty miles away. An eighty-mile round trip three times a week didn't sit well with anyone, least of all Miss Blunt who was an accomplished horsewoman and won many trophies as a three-day eventer on the amateur circuit.

Candice was an experienced rider too and suggested they turn the derelict school at Cross Drummond into an equestrian centre, comprising of a riding school and private hire stables. She would arrange for investors to help finance the venture and put up the rest of the money herself. The idea was met enthusiastically by all, except Miss Blunt who regarded Candice's intervention as a prime example of the super-rich taking over village affairs. She was further offended when Candice asked if she would be willing to manage the riding school.

'The audacity of the woman! How dare she breeze into the village like she owns it and offer me employment,' Miss Blunt had protested to her friends.

Due to this, and the bad start they had gotten off to when Candice moved to the village, the conflict between them escalated into something on a par with the War of the Worlds. It would have continued in that vein had it not been for the intervention of Emily Braithwaite. The mild-mannered woman who wouldn't say boo to a goose rounded on Miss Blunt and told her, in no uncertain terms, that Candice was trying to help and people shouldn't be so quick to judge her. Her outburst had such an effect on Miss Blunt that she reconsidered and agreed to Candice's proposals.

The Council couldn't get the property off their hands fast enough and authorised the sale of the land immediately. They regarded the building as a bomb-site, a costly one that had to be accounted for in their annual budgets despite never spending a penny on it. They were delighted that someone wanted to redevelop the area and did everything in their power to speed things along.

Planning permission was granted and bank accounts were opened to handle the huge amounts of money needed to finance the project. Investors were found and surveyors, architects and contractors were appointed. After six months of backbreaking work those solid oak doors opened again and the new Cross Drummond House rose like a phoenix from the ashes of the bramble and thicket that had once threatened to entomb it.

Miss Blunt managed the riding school and Samantha was brought in to run the stables. In time Samantha would be responsible for managing the whole business but not yet. Miss Blunt had much to offer and wasn't ready to retire a second time. It wasn't just Cross Drummond that had new life breathed into it. Miss Blunt had been rejuvenated too. She had a role to play again, one that was beneficial to the whole community, and that, more than anything, was what made her miss Candice the way she did. The brash, attention-seeking American had given her something no one else could have. She gave her a future born of her past. She gave her Cross Drummond House.

The equestrian centre had just celebrated its first anniversary. It opened on the previous spring bank holiday and business was booming. At the time of its construction it was thought fifteen stables would have been sufficient but demand for stabling was high and it was decided to add a further ten. This would entail building a new stable row adjacent to the existing one. It meant more work for Samantha and her team but they were passionate about horses and dedicated to their well-being.

Harry wasn't a fan of horses. He preferred cows. He spent hours standing in fields mooing with them because they fascinated him. Candice swore he would have been one if he could. He never enjoyed their visits to Cross Drummond and was unenthusiastic as Candice pointed to her personal mount grazing a short distance away. The sixteen-hand chestnut mare had been bequeathed to Melanie but the youngster wasn't allowed to ride her yet. She would have been too much for her to handle.

"Does Jo Jo look okay to you?" Candice asked.

"I can't see anything out of the ordinary," Harry

replied, trying to sound interested. "Why?"

"I don't know. She doesn't seem right. She looks a bit, ploddy."

"Ploddy?"

"You know, floopy."

"I wish you wouldn't use complicated equestrian terms. They go right over my head."

Candice ignored him. The more she watched her, the more concerned she became. "Look how she's standing."

"It's how she always stands."

"Something is wrong. I don't like the look of her."

"Going by the way she's tucking into that grass she's not off her feed. Has Sam said anything about her being unwell?"

"No, but maybe she hasn't noticed. She's been rushed off her feet today. I'm gonna take a closer look at her."

Harry thought Candice was worrying unduly and held his ground as she walked through the fence and started across the field. It was still water-logged in places after the heavy downpour on Monday night and he didn't want to get his shoes muddy.

"I'll wait here," he called.

Candice carried out an inspection of Jo Jo by walking around her. She couldn't identify the problem but was convinced something was troubling her. Candice knew that horse better than anyone. If her instincts told her something was wrong, something was wrong.

She looked at Harry standing by the fence.

"Is she all right?" he asked.

Candice didn't answer. Her gaze went through him and she faded from view.

Harry assumed she didn't want to get muddy either and expected her to re-appear on the dry ground on his side of the fence but she didn't. *It doesn't take this long to spirit yourself twenty feet,* he thought.

He waited ten minutes but she didn't come back.

*

"They must have put something in the water," Harry said to himself when he heard the front door slam shut.

Samantha left Meadow Cottage the moment he returned. She said nothing in response to his greeting as she fetched her keys from the hallway table. A moment later she was gone, reversing her car off the drive at speed. Harry wondered if he should have tried a different brand of deodorant and sniffed under his right arm.

Candice was nowhere to be seen. He thought she had gone home to voice her concerns about Jo Jo to Samantha but a search of the cottage failed to locate her and he was forced to conclude that both his house-mates had tired of his company and done a runner. It was like being the last person on board the Marie Celeste.

He saw the TV guide lying open on the coffee table and picked it up. A different channel was showing *Killing Asia* this evening and Samantha's hurried exit suddenly made sense. Harry would have gone with her had he known it was on again. It may have been a modern-day classic but that film could empty a football stadium in ten seconds flat. It wasn't all doom and gloom however. His spirits lifted when he saw another channel was showing *The Diamond Cutter.*

A sound from the kitchen drew his attention and he

went to investigate. It wouldn't have been the first time Candice had snuck in through the back door. Even as a ghost she was prone to carry her shoes and walk on tip-toe when coming in from a late night out but his spirits dipped again when it saw it was an old adversary.

"Oh, it's you," he said, looking at the cat sniffing around the fridge. "We should have that cat-flap nailed up."

Pyewacket wasn't happy to see him either. *If anyone wants to nail you up I'll provide the hammer,* he thought.

"Why aren't you hanging around Emily's fridge? You don't live here anymore. Go away," Harry said, waving his hand at the door.

Pyewacket took the hint and left. It annoyed him that his least favourite ghost had won the day but in all honesty there was little chance of him getting the fridge open and he was sure that somewhere in the fields beyond Meadow Cottage there would have been a mouse with his name on it. Maybe a vole. Perhaps a rat. That would have been a treat. He hadn't had one of those in ages.

Harry and Pyewacket had spent many an hour scowling at one another when he belonged to Candice. Harry didn't like cats and Pyewacket didn't like ghosts - especially those who took exception to him leaving dead birds and mangled mice all over the place - so the falling-out between them was immediate and irreversible.

A cat's territory could extend to the far side of the moon and Pyewacket was a regular visitor to Emily's cottage before Candice died. After her death she took him in and now the old lady doted on him. Sometimes she didn't have the stomach for what he presented her with. Pyewacket had turned killing into an exact science, but he was loyal and attentive when he wasn't torturing lesser creatures and Emily wouldn't have had him any other way.

Harry went back to the lounge and made himself comfortable on the sofa. He assumed at some point Candice and Samantha would return but there was a plus side to having the cottage to himself. If he had to keep his own company all evening he could have stayed up after the nine o'clock watershed and watched *The Diamond Cutter.*

The thought appealed to him so much he considered locking them out.

Five

'You know what they say about diamonds being a girl's best friend.'

'I don't want to throw a spanner in the works but your best friends are locked in a vault in the home of the Count and Countess DeMarcio. The question is how do we get to them?'

Harry was glued to the TV in the attic room. It would have taken the arrival of the invading aliens Samantha had told him about to have made him surrender his place on the sofa. Even then he would have put up a fight. He was eager for the scene to develop and offered some advice in the hope of helping it along.

"Kelly gets out of bed to fetch the picture of the house she took earlier that afternoon. Then you can work out the best way to break in. It's on the table over there," he said pointing at the screen.

Kelly Johnson got out of bed and fetched the picture of the house she had taken earlier that afternoon. As she was naked and the table was a hundred miles away on the other side of the room, Harry found the next few moments very pleasing.

"This really is a great film," he said, smiling.

It was like Christmas and all his birthdays rolled into one. If he had popcorn he would have been drooling over it.

'We can gain access through this ground-floor window,' Kelly said, showing the picture to her accomplice.

It wasn't a window Harry was looking at.

He heard the front door open.

It was just after 10:00 p.m. and the first of his missing

house-mates had returned, although Harry had been so engrossed in the film he hadn't heard Samantha garage her car. His eyes travelled reluctantly from the TV to the door and he willed it not to open.

There was still no sign of Candice; aside from her plotting to relieve the Countess DeMarcio of her diamonds in the nude. Harry was concerned by her absence, it wasn't like her to go off without telling him, but she was present in the guise of an international jewel thief and that brought certain compensations. He wondered if the actors had bothered to get dressed during the commercial breaks.

A knock came at the door and it opened.

"Hello, Mr Black. Is Candice here?"

"No. I haven't seen her all evening."

"Oh, okay. I'm sorry to have bothered you."

Samantha didn't linger. She closed the door again.

Harry knew something was wrong. He got the impression she had been crying.

He should have followed her downstairs but instead he turned his attention back to the TV and admired the cameraman's skill in the way he had framed his shot of Candice as she noted points of interest on the photograph. The *Diamond Cutter* hadn't pioneered full-frontal nudity but had done much to re-invent it. Then her naked leading man stood up and his backside filled half the screen.

"Oh, I forgot about that bit," Harry said, averting his eyes.

If he had been a gentleman he would have averted them whenever Candice came into view but that would have made watching the film a pointless exercise. Most of it would have been spent examining his fingernails.

Harry turned his thoughts to Samantha and felt bad about her sitting in the lounge alone and upset. The angel knocked the Devil off his shoulder and he elected to do the decent thing, letting out a defeated sigh when the world's most unattractive arse exited the shot and Candice commanded the scene again.

"The things I have to do," he muttered, walking to the door.

The lounge was silent when he arrived. Normally Samantha would have had the TV on too, especially during a weekday at this time of night. She liked to watch the ten o'clock news before going to bed but this evening there was nothing. Just silence and a troubled look that was hidden from view as she sat head-bowed.

"Are you okay?" Harry asked.

Samantha looked at him and forced a smile. It was clearly an effort. "Yeah."

"What did you want to see Candice about?"

"It was nothing important... I'll talk to her tomorrow."

She began to cry.

Some men would have felt uncomfortable in the presence of a woman in distress but Harry was sympathetic to the emotions of others and sat beside her. He wasn't the type to panic, although he wished Candice had been there. That Samantha had sought her out suggested she would rather have confided in a woman.

"Is there anything I can do?" he asked.

"I'm sorry."

"You don't have to apologize."

"I want it to be... like it was."

Harry didn't know what she meant. He couldn't do anything until he was in possession of all the facts.

"It's okay, Sam. I'm here," Candice said, appearing in the room.

Harry rose from the sofa to allow her to take his place.

Candice looked at him gratefully and he stood in his

usual spot by the window. He never considered leaving. He formed the impression, correctly, that Samantha would have been happy for him to stay.

"What's wrong?" Candice asked gently. "Does it have anything to do with your mom's visit?"

Samantha nodded. The evening had overtaken her in a way she hadn't expected and she took a moment to compose herself.

"Dad had an affair. Mum's in pieces over it."

"Oh Sam, I'm so sorry."

"I went to see him, to have it out with him, but I think I've made it worse."

"You went to the house?"

"No, he's not there. He's renting a room in Falworth. Mum gave me the address before she left."

"What happened?"

"I asked him why he did it, who this woman was that he was willing to throw everything away for. He said he didn't mean to hurt anyone. It was a mistake, flirting in the office that went too far and turned into something else. He was in tears when he told me but I didn't care. I called him a thoughtless bastard..." Samantha cried again. "I lost my temper. I wanted to hurt him like he's hurt mum."

Candice looked at Harry. Neither of them knew what to say. Martin was a good man, he was dependable and loved his family. He would have laid down his life for them. Why would he have done something like this? Everyone flirted. It happened every day in all walks of life but good people knew when to stop. Dependable people drew a line. Those who loved their families didn't take the next step.

"Have there been any problems between your mom and dad?" Candice asked.

"No. There wasn't a hint that something like this

might have happened. It came from nowhere."

That made it all the more baffling.

"What about Mel? Does she know?"

"Mum told her dad's working away. She wants to keep it from her for as long as possible."

"She's trying to protect her."

"But it won't do any good, will it? She'll find out. Mel worships the ground dad walks on... I can't bear to think of what that poor girl is going to go through."

Candice felt for all of them. They were a family divided and difficult decisions lie ahead but moreover she felt inadequate. The one thing Samantha needed she couldn't provide. "I wish I could hug you."

"Me too... I don't know what to do, Candice..."

Samantha bowed her head and wept.

Now Harry left. It would have been wrong to stay. Samantha had to come to terms with a bad situation, not in private but in the company of her best friend. That Candice couldn't comfort her in a physical sense didn't matter. It was enough that she was there.

*

Candice stayed with Samantha for an hour. During that time they talked and Samantha felt better but neither were under any illusions. Martin was repentant and desperate to save his marriage but Janet couldn't imagine a time when he would have moved back to the family home let alone repair the damage of his actions. She loved him but she didn't know if she could trust him.

There was little doubt that in the fullness of time she would have forgiven him for what he had done but how could they move forward if there was no trust? That, more than anything, would be the biggest hurdle to overcome. It would determine if they had a future together or not. Anyone could forgive but re-building trust was another matter. How could a person look at someone in the same way after they had been lied to and betrayed? How did loving eyes lose their suspicion? How could the deceived know they wouldn't be deceived again?

"Is Sam okay?" Harry asked when Candice returned to the attic room.

"She's gone to bed. She's better than she was."

"What was Martin thinking of?"

Candice sat on the sofa. It was as if all the troubles in the world sat with her. "I don't know but it's gonna be hard for everyone concerned. Mel especially. Sam's right. She'll be devastated if Janet and Martin can't work through this."

"I wonder if they *can* work through it."

"The coming weeks will tell. The problem is Mel will be drawn into it long before then. Using work as an excuse for Martin not being there is a temporary fix. It could take months for them to sort themselves out and even then there may be no going back."

Harry knew she was right. It was impossible to put a time-frame on something like this and hazard a guess as to what the outcome may have been.

He sat beside her. "I take it you didn't say anything about Jo Jo. It wasn't the right time."

Candice looked puzzled. "What about Jo Jo?"

"The concerns you have about her."

"I don't have any concerns."

That wasn't how Harry remembered it.

"You said she looked ploddy."

"Ploddy?"

"Yeah, floopy."

"Harry, they aren't even words."

"They were when you used them earlier."

"What are you talking about?"

"At Cross Drummond. We watched Jo Jo graze and you said she didn't look right. You went to take a closer look at her but didn't come back. You faded from view. Where did you go by the way?"

"I didn't go anywhere."

"Yes, you did. One minute you were there and the next you were gone."

"I came back with you. When was the last time you had your eyes tested?"

This made no sense to Harry at all.

"You didn't come back to the cottage with me. I assumed you left to speak to Sam but when I got here she was on her own. I said hello, she ignored me and stormed out. Then Pyewacket broke in and tried to raid the fridge. The next time I saw you was at nine o'clock when you had sex in the shower with that tall bloke with the flabby bum."

There wasn't a lot Candice could have said to that but she made an effort.

"Have you been drinking?"

"If you don't remember any of this, the question is how much have *you* had to drink?"

"Aside from the fact that we came home from Cross Drummond together and the last time I had a shower was in 2016, I don't know any guys with flabby bums."

"Yes, you do. He helped you to steal the Countess DeMarcio's jewellery collection. One of those necklaces was worth four million pounds. And I meant to talk to you about the shower thing. Personal hygiene is very important."

"The Diamond Cutter."

"Yeah."

"You're talking about the movie, The Diamond Cutter."

"Yeah."

Candice scratched her head. "Did you have ice in your drink?"

"You went to see what was wrong with Jo Jo and left me at Cross Drummond on my own."

"Was that before or after I had sex with Baines Derrick?"

"Who?"

"The guy with the flabby bum."

"Oh. Before."

"I see. Thank you for clarifying for me."

"Not at all." Harry paused and re-traced his steps in a conversation that had become as puzzling to him as it was to Candice. "Where was I?"

"I don't know. If it was put to a vote no one would know where you are at this moment in time."

"Oh yeah, Jo Jo," he said, carrying on regardless. "When are you going to speak to Sam about her? I know you're worried because she's gone floopy but you'll have to get the timing right while Sam has all this on her mind."

"I'll see how it looks tomorrow," Candice told him, hoping that if she played along he might have stopped talking.

A few seconds would have been nice, a couple of minutes ideal. Thirty or forty years would have been perfect but she couldn't see that happening somehow.

*

In the basement of Brook Cottage Grantley pulled the respirator from his nose and mouth and let it hang under his chin. The chemicals were harmless when used separately but mixed together the fumes became toxic and would have killed if the necessary precautions were not taken. The irony wasn't lost on him. Who would have thought that something so deadly would have held the key to something so inspiring?

Grantley needed to know more about Candice and Harry. He knew they haunted Meadow Cottage and that Samantha, Emily and Ian were aware of their existence but beyond that he was in the dark. It was early days in terms of gathering information but what he had learnt so far would prove useful.

He also knew what happened at Cross Drummond. More importantly, he knew the reason for it.

Six

The police car had become a regular sight around the village but this morning it wasn't there as part of ongoing enquiries into the Ted Cooper burglary. There had been another one. This time the victim had been at home.

Barbara Cullen was a sixty-three year-old widow who lived alone. She had been bound and gagged by the intruders when they broke in during the early hours of the morning. Mrs Cullen was unharmed but she had a heart condition and was shaken by the experience. Her admission to hospital was a precautionary measure.

News of what happened tore through Cloverdale St Mary like a tidal-wave. Anxious residents discussed the situation on the street and over garden gates where they would usually have talked about less important issues like the weather and how many pots of jam Mrs Jenkins would have made for the annual village fête in two weeks time. The previous year she had set a personal best and sold seventy-five. Now home security was the topic of conversation. The village had been targeted by thieves who were determined to add to their haul and people were scared.

Miss Blunt had called an emergency meeting in the village hall to be held on Friday evening but how many villagers would have attended was a matter for conjecture. It was all very well discussing ways to make properties safe and secure but people didn't want to run the risk of being burgled while they were away from their homes. Not that the burglars would have paid much attention to that. As proved in the case of Barbara Cullen, they didn't care if the property was occupied or not.

A crime prevention officer would be present to listen

to concerns and offer advice but Miss Blunt was outraged by this assault on the village and wanted immediate action to be taken. During a visit to the police station in Falworth earlier that morning she demanded that a police presence be maintained in Cloverdale St Mary until the burglars had been apprehended. She didn't want to turn the village into a police state but argued that around-the-clock protection was the only way to safeguard residents at the mercy of thieves who threatened to undermine the very fabric of their society.

Now, as Ron poured a lunchtime glass of Minsk for Emily in the Coaching Inn, all thoughts were on the night to come.

"You have our phone number, Emily. Call me if anything happens. I can get to you a damn sight faster than the police," he told her.

"Thank you, Ron, but I'm sure everything will be all right."

"It's better not to take chances. I don't want to frighten you but Ted and Barbara live alone and so do you. Give me a call if anything is worrying you."

Emily had never known Ron to speak in such a way. It was clear he was concerned and she nodded to reassure him. "I will. Thank you."

What she couldn't tell him was that Harry would be watching over her until the burglars were caught. He had insisted on it the moment he heard of the latest break-in. While he spent his nights at Pine Trees Cottage Candice would look out for Samantha.

Maggie had overheard what Ron said and stood beside him as Emily took her drink to her table. "Have I told you recently that I love you and my world would come to an end if you weren't a part of it?"

"What the bloody hell brought that on?" he asked, stunned.

As a man more accustomed to insults than terms of endearment from his wife, his reaction was understandable.

"What you said to Emily was really nice. It's good to know who your friends are."

"Does this mean you'll forgive me the next time I punch a pick-pocket?"

"As long as it doesn't result in a missed flight." Maggie kissed his cheek. "You're all right, Ron Jones."

"Stop it. You're scaring me."

"Do you remember the outfit I wear for Halloween?"

Ron recalled it fondly and smiled. He liked Halloween. Maggie was the sexiest banshee he had ever seen.

"The basque, suspenders and fishnet stockings?" he asked.

"I'll lay it out for tonight."

He looked at Emily sitting by the fireplace. "Emily, I forgot to tell you. We've gone ex-directory."

She had no idea what he meant by that.

Maggie laughed and nudged him in play.

The seriousness of their situation returned like a bad dream and Ron was solemn again. When he spoke suspicion and caution sounded in his voice.

"Does it strike you as being strange that these burglaries started when Grantley moved to the village?"

"You're not suggesting Norman is behind them surely?" Maggie replied.

"Oh, it's Norman now, is it?"

"It's always been Norman. You're the only one who doesn't like him."

"The fact that I don't like him is neither here nor there. He arrived three days ago and since then there have been two burglaries. It's too much of a coincidence if you ask me."

"You're reading something into nothing. He's a retired doctor, not an international jewel thief."

"That reminds me, I recorded The Diamond Cutter last night."

Maggie raised her eyebrow. "I thought I banned you from watching that film."

"Candice was a good friend and her memory should be upheld."

"I couldn't agree more but I would rather you upheld it by watching films in which she wore clothes occasionally."

"There wasn't that much nudity," Candice protested, sitting on a bar stool in front of them.

"Mind you, Baines Derrick was good in it," Maggie said, slipping into a dreamy smile.

"What, the bloke with the flabby bum?" Ron asked.

"There you are, two viewers can't be wrong," Harry announced, standing beside him. "Oh, they've got *Caribbean Firelight,*" he added, pointing to the back-bar.

That the Coaching Inn had taken stock of his favourite cocktail left Candice largely unimpressed and she rolled her eyes.

"If you ask me Grantley isn't what he seems," Ron said.

"When you take a shower you remove your clothes," Candice pointed out, defending her morals.

"And when you're having sex in it," Harry agreed. "And when you're having sex in bed, and when you're having sex in a hire car, and when you're having sex on a train, and when..."

"Who the hell died and made you a film critic?" Candice snapped.

"They've got *Bermuda Red* too," Harry said, pointing at the back-bar again.

"Norman Grantley is not connected with the burglaries," Maggie told Ron assuredly. "Failure on your part to accept that may result in the basque, suspenders and fishnet stockings remaining in the wardrobe."

"Salt of the earth. Couldn't wish to meet a nicer man. He's just the sort of chap this village needs," Ron replied.

"So okay, it took me three months to find my bra and knickers, that does not mean the picture was overloaded with nudity," Candice said.

"What is *Arabian Delight?*" Harry asked, perusing the back-bar.

Candice left them and went to sit with Emily.

The pub was seldom busy at lunchtimes. Today it was almost empty so Emily was able to speak freely when Candice joined her. She kept her voice down and glanced at Maggie and Ron to ensure they weren't looking in her direction as she raised a subject that was being debated by many. It wasn't just the burglaries that had captured people's interest.

"Have you heard about Martin and Janet?"

Candice wasn't surprised that Martin's affair had become common knowledge. In a way it was inevitable. Secrets were impossible to keep in small villages. The rumour mill cranked at a slow and steady pace until fact took over from hearsay and every last detail of what should have been private became public.

"Sam told us last night."

"I thought she may have. How is she?"

"Struggling to make sense of it. It's understandable I guess. Especially after what happened to her when she was a kid."

"It makes it all the more unbelievable. How could Martin do something like that?"

"I don't know, Em, but it's gonna be a tough road

back."

"Do you think they will reconcile?"

"I hope so, for their sake and for Mel and Sam's. How did you hear about it?"

Emily sighed. "The village grapevine. The gossip-mongers are hard at work already. It's the one side to village life I don't like. When something like this happens it's regarded as a source of entertainment."

Candice shared her view. She didn't like it either.

"Does Mel know what is happening?" Emily asked.

"No. Jan wants to keep it from her for as long as possible but that won't be easy if the whole village is talking about it. I hope Mel doesn't find out from someone else."

They knew there was a chance she would and lapsed into silence.

"Ron might have something about Grantley," Harry said, joining them. "We know he's not a murderer but he may be involved in the burglaries."

"Norman is a nice man," Emily told him.

"A nice man who is head of a crime syndicate and masterminding a spate of burglaries in this village," Harry retorted.

"Here we go again," Candice sighed.

"If we don't do something no one in Cloverdale St Mary will have possessions by the end of the week."

"Mouth, open..."

"If you say crap I'll swing for you," Harry said.

Candice set about putting him right. Someone had to. Grantley would have sued him for defamation of character if he got to hear of this.

"Harry, Ron doesn't like him. I don't know why but that's the way it is. It doesn't make Norman Grantley a criminal mastermind. Just like having a wooden crate doesn't make him a mass murderer. He's an ordinary guy who has retired and moved to a small village. Give him a break."

"Do you still have your scissors?" he asked Emily.

"Or you can ignore me and go skipping off to Loopy Land," Candice said.

"Here's what we'll do," Harry told Emily, paying no attention to Candice whatsoever. "When you go to bed tonight leave your front door open. It will be impossible for Grantley to resist and he'll call his burglar friends. Candice and I will nab them when they come to rob you and the village will be safe again."

Candice didn't offer an opinion. She saw no point but the same couldn't be said for Emily.

"I'm not leaving my front door open after dark."

"How else are we going to catch them? We have to set a trap."

"It doesn't mean I have to be the bait. What if they come to burgle me and you and Candice are delayed for some reason? I could be sitting on orange boxes by the time you arrive."

"It has to be done, Emily. Grantley must be stopped."

"Norman is a retired doctor, not a burglar."

"I know he doesn't burgle anyone. He gets his gang of thugs to do it for him."

"Thugs?"

"The people who break in. Can you think of a better description for men who would leave a sixty-three year-old widow tied up in her own home?"

"And you want me to leave my front door open?" Emily said aghast. "I'm seventy-one. What chance would I stand?"

81

"You won't be tied up because Candice and I will stop them."

"Ten Miles to Denver is on TV tonight," Candice said from nowhere. "There is a lot of nudity in that film," she added thoughtfully.

"What time?" Harry asked.

"Nine o'clock."

"Don't open your front door till eleven," he told Emily.

"It has a running time of 2½ hours," Candice said.

"Better make it midnight to be on the safe side."

As far as Emily was concerned this wasn't one of Harry's better ideas and she went to great pains to tell him so.

"I'm not leaving my front door open at all. Norman is not the monster you're making him out to be. You have no right to slander him in such a way."

"What was that, Emily?" Maggie asked, stopping at her table.

"You're rehearsing for a play," Harry helpfully suggested.

"Um, nothing. I was thinking out loud."

"Oh."

Maggie hadn't heard what she said, only that she had said something, and went on her way none the wiser.

"I suppose *thinking out loud* works too," Harry pondered.

Candice thought of times past when she needed an excuse for talking to herself in public and wished she had used that response. Rehearsing for a play sounded good on paper but it had placed her in a difficult position on more than one occasion.

Harry was about to argue his case for a sting operation further when the door opened and Grantley walked in.

Instead of going to the bar he changed direction when he saw Emily and stood beside her.

"Hello, Emily. May I join you?"

"Yes, by all means," she replied, casting Harry an unseen glance.

He had to move quickly when Grantley chose to sit on the chair he occupied.

"He almost sat on my lap then."

Candice grinned and shook her head.

"What have you been doing with yourself today?" Emily asked the new arrival.

"I'm still unpacking boxes. I had no idea how much rubbish I had accumulated until I moved house."

"I'm sure your possessions aren't rubbish."

Grantley smiled. "It's nice of you to say so, Emily. I still don't know where I'm going to put it all though."

Harry had moved to a fourth chair at the table and made his thoughts on the subject clear. Clear, at least, to those who could see and hear him. "You could put it in the secret hiding place where you stash other people's possessions."

"You could put it... um, how are you finding the village in general?" Emily corrected herself.

"It really is a beautiful place. I'm sure I'm going to be very happy here," Grantley told her.

"You'll need a bigger cottage if you carry on the way you are," a scornful voice said.

"I went for a walk this morning and was left in no doubt that coming here was the right thing to do. Who would want a city and all its traffic and noise when one can enjoy the delights that Cloverdale St Mary has to offer?"

Candice saw the way he looked at Emily when he spoke, the suggestive grin that played around the corners of his mouth and eyes that refused to move from hers. They had a definite twinkle in them. Emily's did too and Candice realised they were attracted to each other. Like Maggie before her, she detected a spark between them that may have ignited given the right circumstances.

"Let us know if we're cramping your style," she said, playfully.

Emily didn't know how to respond to her remark and tried not to blush.

"Are you all right?" Grantley asked her.

"Um, yes. Do you have a big one?"

So much for cramping her style.

"My God, Em. Cut to the chase, why don't you?" Candice said, stunned that she would have been so forthright.

"Your garage," Emily blurted, realising what she had said and desperate to repair. "I was wondering about your car. If it's a small one there'll be lots of room for it but if it's a big one... there might not be."

She wished she hadn't started this.

"I drive a Ferrari California T," he replied.

Now it was Harry who was stunned.

"A Ferrari? Who did he steal that from?" he gasped.

"I got it cheap. It was quite a steal really."

"He's admitted it! He's a thief and a cad," Harry boomed.

Candice was unfamiliar with the term and looked at him questionably. "Cad?"

"It's another word for criminal mastermind."

"Who did you steal it... I mean, why was it cheap?" Emily asked, growing more and more flustered.

"It belonged to a patient of mine. He's in his late-fifties and thought a high-performance sports car was too young for him so he decided to get rid of it. I'm older than he is but that sort of thing has never bothered me. Toys for boys I suppose. If I like something I buy it. I made him a ridiculous offer and he accepted."

"How ridiculous was your offer?" Emily asked. She realised it was a personal question and apologized. "I'm sorry, that's none of my business."

"It's all right, it's no secret. It cost £80,000. I bought it when I retired. Thought I would treat myself."

"The burglary business must be looking up," Harry snorted.

Candice found herself pining for her Porsche 911 when a thought struck her. "What car did you drive?" she asked Harry.

"A Ford Cortina Mk 3."

"Is that good?"

"It is if you like Ford Cortinas."

It was clear from his envious expression that he didn't. He would have sold his soul to the Devil to drive the sort of car Grantley owned.

Harry turned his thoughts to his criminal activities and instructed Emily on the best way to proceed. Grantley and his gang of desperadoes would have been behind bars by this time tomorrow if they handled the situation carefully.

"Tell him you're leaving your front door open at midnight," he said.

Bearing in mind Grantley was attracted to her, Candice didn't think that was a good idea. It was one thing to want to know how big it was but an invitation to stop by in the dead of night may have been misconstrued.

She was about to voice her concerns when a man

entered with a motorcycle crash helmet tucked under his arm. He glanced at them briefly and walked to the bar. He didn't order a drink. He was seeking directions for getting to Falworth.

Ron advised him of the best road to take and underlined his directions by pointing and waving his arms. To watching eyes he was either telling him about the many roundabouts he would encounter or teaching him how to fly. Then Maggie told the stranger to ignore everything her husband had said and suggested a more direct route, one that wouldn't have necessitated an overnight stop in Nepal. The man was grateful for the advice, although none the wiser for it, and left them arguing at the bar.

"He'll end up in China if he follows your directions," he heard her say as he left.

"Of course he wouldn't. He told me he's riding a 1200cc. He'll run out of petrol long before he gets to Beijing," Ron countered.

Grantley allowed the distraction to pass and turned to Emily with those eyes that clearly wanted to get to know her better. "Emily, may I ask you something?"

"Don't tell him where you keep your pension book," Harry said.

"Yes, of course."

"I was wondering, would you care to have dinner with me this evening? I've been told there are some nice restaurants in Falworth."

"Say no," Harry demanded. "It's a ruse to get you out of the house."

"Well, I don't know, Norman."

"Please say yes. I won't lie to you, Emily. I enjoy your company and would like to spend more time with you."

"Goodness," she said, trying not to blush again.

Grantley smiled. "I'll have you home by ten o'clock. Scouts honour."

"He was never a Scout," Harry said. "While other boys that age were doing things with their woggles he was planning his first bank job."

"We all have to eat," Grantley added in gentle persuasion.

Emily melted. The truth was she was flattered. Since her husband passed away no one had paid her a second glance. Then along came Norman Grantley, a courteous man whom she liked immensely.

"Yes, Norman. I would love to have dinner with you."

"Goodbye pension book," Harry said.

Candice didn't want to intrude on what was turning into a private conversation and stood up, urging Harry to do the same. "I think you and I should leave these two alone to sort out their date."

"It isn't a date," Emily said, forgetting herself.

"Of course not. Just two friends enjoying a pleasant meal together," Grantley assured her.

"What? Oh, yes. That's what I meant."

She wrung her hands anxiously.

Harry didn't share Candice's sense of privacy and her willingness to be elsewhere. A good friend needed his protection and he was duty-bound to provide it. "I'm not going anywhere until I talk Emily out of this madness. Having dinner with a criminal mastermind is the last thing she should do. Emily, go to your room," he told her, pointing to the door.

"Is that the best you have?" Candice asked him.

"I might stop her pocket money too," Harry replied, realising how ridiculous he had sounded.

"I'm going for a walk. Bye, Em. Have a nice evening."

Candice faded from view.

Seven

It was a good turn out in the village hall, better than Miss Blunt expected. The crime prevention officer took his seat beside her at the table on the stage and pulled his microphone towards him.

"Good evening everyone. Thank you for attending," she began. "As you know there have been three burglaries in the village over recent days and it pains me to say that in my opinion we can expect more. It is clear to me that Cloverdale St Mary has been targeted by unscrupulous characters who regard our village as easy pickings. This evening we must address this issue and determine what to do about it. Before we go any further I would like to introduce Sergeant Colin Lacey. He is the Crime Prevention Officer based at Falworth Police Station. Sergeant Lacey."

"Thank you, Miss Blunt. Good evening to you all. During the early hours of this morning a third burglary took place at the home of Mr and Mrs Pearce who run the general store and tearoom. Their property is located on the high street, which would suggest the thieves are growing in confidence and becoming more daring. Prior to this the other break-ins were in out-lying parts of the village, isolated properties that presented less chance of the burglars being detected. In view of this latest development it is important that everyone remains vigilant. Please report any suspicious activity to the police immediately. It may be nothing but it's better to err on the side of caution."

"Aside from that, what can we do to protect ourselves from this?" a woman asked from the floor.

"I have literature on home security that I'll be passing around shortly. In addition I can offer advice on the best way to protect your homes. We will go into detail about that this evening but if anyone would like me to come to their homes for a private consultation I am more than willing to do so. There are many ways to make life difficult for burglars, some of which may not be obvious to you. I will do all I can to advise you on the best way to make your homes secure and hopefully provide some peace of mind."

"It strikes me the best way of doing that is to have a stronger police presence in the village," Ian called from the back of the room.

Miss Blunt couldn't have agreed more and readily stated the fact. "I have raised this point with the police in Falworth and I must say, Sergeant Lacey, I was not impressed by the response I received. It seemed to me there was a general lack of interest in what is happening here."

"I assure you that is not the case, Miss Blunt. I'm afraid it comes down to available resources. We simply don't have the manpower to maintain a presence in the village overnight or for a sustained length of time."

"So we're left at the mercy of the burglars," a disgruntled resident called out.

"Pretty soon there will be no one *left* to rob," another said.

"Norman Grantley is behind this," a third voice boomed.

Candice looked at Harry appalled but fortunately he had forgotten to take himself off silent mode and no one heard him.

"I understand your concerns," Sergeant Lacey said. "If it was possible to maintain a police presence in

Cloverdale St Mary we would do so but I'm afraid it isn't. For the next few nights a patrol car will visit but the officers can only stay a short time."

"You mean when they've gone we're on our own," Maggie said from the front row.

This was not what the villagers wanted to hear and discord filled the room as they debated the situation among themselves.

Sergeant Lacey raised his hands in a calming gesture. "No one is leaving you to face this threat alone."

"It doesn't sound like it," a man shouted.

"Arrest Grantley!"

This time Harry had taken himself off silent mode but the mood in the hall had turned ugly and he wasn't heard above the noise.

"Keep out of it," Candice told him.

"I have an opinion that I believe speaks for many here."

"It only speaks for Ron and he *isn't* here. If you say anything else I'll never let you watch The Diamond Cutter again."

"What about Ten Miles to Denver?"

"That too."

Harry sulked in silence.

It was left to Miss Blunt to bring the meeting to order.

"Ladies and gentlemen, we will not achieve anything this evening by arguing. It is clear the police do not have the slightest idea of how to catch these criminals but nothing will be gained by stating their short-comings."

Sergeant Lacey didn't know if he should have thanked her for her intervention or not.

"The important thing is that we stand together as a community," she went on. "That means protecting our homes and businesses by setting up a neighbourhood watch and patrolling the streets ourselves."

Sergeant Lacey had no problem with a neighbourhood watch scheme, it was a good thing and he welcomed it, but residents patrolling the streets screamed *Vigilante* and that gave him cause for concern. "I'm not sure that's a good idea, Miss Blunt. It would be better to leave the policing of the village to the police."

"But the police will not be here when we need them – late at night or in the early hours of the morning when our homes are being robbed," she replied.

"Well said," Harry called.

A look of disapproval from Candice made him feel inclined to refrain from making further comments.

Sergeant Lacey felt the tide of public opinion turn against him but insisted the residents shouldn't act rashly. It would have led to problems that would have been better avoided. "By all means set up a neighbourhood watch scheme, that is something the police can help you with, but I strongly advise against patrolling the streets at night. That side of it should be left to us."

"Two bobbies driving around in a patrol car for half an hour doesn't inspire confidence," he was told from the floor.

As far as Miss Blunt and many in the hall were concerned self-protection was the only way forward in light of limited police resources but Sergeant Lacey found an unexpected ally when Bill Pearce stood up to air his views.

"Speaking as someone who has been burgled, I think the sergeant is right. Susan and I were fortunate, we didn't know they were in the house and no harm came to us, but Barbara wasn't so lucky. She was tied up, a sixty-three year-old woman who presented no threat to them.

If they're capable of doing that what will they do if they're challenged by members of the public? They might turn violent. There's no telling what will happen."

"Thank you, Mr Pearce. You raise a valid point," Sergeant Lacey said. "I know emotions are running high, you're concerned and want protection, but taking matters into your own hands is not the solution."

"It's better than doing nothing and losing everything we own," a man called.

Sergeant Lacey assumed, correctly, that a long and difficult evening was in store for him.

*

The meeting finished at 9:00 p.m. and most residents went home to cottages they had once taken to be secure but now felt vulnerable in. A few went to the Coaching Inn for a drink, Emily, Ian and Grantley among them. Harry and Candice went too. They sat at their usual table by the fireplace and discussed the evening's events at length.

Emily was worried about the burglaries but what concerned her more was Miss Blunt's parting words to her at the meeting's conclusion. The police had made their position clear; no residents were to patrol the streets late at night, but the burglars had to be caught and the Terror of Cloverdale St Mary had other ideas.

"Prudence is going ahead with the night patrols," she told the others. "She's going to ask for volunteers. I wish she would reconsider. It could be dangerous."

"Sometimes the best protection is self-protection," Grantley replied.

"The police don't think so. They advised us against it for a reason."

Ian looked at Harry. It was clear from his ghostly expression that he would have liked to see the residents patrol the village in tanks. If they could have gotten their hands on a couple of fighter jets all the better.

"I think Emily is right. Some things are better left to the authorities."

"Hogwash," Harry said.

Grantley sipped his drink and returned the whisky glass to the table. When he spoke he did so reflectively, stating a point others may not have considered. "It's surprising that something like this hasn't happened in Cloverdale St Mary before. Candice Freeman lived here not long ago. You would have thought a high-profile name would have made the village a prime target for thieves."

The reference to Candice made Harry wary.

"I must admit, that never occurred to me," Ian replied.

"Me neither," Candice said.

"It's occurred to someone," Harry told them, eyeing Grantley suspiciously.

"I wish I could have met her," Grantley told his drinking companions. "What was she like?"

Emily and Ian glanced at her.

Candice smiled. "Make it good, guys. List all my outstanding points and remember to say I liked animals and small children."

"Candice?" Emily said, pausing over her glass of Minsk. "Well, I suppose she was all right."

"If you like that sort of thing," Ian added.

This wasn't what Candice had in mind.

"Was she not popular in the village?" Grantley asked them.

"Oh yes, everyone liked her," Emily said. "It's just

that sometimes she could be a bit, well..." She looked to Ian for assistance. "How would you describe it?"

"Big-headed."

"You are so not getting a birthday card this year," Candice told him.

"Don't get me wrong, she was a very nice woman and she loved animals..."

"And small children," Emily interrupted.

"... but she had a tendency to elevate her position from time to time. You know what these celebrities are like."

Harry grinned. "You asked for that."

Emily decided they had tortured her enough and looked her square in the eyes. "The main thing we can tell you about Candice is that she was a wonderful friend and our lives are all the better for having known her."

"Yes. No one in this village has been missed more than Candice," Ian said.

"I was missed," Harry told him.

"No one in this village has been missed more than Candice," he said again.

Candice laughed. "And you asked for that."

"You're not getting a Christmas card either," Harry informed him.

Grantley didn't know why the vicar had repeated himself. He assumed it was out of respect. He looked at her picture on the wall above the fireplace and took the conversation further. "It must have been hard for you when she died."

"Yes. It was very difficult," Emily replied.

"Had she lived here long?"

"It was almost a year."

"I saw on the news that something happened to her grave soon after the funeral. It was disturbed, wasn't it?"

Ian recalled the incident only too well. Prior to the

burglaries it was the last time the police had been called to the village. "Yes, regrettably so. We think it was trophy hunters. The grave was partially opened and there was some damage to the headstone. Fortunately whoever was responsible failed to open the grave fully. My guess is they were interrupted in some way and abandoned the attempt."

"And it hasn't happened since?" Grantley asked.

"No, that was the only time."

"Did you implement any security measures?"

Ian sighed. It would have been the sensible thing to do but a woman who lived her life in the media spotlight deserved privacy in death. "Security cameras have no place in a churchyard, Norman. Candice should be allowed to rest in peace."

"Quite so."

Grantley realised that Ian was reluctant to discuss it further and dropped the subject. He rose from the table to go to the toilet.

"Why is he so interested in that?" Harry said.

Emily shrugged her shoulders. "He's new to the village. He's sure to have questions to ask us."

"When I arrived in the village I asked what time the pub opened. I didn't try to extract information about grave robbing and what measures had been put in place to prevent it."

"He was hardly doing that," Ian said.

"It sounded like it to me. You'd better do the rounds tonight. Grantley might think Candice had a couple of Oscars buried with her. If he does he'll have that grave open before you can say *'I would like to thank the Academy for this award and will put it with all the other stuff I've nicked.'*"

Candice couldn't believe what she was hearing. This latest excursion into unlawful activities involved her directly but even now she felt Harry was clutching at straws. "So he's gone from being a murderer, to a criminal mastermind, to a grave robber. What does he do on his days off?"

"That man is a walking crime wave," Harry insisted. "He'll get his spade and dig up everyone if we don't do something to stop him. When I'm buried I like to stay buried."

Candice looked at Emily and Ian in turn. "It's time for the pub quiz. What word is commonly associated with the phrase *'Mouth open?'*"

"Refuse to take this seriously if you will but don't come running to me when your coffin has been opened and you're left propped against a lamp post."

"Harry, my Oscars are safe with Sam, Emily, Prudence and Brenda. You need to get a grip on reality."

"All right, have it your way. Just make a note of this conversation in your diary."

Candice elected to ignore him. "I meant to ask about dinner last night," she said to Emily. "How did it go?"

"It was very nice. I think I may have damaged my hip though."

"On the first date?"

"It wasn't a date – and I would thank you for not putting me in embarrassing positions when Norman and I are in conversation."

"I'm more interested in the positions *he* put you in."

"As a man of God should I be party to this discussion?" Ian asked.

"It was nothing of that nature," Emily said. "It was his car. It's low to the ground and I had some difficulty getting in and out."

"Are we buying this?" Candice asked, looking around the table.

"Not in the slightest," Harry said.

"As a man of God I reserve judgement. Although it must be said, Emily, you'll have to do a lot better than that."

Emily frowned at the vicar and sought solace behind her wine glass.

Grantley returned soon after with another round. "I hope you don't mind but I took the liberty of getting you another," he said, setting the drinks down.

"Thank you, Norman. I really should be going but I've always got time for one more," Ian said.

"I'm delighted to hear it."

"You'll notice he didn't get us anything," Harry said to Candice.

"The man is obviously a cad," she replied.

Grantley sipped his drink and looked at the others. "Is there anywhere around here where I can buy a spade?"

If Harry *had* been drinking he would have choked on it.

"Did I hear that right?" Candice asked, equally taken-aback.

"The lamp post outside the butchers is a nice spot," Harry told her.

"Why do you need a spade?" Emily asked.

"The rear garden of my cottage is overgrown. It needs clearing. I'll have to get a good pair of pruners too."

Candice drew a sigh of relief.

"The nearest place would be Falworth," Ian said. "There are a couple of hardware shops in the town centre."

"I thought that would be the case. I'll drive in tomorrow morning," Grantley replied.

Candice looked at the clock on the wall and realised it was getting late. She was mindful of Samantha being at home alone with burglars in the area and decided to leave. "I'm heading back to the cottage. I'll call by tomorrow, Em. You can give me the steamy details about last night."

Emily fidgeted in her seat, trying not to look embarrassed again.

*

"I thought I heard someone moving around downstairs."

Samantha waited by the door to the attic room as Candice took control of the situation.

"Stay here. Close the door after me and lock it. Do you have your cell phone?"

Samantha showed it to her. "Yeah."

"Don't call the police yet, it might be nothing, but be ready to."

"Okay. Be careful."

Candice looked at her in a manner to suggest *I can't believe you said that.*

"You know what I mean."

"Keep calm and listen out for the screams. It won't be me making them," Candice felt compelled to add.

"I know. I don't want to hurry you but could you get on with it? I have to mow the lawn in four hours."

"That grass is a little long. You should have done it weeks ago."

Samantha was dressed in just a T-shirt and hugged herself to keep out the early morning chill. She would have visited her wardrobe prior to raising the alarm had she known they were going to have a debate about gardening. "Could you protect me from the burglars please? I'm cold and want to go back to bed."

Candice saw goosebumps on her arms and legs and grinned as she walked out onto the landing. She made sure Samantha closed and locked the door after her and went downstairs to investigate.

The sound Samantha heard had come from the kitchen and Candice heard it too when she reached the hallway. She couldn't make out what it was but had no doubt that her first citizens arrest was imminent. Or was it?

It occurred to her there was little she could have done in actually apprehending the burglars. At best she would scare them away but she could have followed them to see where they went. This information would be passed to the police and the residents of Cloverdale St Mary could breathe easily again.

"You guys have picked the wrong cottage," she said to herself as she walked through the wall beside the kitchen door.

Pyewacket was used to Candice in her ghostly form and didn't turn a hair when she appeared. Instead he busied himself with what he had been doing prior to her arrival.

If you can get into this fridge you're a better man than I am, Gunga Din.

Candice was disappointed that it was a false alarm. Knowing her luck Harry would have caught the burglars. She would never have heard the last of it if that happened. As a mortal he would have dined out on it for months. As a ghost with eternity at his disposal... God, it didn't bear thinking about.

"What are you doing here?" she said to Pyewacket.

I thought I'd stop by for a snack. How do you open this thing?

"This cottage is out of bounds to you at night. Go

raid Emily's fridge."

I would if she didn't have a padlock on it.

Like Harry before her, Candice pointed to the door.

"You have five seconds in which to vacate the area. If you don't I'll tell Samantha to buy a dog."

Pyewacket took a leisurely stroll to the cat flap. The dog hadn't been bred that would have been a match for him and he was unimpressed by the threat but the fridge had gotten the better of him again and he had no intention of outstaying his welcome.

Candice smiled as she watched him leave. "Be good. Love you, baby."

Pyewacket didn't hear her. He had seen a moth and was chasing it down the garden path. He would have caught it had it not sensed the danger and climbed to an altitude of twenty feet to evade him.

I hate it when they do that, the cat thought.

Candice wanted to be sure that all was well in the cottage and checked the downstairs rooms. When she was satisfied it was burglar-free she checked outside too.

Eight

Melanie Copeland was reading the May issue of *Horse and Rider Magazine* in the lounge. Her mother was polishing the coffee table. "What time is daddy coming home?" she asked, looking at her as she worked the polish into the wood.

"I'm sorry?"

"Daddy doesn't work on Saturdays. What time will he be home?"

"I'm afraid he is today. He's very busy at the moment," Janet said awkwardly.

"Will he be working all day?"

"I think so."

"What about tomorrow?"

"No, he won't be working tomorrow but he's in Scotland. It's a long way to come for just one day."

It was all Janet could do to stop her emotions from betraying her. She had to stay strong for Melanie. She laughed at her silliness and tried to act normally but it wasn't easy. It was hard. It was so damn hard.

Melanie failed to hide her disappointment. She hadn't seen her father all week and missed him. It wasn't the same when he was away. "Where is he living in Scotland?"

"He's not living there. He's staying in a hotel," Janet said.

"He was taking me to see Misty and Jo Jo this afternoon."

"I can take you... I need to fetch a clean duster."

Janet went to the kitchen as an excuse to escape from the room. She wept as she rested her hands on the worktop. It was made of marble and was hard. It was brutally hard. It was bone-crushingly hard. It was *why the hell did you do this to us?* hard.

She heard the front door open.

"Daddy, daddy!" Melanie called, running to greet him.

"Hello, half pint. Have you been a good girl for your mother?"

"I'm always a good girl," she said.

"That's debatable." Martin bent and kissed her hair.

"Are you taking me to see Misty and Jo Jo today or do you have to go back to work?"

"No, I'll take you. Just like I do every weekend. Where is your mother?"

"She's in the kitchen. Do you want to see my magazine?"

"Maybe later. You go back to the lounge. I'll be in shortly."

Melanie ran back to the living room, happy again, everything right with the world now her father was home.

For Martin Copeland everything was wrong.

"Why are you here?" Janet asked when he joined her in the kitchen.

"I heard about the burglaries. I can't stay in Falworth when you and Mel might be at risk. My place is with you."

"The returning hero."

Martin sighed. He didn't want confrontation. He knew this wouldn't be easy but hoped Janet would have understood his reasons for going home. "It doesn't have to be like this, Jan. I know what I did was wrong, and I would undo it in a heartbeat if I could, but please believe me, I never meant to hurt you."

"You made love to another woman. How do you think that was going to make me feel?"

He hung his head in shame.

"I want you to leave."

"What about Melanie? What about us?"

Everything Martin held dear was slipping away from him. He was powerless to stop it. There one moment and gone the next, his life and Janet's thrown into chaos by moments of weakness that he should have been strong enough to overcome. He began to cry.

"Please, Jan... let me fix this."

"You think you can put a plaster on it?" Janet said, crying too. "You think you can walk in here and make it all right? Do you have any idea what you've done?"

"I love you."

"When did you remember? The first time you laid down with her or the last?"

Janet's response left him feeling like the lowest of the low.

You thoughtless bastard, Samantha shouted in his head. *You selfish, thoughtless bastard.*

Who but the thoughtless could have put their family through something like this? Who but the deceitful could have plotted and schemed against those they loved? Who but the repentant could have stood before their wife begging forgiveness?

"Please... don't let it end like this."

"What's wrong?" Melanie asked from the doorway. She was distraught at seeing them in tears.

Neither had seen her arrive and Janet tried to repair the damage.

"Go back to the lounge," she said.

"Why are you crying?"

"Daddy and I need to talk. Go back to the lounge," her mother repeated.

"Tell me what's w-wrong," Melanie pleaded.

"Now, Melanie. Go to the lounge now."

The little girl wheeled away in tears and ran upstairs to her room.

Janet felt bad for being stern with her and broke

down. Martin instinctively went to comfort her.

"GET AWAY FROM ME!" she screamed. "Look what you've brought us to. Was it worth it? Did you think it wouldn't be like this?"

Janet fled the room through the back door and ran into the garden. The grass beneath her feet was hard.

It was so damn hard.

*

Samantha was mowing the lawn. She had been for half an hour but her progress was slow due to the fact that it was the worst lawnmower to ever come off a production line.

"You missed a bit," Harry said, appearing beside her. "In fact you've missed most of it," he added, looking around from his stationary position.

"That's because this thing is rubbish," Samantha replied. "How long have you had it?"

"I bought it from a car boot sale in 1985."

"You would have been better off buying the boot."

"What's wrong with it?"

"The choke slips open and floods the motor, one of the wheels keeps falling off and the blade would struggle to cut through butter. I had more fun sleeping on your sofa last night."

Harry enjoyed his conversations with Samantha. She was witty and entertaining but she did have a tendency to lose him every now and then. This was one such occasion. "Why did you sleep on my sofa? You have a perfectly good bed."

"I was waiting for Candice to come back. She didn't

and I fell asleep on your sofa."

"And where was Candice while you were doing this?"

"She went to catch the burglars."

"There were no break-ins last night."

"I can't be held responsible for that."

"Nor would I expect you to. The question is if the burglars took the night off who was Candice trying to catch?"

"The people who we thought were burglars."

"What people?"

"The people who weren't there apparently."

Harry scratched his head. "Sam, if you don't start to make sense I may have to strike you with a blunt instrument."

"I heard a noise downstairs last night. I sneaked to the attic room to tell Candice and she went to investigate. She didn't come back and I fell asleep on your sofa. I don't know where she is. I haven't seen her since."

"So one of our ghosts is missing?"

"Yes."

"Again. She's doing that a lot lately." A thought occurred to him and he changed the subject. "I meant to ask you, did she speak to you about Jo Jo?"

"Yeah. She asked me to take a look at her. Something didn't seem right so I called the vet to be on the safe side."

"The equestrian term is floopy," Harry replied.

It was the first Samantha had heard of it. She smiled out of politeness.

"Quite. Anyway, Charles said it was nothing to worry about. She had a slight chill. She's okay now."

"Good. I know Candice was worried about her."

Samantha's mobile phone vibrated in her jeans pocket. She rarely set it to vibrate but the lawnmower was louder than a jumbo jet taking off and had it rung she would never have heard it. An erupting volcano would have been quieter. "I'd better take this. It might be important," she said as she fished it out.

She made it sound like it may have been her New York broker.

"By all means."

Samantha walked away to take the call. The next thing Harry knew she was in her car and gone.

Finding himself deserted for the second time in four days, he tried to apply logic to a baffling situation.

"I know it's not my deodorant so they must have put something in the water."

*

"They certainly made a mess. Who would do something like this?"

Ian didn't answer Ron. He bent to retrieve a hymn book from the floor and looked at his vandalised church in silence. He never thought he would have seen such a thing in Cloverdale St Mary.

"How anyone can desecrate a church is beyond me," Miss Blunt said.

Her eyes found excrement smeared over the altar and she was forced to look away.

"Have the police finished here?" Ron asked the vicar.

"Yes. They left ten minutes ago."

"Then let's get it cleaned up. I'll ask Maggie to organize some more help. She'll put the word around."

"Thank you."

Ron placed his hand on Ian's shoulder and forced a smile. It was difficult given the circumstances but he was determined to show his support. "We'll soon have it back to how it was. This place will be full of volunteers before you know it."

Ian didn't doubt that for one moment. He knew the villagers could be relied upon for assistance during his time of need. No one would have left him to clear up the mess on his own. He was just stunned that something like this could have taken place here.

He was unaware of what had happened when he went to the church at 7:00 a.m. Cloverdale St Mary had a reputation for being a safe and trusting village but he always locked the door last thing at night and it was still locked when he arrived. It was only when he went inside that he realised someone had broken in and committed an act of desecration.

The vandals had gained entry through the vestry door at the rear of the church. It had been forced open with a crowbar. Once inside that crowbar had been put to other use. There was damage on a massive scale. Everything that could be smashed and broken was smashed and broken.

Ian was astonished that he and his family hadn't heard anything from the vicarage a short distance away. He couldn't understand how so much destruction could have been caused so quietly. Other cottages stood nearby too but everyone was oblivious to what was going on. Worse still was the pungent smell of animal faeces hanging on the air. It was everywhere. Whoever did this were animals of a different sort.

Ian knelt before the altar among the wreckage of torn Bibles and broken statues and prayed. He wept as he did so.

*

Emily made herself comfortable in her lounge at midday with a cup of tea. She, like many others, had spent a tiring morning helping to clean up the church. Ron had been proved right. Once Maggie put the word out Ian was inundated with residents who had only one thought in mind; let's get this mess cleaned up and show the vandals they won't get the better of us. The Dunkirk spirit was prevalent in cities during times of hardship, it thrived in towns under similar circumstances, but in villages and small hamlets it held the community together and no power on earth was greater.

Emily had gone home for something to eat and would return to the church later but lunch turned out to be her cup of tea and a ham sandwich because she was too exhausted to make anything else. She found the extent of the damage distressing and had been reduced to tears on more than one occasion. Ian didn't want her to go back but Emily wouldn't hear of it. As a regular church-goer she felt duty-bound to be involved in the clean up. She wouldn't have forgiven herself if she hadn't done all she could.

Grantley helped too after he returned from his shopping trip in Falworth. He offered to buy her lunch in the Coaching Inn but she declined in preference to going home. However, Emily did accept his invitation to have dinner there that evening. Now, sitting quietly with her thoughts, she wondered if she should have. It wasn't that she didn't want to have dinner with him. It was the timing.

"Knock, knock. Only me," Candice said, appearing in the room.

"Hello, my dear. How nice to see you," Emily replied.

"I was drifting by on the breeze and thought I would pop in. What have you been up to this morning?"

"Haven't you heard? The church was broken into last night and vandalised. I've been helping to clean it up."

Candice was shocked and appalled by the news. It was the sort of thing that happened to other people somewhere else, not to them. Not in a village like this. "Vandalised?"

"It's in a terrible mess. Ian is very upset but he's trying to put a brave face on it."

"I'll stop by and see him when he's not so busy. How bad is it?"

"Very bad. Bibles and hymn books were torn up and strewn over the floor. The statues of Christ and the Holy Mother were smashed. Lots of things have been broken. What really upset Ian was the excrement."

"Excrement?"

Emily could barely bring herself to speak of it. It was the worst thing she had ever seen. "It was awful, Candice. It was smeared everywhere. Ian wouldn't let anyone touch it. He insisted on cleaning it up himself."

Candice shook her head. This latest incident made it feel like a community under attack. It was as if Cloverdale St Mary had been singled out for every bad thing that could have happened. She wondered when there would be an end to it. "What is going on in this village? First the burglaries and now this. It's one trial after another."

"Do you think the same people are responsible?"

"It's possible but I doubt it. Why would thieves vandalise a church? I can understand why they would steal from one. Churches contain valuable artefacts and most have zero security but why wreck it? Was anything taken?" Candice asked in afterthought.

"It doesn't appear so. Ian has carried out a rough inventory but everything seems to be in place. It's just the damage."

"It doesn't make sense at all. Are you going back later?"

"Yes. I came home for lunch."

Candice pointed at the plate on Emily's coffee table. "A ham sandwich isn't gonna see you through the day."

"After the morning I've had I'm not very hungry to be honest with you."

Candice remembered the reason for her visit and turned the conversation to more pleasant matters. "I guess you're still pretty full after your dinner date the other night. How was it?"

Emily cheered up a little and smiled in reflection of an evening that had been enjoyable from start to finish.

Grantley had been the perfect gentleman. He was charming, humorous and good company. He treated her like a lady, the way her husband had done during a long and happy marriage. If it wasn't for the fact that his car played havoc with her hip she wouldn't have wanted the evening to end.

"It was very nice," she said. "He took me to Milanos. I've always wanted to dine there but it's out of my price range. Norman insisted on paying for the whole thing."

"Quite right. He invited you."

"Yes, but I like to pay my share. Anyway, after an excellent meal we came back here and chatted over coffee. He's a very interesting man. We talked till one o'clock in the morning and he left."

"After a goodnight kiss?"

"I allowed a peck to be placed lightly upon my cheek," Emily replied daintily.

Candice saw that twinkle in her eyes again. "You like him, don't you?"

"Yes, I do."

"Are you in the market for taking things further?"

"Candice, we've known each other less than a week. We're not about to go rushing down the aisle."

"Stranger things have been known to happen. Timing

goes out the window when romance is in the air."

Emily smiled again and dismissed such a notion with a casual wave of her hand. "Romance indeed. I left that sort of thing behind me years ago. We had dinner and it was very pleasant. End of story."

Candice wanted to know more and went fishing, discreetly of course. "Did Norman help out at the church this morning?"

"Yes. He went to Falworth to buy his gardening tools but when he returned and heard what had happened he came over straightaway."

"And you and he worked together during the clean up."

"Well, yes. I suppose we did."

"And then he offered to buy you lunch."

Emily failed to hide her surprise. "How did you know that?"

"Because he likes *you*. So the question is what are you doing here with a cup of tea and a ham sandwich that is curling at the edges?"

"It's not curling at the edges. That's the shape of the bread," Emily bluffed. She met an expression that knew she was trying to side-step the issue and grinned. "Norman did offer to buy me lunch but I declined. Instead I accepted his invitation to join him for dinner in the Coaching Inn this evening."

Candice smiled and rubbed her hands together. "Two dinner dates in three days. Can I be your maid of honour?"

"It's nothing like that. We enjoy each other's company."

"And you get free food out of it. Don't forget he's a retired doctor. He could do something about your hip. Why wait for the NHS when you can go private?"

"Candice Freeman, you're incorrigible."

Candice laughed and Emily laughed too.

The light-hearted moment didn't last long. The old lady stared past her and a troubled look came to her face.

"Is it too much too soon?" she asked.

"What do you mean?"

It was time for total honesty and Emily confided in her.

"You're right about Norman and I. We are attracted to each other. I felt it the first time we met. It could be wonderful if it was allowed to flourish but the only man I ever loved was George." She looked at his picture on the wall. It had been taken three months before he died unexpectedly of a heart attack. "I know it's silly to speak of love. Norman and I hardly know one another but what if our relationship did go in that direction? I don't want to be disrespectful to George's memory."

Candice wasn't surprised she felt that way. She expected nothing less knowing Emily as well as she did. "There's no harm in forming a friendship with another man but the good in you would see it as a betrayal. You're wrong to and George would be the first to tell you so but you feel that way because he was your soul mate."

"It doesn't seem right somehow."

"I know you miss George but he would want you to be happy. The past is filled with memories that we cherish but it's no place to live, Em. That's what the present is for, so we can make new memories to look back on in the future."

Emily recalled telling Miss Blunt the same thing when she reacted badly to the proposed equestrian centre but found it difficult to apply to herself. That was business. This was something altogether different.

"I wouldn't want George to think I don't love him anymore," she said. "I'm not sure what to do."

The answer to that was obvious.

"Take it one day at a time," Candice told her. "Don't put yourself under pressure by making it complicated when it needn't be. Enjoy your friendship with Norman and see where it leads. If it develops into something else you'll have George's blessing. You'll know it by then. You'll know in your heart."

Emily nodded. A good friend had told her what she already knew. She just needed to hear it in words that were plain and simple, reassurance from someone who knew better than most that love never dies. "Thank you, Candice."

"Eat your lunch. You have a busy afternoon ahead of you."

*

"Is Candice back yet?"

Harry had been standing guard over the lawnmower. It may have been next to useless but Samantha left it unattended and he didn't want the burglars to drive by and steal it. "No. I don't have a clue where she is," he told her. "I don't know where you've been for the past two hours either. This is a valuable piece of machinery. You can't leave it lying around for any Tom, Dick or Dave to pinch."

"Sorry. I had to go home. Dad's there."

Missing ghosts and vulnerable lawnmowers suddenly lost their importance and he looked at her anxiously.

"Is everything all right?"

"Mum wanted him to leave but he's going to stay. He insisted on it with burglars operating in the area."

"I think that's a wise decision. Janet and Mel

shouldn't be there alone."

"Yeah, that's what I said. The three of us sat around the kitchen table and talked it through. Things are tense between them and I don't know how they'll get on being under the same roof but it's a step in the right direction. Dad is going to sleep in my room. That was something *mum* insisted on."

"It's understandable given the circumstances."

"The only problem is Mel. She knows what is happening now. Well, in part at least."

"How did she take it?"

"Badly. She stayed in her room the whole time I was there. It was just as well bearing in mind the topic of conversation. She doesn't know the full details, only that mum and dad have things to sort out. She doesn't know about the affair."

Harry felt encouraged by the way Samantha was handling the situation. She had come to terms with it and was calm and objective. She had abided by her mother's wishes and hadn't taken sides. It would have been easy to have done so, to condemn her father as the villain and make life difficult for him, but that wasn't her way and never would be. She wanted her parents to work it out, to reconcile and be a family again. That wouldn't happen if their eldest daughter lobbed grenades at Martin while screaming adulterer.

"I'm sure things will turn out all right, Sam. They just need a bit of time. With your support they can come through this."

"I'll do whatever I can."

"And you'll do it well because you're a caring person."

Samantha grinned. "Thank you, Mr Black."

Harry didn't. His frown was the type normally reserved for lawns that were in need of mowing. "When are you going to start calling me Harry? It's like standing on ceremony. You'll be saluting me next."

She did so out of fun.

"I refuse to take this conversation further. You're too much like Candice sometimes."

"I wonder where she is?" Samantha said, becoming serious again.

"With any luck she's in Falworth buying a new lawnmower." Harry cast it a derisory glance. He would have kicked it if he could. "This thing is rubbish."

Samantha laughed and they went indoors, leaving the grass uncut and the mower at the mercy of anyone who may have taken a shine to it.

Had it not been returned to the garden shed soon after it would still have been there six months later.

Nine

Emily toyed with a meal in the Coaching Inn that was up to Ron's usual high standards but she had no appetite for. It was as good as anything that appeared on the menu in Milanos and came at a fraction of the cost but she simply wasn't in the mood for it. In retrospect going back to the church that afternoon had been a mistake.

Ian knew she was finding it difficult and suggested she went home but Emily insisted on staying and finally left at four o'clock. By then most of the work had been done and the others left too. Miss Blunt stayed well into the evening and helped the vicar and his wife to put the vestry in order. The vandals had spared nothing in their attack. They had taken a holy place and turned it into a bomb-site.

The church played an important role in village life and seeing it wrecked had been a bitter pill to swallow. Emily despaired at what people were capable of. There was no rhyme or reason to it, just mindless vandalism that appealed to some and disgusted many. She wondered who could have done such a thing, what pleasure could they have derived from it? Knowing the answer made her feel worse. It could have been anyone. The pleasure was in the doing.

There was another reason why Emily had taken the vandalism of the church so personally but hadn't spoken of it. Miss Blunt knew. They had talked about it briefly during the day but only to each other. Not to anyone else.

"Is everything all right?" Grantley asked, pausing over his water glass. "You seem to be out of sorts this evening."

"Yes, I'm fine," Emily replied, forcing a smile. "What

happened at the church has made me poor company. I'm sorry."

"There's no need to apologize. It came as a shock to everyone."

"You must be wondering what you've let yourself in for. First the burglaries and now this. I wouldn't be surprised if you wanted to move again and find somewhere safer to live."

It was Grantley's turn to smile but he did so genuinely.

"It would take more than thieves and thugs to make me turn my back on Cloverdale St Mary. I like it here. I like the people too."

Emily began to cry.

Grantley abandoned his meal and took her hand. He was concerned and sympathetic, everything a decent man would have been. "Don't be upset, my dear. I'm sure the police will catch those responsible and bring them to account."

"You must think me very silly."

"Not at all. This village means a lot to you. I can see how you would find something like this distressing."

"It would be best if I went home. I'm sorry, Norman. Please forgive me."

"Of course. I'll walk with you."

"No, stay and finish your meal. I'll be okay. I really am sorry."

"May I call on you tomorrow? To make sure you're all right."

"I would like that. Thank you."

Emily rose from the table and left.

*

"It would help if I knew what you were talking about."

"Last night," Samantha told a bemused Candice in the lounge of Meadow Cottage. "You went downstairs to investigate the sound I heard but didn't come back. I fell asleep on the sofa in the attic room because you told me to stay there."

"That's right. I checked her bed and it hasn't been slept in," Harry said.

Samantha wasn't sure if she liked the idea of Harry going into her bedroom but elected not to comment.

It was 10:30 in the evening and the first time they had seen Candice all day. Where she had been was a question yet to be addressed. That would come but first they wanted to know what happened in the early hours of the morning when she went missing to begin with.

Candice looked at them in turn and came to the conclusion they must have gone mad. "Did they put something in the water around here? I didn't go anywhere last night. We talked for a while, then you went to your room and I went to mine."

She had answered without giving it much thought but when she did she was swept by doubt. It suddenly dawned on Candice that Samantha was right. When she spoke again it was as if a piece of a jigsaw puzzle had fallen into place. A puzzle she had no prior knowledge of.

"Then you came to tell me you heard a noise and I went to take a look."

"That's right, but you didn't come back," Samantha said.

"Didn't I?"

"No. The next thing I knew I woke at seven o'clock this morning with a stiff neck." Samantha looked at Harry with an air of disapproval. "It's not the most comfortable sofa in the world."

"I'll make the manufacturer aware of your comments."

Candice didn't respond. She had retreated to silence and remained there.

"Don't you remember what happened after you came downstairs?" Harry asked her.

"No. Not a thing," she said.

It was Cross Drummond all over again.

"The other day at the stables, when we were watching Jo Jo. You were convinced you came home with me but you didn't. You went somewhere else. Do you know where you might have gone?"

"We've been through this before. I came back..." Candice stopped abruptly. She knew by his concerned expression that there was more to it. "I thought I came back with you."

"No, Candice. I didn't see you again until ten o'clock that evening. Four hours later."

"So where the hell was I?"

No one answered.

Candice stood up from the armchair and paced the room. She had no memory of what she had done or where she had been. Her mind was a total blank and she struggled to apply reason to it. "This is crazy. How can I go someplace without knowing where I'm at?"

"Keep calm," Harry advised her.

"That's easy for you to say. You're not the one who can't remember what they're doing from one moment to the next."

"There has to be a logical explanation," Samantha said.

"Yeah, I'm going insane. Can that happen to a ghost?"

"I can't say I've heard of it," Harry replied.

"Good for me, I'm breaking new ground. I always wanted to be an innovator."

Harry saw the dangers of trying to run before they

could walk and appealed for calm once more. He too was at a loss to explain what was happening but nothing would have been gained by second-guessing the unknown. "I agree with Sam. There must be a simple explanation. All we have to do is work out what it is."

"Maybe you could tag me with a radio transmitter like the cops use. That way we would know my whereabouts 24-7."

Something else was worrying Samantha and she approached it carefully. The situation was perplexing and she didn't want to make it worse.

"I don't want to worry you further, Candice, but the time lapse might be an issue. When you disappeared at Cross Drummond you were gone four hours. This time it's been twenty."

"I've been here with you guys."

Samantha shook her head. "Mr Black and I haven't seen you all day. Not till you appeared ten minutes ago."

Candice looked at them assuredly. The time had come to panic. "Okay. Someone needs to say something positive here to stop me from freaking out."

"Perhaps you slipped into another dimension," Harry offered.

"Not helping."

"Is that possible?" Samantha asked him.

He shrugged his shoulders. "I don't know."

"What we need is an expert in the paranormal," Samantha said.

"The trouble is there's never one around when you need one," Candice told her. "What am I gonna do? I don't know where I'm gonna be in five minutes from now."

"You're going to be here with us," Harry said.

"I appreciate that something needs to be done but I'm too old to be grounded."

Harry looked at the clock on the wall. He had a prior

engagement that was pressing and couldn't be put off. "Actually, you'll be here with Sam. I have to go. I'm due on burglar-watch at Emily's."

Samantha didn't welcome a possible re-run of the previous night and wished he would stay but Emily was a pensioner living alone and these were uncertain times. Harry had given his word that he would look out for her until the burglars were caught and nothing would make him break it.

"She won't be home yet. She'll be in the pub," Candice told him.

"Emily isn't the boozer you make her out to be," Harry replied. "You still hold the record for the most hours spent in the Coaching Inn."

Despite the concerns that existed over her disappearances and memory lapses, Candice was amused.

"She's having dinner with Norman Grantley this evening. I expect they're halfway through dessert by now."

"She had dinner with him on Thursday," Harry said.

"And she's having dinner with him tonight too." Candice was serious again and stared beyond him when a thought occurred to her. "How did I know that?"

"Have you spoken to Emily today?" Samantha asked.

"No... yes," Candice corrected herself, remembering. "I went to see her this afternoon. The church was vandalised."

"Yes, it was," Harry said.

"Emily told me about it. That was when she told me she was having dinner with Grantley this evening."

"That accounts for some of your missing twenty hours," Samantha said. "Can you remember what time this was?"

Candice resumed pacing the floor, trying to connect

fragments of details that were hazy but became clearer the more she thought about it. "She was eating a sandwich. She had been helping to fix up the church and went home for lunch. It was midday." She smiled, heartened by the fact that something had come back to her. "I was in Emily's cottage at midday."

It wasn't much but it was a start.

"All we need to do now is determine where you were before then and in the ten hours since," Harry said, spoiling the moment.

"Has anyone got a radio transmitter going spare?" Candice asked, deflated again.

"We'll pick this up in the morning," Harry said. "I'd better be going. Dessert doesn't take long to eat and the Coaching Inn closes at eleven."

"You can't go now. She might invite him back for coffee," Candice replied.

"All the more reason for me to be there. I wouldn't trust that man as far as I could throw him. Come and fetch me if there are any problems here." It occurred to Harry that Candice wasn't the most reliable of ghosts at the moment and his parting words were directed to Samantha. "If Candice goes AWOL again call Emily."

Candice took exception to this and pulled a face at him as he faded from view.

*

Emily was sitting in her lounge when Harry arrived. Pyewacket was lying on the sofa but when the cat saw him he decided it would be a good time to find something to mutilate and took leave of them.

Even before the burglaries Harry was a regular visitor to Pine Trees Cottage. He and Emily liked to watch old black and white films on TV. They used to watch horror films but Harry was easily frightened despite his claims to the contrary and spent most of his time hiding behind the sofa under the pretext of looking for a missing cuff-link so they changed their viewing habits to something less shocking. The musicals, comedies and dramas they watched now suited him perfectly. He had harboured a secret fear that one evening he might have found a cuff-link and would have to think of another excuse for missing the film.

He expected everything to be ready but was dismayed to find the room silent. "Why isn't the telly on?"

"I don't feel like watching TV tonight. I was about to go to bed," Emily replied.

"At this hour? You're a night owl."

"It's been a long day."

Harry knew she had spent most of it helping at the church but realised something was wrong and immediately assumed the worst. There was only one explanation for Emily's subdued mood and he was determined the guilty party would be held accountable. "What did Grantley do?" he asked angrily.

"What?"

"You had dinner with him this evening. Has he upset you in some way?"

"No."

"Something is wrong."

"I'm just tired."

"You're not your usual self. Something is bothering you. If Grantley has stepped out of line I'll have him."

"Please don't go on at me, Harry."

She began to cry.

Her tears surprised him and he tried to be of comfort.

"It's all right, Emily," he said, kneeling beside her chair. "I'm sorry. I didn't mean to speak out of turn."

"You haven't done that."

"I care about you. You know I get a bit carried away sometimes."

Emily dabbed her eyes with a handkerchief and smiled weakly. Harry was the master of the understatement.

"Is there anything I can do to help?" he asked.

Emily composed herself. A difficult day had claimed victory over her. She just wanted it to be finished but Harry was concerned and deserved to know the truth behind it. They knew each other too well to keep secrets.

"The problem isn't Norman. Well, it is, but only partially and not in the way you think. He hasn't done anything to upset me."

"So what has upset you? Have you seen anyone acting suspiciously around the cottage? Has something frightened you?"

"No, it's nothing like that. It's what happened at the church." She paused in a moment of reflection, happy memories tainted by recent events. "George and I were married there. Today is our wedding anniversary."

Harry understood now.

"Seeing it vandalised was heartbreaking. It was the happiest day of our lives and today I watched Ian clean animal faeces off the very spot where George and I took our vows. How can people do something like that? How can they desecrate something that means so much to others?"

Harry wished he knew. One thing was certain. Those responsible would have shown no remorse if they heard Emily speaking now. They would have taken delight in her distress and done all they could to have made it worse.

"Have you spoken to anyone about this?" he asked.

"Only Prudence. She was one of my bridesmaids. You know what an excellent memory she has for important dates. She took me aside this morning and told me how sorry she was. I didn't mention it to anyone else."

"You haven't told Grantley?"

"No. He knew I was distraught but I didn't tell him why. I didn't stay for dinner this evening, I left early. He said he would call on me tomorrow to make sure I was all right. In hindsight I shouldn't have gone out with him. Not today."

Her eyes travelled to George's picture on the wall.

Harry knew there was more to it. "Grantley means a lot to you, doesn't he?"

"I know you don't like him, but yes, he does. He's a good man."

Harry couldn't see what the attraction was but this was no time to question her judgement. He still didn't trust Grantley but Emily liked him and he had to accept that she wanted to spend more time in his company. In future he would bad-mouth him in private and not in her presence. He felt like a fraud because of it but Emily's feelings had to come first.

"You said he was part of the problem. In what way?"

Emily recalled her conversation with Candice. Everything they said to each other still held true but returning to the church that afternoon had made her doubts resurface and it wasn't as straightforward as it was over lunch. If anything it had given her greater cause for concern.

"Norman and I get on well and I would like to see more of him but I don't want to be disloyal to George's memory." She realised what she said may have been open to misinterpretation and tried to repair. "Not that I'm looking for that sort of relationship. I don't mean in a physical way or anything like that."

Emily felt uncomfortable and wrung her hands.

Harry knew what she meant and smiled to reassure her. "George played a large part in your life. There was a bond between you that not only survived the test of time but grew stronger as it went by. That sort of love is rare, Emily. George would want you to be happy. He wouldn't think badly of you if you found it again."

"That's what Candice said but I can't help thinking badly of myself."

Harry had no answer for her. There was nothing he could have said that would have made her view things differently.

A change of mood was called for and he seized the moment to be positive.

"Come on, Braithwaite, put the telly on. Let's watch a film and forget our troubles for a hour or two."

"I would rather go to bed."

Oh, the sadness in her eyes. It tore into his very being.

Emily walked out of the room slowly.

Harry sat on the sofa to begin his all-night vigil.

Countless troubled thoughts swamped his mind. The situation regarding Candice defied explanation. Emily's dilemma had been easier to address but his words of reassurance couldn't be accepted by a woman who loved her dead husband and felt guilty for liking another man. Harry could see no easy way around it. It was what it was; a good heart being pulled in two different directions.

The village braced itself for another uncertain night and the church stood dark and empty, licking its wounds after suffering a brutal attack. Daylight was hours away but a solution to their problems was even further out of reach.

*

Miss Blunt lay bound and gagged on her bedroom floor. She was bleeding from a cut to her forehead.

"This should fetch a couple of quid," one of the intruders said, admiring the Academy Award now in his possession.

It had been presented to Candice for her portrayal of Doctor Helen Daniels in Jon McGuire's 2014 film *The Eternity Child*.

His partner in crime was more interested in the haul of three-day eventing trophies that had been taken from their display cabinet and put in a black refuge sack. They would have fetched a handsome price too when melted down.

For him this burglary was personal and he looked at Miss Blunt without comment. He was wearing a mask so he had no fear of being recognized but he couldn't speak because she may have placed his voice.

Vandalising the church that Miss Blunt devoted so much time to and robbing her of her most prized possessions was only the beginning. Vengeance belonged to the man in the mask and he would have it.

Cloverdale St Mary hadn't begun to suffer yet.

*

It was 3:17 a.m. Candice stood in Samantha's bedroom as she slept. She stared at her through trance-like eyes. Over the past couple of days she had watched her shower and dress but this was the first time she had studied her at rest. It wouldn't be the last.

Candice was unaware that she was in Samantha's bedroom. She didn't know she was being controlled by a force that was powerful and all-consuming. She followed when her Master called, she went where he told her to go. She obeyed without question because when she was under his influence she had no mind or will of her own. It was her duty to serve him and serve him she would.

It had been a hot day and wasn't as chilly as the previous night. Samantha had discarded the T-shirt she wore in bed to sleep in the nude. The duvet covering her lay at her waist. She stirred, rolling on her back, but didn't wake. Arms above her head, she arched herself as she stretched and settled down again.

The twenty-one year-old looked after herself and it showed in a body scrutinized by those trance-like eyes. It didn't matter that the force wasn't present. There was no need for him to be in attendance when he could rely on his unknowing assistant. He could have done what he wanted when he wanted, secure in the knowledge that no one was in a position to challenge him. There were no limitations for a man as powerful as he. What mattered was that Norman Grantley had made his choice and was ready to proceed to the next phase.

Samantha was destined for greatness.

Ten

The Church of St Mary may have been vandalized but Ian had no intention of allowing it to disrupt his Sunday morning service. It was open as usual and because of it Miss Blunt's plight was discovered.

She set out fresh flowers on service days. For that reason she got to the church early and was one of the first to arrive. When she failed to appear that morning Ian was concerned and went to her cottage. Receiving no answer when he knocked on her door, he looked through the lounge window and saw the room had been ransacked. The police and paramedics were there in twenty minutes.

Miss Blunt was shaken by her ordeal but none the worse for it in a physical sense and recovered quickly. The cut to her head wasn't serious and she flatly refused to go to hospital for a detailed examination. *'There are people more deserving of your time. I suggest you tend to them and leave me to go about my business,'* she had told one of the paramedics forcibly.

He didn't want to engage in a shooting war and bowed to her wishes. There was as much chance of Miss Blunt going to hospital for a check-up as there was of the burglars returning her possessions.

Ian insisted that she stayed at home to rest. Miss Blunt insisted that she would attend the service. Ian put his foot down and ordered her to rest but he was talking to himself because she had already left.

That woman is indestructible he thought, going after her.

Now, with the service concluded and at home again, she told Emily and Maggie what had happened over a cup of tea.

"I heard a noise at two o'clock this morning. It sounded like the sideboard drawer being opened. It is tight-fitting and difficult to open if one is not aware of the problem. When I came downstairs to investigate I found two men in the lounge."

"What did you do?" Maggie asked.

"I told them in no uncertain terms that I was going to call the police."

Neither of her visitors were surprised to hear this. It was typical of Miss Blunt to seize the bull by the horns. Anyone else would have fled the room and barricaded themselves in the kitchen but that wasn't her way. A challenge had to be faced, not avoided by hiding behind the refrigerator.

"Before I could go to the phone one of them struck me on the head. I lost consciousness and woke soon after tied up in my bedroom."

"I wonder why they took you back upstairs?" Emily said.

"Presumably they did not want me cluttering up the lounge while they were in the process of emptying it," Miss Blunt replied, less than charitably. "The nerve of those people. They must be caught. This cannot be allowed to go on."

"But what can we do?" Maggie asked. "They seem to have a free hand to go wherever they want. Who knows where they'll strike next."

"It is all the more reason for us to start the night patrols as soon as possible," Miss Blunt said. "The police are quick to act after the event but they cannot be relied upon to prevent these burglaries from being committed. We must take matters into our own hands. There will be no end to them if we do not."

Emily still didn't think self-policing was a good idea but didn't comment.

There came a knock at the door.

"Would you like me to see who it is?" Maggie asked Miss Blunt.

"That will not be necessary. I will go."

Her response had *I'm quite capable of opening a door* written all over it but Maggie didn't take offence. She knew her too well.

She and Emily grinned.

"Norman. How nice to see you," they heard her say from the hallway.

"My dear Prudence. I didn't go to church this morning and had no idea what had happened. I came as soon as I heard. Are you all right?"

"Yes, thank you. Please, come through. Emily and Maggie are here."

Grantley followed her to the lounge.

"Good afternoon, ladies," he said on arrival.

"Hello, Norman," Maggie replied.

Emily smiled but said nothing.

"Would you like a cup of tea?" Miss Blunt asked.

"I don't want to put you to any trouble."

"Nonsense. There is plenty more in the pot. Would you attend to it, Maggie?"

Maggie grinned again and poured one for him. "Milk and sugar?"

"Sugar but no milk please."

Grantley looked around the room and was heartened by what he saw. Now it had been cleaned up it appeared normal. The electrical items were missing of course; the TV, DVD player, stereo, but it wasn't as bad as he expected. He saw the display cabinet was empty but didn't know what it had contained.

"Thank you, Maggie," he said, accepting his tea. "Did they take much?"

"The usual things burglars steal," Miss Blunt replied. "Most of what I own is personal to me and would be of no use to others. There would not be much re-sale value attached to it."

"I'm sure that isn't the case, Prudence. I'm sorry this has happened to you."

The truth was Miss Blunt's possessions meant the world to her. Most were irreplaceable and she bowed her head to hide her distress.

"If there is anything I can do don't hesitate to ask," he said.

"Thank you, Norman. It is very kind of you to offer."

"They stole her trophies," Emily told him with a heavy heart.

"Trophies?" Grantley asked.

"Prudence is an excellent horsewoman. She used to be a three-day eventer. She won competitions all over the country."

"On the amateur circuit," Miss Blunt said, embarrassed by Emily's compliment.

"And they took them," Grantley said, appalled to hear it. "I can't imagine what you must be going through, Prudence."

"They are merely material things, Norman. One rises above their loss and carries on. I was fortunate. Aside from a bang on the head I came through it unharmed. It could have been much worse."

"Quite so," he replied, not sure what to say.

"They stole an Oscar too," Maggie said.

That he didn't expect to hear.

"You had an Oscar?"

"It was bequeathed to me by Candice Freeman."

Miss Blunt found the loss of the Academy Award more upsetting than anything else. Not because of its value, that didn't matter to her, but because it had belonged to a good friend who entrusted it into her care. It was a reminder of better days, of the bond that had developed between them, of a young life taken too soon. A woman who was loved by millions but cherished by just a few.

Miss Blunt rose from her chair. "Please excuse me."

She walked hurriedly from the room in tears.

Emily went after her and provided comfort as she broke down in the kitchen.

"Oh, Maggie. Something needs to be done about this," Grantley said in their absence.

Maggie offered nothing in reply but their thoughts were the same. Something did need to be done and it had to be done now.

This was one burglary too many.

*

"If I could get my hands on them they wouldn't know what day of the week it was," Harry said, angered by the news of the latest break-in.

"What we need is a plan," Candice told him. "It's all very well watching over Emily after dark and keeping an eye on Meadow Cottage but when they hit someone else we're in the wrong part of town."

"We can't be everywhere."

"That's why we need a plan. There must be something else we can do."

"We could draft in some of our friends from the afterlife. Bert would be willing to help and there are hundreds more like him."

"Harry, we can't put a ghost in every cottage. Even if we could what good would it do? We can't call the cops when the burglars show up. All we can do is pull faces at them in the hope of scaring them off. It's hardly the ultimate in home security, is it?"

"I don't know about that. Not many burglars would survive number twelve on the list. I did it to myself once. I thought I was going to have a heart attack."

"It's better than electrocuting yourself with a power drill."

"I'd like to electrocute those thieves. Technically you're a victim too. How do you feel about your Oscar being stolen?"

"That's not important. I'm just glad Pru is all right. I dread to think what might have happened."

"I wonder why they took her upstairs. When they tied up Barbara they left her in the lounge."

"That's what worries me."

The possible scenario of what lay behind their actions didn't bear thinking about and they were silent for a moment.

"I'm glad nothing happened here," Harry finally said.

"Let's hope it stays that way. Now the burglars have an Oscar as part of their haul it might make them wonder if there are any more in the village. That would make this place an obvious target. It's common knowledge that I lived here and Sam and I were friends. If Pru had one of my Academy Awards why shouldn't she?"

"Not to mention the Golden Globes and BAFTAs," Harry agreed. "I know most of them were sold for charity at auction and the others are safe with Brenda in London but the burglars might think they're here."

"Maggie and Ron have a BAFTA. Ian and Sheila have a Golden Globe," Candice reminded him.

It occurred to Harry that when Candice moved to Cloverdale St Mary the village had become a treasure trove. The combined value of her awards made it one of the richest in the country. It was no wonder thieves had staked a claim to it but perhaps that would have been their undoing.

"Wait a minute. We could turn this to our advantage."

"What do you mean?" Candice asked.

"What if the burglars did know there was an Oscar here?"

"They would come to steal it."

"Exactly. And when they do we catch them. We don't have to put a ghost in every cottage. We make them come to us."

"You mean use Meadow Cottage as a trap?"

"Yes."

"Samantha will love that idea. She could put up a big sign outside: *'Attention all burglars. I have an Oscar left to me by Candice Freeman. Why don't you hit me over the head, tie me up and steal it?'* We could help with the lettering."

Harry didn't appreciate her sarcasm and responded accordingly. "Am I to gather from your comments that you're not in favour of my plan?"

"Sam is our friend. We can't put her in danger like that."

"She won't be in danger. We will be here to protect

her."

"You perhaps. There's no telling were I might be. I don't even know if I'm gonna stick around long enough to finish this conversation."

Candice's wanderlust had become secondary in light of recent events, overshadowed by what had happened to Miss Blunt and the threat of more burglaries to come. It should have been addressed sooner and Harry felt guilty for not doing so.

"Was everything okay last night? You didn't feel an overwhelming desire to visit Australia?"

"I was going to but I left it too late to get my shots."

"I know travel broadens the mind but it might be better if you stayed at home for a while."

"Have you had any more thoughts on that?"

"I thought of nothing else all night."

Candice had been thinking about it too and was no closer to finding an explanation. All sorts of possibilities had entered her mind and taken up residence there, worst case scenarios too horrible to contemplate that were impossible to dismiss. She didn't know what was happening to her or why but something had to be done about it. She felt in limbo, waiting for it to happen again and dreading the consequences.

"What if it's something bad, Harry? What if I go away and don't come back?"

"That won't happen. Whatever it is we'll sort it out," he said assuredly.

"I don't wanna lose you. I couldn't bear it if I never saw you again."

Harry sat beside her on the sofa. For both of them eternity had become nothing more than a word, something permanent that could have ended any moment, but he refused to surrender to the possibility. He would fight it with everything he had. "You're not losing me and I'm not losing you. We're like glue you and I. We're stuck with each other."

Candice smiled. She hoped he was right but what if he was wrong? Harry had no idea how scared she was.

The actress in her hid it well.

*

Melanie watched Samantha exercise Jo Jo at Cross Drummond and sighed as she sat on the gate to the field. To say she was envious of her sister at times like this would have been an understatement. "I wish I could ride her, daddy. When can I?"

"I think you need to be a bit older before you can handle a horse of that size," Martin replied.

"But she's mine. Candice gave her to me."

"I know. It must be hard for you seeing Sam and your mother ride her but that's the way it has to be for now. Be patient, Mel. Good things come to those who wait."

"By the time the good thing comes to me Jo Jo will be too old for anyone to ride," Melanie sulked.

Martin couldn't help himself. He roared with laughter.

Melanie looked at him through adoring eyes. She didn't know what the problems were between her mother and father, only that they were awkward with one another and everyone was sad, but hearing him laugh lifted her spirits. He hadn't done so in a long time and she was glad of it.

"Are you happy again?" she asked him.

Martin smiled and smoothed her hair. "Of course I am. I'm here with you. You always make me happy."

"And Sam."

"Yes, and Sam."

"When will you and mummy be friends again?"

The innocence of youth. Deception, loss, betrayal and pain had no place in a child's world. There was no time-frame, no negotiations, no agenda that had to be kept to. It was simply a case of when things would return to normal, when the awkwardness and sadness would be gone and mummy and daddy would be friends again. What was difficult for adults was easy for children because they didn't complicate matters by applying adult rules. For them it was candy-floss and magical castles in the sky. For Martin Copeland and people like him it was so damn hard.

"I don't know, Mel. We have some things to sort out."

"What things?"

"You needn't concern yourself with that. We'll make it better again. I promise."

In wanting to spare her the sordid details, Martin unwittingly opened the door to doubt and self-recrimination.

"Is it because of me? Did I do something wrong?" she asked.

It was the worst thing a cheating husband could have heard. It devastated him to think that Melanie would have held herself responsible for the breakdown of his marriage, that without knowing anything about it she would blame herself.

"No, Mel, you haven't done anything wrong. It was me. I did something bad and upset your mother. It was foolish of me and I wish I hadn't done it. You're not to blame in any way. It isn't your fault. Your mother and I love you. We love you very much and I'll do everything I can to make things right."

"Did you have an affair?"

Martin should have been surprised but he wasn't. Melanie was of an age where she knew about such things through social media and playground talk. She may not have fully understood the implications that lay behind it but she knew that marriages had failed for less.

"Yes, I did."

"Who is she?"

"A woman I work with. It's over now. It should never have started in the first place. I'm sorry, Mel."

"Were you in Scotland?"

A single tear ran down his cheek.

"No. I wasn't in Scotland."

He kissed her head and regretted the lies he and Janet had told Melanie to protect her from the loss, betrayal and pain. In doing so they had allowed something else that had no place in a child's world to enter. It was the same thing he had done to his wife, the unforgivable crime for which he had to atone. They had deceived her.

Melanie stared across the field in silence.

She came back to herself when Samantha walked Jo Jo to the gate. They came to a halt in front of them and her sister dismounted.

"Come on then, Mel. Your turn," she said.

Melanie looked at her father. Her eyes were wide with surprise and excitement. "What?"

Martin smiled. "You asked when you could ride her, I said when you're older. That was five minutes ago. You're older now."

"Can I? Can I really?"

"Yes, you can, but there are some rules you have to follow," Samantha said.

Melanie took her hard hat from the gate post and jumped to the ground. Jo Jo didn't flinch despite the sudden movement.

"The rules are no trotting, cantering or galloping," Samantha told her. "You just walk around for now. I know you're a good rider but Jo Jo is more powerful than Misty. You won't be able to stop her if she gets her head and decides to take off."

"So it's walking only," Martin reiterated.

"Okay."

Melanie took the reins from Samantha and pulled herself up into the saddle.

Martin took a picture of her on his mobile phone.

They watched them walk away with contrasting opinions. Now Melanie was actually moving Martin was concerned.

"Are you sure she's ready?" he asked Samantha.

"Truth be told, she's been ready for months. We've been too protective of her. Mel knows what she's doing. She'll be all right."

"She knows about the affair," he said.

Now it was Samantha who looked concerned.

"How?"

"She asked me straight out."

"What did you say?"

"I told her the truth. I didn't go into details of course but I admitted to being unfaithful." He watched Melanie walk Jo Jo in a wide circle. He had never seen her so content. "She had a right to know. Mel's been lied to enough."

"I'm glad you told her."

"Do you think your mother will ever forgive me?"

"I'm sure she will. You haven't become a different person, you're the same man you always were. Mum will come to realise that in time."

"And you? Can you forgive me for what I did?"

That was less clear-cut and Samantha hesitated.

"I've accepted it. I'm not angry like I was but I still don't understand why you went with her. I don't think I ever will. I love you, dad, and nothing will change that. You sacrificed so much for me in bringing me up on your own. I know it wasn't easy for you but I need time too, like mum does."

Martin couldn't have wished for a more honest answer. He had raised his daughter well. He reached for her hand and she took his instinctively. "I'll make it up to you, Sam. I'll make it up to all of you. I promise."

"You don't have to do that. All you have to do is love us."

Samantha embraced him and suddenly hard seemed a little bit easier.

Eleven

It had been a busy morning for Bill and Susan in the village shop. Their Tuesdays were known to be slow but a constant stream of customers had kept them on the go from the moment they opened. It used to be a shop and post office but the post office had gone the way of many in small villages and was closed as part of cut-backs six months previously.

The villagers fought the closure vigorously. Miss Blunt had taken their protests to the highest level of local government but austerity was key and their protests were doomed to failure. It was like everything else that served the public interest. Why have hospital beds when patients could have been left on trolleys in congested corridors? Why did schools need books and learning materials when there was a teacher at the head of the class who could have muddled by without them? Why should a village have a post office when there was a perfectly good one in a town fifteen miles away? Those without transport could have got there by bus - or they could before the bus service was cut too.

Susan was devastated by the decision to close it. She had been a postmistress for twenty years and knew nothing else. She and Bill owned the premises. The shop was an extension of their cottage. She needed something to fill the void left by a business taken away from her and embarked on a new venture.

The space once occupied by the post office was now a tearoom where locals and visitors to the village could pass the time of day over tea and scones. It was an instant success and proved to be very popular. Two months previously wash room facilities had been added and it was now a thriving business in its own right. It was the worst place to go if someone wanted to renew their passport but as somewhere to catch up with village gossip it was perfect.

Miss Blunt had to go to Falworth for a dental appointment and stopped for tea and a butterfly bun prior to driving into town. She joined Emily sitting at a table but her arrival went unnoticed. Emily's attention was directed elsewhere.

The front page of the morning newspaper had taken everyone in Cloverdale St Mary by surprise. Reports of strange lights in the sky over the village was one thing, seeing a picture of an actual UFO above Cross Drummond was another. After the week the villagers had endured, this latest news was not welcome by some.

"I take it you know what this means," Miss Blunt said, sitting down.

"Oh, hello Prudence," Emily replied, looking up from her paper.

"Because of this ridiculous story the village will become swamped by UFO watchers and a curious public. Aliens from outer space indeed. It is clearly a hoax. They must think we were born yesterday."

"The picture looks genuine to me."

"You are an authority on such things, are you? That the picture was submitted anonymously speaks volumes for its authenticity. This is obviously the work of some fool with a computer who has nothing better to do with their time. One simply superimposes an image of what is allegedly a UFO on a photograph of Cross Drummond and passes it off as the real thing. The gullible and easily-led see little green men from Mars and before you know it Cloverdale St Mary is full of strangers watching the skies and interfering with village life."

Susan arrived with her tea. As far as she was concerned being the centre of attention in the national press wasn't a bad thing. More visitors to the village meant more custom. "It will be good for business. Ron and Maggie have had several calls asking about accommodation. All their guest rooms have sold out."

"You see? It has started already," Miss Blunt said.

"It will be nice to have new faces in the village," Emily ventured.

It wasn't an opinion Miss Blunt shared. It was the worst thing that could have happened, especially in light of the recent burglaries. An increase in custom for local business meant more opportunities for the thieves.

"It is an ill wind that will blow no good," she said over her teacup. "Mark my words, we will have cause to rue this day. The Coaching Inn cannot accommodate everyone who will come here. People will park caravans and goodness knows what else on the green. And what of our night patrols? We only started them yesterday. A village over-run with thrill-seekers will be impossible to protect."

"There haven't been any burglaries since you were robbed. Maybe they've moved on," Emily said.

"If you believe that you are deluding yourself. Cloverdale St Mary is still under threat and this UFO nonsense will only serve to make matters worse."

Susan pointed to Emily's empty cup. "Would you like a refill?"

"Yes, that would be lovely. Thank you."

Miss Blunt's expression was like vinegar. She was renowned for sucking on invisible lemons and that was how she looked now. "I would put in an order for more supplies if I were you. Something tells me you will need it."

"I hope so," Susan replied, taking leave of them. *I might have to invest in a larger oven too*, she thought.

*

A copy of the morning paper had found its way into the attic room of Meadow Cottage. Like Miss Blunt, Candice was convinced it was a hoax and refused to take it seriously. The idea of UFOs flying over Cloverdale St Mary was ludicrous. If that picture was authentic she was a direct descendant of Captain Kirk. Perhaps Mr Spock. Maybe both.

"How anyone can buy into this is beyond me," she said to Harry. "You would have to be a complete and utter idiot to fall for it."

"People have been led astray by less," he replied.

"Look at it. That's not a UFO. It's a Frisbee with coloured lights drawn on it. Two seconds after that picture was taken a dog plucked it out of the air."

"I assume it's meant to resemble the lights that were seen during the storm last week," Harry said, looking over her shoulder at the newspaper.

He walked around the sofa and stood by the window.

"That couple from East Anglia wouldn't know lightening if they were struck by it," Candice replied dismissively.

Harry lapsed into thought. He could see only one explanation and had a eureka moment. It was so obvious he couldn't understand why he hadn't made the connection before. "Wait a minute. Maybe the storm wasn't a storm. It might have been a smokescreen to hide something else."

Candice looked puzzled because it was the natural reaction to being puzzled. "What?"

"Consider the facts," Harry went on. "Strange lights are seen in the sky over Cloverdale St Mary and we experience one of the worst thunderstorms on record. The next day Grantley arrives in the village." He was convinced he was onto something and looked at her assuredly. "It's too much of a coincidence."

"Harry, what are you saying?"

"Norman Grantley is not of this world."

"You mean he's an alien?"

"Sent here to pave the way for a mass invasion no doubt."

Candice was stunned. This was off the wall even for him. "Are you telling me that Norman Grantley is from outer space?"

"Stranger things have been known to happen," he said.

"Only in the movies. In the week he's been here you've accused him of being a murderer, a criminal mastermind and a grave robber. Now he's an alien from Planet X. It must be said, Harry. Even in death you need to get out more."

"You'll sing a different tune when he runs amok with a ray-gun and starts pickling people's brains."

"I wonder if there's a cure for what you've got?"

"Everything fits," he insisted. "That crate didn't contain a skeleton when he moved in. He put it inside afterwards to throw us off-track."

"You came off the tracks long ago," Candice told him.

Harry wasn't listening. He was focused on eureka moment number two. "That crate was filled with alien spores," he said, snapping his fingers. "He'll let them loose on the wind and take over the planet. If we don't stop him we'll be colonized and made to serve beings who have far greater intelligence than we possess."

"From where I'm sitting that wouldn't be difficult."

He heard her that time.

"What's that supposed to mean?"

"Let me abbreviate it. M.O.C."

Harry wouldn't be reasoned with. The situation was critical and demanded immediate action. "The question is what do we do about it? The future of the human race is at stake."

"I wore a blue dress. It had a bow on the front, a pretty white thing."

"Thank you for sharing that with me. Now, about Grantley and his dastardly plans to take over the world..."

"I can't remember what day it was but it was in the summer. When the soldiers came papa hid me in the barn. He told me to be really quiet and went back to the house."

Harry stared at Candice in silence. Her gaze went past him, as if he wasn't there. Like it had that day at Cross Drummond.

"The sound of horses drew closer until their hooves became a thunderous roar. I heard gunshots and men shouting. *'Burn them out,'* someone called. *'Get them Union dogs out of there,'* and they threw the torches. I heard mama screaming. I didn't know they were raping her. They shot papa when he tried to stop them. Jack died in the flames. When the soldiers set fire to the barn I got out and ran away. I hid in the woods and stayed quiet like papa said. They didn't know I was there."

Harry knew it wasn't Candice speaking. She looked and sounded the same, nothing about her had changed in that respect, but it wasn't her.

"Who are you?" he said.

"Excuse me?"

"Who are you?"

"Have you gone nuts?"

"Answer the question."

"I'm Candice Freeman, medically deceased but still a resident of this parish. Why have you gone weird on me?"

"What have we been talking about?"

"The price of gasoline. Harry, what's gotten into you?"

"What have we been discussing?"

"How to make Frisbees look like UFOs. Are you giving out prizes for this?"

Candice was back to normal. The spirit of a ten year-old girl recounting how her family had been butchered by Confederate soldiers during the American Civil War had left her. She had no knowledge of what had happened.

Harry elected not to tell her. "Yeah. I'll buy you a packet of chocolate digestives."

"I miss those. Do you miss anything about not being alive?"

"No, not really."

"Not even your Ford Cortina?"

"Yes, I miss that."

And I miss you when you go away.

Harry didn't know who the child was or why she had chosen to speak through Candice. He had never believed in reincarnation but was open to the possibility now. Could it have been a past life resurfacing? Was that where Candice went when she disappeared, into the void of long ago and who she used to be? There was another possibility but for Harry it didn't bear thinking about.

One thing was certain. This was more serious than he imagined.

*

It didn't take long for the invasion to begin. There was no sign of the one foreseen by Harry but Miss Blunt's warnings proved to be correct and the first UFO investigators arrived in the village later that afternoon. It was as she had feared; two 4x4s parked outside the Coaching Inn and a third attached to a caravan on the village green. It had a bug-eyed monster painted on it with the words *'We're out to get you, ET'* written underneath.

"I hope you find the room to your satisfaction," Maggie said, dropping the key into the palm of Rafe Turner. "Breakfast and dinner can be taken at any time. As long as breakfast is at breakfast and dinner is several hours later."

"What time do you serve breakfast?" he asked.

"What time do you get up?"

"About ten o'clock usually. We do most of our work at night you see."

"Why do aliens fly around after dark?"

"That has baffled ufologists for many years, ever since the first sightings were reported in fact. There is, no doubt, a scientific reason for it, but our research into that area is ongoing. I couldn't commit to an answer until all the data is in."

He had lost Maggie after *'that has.'*

"We serve breakfast between seven and ten but as you're vampires we'll make an exception in your case. You can take it whenever you want," she said.

"We're not vampires. We're paranormal investigators specializing in the UFO phenomenon."

Maggie made a mental note for future reference. *Don't try to be humorous around this man. He doesn't get it.* "That will save us money on garlic."

"I don't like garlic."

"I've yet to meet a vampire who does."

"I'm not a vampire."

Maggie made another mental note. *Pay attention to previous mental notes.*

"Well, I'll leave you to unpack and settle in. The first drink is on the house," she said, walking to the door.

"I don't drink," he told her.

Maggie wanted to make a comment about bloody Mary's and how it was the preferred tipple in Transylvania but as she was paying attention to her mental notes she elected not to. "Ron and I are up till around midnight so the front door is open until then. After that it's locked and bolted till six the following morning."

"That won't be an issue for us. We go out when it's dark and come back when it's light."

No, don't bother, Maggie thought.

She left the new arrival and went downstairs to the bar. Of everyone she had checked in that afternoon, he had struck her as being the most normal.

The Coaching Inn had five guest rooms and all were occupied in light of Cloverdale St Mary becoming the centre of the universe in terms of invading aliens and their interest in the Kent countryside.

The newly-arrived guests were members of a paranormal investigating team from London. They consisted of Rafe Turner, his estranged wife, Karen, and the woman she had left him for, Siobhan Drake. The leader of the team was Brian Watson, a dedicated man with thirty years experience in the field. The final room was occupied by the youngest member of the team, Neil Bradshaw. He claimed to have been abducted by aliens when he was twelve years old but no one believed him. His colleagues considered him to be a bit of a twit.

Brian was unable to give Maggie an indication of how long their stay might have lasted. He said it was impossible to apply a time-frame to matters relating to the paranormal and they may have been there for quite a while. That had given rise to a problem. One of the rooms had been reserved in advance and if their stay was in excess of eight days Brian and Neil would have to share.

Maggie assumed their investigation would have been concluded by then and tried to appear enthusiastic when Brian told her that during a field-trip to Yorkshire the previous August their stay had lasted three weeks. The thought of being host to them for that length of time made her consider divorcing Ron and moving to the Outer Hebrides but she drew comfort from a room rate of £80 a night. The money would have come in useful. They were planning their holiday for next year and Las Vegas didn't come cheap.

The caravan parked on the green was home to the first of the thrill-seekers as Miss Blunt had called them. They were a family of three from Bristol. The husband was a UFO fanatic who saw aliens everywhere he looked. His wife supported him in his views and dressed as an extraterrestrial at parties. Their fifteen year-old daughter was constantly embarrassed by her parents and wanted nothing to do with them.

She would rather have been at home with friends

than stuck in a caravan with two people who had lost their marbles and didn't understand her. It wouldn't have been so bad if they had allowed her to have her nose pierced but on that they had stood firm. Chasing aliens was one thing, being led around a field by a rope through a ring in her nose like an Aberdeen Angus was another.

*

Miss Blunt had gone to the equestrian centre after her dental appointment and was appalled to see the caravan on the green when she returned home at 6:00 p.m. The nerve of those people. Something had to be done. She parked her car outside her cottage and walked purposely towards it.

Ron was watering the hanging plants outside the pub when he saw her approach. She looked like an army marching on a small, undefended country. "Take a look at this," he called to Maggie, just inside the entrance. "Prudence is on the warpath."

She went outside to watch. "This should be good."

"I wonder if they have life insurance?"

Miss Blunt arrived at her objective and knocked loudly on the door. "Are your parents at home?" she asked Natalie Collins when she opened it a moment later.

"No, they're in this bloody caravan," the teenager replied. She put on a set of headphones attached to her mobile phone and stepped outside, calling over her shoulder as she did so. "Mum, dad. There's an alien out here to see you." She didn't wait for a response. She elected to go for a walk in preference to being bored indoors.

"Hello. Can I help you?" David Collins asked, appearing soon after.

"Are you the owner of this..." Miss Blunt was reluctant to use the word caravan. It was too uncouth. "... Establishment?"

"Yes."

"You cannot park it here. This is public property."

"I know. I'm a member of the public."

Collins had answered tongue-in-cheek. There was nothing in his manner to suggest he was being confrontational but that was how it came across. Unknown to him, his light-hearted response had released the baying hounds of hell.

Miss Blunt sucked on her lemon and glared at him. "It is a village green, communal land set aside for the enjoyment of local residents. It is not somewhere to park a monstrosity such as this with the intention of living here. I demand that you move it at once."

He knew it now.

"Where else can I park up?" he asked, perplexed.

"I hear the Orkney Islands are nice at this time of year."

"The roads and lanes around here are very narrow. If I park somewhere else I'll cause an obstruction."

"That is of no concern to me. I have made my position clear. I expect this vehicle to be removed immediately. If it is not I will report the matter to the police."

Miss Blunt had nothing more to say on the subject and turned abruptly on her heel.

Collins watched her go in stunned silence. If his daughter was right and she was an alien planet earth wouldn't have stood a chance if they were all like her.

*

Ian sat on a riverbank fishing. It was one of his favourite places, a nice, quiet spot to spend lazy afternoons and early evenings while the world and all its troubles hurried by out of sight and out of mind.

He used to go there with Harry when he was alive, two friends fishing together with beer in the cooler and important issues to discuss. Would Manchester United win the Premier League that season? Could the latest Lamborghini to roll off the production line really do nought to sixty in two seconds? Did American astronauts walk on the moon or was the whole thing filmed on the back lot of Twentieth Century Fox? They solved mysteries that had evolved over a thousand years and still found time to talk about cricket. They were good days. Then Harry died and they were gone. For a while at least.

"What happened then?" Ian asked him.

Harry stared across the water in troubled thought. A bad situation was getting worse and he had turned to the vicar for guidance. It was another mystery to be solved but he didn't know where to start.

"Candice returned to normal. It was as if someone had flicked a switch, there one moment, gone, then back again. She had no memory of what had happened. I don't know what to do, Ian. How can another spirit speak through her without her knowing it?"

"Have you heard of anything like this before?"

"No. If I had I wouldn't be so worried. I think I'm losing her."

"How could that happen?"

Harry considered the one possibility that filled him with dread. It was the only explanation that made sense in a mind struggling to work it out. "I think she's being called. This might be the start of her passing over to the other side. Candice said as much herself. She said *'what if I go away and don't come back?'* I told her it wouldn't come to that but I was lying. There's a chance she might."

Ian was lost for an answer. If Candice was passing over what could have been done to stop it? How could a ghost be made to stay when God or something as powerful demanded otherwise? To prevent it from happening would have been beyond spirits and mortals in their limited understanding of such things.

"I don't know what to tell you, Harry. I wish I did."

"I won't let her go, Ian. I can't."

"But what could you do? If you're right, if Candice is being drawn to eternal rest, it would be out of your hands. No power on earth could stop it."

Harry stared across the river again. To him it was symbolic. It represented the void that he was desperate for Candice not to cross. "I'll find a way. I have to."

Twelve

"It's Samantha Copeland, isn't it? You live in Meadow Cottage."

It was Wednesday morning and Samantha was paying Bill for her newspaper in the village shop. She turned to look at the man standing behind her.

"Yes, that's right."

"Allow me to introduce myself. I'm Norman Grantley."

Samantha smiled and shook his hand. She hadn't ventured into the village during the past week and only knew of him through others. Now she could form her own opinion. "It's nice to meet you. It's amazing we haven't met before in a village as small as this. Have you enjoyed your first week here?"

Grantley returned her smile with a natural confidence. "It's a week and one day now. I feel like a local. Yes, I really like it here. Best move I ever made."

"I'm glad you're settling in well."

"Thank you. You work at the stables at Cross Drummond, don't you?"

"Yes. I'm the manager there."

"I must admit to knowing nothing about horses but would it be possible for me to visit one day? I would love to see it."

"By all means. We're always open to visitors. Feel free to pop in any time. If you play your cards right we might give you a fork and a stable to muck out."

Grantley laughed. "My dear Samantha, I wouldn't know where to begin."

"Full training would be given. I'm sorry to cut this

short but I'm running late. It really was nice to meet you."

"Of course, I don't want to hold you up. It was nice to meet you too."

Samantha said goodbye to Bill and Susan and left the shop. *What a pleasant man,* she thought. *He's nothing like a serial killer.*

Grantley watched through the window as she got in her car and drove to work. Thoughts of a different nature went through his mind. *I hope you won't find the restraints too uncomfortable. I wouldn't want to damage such delicate skin.*

"What can I do for you, Norman?" Bill asked.

"Just a newspaper please, Bill." Grantley took one from the stack beside the till and frowned when he read the headline. "Not more UFO sightings? Cloverdale St Mary will become another Area 51 if it carries on like this."

"I wish I knew what to make of it," Bill said. "I stayed up till three o'clock this morning and didn't see a thing."

"Don't tell me you believe this nonsense?"

"I have an open mind."

"And an open till," Susan added from her side of the shop.

"It's true this will be good for business but it's not about money. This is very important to the scientific community," Bill said in his defence.

"Does that mean I can have my newspaper for nothing?" Grantley asked.

"Certainly not. Give me 50p or I'll set the dog on you."

"You don't have a dog."

"Then I'll rent one. Come on, pay up."

The light-hearted banter between shopkeeper and customer was interrupted by the sound of a police car speeding along the high street. It was followed by an ambulance.

*

Not for the first time over recent days, the residents of Cloverdale St Mary were in a state of shock. The fifth burglary to befall the village had been by far the most serious.

Albert Preston and his wife Sarah had been robbed during the early hours of the morning. He was seventy-one years old and she was sixty-nine. Mr Preston tried to defend their home and received a severe beating because of it. He was admitted to hospital with a fractured skull. His condition was critical. The burglars had armed themselves with baseball bats to counter the threat of the night patrols and demonstrated their willingness to use them against anyone who stood in their way.

It was a point Emily raised with Miss Blunt when she met her for lunch in the Coaching Inn at midday. They usually met for lunch on Fridays but this coming Friday was Emily's birthday and a celebration was planned for that evening. Candice may have held the record for the most hours spent in the Coaching Inn but Emily didn't want to challenge it by going there twice in one day so she and Miss Blunt had brought their lunch date forward.

"You have to stop the night patrols, Prudence. It's too dangerous," she said over her salad.

"What happened to Mr Preston was truly terrible but the night patrols have no bearing on it," Miss Blunt replied.

"The burglars were armed with baseball bats. They didn't use weapons before. They're using them now because of the threat from the public. If the night patrols go on there is no telling what they will do."

Miss Blunt looked at Emily sternly. She didn't like the implications behind her comments. "I hope you are not suggesting that I am responsible for what happened to Mr Preston?"

"No, not at all. I know you want an end to this, we all do, but policing the streets ourselves is not the answer. Now the burglars are armed anything could happen. It's too dangerous to continue with it."

"The police are woefully inadequate when it comes to providing the protection we need. The night patrols are the only deterrent we have at our disposal to see that our homes remain safe and secure. To stop them would be an open invitation to the burglars to strike whenever they have a mind to."

"It didn't stop it from happening to the Preston's, did it? There is a risk of someone being killed if you continue with this course of action. Please, Prudence, stop the night patrols now, before it's too late."

Miss Blunt refused to back down. To have done so would have been surrender and she was not the surrendering type. "The night patrols will continue and that is all I have to say on the matter. I refuse to debate this with you any further."

Both women fell silent.

Miss Blunt looked across the room at the ufologists taking lunch at a table near the window. They were comparing notes on their first night in the field. They hadn't seen any alien spaceships but were amazed by the amount of cats in the area. One in particular spent a long time sniffing around their sandwich boxes and seemed reluctant to leave. Then a mouse came to its attention and carnage followed. Karen was physically sick. She would have nightmares for months to come. Miss Blunt noticed that she was the only person at the table not eating.

"I see that awful caravan is still parked on the green," she said. "I have told them twice to move it but they clearly have no intention of doing so."

"It is public property," Emily said.

"It is a village green, not a caravan site for people who have no right to be here. They show a total lack of consideration for others. As for the wife, I have never met someone so devoid of taste and decorum. Have you seen how she has chosen to dress this morning? A T-shirt cut off at the waist is bad enough but her jeans are so low over her hips they are almost down to her ankles. It is disgraceful."

"Yes, Prudence."

Emily formed the impression, correctly, that this was going to be a very long lunch.

"The husband is no better. Every time I see him he has a cigarette in one hand and a tin of lager in the other. It looks like he has not shaved in days."

There was a reason for that.

"He has a beard, quite a long one," said Emily, surprised.

"That is my point. If he came into possession of a razor he would be at a loss to know what to do with it. Anyone who took pride in their appearance would not grow facial hair. It is a sign of laziness and slovenly behaviour."

"Ian is growing a beard."

"And I must say it does not suit him. I have told him

so."

"No, Prudence."

"As for the daughter, goodness me," Miss Blunt tutted, turning the conversation back to the family from Bristol. "Someone should tell that child there is more to life than mobile phones and social media. The girl has no idea what is going on around her. She walks everywhere head-bowed, reading and sending text messages. We may have to chop the trees down to prevent her from colliding with one."

"Yes, Prudence."

Maggie appeared at their table. "Can I get you ladies anything?"

"Do you have a cyanide capsule?" Emily asked her.

Miss Blunt chose to ignore the comment.

Maggie smiled at Emily sympathetically. She assumed her request had resulted from Miss Blunt not being in the best of moods – one look at her was enough to know she was still on the warpath – but she decided to have some fun with her and put it down to another reason. "I know it's your birthday on Friday and you're really old now, almost archaic it might be said, but Ron is baking you a cake and suicide wouldn't be a show of gratitude."

"If there was another pub in this village I wouldn't come here," Emily said.

"If there was another pub in this village neither would I," Maggie replied. She glanced at the ufologists and hoped the alien invasion would have come sooner rather than later. It was only day two and she was tired of them already. "I spent three hours this morning being bored to tears about the likelihood of extraterrestrial life in the Boggle galaxy."

"Boggle?" Emily asked.

"I don't name these places."

Miss Blunt frowned behind her water glass.

"It was that man sitting next to the blonde woman."

Emily cast Neil a subtle glance that went unnoticed by him.

"He said he was abducted by aliens when he was twelve," Maggie went on.

"And they took him to the Boggle galaxy?" Emily asked.

"No, Barrow-in-Furness. He said it worked out okay really. His gran lives there. I told him I had things to do but couldn't get rid of him. He followed me around the pub like a lost puppy. I can't see why aliens would want him. He's a bit of a twit."

Emily sneaked another look at him in conversation with his colleagues. They were trying to determine not how to track a UFO if they saw one but how to keep inquisitive cats away from their sandwiches.

"It must be a lot of work for you having a full house," she said to Maggie.

"It's not too bad. The rooms are easy to do but if the bar gets any busier I'll have to ask Jill and Deborah to do some extra shifts. They've been great. They said they'll come in whenever I need them."

"Everyone stands to make a profit," Miss Blunt remarked snootily.

Maggie felt her hackles rise. She was about to take Miss Blunt to task over her comments when the door opened and forty people walked in, all of them strangers. The noise that accompanied their arrival turned a quiet country pub into a loud city one.

"Oh my God," the landlady gasped.

"It looks like Jill and Deborah will be needed sooner

than you thought," Emily said, watching them converge on the bar.

Maggie left them and went back to work.

Miss Blunt dabbed the corners of her mouth with her napkin and took satisfaction in knowing she had been proved right. There were more people inside the pub than in mission control at NASA. "Mark my words, this is only the beginning. By the end of the week this village will be over-run by outsiders."

Emily watched Maggie and Ron rushed off their feet behind the bar and didn't welcome that prospect at all.

*

Miss Blunt had more reason to suck on her lemon when she left the Coaching Inn to go back to work. There were now three caravans on the green, two pick-up trucks and enough cars to fill a Formula 1 grid. Her car had been blocked in and she had to return to the pub in order to ascertain who the owner was to ask him to move it, although there was greater emphasis on biting his head off than a polite request for him to move his vehicle. The owner was a big man built like an outhouse with tattoos on biceps that resembled steel girders but Miss Blunt left him shaking in his boots.

Her anger reached boiling point on the road to Cross Drummond when she saw a TV unit head towards the village. It consisted of three cars, a van and the biggest satellite dish she had ever seen. She dreaded to think what she would have found when she got home at six. Cloverdale St Mary was being turned into a circus and the besieged residents now faced the prospect of having microphones shoved under their noses every time they ventured outside their homes.

It had happened before. When Candice died TV crews from around the world descended on the village but that only lasted a few days. They left immediately after the funeral and normality soon returned. This was different. This media event was set to go on until people lost interest in the story. What made it more unpalatable for Miss Blunt was that this invasion of privacy would coincide with the first anniversary of Candice's death. It was one week from today. Many others felt the same way.

Ian had planned a simple service to give the villagers an opportunity to reflect on the loss of a good friend and to pay their respects but how could they have done that under the gaze of public scrutiny? What should have been private and kept within the village would be televised around the globe and witnessed by all. They expected some media involvement, the press was always going to mark the first anniversary, but it shouldn't have been like this; people coming from miles around to watch the skies in the hope of seeing flying saucers. Where was the respect in that?

*

Candice and Harry watched the TV crew set up on the green. She was in her element being around cameras again. It reminded her of a glittering career that would give pleasure to millions of people for years to come, when she was the most sought after actress in the world and everything she touched turned to gold.

"I would go with two on the far side and pan across to the centre," she said. "That would give them a great long shot to the church."

Harry sighed. His intention had been to go for a pleasant walk, not take a crash course in cinematography. "Candice, it's a news report. They're not filming a remake of The Diamond Cutter."

"I know they're not. Everyone has their clothes on." Something else caught her eye and she pointed to the distance. "That backdrop is all wrong. It's too cluttered. They should knock those cottages down so we get a clear view of the fields beyond them."

"One of them is Emily's."

"There are plenty of caravans around here. She could move into one of those."

"Were you as brutal as this when you made films?"

"It has to be done right." Candice frowned and creased her chin. "I'm not sure about Bill and Susan's place either. That might have to go too."

Harry elected not to comment.

Candice was like a kid in a sweet shop. Her eyes were everywhere. "Don't you find this exciting? All the cameras and sound equipment 'an stuff. It's great."

"It's a news report."

"That will be beamed into the homes of millions of people. I wonder if they would let me say a few words."

"What!"

She looked at him accusingly. "You don't think I could read the news?"

"I'm sure you could have when you were alive."

"Oh yeah. I forgot about that."

"Clearly."

"What a bummer. The one time cameras come to the

village and I'm dead."

Harry didn't answer. He had seen something that concerned him. "Is it me or is that woman staring at us?"

He pointed to a solitary figure standing beside a camper van.

Candice looked at her too. "It's you. How can she stare at something she can't see?"

The woman fetched her mobile phone from her pocket and took their picture.

"There must be something of interest behind us," Candice said.

She and Harry turned around but saw nothing worthy of a photograph. There was an empty packing case belonging to the TV crew but who would have wanted a picture of that?

The woman nodded and smiled at them.

"Okay, now I'm worried," Candice said.

"Stay here."

Harry walked across the green to where she was standing. He had never seen her before. Presumably she was one of the new arrivals who had come to the village in search of aliens and all things extraterrestrial. She was in her mid-thirties and smartly dressed in jeans and a black jacket, although the tartan scarf wrapped around her neck seemed unnecessary for the time of year. Her waist-long auburn hair was tied in a loose ponytail.

She watched Harry approach and appeared startled when he walked through a light reflector in preference to walking around it.

"Can you see me?" he asked on arrival.

The woman looked him up and down. She was amazed by what she had witnessed and found it difficult to speak.

"Yes. My God, yes." She tried to compose herself. She felt awkward and forced a tentative smile. "My name is Delia. It's jolly nice to meet you." She offered her hand in greeting, only to withdraw it when she realised how pointless the gesture had been.

Despite her age and appearance she had the manner of a much older woman. She struck Harry as someone who would have been ideally suited to a private girls school in the 1940s, a sports teacher who coached the hockey team and called *'I say, Daphne, jolly good shot'* while they gave the opposition a damn good thrashing. St Trinian's came to mind but to look at her she was ultra-modern.

"How can you see me?" he asked.

Delia Truebody laughed nervously and blurted her reply. "I don't know." She took a deep breath and composed herself a second time. "Goodness, I'm actually speaking to a ghost. You're my first one you know."

"Can you see her?" Harry asked, pointing at Candice.

"Miss Freeman? Yes, I can see her too. Such a wonderful actress. She was excellent in The Diamond Cutter. Do you think I could get her autograph?"

"That might be a bit difficult," he replied.

She felt embarrassed and slapped her forehead with the palm of her hand. "Of course, how silly of me. She probably doesn't have a pen on her. Do you have one? No, don't answer that. Get a grip on yourself, Delia."

"Are you all right?"

"I'm a teeny bit nervous to be honest. I didn't think you would come over to speak to me."

"I didn't think I would have my picture taken today."

Delia was consumed by guilt and apologized for all her worth. Good etiquette was important to her and she had made an unforgivable error. "Oh, I'm terribly sorry. I acted without gaining your consent. One should always seek permission before taking someone's photograph. How rude of me."

"No, I didn't mean it that way. What I meant was..." Harry stopped and scratched his head. "Who are you?"

"Delia Truebody."

"Ah, but who *is* Delia Truebody? It's the person behind the name that I want to get to know," he said philosophically.

"Goodness. You want to get to know me?"

"How would you feel about joining me for drinks at my place this evening?" he asked, now sounding suave and sophisticated.

"Unchaperoned?"

"I don't think you need worry about that."

"Oh."

Delia looked hurt. She had taken it to mean he found her unattractive.

"I'm a ghost. You're perfectly safe with me."

"Oh yes, of course," she replied, smiling again. "Drinks would be jolly nice. Thank you. May I ask a question?"

"By all means."

"What is your name?"

Harry answered in a voice that Roger Moore would have been proud of. "The name is Black. Harry Black. Until this evening, Delia. Ashanti."

He would have kissed her hand if he could.

It was a shame Harry had gone to so much trouble to appear debonair because she called after him as he turned to leave and ruined the moment.

"Excuse me. Where should I go for these drinks and

what time do you want me to be there?"

"Meadow Cottage, eight o'clock. Ask anyone, they'll tell you where it is."

"Jolly good. I'll see you then."

Delia looked at Candice as Harry walked away and waved to her. Candice felt compelled to wave back.

"What the hell is going on?" she asked when he rejoined her.

"I'm not sure but I have a date for eight o'clock this evening." Harry saw Delia wave to him too and returned it with a courteous smile. "Let's go home. I have to practice making vodka Martinis."

*

Melanie sat head-bowed in the corridor outside the headmaster's office. She was the kind of girl who never got into trouble at school. She worked hard and all the teachers liked her. They had nothing but good things to say about a child who was thoughtful and considerate to others and always did the best she could. For her to have gotten into a fight with another girl was completely out of character.

Melanie used to speak with a stammer and was bullied at school because of it but she wasn't the withdrawn, self-conscious child she was then. She had blossomed into a confident young lady who could take care of herself. Her stammer re-appeared sometimes, when she was excited or upset, but it was a rare occurrence and there would be no going back to the insecure little girl she used to be.

Her parents saw a bright future in store for her but

Janet hadn't expected to be summoned to the school to be given details of a playground spat that resulted in Melanie planting her fist in the mouth of a fellow pupil. The girl on the receiving end had been one of her tormentors during those bullying days and thought she remained a safe target. She wouldn't make that mistake again.

It was the end of the school day and Melanie's eyes lifted to the headmaster's door when it opened. Janet did not look pleased.

"Thank you for being so understanding, Mr Rogers," she said to the principle.

"Not at all, Mrs Copeland. But like I said, if there is a re-occurrence of this I would be required to take it further."

"Yes, of course."

Janet shook his hand and she and Melanie left.

Neither spoke in the car going home. Janet knew she should have chastised her daughter for acting in such a way but how could she when their lives had been turned upside down? Melanie had reacted to things said, the cruel taunts of someone who had overheard her parents talking about the Copeland's troubled marriage. She had taken great delight in telling Melanie who her father had screwed and how often, all of it made up because she had no way of knowing the actual details. It was better to lie than say nothing. Melanie lost her temper and lashed out. During the scuffle that followed she landed a punch that put the girl on her back and she was brought before the headmaster.

When they arrived home Janet sent Melanie to her room. What to do about it would be decided when Martin got home from work. In that respect nothing had changed. The discipline of their children when they misbehaved had always been a joint decision. This would be no different. They would decide on the best course of action to take as a couple, not two halves of the separate they had become.

*

Grantley knocked on Emily's front door at 7:00 p.m. It was to be a brief visit as he had things to do at home. This would suit Emily because she had to go out. Harry had visited earlier and told her about Delia Truebody. He wanted Samantha, Emily and Ian to be present for their chat over cocktails.

"Hello, Norman," she said, opening the door to him.

"Good evening, Emily. I hope I'm not disturbing you?"

"No, not at all. Come in."

She stood aside in the doorway to allow him entry.

"Thank you. I can't stay long but I wanted to talk to you about something that is really quite urgent."

Emily had no idea what it could have been about and led him to the lounge. "How intriguing. What can I do for you?"

"It's more a case of what I can do for you," he replied, accepting her invitation to sit down. "A little birdie tells me it's your birthday on Friday."

Emily grinned. "Is this birdie a redhead who runs a pub not far from here?"

"I believe she does dabble in that field, yes." Grantley smiled and bridged his fingers under his chin. "I popped in for a swift half earlier and Maggie told me about it. Which is more than you did it must be said. If I didn't know better I would say you were trying to keep it from me. A big celebration at the Coaching Inn and I would have been sat at home with a mug of cocoa watching TV."

"I was going to tell you tomorrow and offer an official invitation." A thought struck her and she looked concerned. She hoped she hadn't taken anything for granted. "You're not busy, are you? You can make it?"

"Try keeping me away. The thing is I would like to treat you to a small gift. Just a little thing between us."

"You don't have to go to any trouble on my account."

"Nonsense. It's a special occasion. May I be permitted to take you out tomorrow? We could make a day of it, perhaps go to London. I know some excellent restaurants there. We could have lunch, see the sights in the afternoon and round it off with dinner. It will be your day from start to finish. As your chauffeur I am more than happy to take you wherever you want to go."

"It's very kind of you to offer, Norman, but I couldn't. It's too extravagant."

"It is no more than you deserve. Please say yes."

"Yes."

He laughed. "That has to be the fastest U-turn in history."

Emily slipped away to a private moment. When she returned she saw everything clearly, the way she should have seen it five days previously. "A good friend once told me the present is for making memories to look back on in the future. We never forget our past but that shouldn't stop us from looking ahead."

Grantley didn't understand what she meant. He knew there was more to it but didn't question her. He didn't want to pry into something that was personal. "The words of a very wise friend, I think."

"Yes. She is."

He stood up. "The car will be outside your door at ten o'clock. I expect you to be there on the dot."

"And forgo my right to keep a gentleman waiting?" Emily replied, tongue-in-cheek.

"Very well. One minute past but no later. If I get a parking ticket you can pay for it."

They laughed at their silliness and Emily showed him out.

She looked at George's picture when she returned to the lounge. His smile still melted her heart. It always had and always would. It was what she loved about him most, that and the fact that never had she known a more caring and decent man.

"You don't mind that I spend time with Norman, do you, George?" she said quietly. "Because if I thought you did..." She stopped in mid-sentence and smiled. "We wouldn't be having this conversation."

Emily kissed her fingers and held them to his lips.

Thirteen

Samantha looked at Harry bemused in the lounge of Meadow Cottage. To have been told he had invited a stranger to their home for drinks hadn't phased her, they had to find out how Delia Truebody could see Harry and Candice when others couldn't, but she hadn't expected what came next.

"Why do you want a tuxedo?" she asked him.

"I have to create the right impression."

Samantha was sure there was an appropriate response to that but it didn't come to her. "I'm afraid I don't have one," she offered instead.

Harry sighed. "I hate to say this, Sam, but you're being of no help to me whatsoever."

She actually apologized.

That Harry saw himself as a secret agent on a mission to save queen and country didn't concern Candice. She was more worried about his date.

"I'm not convinced this is a good idea. We don't know the first thing about this woman. How do we know we can trust her?"

"We won't know anything until we talk to her. That's why I arranged this meeting," Harry replied.

Samantha nodded in agreement. She understood why Candice would have been wary, it was a complication no one had foreseen, but there was no choice. They had to find out who Delia was.

The doorbell rang.

"That will be Emily and Ian," she said.

"I'll get it," Candice told her, leaving the room.

A moment later they heard her curse from the

hallway.

Samantha followed her out and opened the door that Candice had failed to open. It wasn't the first time it had gotten the better of her.

"I can walk through walls and touch solid objects so why can't I open this damn door?"

"The lock is a bit stiff," Samantha said, trying to make her feel better.

"Hi Sam, Candice. I'm sorry we're damn early," Ian said, crossing the threshold.

"Hello, Sam. I like what you've done with your damn hair," Emily remarked, going in too.

"Thank you. I thought I would wear it a bit damn shorter."

Candice smiled and followed them to the lounge. She felt nervous about this evening but not for the first time her friends had put her at ease.

"This is a turn up for the books," Ian said, sitting down. "Do you know anything about this woman?" he asked Harry.

"Not a thing. Only that she could see Candice and I as clear as day."

Emily was surprised by their reaction to Delia. It was unusual for a mortal to see a ghost when they didn't want to be seen, for that ghost to be Candice Freeman brought its own set of problems in a world dominated by instant news, but it didn't constitute an emergency meeting and a lengthy debate over whether or not she owned a tuxedo. What Emily didn't realise was that she wasn't in possession of all the facts.

"Did she say anything to suggest she would go public about your existence?" she asked Candice.

"I didn't speak to her. 003½ did the talking."

"That reminds me, why did you ask if I owned a cigarette case?" Ian said to Harry.

"It can be used to engage the ejector seat when you're not in the car."

"Good answer." He looked at Samantha. "Do we have to wait for Delia to arrive or can we start drinking now?"

She laughed and poured him a glass of wine. Emily received one too.

"So did she say she was going to go public?" she asked again.

All eyes turned to the secret agent in their midst.

"Well, no. To be honest she found it difficult to say anything. She was a bit nervous. The thing is, Emily, this isn't the only strange occurrence to have happened recently. Over the past week Candice has experienced problems. She's been disappearing against her will."

"Disappearing?"

Candice looked at her sadly. "Yeah. Where I go is unknown because we don't have a radio transmitter but I have no idea when I'm going there and can't remember anything when I get back."

"Then this woman arrives and takes her picture on the village green. It leads me to wonder if there's a connection," Harry said.

Emily realised from Ian's expression that he knew about it, Samantha too. She was the only person in the room with no prior knowledge of these events. "Why didn't you tell me about this sooner?"

"We thought it better not to say anything until we knew what we were dealing with," Ian replied.

Emily was swept by guilt. As a reason for keeping it from her it made sense but she knew the truth of it, or what she mistakenly took to be the truth. "It's not that at all, is it? I've been too busy doing other things. Having lunch with Norman. Having dinner with Norman. Going shopping with Norman."

"Em," Candice started.

"No, my dear, don't make excuses for me. Something bad is happening to you and I didn't take the time to notice. I'm meant to be your friend. Do you know what your friend is doing tomorrow? She's going to London with Norman."

"Really? That is so cool," Candice said smiling.

Emily was close to tears.

"I mean, that is so not cool." She looked at Ian and pleaded with her eyes for him to do something.

He sat beside Emily on the sofa and held her hand. "You haven't deserted your friends and no one thinks badly of you. We know how much you care, Emily. That's why we didn't damn well tell you."

It was typical Ian and it worked a treat.

Emily smiled and forgave herself.

The doorbell rang.

"You'd better get that, Sam. Be assertive though, the lock's a bit stiff," Candice said. She looked at Emily. "Are you okay?"

"Yes. But in future tell me if there is a problem, you silly girl."

Candice liked it when Emily called her a silly girl. It was what her mother used to say when the occasion demanded it. She saw a lot of her mother in her. It was why she loved her so much.

Harry stood up to greet their guest when Delia followed Samantha into the lounge. Being a vicar of impeccable manners, Ian stood too. Candice prowled in front of the fireplace like a mountain lion intent on ripping out someone's throat.

"Goodness," Delia said, casting around the room.

She felt more nervous now than she had that afternoon. She expected drinks and nibbles with two earth-bound spirits, not half the population of the village and presumably more on the way.

"It's wonderful to see you again, Delia. You look as stunning as ever," the secret agent said, flashing a smile.

"Thank you. I'm sorry, but my memory is a bit of a colander when it comes to names. What was yours again?"

"Harry Black," he answered shortly.

"Oh yes, Mr Black." Delia looked at Candice standing by the fireplace and gulped. Never in her wildest dreams had she expected to be in the presence of greatness. "And you're Candice Freeman."

"I might be," the voice of greatness replied suspiciously.

"It's awfully nice to meet you. It's a privilege, an honour, a moment I'll cherish always."

Candice was staring at her throat. "Likewise."

It was left to Harry to rescue the moment.

"That's the dead people in the room taken care of. Allow me to introduce the living. This is Samantha Copeland, Emily Braithwaite and the Reverend Ian Dawson."

"Hello," Delia offered in a blanket greeting.

"What blood type are you?" Candice asked her.

"Excuse me?"

"It's not a difficult question."

"O Negative."

"Sit down."

"Okay."

"Do you wanna drink?"

"Yes."

"What?"

"Whisky?"

"Fix her a whisky."

"No ice."

"We can do that."

"Thank you."

"I might kill you later."

Harry appreciated that Candice was anxious but threatening to assassinate their guest was taking her concerns to extremes. Delia would have hired a bodyguard and gone into hiding if they carried on like this. She might have become the first mortal to take out a restraining order against a ghost.

"Delia, let me say at this point that Candice is a nice person and you're not seeing her at her best. Can I ask you one simple question that will set everyone's minds at ease?"

"By all means, Mr Pink... Blue... Orange... Purple... Black!"

She punched the air when she finally got it right.

"How the hell can you see us?"

"I'm a psychic."

"A sidekick to who?" Candice asked.

Ian clarified for her. "No, not a sidekick in terms of a comedy double act. A psychic, as in someone gifted in the ways of the paranormal."

"You know, sometimes, Ian, when you open your mouth a really annoying sound comes out."

"Don't start on me because we won't let you kill her," he protested.

"Why do you want to kill me?" Delia asked.

"Because I don't know if I can trust you."

"I don't know if I can trust my energy supplier to send me an accurate gas bill but that doesn't mean I'm going to kill them."

"That's a good point," Ian said. "That's an excellent point."

"Mouth, open, crap," Candice replied.

"Miss Freeman, meeting you is a dream come true," Delia assured her. "You have no idea how I've longed for this day. I have nothing but the greatest of respect for you and Mr Green... Scarlet... Pimpernel... Black!"

Candice didn't see it that way. In the cut-throat world of show business she had been taught to think the worst of people first and believe later. She only took them at their word after they had been tortured and connected to a lie detector.

"You could get a lot of media coverage out of this. I can see the headlines now; *The Ghost of Candice Freeman, alive and well and living in Cloverdale St Mary.*"

"I don't think the term 'Living' can be applied to ghosts," Ian pointed out to her.

"Oh, there's that annoying sound again," Candice said, cupping her hand to her ear.

As before, it fell to Harry to restore order.

"In the interest of this discussion serving a useful purpose and not descending into chaos, I suggest you belt up and leave it to me."

"Well said," Candice replied.

"I was talking to you, not Ian."

"Oh."

"Do you know what your blood type is?"

"RH Positive."

"Bear that in mind."

Even Harry didn't know what he meant by that but it had the desired effect. Candice fell silent.

"Delia, please take my word for it when I say you're not in danger and no harm is going to come to you."

"Thank you, Mr Lilac."

"I might kill you if you don't get my name right but let's not get ahead of ourselves. You say you're a psychic but what brought you here?"

"My camper van."

"And I'm sure it's a very nice camper van but that isn't what I meant. Why did you come to Cloverdale St Mary?"

"G.A.G.A."

"Pardon me?"

"Ghosts and Ghoulish Apparitions. It's a paranormal society that I'm a member of. I heard there was an event taking place here."

"An event?" Emily asked.

Delia's eyes lit up excitedly. "Yes. I read about it in the paper. The whole country is talking about it."

"Cloverdale St Mary is in the news because of UFOs, not ghosts," Harry said.

"I know. I came to the wrong village. It turns out the ghost thing is happening in another one thirty miles from here. I was going to leave when I realised my mistake but then I saw you and Miss Freeman on the green. I thought why do I need to go to Brispane when there are ghosts here? It was awfully exciting. I couldn't believe my luck."

There was an enthusiasm about Delia that left them breathless. She was a little eccentric perhaps but they got the impression that if Daphne had played a poor shot the hockey teacher would have been the first to put her arm around her shoulder to offer encouragement.

"When we spoke earlier today you said we were the first ghosts you've encountered," Harry said.

"That's right. I've been a member of the society for ten years. I was only slightly GAGA to begin with but the more I got into it the more fascinated I became. The trouble was I never saw a ghost. This is the first time I've had a whiff of one. I always knew I had the gift. My mother had it, my grandmother too, but the spirits refused to show themselves to me. I've stayed in haunted hotels and visited paranormal hot-spots all over the country and never saw a thing. I was beginning to think I never would and came jolly close to packing it in. I told myself I would go on one more field trip and if nothing happened that would be an end to it. You can imagine how chuffed I was to see you. It was a life-defining moment for me. All those barren years suddenly became worthwhile."

"What will you do now?" Samantha asked.

Delia sighed. All at once her enthusiasm was gone, replaced by the regret of if only. For her it was a case of seeing the wrong ghost at the wrong time.

"Pretend it never happened and go to Brispane." She looked at Candice and smiled in sad reflection of what might have been. "It's ironic that when I do encounter my first ghosts I find myself meeting one of the most famous people to have ever lived. I couldn't go public with my findings, Miss Freeman, it wouldn't be fair on you. The paranormal community would hound you relentlessly. I couldn't allow myself to be responsible for such a thing. I will never tell a living soul of your existence."

"Thank you," Candice said, believing her at last. She recognized Delia's disappointment and apologized for being less than friendly towards her. "I'm sorry I gave you a hard time. There was no call for that."

Delia felt an apology wasn't necessary and was about to dismiss it but she turned quite pale and raised her hand to her forehead. For one horrible moment they thought she was going to faint.

"Are you all right?" Ian asked.

She found it hard to focus and swayed in her chair.

"I'll fetch you a glass of water," Samantha said, leaving the room.

"I don't know what is... I feel... oh gosh. Something is wrong. Something is most definitely wrong."

"What is it?" Harry asked.

Delia looked at Candice. She felt a sense of dread, a feeling of impending doom that came to her the moment she made her apology. It was as if a barrier had been lifted and she was seeing her for the first time. "It's you, Miss Freeman."

"Me?"

"Goodness. I detect an aura about you."

"Is that a good thing?"

"It depends on your definition of good."

Samantha returned with the water. "Drink this."

Delia drank and took a moment to gather herself. The colour returned to her cheeks and she appeared to be over the worst of it but she was clearly troubled by the experience. When she felt able to continue she turned to Candice once more.

"Has anything strange happened to you recently?" she asked.

"In what way?"

"Have you been unsure of where you are? Suffering from memory lapses?"

The others were as surprised by this as Candice and

hung on every word.

"Yes."

"Have other spirits spoken through you?"

"No."

"Yes," Harry said.

Candice looked at him. She didn't speak. She was too taken aback.

"It happened yesterday. I didn't say anything because I didn't want to worry you."

"Tell me what took place," Delia said.

"We were talking, then it was like Candice wasn't there anymore." He directed the rest of what he had to say to Candice herself. "Your voice didn't change but a young girl spoke through you. She recounted the day her family died. I got the impression it was during the American Civil War."

Candice remained silent.

"It only lasted a few moments. Everything was normal prior to it happening. There was nothing to suggest someone else was present. She came, said her piece and then left you." He turned to Delia. "What do you think caused it?"

"I have no idea but it's jolly exciting, isn't it?" she replied smiling.

"That would depend on your definition of jolly," Candice told her.

"And exciting," Harry said.

Delia put aside her intrigue over these events and was serious again. "Yes, I'm awfully sorry. I appreciate this must be very difficult for you."

Samantha recalled the discussion that had taken place in this room on Saturday evening, when Candice returned after her long absence and they realised something was wrong. She had remarked that the services of an expert in the paranormal would have been useful but no one expected to meet such a person by chance four days later. They would have been no closer to finding an answer if Delia had gone to the right village in search of her event. Now there was hope.

"Is there anything you can do to help?" Samantha asked her.

"I'm rather out of my depth, I'm afraid."

Harry seized the moment and raised his worst fear. "Do you think Candice might be passing over?"

"I don't know. It's possible." Delia looked at her curiously. "Do you want to?"

"No. That's the last thing I want," Candice said.

Delia cast around the room again. It was clear from the faces of everyone present that they didn't want it to happen either.

There was a bond between them, one of the strongest she had seen. This wasn't about mortals and ghosts sharing a brief passage in time, of living, dying and moving on. What she saw were friendships that went beyond life and death and would never diminish. Friendships like that were worth preserving. Yes, she was out of her depth but how could she have turned her back on something so important?

"I know a college professor who came across something similar to this. A brilliant man in his field. I could call him and ask his opinion."

Harry was glad of the offer but responded to it cautiously. "There can be no names. He mustn't know it's Candice."

Emily saw the need for secrecy too. They all did. "I don't think you should divulge the location either. He might make a connection if he knows it's Cloverdale St

Mary. We can't take any chances."

"Don't worry, mum's the word," Delia said, rising to the challenge. "I've been known to talk for hours without saying a thing."

For some reason they didn't doubt that at all.

"When are you gonna call him?" Candice asked.

Delia took her mobile from her pocket. "No time like the present."

She one-touched the number and waited for it to connect, providing a running commentary on what was happening. "It's ringing. Bit of crackling on the line. Still ringing. Ah, hello... It's going to voicemail. It's gone to voicemail. Hello... It's cut me off." She put the phone away. "I'll try again tomorrow. I might get better reception then."

The appearance of the mobile prompted Candice to re-visit events on the green that afternoon. She was confident they could rely on Delia's discretion but mobile phones could be lost or stolen and she didn't feel comfortable having her picture on it.

"Can I see the picture you took of us today?" she asked.

"I'm afraid there's nothing to see. All I got was a picture of a packing case belonging to the TV crew. It was silly of me to try really. Ghosts are notoriously shy when it comes to having their picture taken. I know people who have had them in their viewfinder as clear as you like but all they ended up with was an orb or a blurry mist."

"That's probably just as well taking into account the sensitive situation we find ourselves in," Ian remarked.

"Quite so," Delia said. "If it had come out I would have deleted it."

The last of Candice's fears regarding Delia had been

dispelled. She knew without doubt that she could be trusted. She wouldn't have done anything to put her or Harry at risk. She wouldn't have let something slip in an unguarded moment. She would have done all she could to help them despite being out of her depth. Of that Candice was sure. All she had to do now was deal with her fears over what was happening to her.

"I couldn't bear it if I had to leave you guys."

Her comment was unexpected and had a sobering effect on everyone. It was as if she had reached out to them emotionally but of course that couldn't be. Delia wondered what to make of it. Here was a ghost showing love and affection but how could Candice be capable of those emotions? It defied explanation.

"I'll do everything I can to make sure that doesn't happen, Miss Freeman," she said.

"The first thing you have to do is call me Candice. We're all friends here."

"The second thing you need to do is park your camper van on the drive," Harry said. "There have been a spate of burglaries in the village recently and I would rather you were close by." He turned to Samantha. "Would you be okay with that?"

"I can go one better. I would be happy to make up the spare room for you. Why sleep on a drive when you have access to the house?"

Delia failed to hide her surprise. She didn't know these people, they had only just met, but Samantha was offering to put a roof over her head. "It's jolly kind of you but I couldn't put you to all that trouble."

"It's no trouble."

"I think it's an excellent idea," Ian said. "The burglaries are a cause for concern and there is safety in numbers. I don't want to alarm you but the people committing them can be violent. Aside from that, if you park on the green you'll have Prudence Blunt banging on your door demanding that you leave. That can be scary too. You'll be more comfortable here."

"Well, if you're sure," she replied.

Samantha was committed to her offer. The arrangement suited her too. She was glad of the protection Candice provided but her continued presence was uncertain and it would have been nice to have another person in the cottage.

"You're welcome to stay for as long as you like. I only ask one thing in return. Keep calling him Mr Pimpernel," she said, pointing at Harry. Samantha found it impossible to keep a straight face and laughed. "That was so funny."

The others laughed too, except Delia who was a little embarrassed and Mr Pimpernel who did an excellent impersonation of Miss Blunt and sucked on an invisible lemon. He would have turned Samantha's chair into an ejector seat if he could.

Fourteen

It was two o'clock in the morning and Maggie and Ron had gone to bed. She had fetched her banshee Halloween costume from the wardrobe so sleep didn't appear high on their list of priorities. Ron couldn't believe his luck as she threatened to spill out of a basque that seemed to be a size too small for her.

"HELP! LET ME IN... LET ME IN!" they heard a voice shout amid pounding on the front door.

"You said that without moving your lips," Ron remarked.

"What's going on out there?" Maggie asked, looking over her shoulder at the window.

"I don't know but if we ignore it it's sure to go away."

"HELP ME... PLEASE, LET ME IN!"

Ron frowned and got out of bed. "Typical. Just when things were getting interesting," he muttered, putting on his dressing gown.

"Where are you going?"

"I'm going downstairs to see who is making that racket."

Maggie feared for his sanity and safety. The disturbance had to be investigated but not on the doorstep at this hour of the morning. It could have been anyone out there. "You can't go downstairs. It might be the burglars. They're armed with baseball bats."

Ron sighed. He loved Maggie, especially when she wore a basque and suspenders, fishnet stockings, high heels and a wig of wild, out-of-control hair, but she clearly didn't understand the workings of the criminal mind.

"Burglars don't bang on doors asking to be let in.

They phone to make an appointment," he said.

"Don't go downstairs. It's too dangerous. Call the police."

"And say what? *'Someone is outside my pub pleading with me to let them in?'* I can't see them responding to that."

"Look out of the window then. They can't get you with a baseball bat if you're up here."

Ron conceded. The pounding had grown louder. It could have carried on all night if he didn't do something. "Okay, I'll go to the window."

"Wait a minute. He might have a ladder. Or a trampoline."

He decided the best response to that was to ignore her completely.

Ron walked to the sash window and pulled it open. When he looked down he saw a familiar face outside.

"LET ME IN!" Neil Bradshaw shouted, pounding on the door again.

"Could you be careful with that please? We've recently had it painted," Ron called to him.

Neil looked up and pleaded for all his worth. "Please let me in... I'm being chased by aliens."

"Who is it?" Maggie asked from the safety of their bed.

"It's one of the ufologists, the chap who was abducted by aliens when he was a kid. I think he's a bit of a twit."

"You have to let me in. They're coming for me," Neil panted. Lights appeared on the far side of the green and he went into hyper-drive. "My God, they're here... LET ME IN... LET ME IN!"

If he had pounded on the door any harder it would

have come off its hinges.

Being calm and rational, Ron watched the advancing lights with a heavy sigh.

"You know a lot of aliens who drive 4x4s, do you?" he asked.

The car came to a halt outside the pub and Neil's colleagues stepped out.

"Are you all right?" Brian asked.

Neil was so relieved to see him he would have dropped to his knees and kissed his feet if he could have got his legs to work. "I only just escaped with my life. It was horrendous. It was as close to me as you are now." The thought of monsters lurking in the darkness waiting to take him to a galaxy far far away did nothing for his peace of mind and he pounded on the door again. "LET ME IN... LET ME IN!"

"It was very expensive paint," Ron said to him.

Brian didn't know what had happened, only that their work for the night had been ruined by one of his team freaking out in the Kent countryside. He was eager to get to the bottom of it but a village street at two o'clock in the morning wasn't the best place to conduct a scientific debriefing.

"I think it might be best if we came inside," he called to Ron. "Neil has suffered a traumatic experience. A group hug may be in order."

"Couldn't you do that out there?"

"There are aliens out here!" Neil wailed.

Ron waved his hand at them in a gesture of compliance. The truth was he didn't know if his front door would have survived another attack from a man who clearly had no respect for oak. "All right, I'm coming down, but I must insist that any hugging is done in your rooms. There are some things I don't want to see."

He closed the window and went downstairs.

The ufologists assembled in the bar awaiting Neil's account of an evening that was destined to live long in his memory. He asked Ron if he could have a brandy to settle his nerves. He was clearly distressed and the landlord felt for him but after-hours drinking carried a heavy fine and he flatly refused.

Making do with a bottle of water given to him by Rafe, Neil prepared to tell them about his terrifying ordeal, but before he could start he had reason to be more afraid when he saw a banshee walk towards him.

Unlike Ron, Maggie hadn't put on a dressing gown and the sight of the apparition drove fear into Neil's heart. He let out a cry and stumbled backwards.

"Oh my God... make the hideous creature go away!"

"Steady on. That's my wife," Ron said.

"There's nothing hideous from where I'm standing," Brian drooled.

"At the risk of repeating myself, that's my wife," Ron said again, narrowing his eyes at him.

"I would have been safer with the aliens," Neil protested.

Ron wanted to go back to bed but Maggie's arrival had put paid to that. Neil would have fled the room in an instant if aliens hadn't been waiting for him outside but Brian and the others seemed reluctant to go anywhere. Siobhan in particular liked what she saw. She made a mental note to buy a basque for Karen.

"Couldn't you have put something on before you came down?" Ron said.

Maggie didn't see what the fuss was about and shrugged her shoulders. "I work in the bar dressed like this on Halloween."

Siobhan made another mental note. *I have to come back for that.*

"I know, but today is the 8th of June," Ron pointed out.

Neil marked himself with the sign of the cross. "It's 'orrible... and it talks."

"I won't tell you again," Ron warned him.

A long night showed signs of becoming even longer when a new face joined them. Ron had left the front door open and regretted his oversight as Grantley walked in.

"Is everything all right?" he asked, striding through the bar. "I heard a terrible commotion and thought I should... goodness me," he interrupted himself, breaking into a smile when he saw Maggie.

"What part of *'That's my wife'* do you people not understand?" Ron asked.

Maggie tried to pull up her basque. It was a valiant effort but there was simply too much filling it.

"Is everything okay? You're not being burgled, are you?" Bill asked, arriving with Susan.

I'd may as well open up, Ron thought.

He saw where Bill's eyes had wandered and sighed in defeat. "We're having a chat. You know, the ufologists, Maggie and I. You remember Maggie. My wife."

"Why are you wearing your Halloween costume? It's months away," Bill said.

Susan looked at him in a manner to suggest *I can't believe you asked that question.*

"Ah," Bill said, realising.

He turned to Ron and voiced his concerns again. "We heard a lot of banging going on and wondered if you needed help."

"No, we hadn't got to the banging part yet," Maggie

answered for him.

"What do you mean?"

There was that look from Susan again.

"Oh, I see."

Ron was more concerned about the amount of people in his bar. He considered opening the beer garden to accommodate them all. "It's just as well there isn't a police presence in the village at night. We could lose our licence if they saw you lot in here."

"So you're not being burgled?" Grantley asked.

"No," Ron replied.

"Why are you up then?" Susan enquired.

"Chance would be a fine thing. We hadn't got to that part either," Maggie muttered.

"This chap is being chased by aliens," Ron said, pointing to Neil.

"I heard something in the trees. I thought that cat had come back to pinch my sandwiches but then I saw it. It was an alien."

"Illegal or extraterrestrial?" Grantley asked.

He knew from Brian's pained expression that his question hadn't been appreciated and elected not to comment further.

"What did it look like?" Karen asked her colleague.

"It was horrendous. Big lifeless eyes, leathery skin and a huge, slobbering mouth."

The description fitted Brian's mother-in-law but she hadn't come on this trip.

"Did it try to make contact with you?" Siobhan asked.

"I didn't give it a chance to. I ran like the clappers. I knew it was chasing me. I could feel its hot, rancid breath on the back of my neck."

Maybe she got the train? Brian thought.

Ron had never heard so much nonsense in his life. There was as much chance of aliens running amok in the village as there was of Maggie putting some clothes on. "It was a prankster dressed up to look like an alien. Someone was having a laugh, a bit of fun at your expense."

"It was real I tell you," Neil insisted.

Ron didn't feel inclined to debate it further. It was late and he wanted an end to all this. He wanted normality to return, for the world to go away. More importantly, he wanted to reacquaint himself with the banshee standing at his side. "Okay, it was real. Shouldn't you be having a group hug in your rooms?"

"What's going on? Are you being burgled?" Terry Driscol asked, arriving with one of three patrols that roamed the village at night.

"And then there were eleven," Ron said.

"Can I have some breakfast?" Neil asked.

"Not at two o'clock in the morning, no," Ron snapped.

"Is everything all right? You're not being burgled, are you?" John Francis said, leading in the second patrol.

"Does it look like they're being burgled?" Brian said to him.

"It looks like they're getting ready for Halloween," Francis replied.

"Are you being burgled?" Dan Tyler panted out of breath, arriving with his patrol immediately after.

Ron found Bill through the sea of people filling his pub and held out his hand. "Give me your door key. Maggie and I will sleep at your place."

"I left the front door open," he replied, staring at Susan horrified.

That got rid of two of them at least.

*

Candice stood beside Samantha's bed as she slept. As before, she didn't know she was there. Candice knew nothing when she went away and became the servant of the powerful mind controlling her.

She whispered. "Rise."

Samantha opened her eyes. She pulled the duvet aside and stood up. She too had gone away.

"Go to the dressing table."

Samantha did as instructed and stood motionless in front of it. She didn't see her reflection in the mirror. She was oblivious to it, like she was oblivious to everything that was happening to her.

"Pick up the knife and hold it to your throat."

She retrieved the carving knife that Candice had put there. The blade was cold and sharp against her skin but she didn't feel it. Samantha awaited her instructions, unaware that she would have cut her throat there and then if she had been ordered to.

Candice considered her without comment; the slave of the servant staring at a reflection unseen, submissive and with no will of her own, one command away from slitting her throat and bleeding to death at her feet. It would have been that easy, that simple, but this was just an experiment. It wasn't her time.

Yet.

"Put the knife down and go back to bed."

Samantha obeyed and fell into a deep, lasting sleep. When she woke at 7:00 a.m. she had no recollection of what had happened.

Neither did Candice.

*

Breakfast at Meadow Cottage was busier than usual. Delia dug into a bowl of cereal while Samantha made do with her customary tea and toast. That she would have been late for work was nothing out of the ordinary. She never allowed herself enough time in the mornings.

Candice and Harry watched as she dashed across the room in a panic over where she had left her car keys, toast in mouth and jacket half on and half off.

"They're on the hallway table where you always leave them," Harry told her.

Samantha's reply would have been intelligible if she hadn't been eating.

"It's amazing how that girl doesn't suffer from chronic indigestion," he said as she bolted out of the kitchen.

Candice smiled. "Was everything okay at Emily's last night?"

"Yes, nothing to report there. The Coaching Inn got a bit busy around 2:00 a.m. though."

"They didn't have trouble, did they?"

"Not in a burglar sense. Going by what I can gather, Ron and Maggie were preparing for Halloween when the ufologists returned unexpectedly."

Candice made the connection and smiled again.

"How many burglaries have there been in the village?" Delia asked.

"Five," Harry replied.

"Gosh. And you say they've resorted to violence?"

"Yeah. The last one was particularly bad. They set about a pensioner with a baseball bat," Candice said.

"Goodness me. It must be awful for everyone having

to live under threat of such a thing."

"The sooner they're caught the better," Harry replied. "What are your plans for today?"

"I want to wander around the village, see if I can pick up on anything. I'll try the Professor again too."

"Who is he?" Candice asked.

"A brilliant man, truly brilliant. It's thanks to him that I got involved in paranormal research. He's a lecturer at Chamford College in London. I haven't seen him in a number of years but he still plays an active role in our profession. Some of his papers are ground-breaking, legendary one might say."

"You hold him in high regard," Harry said. "Do you think he'll be able to help us?"

"I'm sure he'll do all he can. If anyone can help it's Professor Grantley."

"Grantley?" Harry asked.

"Yes, Professor William Grantley."

"That's a coincidence. We have a Grantley living in the village," Candice said.

"Do you?"

"Yeah, Norman Grantley. He's a retired doctor."

"From London," Harry added. "Could they be related?"

Candice scoffed at the idea. He had been wrong on many counts but this one wasn't worthy of a second thought. "Harry, Grantley is a common name and London is a big city."

"Yes, of course," he said, dismissing it.

Delia finished eating and washed up her breakfast things. She had spent a very comfortable night in the guest room and didn't want to repay Samantha's kindness by leaving her to do the washing up when she got home from work.

"What about you two? What are you doing today?" Her curiosity got the better of her and she plunged. "That is to say, what do ghosts do?"

Candice answered on Harry's behalf. "We have a busy schedule. There's always something that needs doing. Today we might... well... we could, um..." She was damned if she knew and turned to him for clarification. "What *do* we do?"

"We hang around."

"Yeah," Candice said.

"You know, we haunt," Harry went on, struggling too.

"That's right. We haunt and do stuff like that."

It dawned on them that it wasn't the most productive of pastimes and they fell silent.

"That sounds jolly nice," Delia said, wishing she hadn't asked. "I'm going to take a stroll into the village. Try to get a feel for the place."

"Do you want us to come with you?" Candice asked.

"It might be better if you didn't. I want to know if there are any psychic vibes around. That might prove difficult if I was in the company of ghosts. I wouldn't know if I was getting them from you or elsewhere."

"That makes sense," Candice was forced to agree.

"If you need us for anything we'll be here. You know, haunting," Harry said.

"We could go to Falworth," Candice suggested, trying to sound upbeat. "We haven't haunted that for a while."

"Yes, good point."

Neither were thrilled by the prospect and they retreated to silence again.

Delia smiled awkwardly and took leave of them.

*

Nathan Baker had been employed as a yard hand at the Cross Drummond Equestrian Centre, until Miss Blunt fired him over an act of cruelty. Now he was in the burglary business and doing very well for himself.

"We're taking a chance coming here."

Baker thought Liam Tate was worrying unduly. Why shouldn't they have gone to the Coaching Inn for a drink? The arrival of the ufologists and thrill-seekers provided perfect cover for thieves like them. There were so many strangers in the village who would have paid attention to two more?

"Don't worry about it. We're safe enough," he said.

"Someone might recognize you."

"Among this lot? You must be joking. They're packed in like fucking sardines."

Tate looked at the bar staff rushed off their feet. The lunch trade had become busy and it was all that Maggie and Ron could do to keep up. Jill and Deborah worked extra shifts as agreed but it was an uphill task for all of them.

"When are we going to do Meadow Cottage?" he asked.

"All in good time."

"We can't stay here indefinitely. The longer we delay, the greater risk there is of getting caught."

Baker grinned smugly. Everything was going according to plan and there was no reason to think it wouldn't continue that way. He wasn't the decision-maker when it came to staging the burglaries, Baker didn't have the final say in who would be targeted and when, but he oozed confidence in a manner to suggest he was. As a yard hand he was out of his depth. As a burglar he was in his comfort zone but only when someone more competent called the shots and told him what to do.

"Something like this can't be rushed. We'll do Meadow Cottage when the time is right," he told Tate. "Pine Trees, the vicarage and this place too. We've got a few more house calls to make before we move on."

"Having the pub on our list makes being here even more risky," Tate said.

Baker paused over his beer glass. "They have things I want and when I want something I acquire it."

Tate didn't know if he could trust his judgement but pursued it no further. It wasn't his place to ask too many questions or raise concerns. He was the muscle, the hired help who beat pensioners with baseball bats if they dared to stand in their way. His job was to put his shoulder through doors and carry what they stole to the van. It was better to leave the finer points of their profession to those with a clearer understanding of it.

He and Baker hadn't known each other long. They met by chance in a pub one evening and the conversation turned to how to make some easy money. Tate didn't know anything about him. Only now was he beginning to work him out.

"It's not about the haul for you, is it?" he said.

"What you take doesn't matter. It's who you take it from that counts."

Baker looked at the picture of Candice above the fireplace. It wasn't just Miss Blunt that he disliked. He laughed till he hurt when he heard the great Candice Freeman had died in a plane crash. If it hadn't been for the man walking his dog in the early hours of the morning he would have done more than desecrate her grave. He would have dug the bitch up and left her on the ground with the spade embedded in her chest.

*

"I spy with my little eye something beginning with... Oh, this is ridiculous," Candice said, sitting on the back porch of Meadow Cottage with Harry.

"How am I meant to get it from that?" he protested.

"We've been sitting here playing I Spy for two hours. There has to be more to death than this."

It was unexpected but Delia's question of *What do ghosts do?* had thrown them. They spent their time glad to be in each other's company and were seldom bored but what did they actually do? They never analysed it before because they had no reason to. It was unfortunate that on the day the question had been raised they *were* bored.

They thought of Emily sightseeing in London and came to the conclusion they should have gone too. After hearing what was happening to Candice the previous evening Emily insisted she wouldn't go. Despite their reassurance to the contrary she felt she had let them down and her place was in the village. If anything happened how could she have helped if she was gallivanting around the capital?

Candice wouldn't hear of it and demanded she went. Harry too, despite his loathing of Grantley and continued mistrust of him. The trip to London formed part of Emily's birthday celebrations and should have been enjoyed, not cancelled over something that was beyond her control.

"Do you want to go to Cross Drummond?" Harry asked.

"No."
"Falworth?"
"No."
"Cape Town?"
"No."
"We could try to get the lawnmower to work."
Candice didn't bother to respond to that at all.
"What are we going to do then? We can't sit here all day."
Renewed determination swept over her, a sense of purpose that had been lacking since breakfast and that question that had given them too much time to think.
"I'll tell you what we're gonna do. While Delia sorts out the problem regarding me we're gonna catch some burglars and solve the mystery of invading aliens. That should keep us busy for a while."
Harry agreed that steps had to be taken to address those issues, the burglaries especially, but first they had other business to attend to. Things were going on in the world that couldn't be ignored or made light of, important things that demanded immediate action. Burglars, Candice's disappearances and aliens from outer space formed only a small part of the trials that had been sent to test them.
"Okay, but let's finish playing I Spy. The score is thirty each and we need a tie-breaker."

Fifteen

Delia turned off her mobile phone. Again her call to the Professor had gone to voicemail and again she had been cut off before she could leave a message. She met her failure to contact him with a heavy sigh and resolved to try later.

The village green was packed with vehicles. Even the space she had vacated by moving her camper van to Meadow Cottage had been filled. It was now occupied by an ambulance made in 1967 that had been converted into a mobile home by a couple from Inverness. People had come from far and wide in response to the UFO story and were still coming. A man from Wales had arrived on a motorbike and was setting up a tent as Delia continued her walk around the village. Miss Blunt would not have been amused when she got home from work. It was practically in her front garden.

By midday Delia was in need of refreshment and went to the tearoom.

"Hello. What can I get for you?" Susan asked as she sat at a table.

"Just a cup of tea please."

"The scones are good."

"I'm not really a scones person."

"Cake?"

Delia didn't like to refuse a second time and nodded.

Her eyes travelled to a table by the door where two women sat. They were kissing.

"I wish you wouldn't do that in public," Rafe said when he returned from the wash room.

The comment had been directed to his estranged

wife.

Karen fetched her teacup from its saucer and smiled. She saw nothing wrong in her and Siobhan's show of affection. He had seen them kiss many times since she left him for the attractive brunette sitting beside her.

"Have you spoken to Neil this morning?" she asked.

"Yeah. He's still stressed out. I don't think the group hug helped."

"It did me the world of good," Siobhan said, holding her lover's hand.

Rafe looked down his nose at her as he always did. "I don't know if he'll be in the right frame of mind for going out tonight. He's been really shaken by the experience."

"Do you think something chased him?" Karen asked.

"I'm sure something did. Whether it was an extraterrestrial is another matter. The landlord could be right. It might have been one of the locals messing around. I wouldn't put it past anyone in this village."

"It seems like a nice community to me," Siobhan said.

"I wouldn't trust any of them," Rafe replied dismissively.

He saw his wife gaze lovingly into Siobhan's eyes and realised she had left the conversation. When they kissed again he decided to leave the premises.

"I have some notes to type up. I'll see you later."

Neither of them acknowledged him. They didn't even see him go.

"Your tea and cake," Susan said, returning to Delia's table.

"Thank you. I take it the village isn't normally as crowded as this."

"No, we have aliens to thank for our sudden population boom. Is that what brought you here?"

Delia played her cards close to her chest. She didn't want to announce that she was a psychic involved in paranormal research. In her experience it wasn't always well met. On hearing the word psychic most people shouted nut-case.

"I'm just passing through," she said.

"Oh. I assumed you were a UFO watcher. Will you be staying long?"

"I'm not sure yet. Perhaps a day or two. It's awfully nice here."

"Yes, we're very fortunate. It's a lovely village."

It was a busy one too and Susan left her to serve a new customer.

Delia looked at the cake she didn't really want and took a bite. Finding it to have been the best thing she had ever tasted, she proceeded to make short work of it.

"I see Susan has been tempting you with her culinary delights," Ian said, appearing at her table. "May I join you?"

"Please do," Delia replied, cheeks bulging. "I have no idea what I'm eating but it's simply fabulous."

"It's Red Velvet cake. She excels at those."

"Hello, Ian. Would you like a cup of tea?" Susan asked, stopping on her way to the kitchen.

"No thanks. I've brought a flask. The tea you serve is horrible."

"I haven't got time to serve you anyway," she said, taking leave of them.

The vicar smiled.

"What sort of night did you have at Meadow Cottage?" he asked Delia.

"A very pleasant one. I've never slept in a more comfortable bed. It was jolly decent of Samantha to take me in."

"That's Sam all over. And we are batting for the same team. I know it's early days but have you made any headway?"

"Not yet. I tried to call the Professor again but still couldn't get through. I've been walking around the village to familiarize myself with it. This afternoon I might go to that woodland area to the north of here. Cross Drummond, isn't it?"

"Yes, that's right."

"I'll see how I get on there. I thought I may have picked up on some paranormal activity but nothing has leapt out at me."

Ian was puzzled. "Why should it?"

"The spirit that spoke through Candice intrigues me. I didn't say anything last night but that sort of thing is jolly unusual. It leads me to wonder if there is another supernatural force in the village. Something that may be influencing her."

"You mean another ghost?"

"It's possible. It may go some way to explaining her disappearances and memory lapses... Excuse me, could I have another slice of cake please?" she asked Susan when she returned from the kitchen.

"Yes, of course."

"Thank you. The problem is if another ghost is present in the village why isn't Mr Olive aware of it?"

"Harry?"

"Yes."

"His name is Black."

"Oh, of course it is. I really am a sieve when it comes to names."

Ian couldn't think why. She was spot on with

everyone else's.

"Maybe he's been a ghost for too long," he pondered.

"What do you mean?"

"I don't know the first thing about this so forgive me if I'm talking nonsense but Harry has been dead for seven years. He's had time to adjust. The same can't be said for Candice. She's coming up to her first anniversary. Could that have something to do with it?"

"When is the anniversary of her death?"

"Next Wednesday."

Delia thought long and hard. Her instincts told her there wasn't a connection but nothing could be ruled out. The simple fact was she didn't know. "Again it's possible but I couldn't say for sure. This is where the Professor would prove invaluable. He's the man we need to answer these questions."

"Your cake," Susan said, setting her plate down.

"Thank you, Mrs Black," Delia replied, her mind elsewhere.

Ian smiled. "Where is my tea?" he asked.

"You said you didn't want one," Susan answered.

"And you call yourself a saleswoman? I expect to see tea and cake on this table without delay."

Susan assured him she would return with his order but something had been brought to her attention by one of her regular customers that needed to be dealt with. Some activities were not suited to a village meeting place.

"Can I get you anything?" she asked, standing at Karen and Siobhan's table. "Tea? Scones? A room?"

They untangled their tongues and looked at her.

"I don't mean to be a killjoy but some of my customers don't feel comfortable with public shows of affection."

"Of course," Karen said. "Sorry."

Susan smiled. "Would you like anything else?"

"Can we have two teas? And some more of this brilliant cake."

*

Harry paced the attic room in Meadow Cottage with his hands clasped behind his back. That he had lost the I Spy tie-breaker by not working out that Candice had spied a bird feeder hanging from a tree branch continued to annoy him – how was he supposed to have got it from *D for dangling bird feeder?* - but he put aside his disappointment as he ran through the schedule regarding the burglaries.

"The first break-in happened at Ted Cooper's cottage on the 31st of May. The second was Barbara Cullen on the 1st of June. The third was Bill and Susan on the 2nd. The church was vandalized on the 3rd and Prudence was burgled on the 4th. The fifth burglary was at Albert and Sarah Preston's cottage on the 7th. These are the facts of the matter. What are we to deduce from them?"

"The burglars wanted three days off before they hit the Preston's," Candice replied.

"Location," Harry said, lifting his finger in the air. He waved it for good measure. "We must concern ourselves with the location of these crimes."

Candice felt like she was in a courtroom. She wanted to identify and catch the burglars, not listen to Harry's impersonation of a QC cross-examining a murder suspect. "You're not gonna say *'I put it to you that on the night in question'* are you?"

"What do you mean?"

"You're making *me* feel guilty and I haven't done anything. Can we have less theatrics and more emphasis on how we catch these people?"

"In order to catch them we have to get inside their minds."

"No, we have to work out where they're likely to strike next and be there to stop it."

"And how do you propose we do that?"

"I don't know but we're not gonna do it from the Old Bailey. Before we can get 'em to court we have to catch the sons of bitches."

"Objection..."

"Harry."

He sulked in silence.

Candice turned on the stereo for some background music. She thought better while listening to The Eagles. "What we do know is there is no pattern to these burglaries. They seem to be striking at random."

"I don't think so."

"Overruled," she said, ordering Harry back to silence. "The questions we need to answer are why did they start with Ted, why did they hit Pru and why haven't they hit anyone since the Preston's?"

"May I say something?"

"Yes, but I reserve the right to take it under advisement."

"Do you remember what Grantley said in the pub that evening, how he was surprised that Cloverdale St Mary hadn't been targeted by thieves before in view of the fact that you lived here?"

"Yeah."

"What if the village has been targeted for that reason

now?" Harry began to count on his fingers. "Ted Cooper. Not a close friend but you dated his son..."

"Only once."

"Irrelevant, move to strike."

It was Candice's turn to retreat to silence. In a way it suited her because it was something she didn't want to talk about and would rather have forgotten. Her one-night stand with Alan Cooper happened a long time ago, they slept together after a party, but it was a mistake and to this day she regretted it.

Harry continued with his assessment. "Barbara Cullen. You wouldn't know her if you passed her on the street. Bill and Susan. Close friends. Prudence. One of your *closest* friends. Albert and Sarah Preston. Unknown to you. What do you deduce from that?"

Candice got it immediately. It wasn't difficult to work out. "Of the five victims I know three of them well. It's about me."

Harry nodded. "It has been from day one. The burglars know you had friends in the village. It's likely you would have bequeathed something to them when you died, things that were personal to you and would fetch a good price. They already have one of them, the Oscar that belonged to Prudence. The others can be found at Emily's, the vicarage, the Coaching Inn and here. That gives us the where but it doesn't give us the when. They're muddying the waters by also robbing people you *didn't* know. That disguises their true intentions and keeps the police guessing."

"Location," Candice said, deep in thought.

"Location is key. At some point Meadow Cottage will be burgled. So will Emily, Ian and Sheila and Maggie and Ron."

Candice conceded the point. "The next time I

complain about your Old Bailey routine tell me to shut up."

"It doesn't solve our problem. We still don't know where they will strike next."

"It raises another question. How do they know where to find these things?"

Harry wondered how someone so smart could have been so dim. The answer to that was obvious. "They know who your friends are and where they live. That makes it a sure bet they knew you."

Candice was stunned. "Are you saying I know them?"

"Not necessarily but one thing is certain. They're locals. They might live in Falworth. They might even live in Cloverdale St Mary or a village nearby. How else would they know who to target?"

The thought of the burglars living among them was disconcerting to say the least. It was a close-knit community. The possibility of thieves living on their doorstep went against everything that was decent. It wouldn't have been the first time people had stolen from their own but it was inconceivable that it could have happened there. That they had been violent towards villagers they knew made it worse.

Candice sat on the sofa. "Okay, Harry. You're a burglar with a liking for Oscars and other things that glitter. What would you do?"

"The way it stands I have two choices when it comes to who I rob next. Emily or Samantha. I wouldn't select a house that was home to a family or a couple when I could target one with a single occupant. I would play the safe option. The more burglaries I commit the more chance there is of my being caught. It's getting risky so I would do an easy one next and then stop for a while. I can come back for the others when it's safer."

"Why is it risky?"

"There are night patrols on every street corner and UFO watchers on the green."

"Who would you go for?"

Harry didn't hesitate over his answer. The was only one candidate. "Emily."

Candice wasn't ahead of the game but at least she had caught up with him. Or so she thought. "And today she's in London. By the time she gets back it will be gone midnight. It's a perfect opportunity for the thieves to add to their haul."

"It would be if you weren't overlooking the obvious."

"What am I overlooking?"

"I said the way it stands I have two choices. If I wait twenty-four hours I've got three. As you rightly pointed out Emily is in London but tomorrow she'll be in the Coaching Inn celebrating her birthday. All her friends will be there, including Samantha, Ian, Sheila and Becky. We can rule out the pub as a target but Emily's cottage, the vicarage and this place will be open for business. They won't have time to rob them all but they can do one or two."

Now Candice had caught up with him.

"The vicarage would be a good bet because the whole family will be out," he went on. "Emily would be their second choice because Sam could leave early for some reason. The guest of honour would stay till the end."

Candice nodded in agreement.

They may have been on the same page but she was at a loss to know what they could have done about it.

"So what are we gonna do? Ian and Sheila won't attend Emily's party if we tell Ian it's likely they'll be burgled next. That will ruin it for her. She dotes over Becky as much as she does Mel."

"We don't tell him," Harry replied simply.

Not for the first time during this conversation, Candice was stunned.

"And we sit with them in the Coaching Inn all evening knowing that while they're enjoying themselves they're losing everything they own? With friends like you I'm guessing Ian doesn't need enemies."

"Were you asleep when God handed out rational thought?"

"What's that supposed to mean?"

Harry waved at her. He sounded more American than she was. "Um, hello. Ghost. We can come and go whenever we please without being noticed. While everyone is having a good time we check on their houses once every half an hour. We can keep an eye on the vicarage, Emily's and Meadow Cottage. Best of all we'll be on hand to catch the sons of bitches if they do break in."

"Oh."

Harry sat beside her and blew out his cheeks. "Talking to you is hard work sometimes."

"Unlike you, I don't have a devious mind."

"You don't have a devious mind? *D for dangling bird feeder.* Where did that come from?"

"I won that tie-breaker fair and square."

"It would have been like saying *F for furry thing* while spying a squirrel."

He clearly hadn't paid attention. That was how she won round eighteen.

Candice elected not to comment and turned her thoughts to a village celebration that could have spelt the end of a spate of burglaries that had left everyone feeling vulnerable. At last they were in a position where they could have done something positive to help. But.

"How do we catch them?" she asked. "I know it's not pretty but number twelve on the list isn't gonna stop them from running before the cops arrive. If anything it will prompt an exit. And how do we get the cops involved in the first place?"

She must have been asleep. Harry could think of no other explanation.

"We don't catch them. We let them commit the burglary and follow them when they leave. They'll either go back to where they're hiding the stolen goods or move on to the next job. Whatever they do one of us will return to the Coaching Inn to tip off Ian who will call the police and inform them of their whereabouts. No one has to know it's him, he can do it anonymously. The burglars are caught and will spend the next ten years doing muesli."

"Porridge."

"I knew it had something to do with breakfast."

Candice grinned. She was impressed. "You're not just a pretty face, are you? When did you work all this out?"

"While I was looking for something that began with D."

It was time for total honesty and she levelled with him.

"Actually, you won the tie-breaker. You got what I was looking at with your first answer. I changed it."

"Daffodil?"

"Yeah."

"You cheated!"

"I don't like losing."

Harry didn't like losing either. For that reason he didn't tell her he had changed what he was spying faster than some people changed their socks. In one round Candice got it right thirty-two times before she finally admitted defeat.

"Okay, we've made a start as far as the burglaries are concerned. What about the aliens?" she asked.

"We'll be rid of that problem when we get rid of Grantley."

"Harry, Norman Grantley is not an alien."

"Of course he is. You can tell just by looking at him."

"What?"

"He has one eyebrow higher than the other. You didn't notice that, did you?"

"No, that got past me."

"The reason for this deformity is because the transformation from his alien body to his human form went wrong. The machine that does it must have been on the blink."

"I spy with my little eye something beginning with M.O.C."

"Magazine on chair," he answered, pointing across the room.

Candice laughed. "You idiot. You goddam idiot. GET OUT OF MY FUCKING HOUSE AND DON'T COME BACK!"

Her eyes were on fire, teeth clenched. A twisted, furious face met his astonished eyes as she stood up and glared at him.

Harry stood too. "Candice?"

"You think you're so smart, don't you? You think you can walk in here like nothing happened after all you've put me through? It doesn't work that way. I won't let you treat me like shit again."

Harry raised his hands in a calming gesture. He had no idea who he was speaking to but this spirit was angry and may have been dangerous, not to him but to Candice. "I want you to leave. Release her and go."

"My friends were right about you. They warned me but I didn't listen. I'm listening now. If I'd done it sooner I wouldn't have been your punch bag for the past eight years."

"Drive her out, Candice. You have to drive her out."

"You didn't think you'd see me with a gun, did you? Thought I was too weak to defend myself? You shouldn't have come here, Nick. It wasn't one of your better decisions."

Candice levelled the imaginary gun at Harry's chest and pulled the trigger six times. Seeing Nick Babarati fall, she looked at him dead on the floor and smiled. "You won't hurt me again. You won't hurt anybody again."

Candice looked up, straight into the eyes of Harry Black. She was horrified and scared in her moment of realisation. The spirit had left her but it was too late.

"Harry?"

She vanished in a micro-second.

"CANDICE!"

Sixteen

Sylvia Patcher killed Nick Babarati in June 2003 after years of mental and physical abuse. He had beaten and raped her so often it became a part of everyday life, until she couldn't take any more and left him.

The violent acts committed against her in the past and his motive for going to her home on the day he died failed to have a bearing at her trial and she was sentenced to death by lethal injection. She spent ten years on death row until a wretched life ended on the 14th of March 2013. Sylvia Patcher wasn't the first person to be let down by the U.S. legal system and she wouldn't be the last. The State of Arizona was one of thirty-one that continued to impose the death penalty.

"Let me go," Candice said in the darkness that surrounded her.

"Go where?" a man's voice replied.

"Home. I want to go home."

"You are home."

"I can't see you. Where are you?"

"Far from here."

"Where is here? Why are you doing this to me?"

"Does there have to be a reason?"

"I'm afraid."

"We have things to discuss you and I."

"What things?"

"I want to talk to you about Samantha Copeland."

"Samantha?"

"Her time is coming. Yours too."

"I don't understand."

"Do you believe?"
"Believe in what?"
"Do you see?"
"See what? You're not making sense."
"It will be clear to you in time."
"What are you talking about? Where am I? Who are you?"
"I am your creator."
"God?"
"No, not God. I am *your* creator."
"I don't know what you mean. I'm frightened. Please let me go home."
"Walk forward three paces. Do you see?"
"Yes."
"Pick it up. Do you remember?"
"Yes."
"Samantha is almost ready but not quite. I have things to do that will change that. Do you understand?"
"Yes."
"Do you believe?"
"Yes."
"We will talk again later. You will stay here until then."

The voice fell silent in the dark void in which Candice was imprisoned. She was anxious and alone, caught not between heaven and earth, not between heaven and hell, but a place decided by the Creator who had total control over her. A place from which there would be no escape until her Master decided otherwise.

She looked at the knife in her hand.

*

Harry was frantic, out of his mind with worry. The way Candice had disappeared made him fear she wouldn't come back.

"She's gone, Ian. There was nothing I could do to stop it."

The vicar appealed for calm. He too was concerned but they had to keep their wits about them. They couldn't allow themselves to panic.

"I know this is hard for you, Harry, but we shouldn't second-guess anything. Tell me exactly what happened."

"She was taken from me. Where is Delia? I need Delia."

"She said she was going to visit Cross Drummond this afternoon."

Harry stared across the churchyard. His eyes travelled beyond his grave to the vast woodland area that stood to the north of the village. He didn't know where Delia was but had to find her. She was the only person who could have helped him.

A moment later he was gone.

Ian returned hurriedly to the vicarage and fetched his car from the garage.

*

Samantha welcomed Delia's visit. They chatted over coffee and she showed her around the stables when she expressed an interest in seeing them. Afterwards she gave her a tour of the rest of the equestrian centre.

Miss Blunt didn't approve of strangers wandering around her school and did all she could to discourage it. The stables were open to visitors but the riding school was not. She allowed the intrusion because Delia was clearly a friend of Samantha's and she didn't want to embarrass her by refusing but she did protest when Delia asked if she might be permitted to see Candice's office. That part of the school was private and Miss Blunt wanted it to remain so. Even members of staff were not allowed access. It was where Candice worked tirelessly to make the equestrian centre the success it ultimately became, a space that was hers and not for the eyes of a curious public. It was where Miss Blunt went when the pain of loss became too much and she wanted to be close to her.

Samantha promised they wouldn't stay long and she relented. The truth was Delia needed to see it because it may have provided a clue to what was happening to the ghost of Candice Freeman. That office and everything connected with it was as important to her investigation as Meadow Cottage and other places Candice had frequented. The moment they entered Delia felt her presence. Not now but over the past year. Candice went there often. It meant a lot to her too.

Candice had seen Miss Blunt cry in that room. She had seen her cry at home. She had witnessed the private sorrow that was never shown in public. She had seen her pull at her hair screaming why? *Come back to us, Candice, we need you,* and felt devastated because of it. What she would have given to ease her pain. Prudence, Maggie and Ron, Melanie and Brenda. People who loved her and she loved from beyond the grave. It wasn't fair but when did death wear an acceptable face?

Delia left the equestrian centre at ten to four and roamed the lanes and roads beyond it. It was here that Harry found her and Ian found them.

"Get in the car. I'll take you back to Meadow Cottage," he said through his open window.

"Mr Jennings told me what happened," Delia replied, urgency in her voice as she climbed into the front seat. It wasn't even a colour but neither Harry or Ian felt inclined to correct her. "Don't go to the cottage. I must return to the riding school immediately."

"Why there?" Ian asked.

"It is of the utmost importance. Please, there is no time to lose."

"In other words floor the pedal," Harry said.

Ian didn't know what was going on but set a new record in reaching their destination. Both Harry and Delia were as white as ghosts when they arrived.

"Where did you learn to drive like that?" Harry asked, stumbling out of the car.

"I watch a lot of American TV."

Delia felt her pulse. "I'm still alive."

"You said you wanted to get here fast," Ian said in his defence.

"Quite so."

Delia left them in her wake as she ran into Cross Drummond House.

"Back again?" Miss Blunt asked as she bolted past her.

"Can't stop."

"Vicar, what is the meaning of this?" Miss Blunt called as Ian followed Delia inside.

"Sorry, Prudence, in a bit of a rush."

"We'll be out of your way in a moment," Harry said, running past her too.

Miss Blunt didn't hear that final apology and was left stunned as she watched Delia and Ian take the stairs two at a time to the second floor. "Have you gone mad? I demand an explanation for this reprehensible behaviour," she called after them.

Delia arrived at Candice's office first. Ian arrived seconds later.

"Close the door and lock it. We can't allow Miss Blunt to follow us in here," she said.

Ian secured the room.

"It's just as well I don't need doors," Harry protested, walking through the wall beside it.

"Shhh," Delia said.

She stood in the centre of the room and cast around it. It was as she had left it an hour previously; empty but for them, a private place seen by a select few. Again she felt Candice's presence but didn't know if it was now or from times past, a part of her that always remained within those walls.

"Candice, are you here?" she asked quietly.

There was no response.

"Can you hear me?"

"What is happening?" Harry asked.

"Please, Mr Brown. I must have silence. Candice, if you can hear me make your presence known. I know you're close by."

There came a loud pounding on the door.

Ian jumped out of his skin.

"What is going on in there?" Miss Blunt called from outside. "Why is this door locked? I demand to be let in at once."

"Candice, there isn't much time," Delia said desperately.

"Open this door immediately!"

"Make your presence known to us."

"Vicar, if you do not open this door you will leave me with no alternative but to call the police."

Delia shook her head. "She's not here."

"Why did you think she would be?" Harry asked.

"I don't know. I had the strangest feeling..."

"Father Ian, I demand that you open this door!"

Ian walked to it and turned the key in the lock. He braced himself for the storm that was about to break. "We have some serious explaining to do," he said to Delia.

Miss Blunt strode into the room and looked at them with daggers in her eyes. "What is the meaning of this intrusion? How dare you force your way in here. I would have expected better of you, vicar."

"I'm sorry, Prudence."

"An apology is appropriate given the circumstances but it does not explain your outrageous behaviour. I want to know what you are doing here and why that door was locked," she barked, pointing at it.

"It was my fault, Miss Blunt," Delia said. "I wanted to take a picture of the office. I asked Father Ian to lock the door because I knew you wouldn't allow it."

"And you agreed to this?" Miss Blunt asked him in astonishment.

Ian was thrown by Delia's response but had to go along with it. "Um, yes."

Miss Blunt felt angry, upset and betrayed. For the vicar to have helped a souvenir hunter was unforgivable. There could have been no excuse for his actions. She walked to the open door and stood beside it.

"I want you to leave immediately. I will not take the matter further but rest assured, if there is a repeat of this I will have no hesitation in doing so."

Ian saw the hurt in her eyes and understood the reasons for it. He knew at once that the Prudence Blunt they saw in public was not who she really was. She was a woman still in morning for her friend and they had invaded her privacy by going into a room that was special to her. To have locked her out of it was the ultimate in cruelty.

"I really am sorry, Prudence. It will never happen again."

She couldn't bring herself to look at him and bowed her head.

Ian and Delia left. Harry followed them.

Miss Blunt closed and locked the door. She took the key with her. No one spoke as they descended the long, curved staircase to the ground floor.

Delia and Harry left the building without looking back and returned to Ian's car but the vicar paused in the entrance in the hope of consoling a woman who was a heartbeat away from breaking down.

"Will you be all right?"

"Please go."

"I'm sorry my actions today have caused you distress, Prudence. If you need to talk you know where to find me."

"That will not be necessary. If you will excuse me, I have work to do."

Ian walked to his car and Miss Blunt returned to her office. She held it together for a brief time, doing all she could to put the incident out of her mind, until it became too much for her and she wept. Delia's excuse of wanting to take a picture had been a mistake. A less intrusive one should have been found. Some things were kept private for a reason.

In an empty office on the second floor a lost and

lonely voice carried on the air, heard by no one.
 "Help me."

Seventeen

Samantha gave Delia a glass of wine and retook her seat on the sofa. The mood inside Meadow Cottage was quiet and subdued.

Ian's thoughts were divided. He was concerned about Candice and felt guilty over events that transpired at the riding school that afternoon. It was eight o'clock in the evening but so vivid in his mind it could have happened just a moment ago.

Samantha knew he was troubled by it but didn't ask for further details. Instead she turned the conversation to why Delia had felt compelled to go back to the school. She had said nothing to suggest she wanted to see the office again when Samantha showed it to her. "What did you expect to find there?"

Delia sipped from her glass and set it down on the coffee table. Even now she wasn't sure. It was a feeling, a gut reaction to something that didn't seem right. "When I was in Candice's office with you I felt her presence. I assumed it was something that lingered, a presence that was always there. Then I heard another spirit had spoken through her and she had disappeared. It made me wonder if my first assessment had been wrong and she *was* there. I had to go back to be sure."

Samantha looked at Harry standing by the window. He hadn't said a word in fifteen minutes. An air of defeat hung over him.

"What did the spirit say?" she asked.

"I didn't really understand it. She was angry, confrontational. She was speaking to someone called Nick. She said he shouldn't have gone to her house.

She wouldn't be his punch bag like she had been in the past. Then she shot him." Harry remembered it clearly; the fire in her eyes, the venom in her voice. The smile of satisfaction when Nick Babarati died at her feet. "She said he wouldn't hurt her again. He wouldn't hurt anyone again."

"What happened after that?"

"The spirit left her. Candice looked at me. She was scared. I've never seen her so afraid. She said my name and disappeared but not like we usually do. She didn't fade away. She went in a split-second."

Samantha knew by Harry's response that he had never seen anything like it. She wasn't surprised when he retreated to silence.

Delia was intrigued. Harry had said something that she had been unaware of, something important that he neglected to tell her when they spoke on the road beyond Cross Drummond.

"You said Candice was scared. She looked afraid?"

"Yes."

"That's wonderful!" she exclaimed.

Delia leapt to her feet, hands clasped below her chin. She couldn't get the smile to leave her face.

"What is wonderful about being frightened?" Harry snapped.

"No, you don't understand. This puts an entirely different complexion on things."

"What do you mean?" Ian asked.

Delia didn't answer. She paced the room deep in thought, trying to apply reason to a puzzle that had too many missing pieces.

"Yes, that must be it," she muttered, talking to herself. "But what of the other spirits? How are they involved?

Perhaps... no, that can't be right. It wouldn't be possible. What if?... don't be silly, Delia. That's not just impossible, it's ridiculous. They might..." She stopped pacing and clicked her fingers, seemingly in triumph. "Oh gosh, of course they do!"

"Have you worked it out?" Samantha asked.

"Sorry?"

"Do you know what's happening?"

"Oh, not really. It's all rather perplexing."

"It didn't sound that way a moment ago. You said *'that must be it,'*" Ian reminded her.

"Yes, it has to be."

"So what is *it?*" he prompted.

Delia sat down and tried to explain. "The key to this is that Candice was afraid. That means she knew what was happening to her. She still has freedom of thought. While she has that she has control over her own actions. That will help us to get her back."

"From where?" Harry asked.

"Wherever she is."

"Yes, but how do we find out where she is?" Ian said.

"That's the perplexing part."

Hopes that had been raised were immediately dashed.

Delia looked at their disappointed faces and did her best to clarify. She felt she was onto something but had made a mess of explaining it to them.

"I believe Candice is being influenced by an unknown force. It's taking her over in some way but doesn't have total control. As far as we're aware this force has manifested itself on two occasions but there may have been other times that we don't know about. Because Candice hasn't succumbed to it completely she has been able to come back to you. She doesn't know where she has been and has no memory of it but that's where the force is strong. Candice is unable to see beyond it. She only knew something was wrong when you told her. That she was afraid today is most encouraging. It would suggest to me that the force still doesn't have her fully in its power."

"What could this force be?" Ian asked.

"I'm afraid the answer to that eludes me. I don't think Candice is passing over to the other side. It would happen quickly if that was the case. It wouldn't be gradual like this. This is something different."

Delia hesitated. She didn't want to cause them more upset but if she had to hazard a guess there was only one explanation as far as she could see.

"I'm convinced it's of a supernatural origin but what worries me is that it may be evil. When I spoke to Candice last night I felt that something terrible was going to happen. I sensed it again over breakfast this morning."

No one commented.

"I'm sorry. I know that isn't what you want to hear."

The room was silent as they wrestled with possibilities they hadn't considered. Was Candice under the influence of an evil force, a slave to do the Devil's work? What was happening? Why was it happening to her? They didn't know and felt helpless because of it.

"What about the spirits that have been speaking through her?" Samantha finally asked.

"I don't think the two are connected," Delia replied. "It's very unusual for one spirit to speak through another, almost unheard of in fact. I think the reason for it is because Candice is going through some kind of transition which has made her susceptible to the presence of other spirits. I don't mean they're here in the village. I thought they may have been but I've uncovered nothing to substantiate that theory. These poor souls are trapped between this world and the next. They're not earth-bound spirits. They wander between the two planes. They're weak and don't know how to find peace.

"When the force exerts its influence over Candice she is weakened too and the spirits are able to communicate through her. They're trying to find release. In the case of the young girl she needed to recount the story of how her family was killed. She may have thought that by telling someone it would have allowed her to move on. She is lost and lonely and doesn't know where to turn. Today was a different matter. The woman was angry. The impression I formed was that she killed someone out of self-defence but was punished instead of helped. When Candice is under the influence of the force these spirits are drawn to her as an outlet for their personal pain."

"How do we get her back?" Harry asked.

"We may have to wait for her to come to us."

"And if she doesn't? What if this force assumes total control of Candice while she's away?"

Delia looked around the room. It was a question that concerned them all. "Then we hold a séance and do everything in our power to bring her back."

*

Grantley walked Emily to her door and received a goodnight kiss in thanks for what had been a perfect day.

"Thank you, Norman. It's been a wonderful day from start to finish."

"I'm glad you enjoyed it. I certainly have."

"Are you sure you won't come in for coffee?"

"As much as I would like to I feel I should decline. If I came in for coffee you'll never get your beauty sleep." He looked at his watch. "In ten minutes it will be your birthday. I'll see you tomorrow, bright-eyed and bushy-tailed."

"Thank you again."

"Not at all. Pleasant dreams."

He turned and walked along the path to the gate.

"Norman," Emily called after him.

"Yes?"

She smiled and shook her head. "Nothing. It doesn't matter. Goodnight."

"Goodnight, Emily. Tomorrow evening the first drink is on you."

She laughed and went inside.

Grantley drove the short distance to Brook Cottage and garaged his car, admiring the stars filling a vast black sky as he closed the door. There wasn't a cloud in sight, no dramas on his horizon. In thirteen days from now he would kill Samantha and everything would be right with the world.

He entered a cottage that was as dark as the night outside. Turning on the light in the lounge, he found Nathan Baker sitting in his armchair.

"What are you doing here?" he asked.

Baker grinned and swirled the glass of brandy he had helped himself to. "Haven't you heard? There are burglars in the area. I knew you were out today so I thought I would make sure the place was safe and secure."

"Get your feet off my coffee table."

Baker dropped his heels to the floor.

Grantley walked to the drinks cabinet and poured a brandy too. He made himself comfortable on the sofa. "Is everything ready for the vicarage tomorrow evening?"

"We'll have the place empty by ten o'clock. We'll have time for another. We could do Pine Trees too."

"No, the vicarage only." Grantley leaned forward. He wanted to make himself absolutely clear. Direct eye contact was important at times like this. "Pine Trees and Meadow Cottage are not to be touched until I give you permission to do so. Is that clear?"

"We're missing a great opportunity. Everyone will be at your girlfriend's party. Those cottages are there for the taking."

Grantley didn't like Baker. He was an ant to be stepped on, a nothing who thought he was something, a nobody who was a means to an end and served no other purpose. No one would have mourned his passing if Grantley had taken him down to the basement. Nor did he like his choice of words.

"1. Emily Braithwaite is not my girlfriend. 2. You will do what I say when I say. 3. If you come here again I will dispense with your services in a way that you would not find agreeable. Do you understand?"

"Yes, boss."

"4. Do not call me boss. Have you confined your occupation of my home to just this room?"

"Why do you ask that?"

"I wouldn't like to think you had taken the opportunity to... what is the correct terminology? Case the joint."

Baker laughed. "It's correct if you lived in America in the 1930s."

"An Englishman's home is his castle, Mr Baker, and

mine is not open to visitors, be it legally or otherwise."

"I wouldn't steal from you. Why would I? There are so many Oscars and Golden Globes in this village where's the point in pinching a cheap stereo?"

Grantley looked at it across the room. "It doesn't meet with your approval?"

"I've seen better."

"Have you seen anything else here tonight?"

"No. I didn't take the tour. Castles have never really interested me."

Grantley was forced to take him at his word. His fear was that while Baker had enjoyed the freedom of the cottage he may have seen something he shouldn't have but he couldn't make an issue of it or labour the point. To have done so would have given himself away. The basement was locked but the man was a burglar. It wouldn't have taken much for him to gain access if he had put his mind to it.

"Why did you come here tonight?" he asked his unwelcome guest.

"I'm worried about Tate. He's getting jittery. I think he might pull out and do a runner."

"That would be unfortunate. However, it is not my problem. I enlisted your services for this venture. Who you chose to assist you was your decision, not mine. Why should your concerns be of interest to me?"

"Because if he does do a runner he'll panic. When people panic they get caught and when that happens they talk. They talk to anyone who is willing to listen. The police, defence lawyers, people like that. Are you interested now?"

"Never has my attention been more focused. What do you intend to do about this problem?"

"Well, you're the man calling the shots. It's more a case of what you intend to do about it."

"I am not in the habit of rectifying other people's mistakes, Mr Baker."

"I thought I should make you aware of the situation."

"Your comments have been noted." Grantley stood and walked to the door in a veiled gesture that it was time for Baker to leave. "Pine Trees and Meadow Cottage will not be burgled tomorrow and you will keep Mr Tate loyal to the cause. Do we have any other business?"

"Not that I can think of."

"Then our meeting is concluded. I suggest you leave the way you came and make sure no one sees you."

Baker drained his glass and stood too. He stopped in the doorway en route to the kitchen where he had entered through a window that hadn't been properly secured. "Always a pleasure. Give my regards to your girlfriend."

Then he was gone, the scum of the earth lost to the darkness of the night.

Grantley locked the window and stored away for future reference a conversation he would rather not have had. He had options. A man like him always did. When Samantha was dead and his work was finished he could have killed Baker too. Who would have missed him? Who would have cared? The world would have thanked him for removing a pile of shit that sat on the pavement tainting the air.

He went to the basement to satisfy himself that everything was all right. It was. Baker had, for once in his life, been true to his word and hadn't gone there.

Grantley looked at the restraints fixed to the wall and imagined Samantha confined in them, naked, terrified, pleading for mercy as her death loomed closer. It was regrettable that she had to die but necessary in order for his dream to be realised. His obsession demanded nothing less. If his goal was to be reached an innocent life had to be taken.

Grantley returned to the lounge and turned off the light. In the darkness he spoke once more to Candice trapped in *her* darkness. She listened to every word and did exactly as her Master instructed.

Eighteen

It was not a happy birthday.

Emily had passed a restless night, troubled by what Harry had told her when he arrived at her cottage to commence his vigil. That Candice had disappeared was the worst news she could have heard. That Delia harboured fears of some kind of force controlling her made it more worrying. What could they have done in the face of the unknown? How could they have helped her if they didn't know what they were dealing with? It may have been a day of celebration but Emily paid her birthday no thought.

Harry didn't stay as she prepared breakfast. He was anxious to return to Meadow Cottage in the hope there may have been news. There wasn't.

*

Samantha was late for work as usual but unlike other mornings she didn't rush to make up lost time. Candice's disappearance weighed too heavily on her mind. Work took second place to her concern. Today she would get there at half past ten. Between now and then the staff and horses would have to muddle by without her.

Harry watched in silence as she stared into a cup of tea at the kitchen table. Delia munched on her cereal. Not a word was said. Never had silence sounded so loud.

Samantha didn't know that at three o'clock that

morning she had sat in a bath filled with cold water, that she had laid back in the tub until she was completely submerged. If the order had been given she would have drowned herself while Delia slept and Harry watched over Emily. The threat to Samantha didn't come from burglars. It came from Norman Grantley and Candice Freeman.

"What are we going to do this evening?" she asked. The silence grew louder until it was ear-shattering. "It's Emily's birthday. Are we going to the Coaching Inn?"

A weight of uncertainty hung on Harry's shoulders. He had lost his wife in a car accident in 2005. Judith was the love of his life, she saw the good in a man that others had used and abused. Now he had lost Candice, the woman who had taken away his pain and gave him love in death.

"I don't know."

"We have to go, Harry. It wouldn't be fair on Emily."

The moment wasn't lost on him and he forced a smile.

"You called me Harry."

Samantha smiled too. "Why not? It's your name."

Yes, it was. Harry Black and Candice Freeman. Two souls who should have been together forever.

"What will I do without her, Sam?"

"She'll come back to us. I know she will."

"I wish I could believe that. You didn't see the way she went. It was so sudden. Final."

A single tear ran down Samantha's cheek.

For a moment Delia thought Harry's cheeks were wet too but it was her imagination or a trick of the light.

Ghosts couldn't cry. They could respond to human emotion but couldn't feel it. Cut them and they wouldn't bleed but they could show concern when someone else bled. They could react to their sorrow and share in their happiness but were unable to experience those things for themselves. Yet here was something different. Harry was devastated by the loss of Candice.

Delia wished she could have said something encouraging, something positive that would have given him hope, but nothing came to her. All she could do was watch as the weight of uncertainty pressed down on him.

No greater love had she known.

*

Janet wasn't looking forward to going to the Coaching Inn that evening. She had been to the village many times since news of her troubled marriage became common knowledge but this was the first time they would have gone there as a family. All eyes would have been on them and she wasn't sure how to handle it.

She and Martin had considered grounding Melanie as punishment for what happened at the school but decided against it. Emily would have been disappointed if she hadn't attended. It was her evening and they didn't want to spoil it. In the end they decided on no punishment at all. They told Melanie she was wrong to do what she did, she should have risen above the taunts and not lashed out, but they didn't take it further. In a way they had no choice. How could a child be punished for loving their parents?

Now, sitting in a coffee shop in Falworth, Janet watched the woman approach her table with an air of detachment. It was almost as if she had stepped outside herself to gain an overview of what would follow, to see it through eyes that hadn't shed so many tears.

"I was surprised to get your call," Anne Jackson said, sitting down.

"Martin gave me your number."

"He knows about this meeting?"

"Yes. I told him I wanted to see you. Thank you for coming. I know you didn't have to."

Jackson didn't answer. There was no sign of remorse or apology in her expression.

"I won't keep you long. There are some things I need to say."

"Okay."

Jackson looked at the self-service counter to their left.

"You can get a coffee first if you want," Janet said.

"No, that's all right."

To Janet's surprise, she took her cigarettes from her bag and lit one. A member of staff appeared at the table thereafter.

"I'm sorry, it's no smoking in here," he said.

Jackson frowned and stubbed it out in a sugar bowl, using it like a sand bucket. Her actions told Janet everything she needed to know about her. The young man looked disgusted as he took it away.

"What do you want to talk to me about?" Jackson asked.

She had made the question sound casual, like she had done nothing wrong and didn't know why she was there.

"I want to..."

"I think I'll get a coffee after all," Jackson interrupted, looking at the counter again as she rose from the table.

"Sit down," Janet said sternly.

As before, Jackson didn't answer. She retook her

seat.

"Let me make this clear. I didn't come here to be pissed around by the likes of you," Janet said. "Martin and I are still together despite your best efforts to break us up and that's how it's going to stay. I have no interest in how the affair started, how long it lasted or that you didn't want it to end. The fact is it *has* ended and there will be no going back. Martin has assured me of that and I believe him."

"If you think..."

"Shut up. I haven't finished."

Jackson was embarrassed and shifted uncomfortably on her chair. At last she was taking this meeting seriously.

"My marriage will survive because it will take more than a cheap tart to wreck it. Martin told me you're still flirting with him in the hope of re-starting your affair. That won't happen so stop wasting your time. If you so much as look in his direction you'll have me to answer to and you wouldn't like that.

"What matters to me now is my family and repairing the damage that has been done to it. I don't hold you solely responsible, Martin is to blame too, but my daughters are the most important thing in the world to me and they've been crushed by this. There will be consequences if you try to come between Martin and I again. I will do whatever it takes to protect my girls."

"Are you threatening me?"

Jackson's voice was shaky. Scared.

"No, I'm making you a promise, you bitch. Stay away from my husband. If you want some fun at work I suggest you drop your knickers for someone else."

Janet stood up and looked at the man who had cleared away the sugar bowl. He was now working on the till. "My friend is paying for the coffee."

She left.

Closure. Now she could get on with re-building her marriage.

*

"Drink this," Brian said, handing Neil a glass of brandy.

"It was 'orrible. 'Orrible," he gasped, prior to gulping it down. "I don't think I want to do this sort of work anymore."

For Neil to have been chased by an alien in the dead of night had been bad enough. For it to have happened again in broad daylight while he had been out for a walk took misfortune to extremes.

"What happened?" Rafe asked him.

"I was walking through the fields beyond Cross Drummond, where we went on our first night here. I saw that cat again."

"Forget the cat. What happened?" Rafe repeated.

"I was on my way back to the village when I became aware of an evil presence behind me."

Brian nodded. He knew the feeling well. His mother-in-law was always sneaking up on him.

"When I turned around I saw it. It was 'orrible."

Siobhan and Karen were standing beside the table in the Coaching Inn where this lunchtime meeting was taking place. Siobhan had slipped her hand inside the back pocket of Karen's jeans to give her a buttock massage. As Karen was enjoying the moment, she played no part in the discussion.

"What did it look like?" Siobhan asked. "Was it the same as last time?"

"No. This one looked like a woman."

Rafe scratched his head. He saw reason to doubt a UFO connection. "How do you know it wasn't a woman?"

"Because it disappeared in front of my eyes. Then it reappeared a second later twenty feet from its original position. The alien kept doing it. It was popping up all over the place. I got giddy just watching."

"They must have some sort of teleporting device," Brian said to his colleagues.

"Or a pogo stick. I've never seen anything like it," Neil replied. "Can I have another brandy?"

Brian returned to the bar to fetch one.

"How was it dressed?" Siobhan asked. "Was it wearing a biochemical suit to protect itself from our atmosphere?"

"Ouch!" Karen exclaimed, standing bolt upright. "You did that a bit hard then."

"Sorry."

Rafe rolled his eyes when a dreamy smile returned to her face.

"No, it was wearing ripped jeans and a T-shirt," Neil answered. "And suede boots."

Siobhan was a prisoner to fashion and looked at him eagerly. "What sort?"

"Ankle, four-inch heel, buckle straps over the front."

"Nice."

Sitting alone at the next table, Delia had heard enough. She just needed clarification on one point.

"Was she blonde?" she asked, standing beside Siobhan.

"Yes," Neil replied.

"Jolly good. Thanks awfully." Delia turned to the masseuse. "I think the left one is done. You might want to start on the right now."

They watched her leave in astonishment.

*

Ian wondered what to do. He knew the burglars would strike again sooner or later but to be warned that the vicarage was the next likely target made him appreciate the problem all the more.

"And you think it will happen tonight while we're at Emily's party," he said to Harry.

"Yes. I wasn't going to tell you but Candice said I should."

"You weren't going to tell me?"

"I have it under control. Candice and I were going to keep an eye on the properties at risk during the course of the evening. If anything happened I was going to tip you off so you could call the police. The burglars would be caught red-handed. I can still do that on my own. You have nothing to worry about."

"Aside from thieves ransacking our home. It might be better if I didn't go this evening."

"The important thing is that you, Sheila and Becky are safe. If you don't go to the Coaching Inn Sheila won't either. That puts all three of you at home. You know what the burglars are capable of, you saw what they did to Albert Preston. Do you want Sheila and Becky to be around people like that? The safest place you can be is at Emily's party."

Ian didn't have to think about it. Harry was right of course.

"Okay, but let me know the moment something happens."

"That goes without saying."

"Thank you, Harry."

They were silent for a moment.

"Is there any news on Candice?" Ian finally asked.

"No. It's been twenty-four hours. It's the longest she's been away."

"I know she will come back. Try not to worry."

Ian had echoed Samantha's words but still Harry drew no encouragement from them. He had a feeling, a sense of dread, an unshakable thought that he would never see her again. It festered and spread like a cancer, consuming him to the point that he could see no hope, no happy ever after, no point in going on without her.

"I'll go if Candice is lost to me."

"Go where?"

"Through the gateway to God's greater creation."

Ian was surprised. It was something he and Harry had spoken of when Candice was alive, of taking the final journey and giving oneself to eternal rest, but he never thought the day would come when Harry would have considered doing it. Some spirits were trapped against their will and destined to remain forever in the place they occupied but Harry had a choice. He had chosen to stay because he didn't want to leave but without Candice there was nothing to stay for.

"I'm sure it won't come to that," Ian said.

Harry didn't answer. He forced a smile but how sad he looked.

"Mr Cream! Mr Cream!" they heard Delia call as she

hurried through the churchyard towards them.

"When is that woman going to get my name right?" Harry sighed.

"I have news."

Suddenly names didn't matter. Harry and Ian looked at one another and went to meet her.

"What news?" the vicar asked.

"Candice has been seen at Cross Drummond. I called Samantha and she told me I would find you here. I thought you should know straightaway."

Harry struggled to take it in. There was hope at last but his mind was spinning. "Who saw her? When? Is she all right?"

"It was one of the ufologists. I don't know how he was able to see Candice but he encountered her while he was out walking on the hills. He was jolly taken aback. He thought she was an alien."

"An alien?" Ian asked.

"Yes. She kept appearing and disappearing. He told his colleagues she was popping up all over the place, even without a pogo stick."

A mind that was spinning was now hurtling out of control.

"Delia, what are you talking about? Is Candice still at Cross Drummond?"

"No, Mr Silver, but she isn't far away. I think this is awfully exciting."

"I'm glad one of us does," Harry said, nearing exasperation.

Delia realised she had left them behind in her excitement and tried to explain. Candice had acted erratically when she was seen, it wasn't normal behaviour for a ghost, but it was good news and something to be positive about.

"I believe that Candice is being held against her wishes by the force that wants control over her. Because it doesn't have *full* control she is trying to come back to us. The man I overheard in the Coaching Inn said she disappeared and reappeared. It happened repeatedly. Every time she reappeared she was in a different place. Don't you see? She's trying to break through."

"Break through what?" Harry asked.

"The barrier that is stopping her from breaking through. Do pay attention, Mr Pink."

Ian thought it would be better if he spoke on Harry's behalf. He had a horrible feeling he was about to punch her.

"This barrier that Candice is trying to break through. Is it at Cross Drummond?"

"No, it's all around us. You're thinking of it in terms of a fence that extends from one point to another. It isn't like that. It's a barrier that separates two worlds. It's a bit like being in a different dimension. Candice is in limbo."

"What's she doing in Wales?" Harry asked.

"That's Llandudno," Ian corrected him. "So if Candice can find a way through this barrier she will come back?"

"Yes. All she has to do is find its weakest point. Of course, she would have to do it before the force takes complete control of her. If that happened she would have no will of her own and wouldn't be able to escape."

Ian wished Delia hadn't ended on a negative note.

"I'm going to Cross Drummond," Harry said.

"She won't be there now, Mr White."

"Where might she be?" Ian asked.

"It's impossible to say. The barrier is everywhere. Candice could be five metres from where we're standing or ten thousand miles away. While she is trapped beyond it there is simply no way of knowing."

"She was last seen at Cross Drummond so that's where I need to be," Harry said.

He faded from view.

Ian stared at the hills, lush and green in the distance. He hoped Harry would find her there but knew he wouldn't. If Delia was right it wasn't a case of finding her. Candice had to find them.

"Have you tried the Professor today?" he asked.

"I called him from the village but still no joy I'm afraid. It went to voicemail and cut me off again. I wish he would buy a new phone."

"Couldn't you text or email him?"

"I've done both but I doubt if he will read them. The Professor doesn't do texts and emails. He's not a big fan of technology."

Ian was disappointed to hear it.

"Are you going to the Coaching Inn this evening?" she asked, changing the subject.

"Yes. Are you?"

"Samantha invited me but I don't want to intrude in a private celebration."

"You wouldn't be intruding. I'm sure Emily would want you to be there."

"Do you think so?"

"Why wouldn't she?"

"She is a nice lady."

"And it's her birthday so you're joining us at the Coaching Inn."

Delia reconsidered. People she had known for just a short time had befriended her under difficult and trying circumstances. They were involved in something extraordinary and that made them special. It would have been good to forget their troubles for a few hours and celebrate an event that was important to all of them.

"Okay. I'll see you there," she said.

"Thank you for coming to find Harry so promptly. He's very concerned. He needs all the help he can get."

"I'll do whatever I can."

Delia turned to walk away but only took a few steps when she stopped and looked back at him. "His name isn't White, is it?"

Ian smiled. "No. It's Black."

She closed her eyes. "Of course it is. I really must try to remember that."

Nineteen

Harry returned to Meadow Cottage at 7:20 p.m. Samantha and Delia were ready to leave for the Coaching Inn.

"Any luck?" Samantha asked him.

Harry shook his head. "There was no sign of her. This barrier. How much do you know about it?" he asked Delia.

"Very little I'm afraid. The Professor is the expert on that subject. A great many others too. I wish I could get through to him."

"You said he works at Chamford College. London isn't far from here. Could you go there to see him?"

Delia hadn't considered it but was willing to try. In the short time she had known Harry she had never seen him look so lost, never heard him sound so deflated. She had never seen someone in love suffer so much. She had to give him something to cling onto. "Yes, if you would like me to," she replied.

"I don't know what else to do."

"I'll go tomorrow."

"Tomorrow is Saturday. The college will be closed," Samantha pointed out.

"To the students, yes, but the Professor usually goes in for an hour or two. I'm sure he will be there."

"Okay. Thank you," Harry said.

Samantha took her jacket from the back of the sofa and walked to the door. Since Candice disappeared she had been dreading this evening. She, Emily and Ian faced the difficult task of pretending that all was well when secretly they were worried out of their minds. Their acting skills would be put to the test. It was ironic that the one person qualified to put in a performance wasn't there.

"We'd better be going."

"I'll see you later," Harry replied.

Delia followed Samantha to the hallway but turned and went back. "I could go to London now. It wouldn't be any trouble. I can sleep in the van and see the Professor first thing in the morning. It would save time."

Harry appreciated the offer, he knew it had been made in a genuine attempt to help, but he declined. "Thank you, Delia, but you should go to the Coaching Inn and enjoy yourself. You deserve it."

Delia didn't answer. She smiled a smile that was every bit as sad as his and went outside.

Harry heard the front door open and close and sat on the sofa. A busy evening lay in store for him. While his friends pretended to be happy celebrating Emily's birthday he had burglars to catch. He would apprehend them for the good of others, to make the village safe again, but more importantly he would do it for Candice. They wouldn't steal her most prized possessions and get away with it.

Not now. Not ever.

*

"Goodness me, not another present?" Emily said, accepting a gift from Melanie.

"Happy birthday, Mrs Braithwaite. I hope you like it," the youngster replied.

"That depends on what it is." She struggled with the paper it was wrapped in. "How much tape did you put on this?"

Melanie smiled.

Emily peeled loose a corner and gained a finger-hold. When she managed to get it open she found it was a bottle of her favourite perfume. "Oh, thank you, my dear. That's very sweet of you."

Melanie drew attention to a past gift. "You're wearing the necklace Candice bought for you last year."

Emily smiled and lifted it between her thumb and forefinger. Oscars, BAFTAs and Golden Globes counted for nothing. The mother-of-pearl necklace and matching bracelet and earrings were *her* most prized possessions. "It seemed appropriate. And this is wonderful," she added, returning to Melanie's present. She leaned forward and kissed her cheek. "Thank you."

Melanie's reaction surprised everyone watching. The little girl flew into her arms and hugged her tightly. It took an age for her to let go. While they were locked in their embrace Emily was stunned by what she whispered to her.

"Candice is coming back."

Emily watched her return to her parents' table transfixed. She had no idea her mouth had dropped open.

"Are you all right, my dear? You look like you've seen a ghost," Grantley said, returning from the bar.

"What? Oh, yes. For a moment I thought I left the gas on."

Her response was torn from a divided mind but it was the best she could do.

What did she mean by that? she wondered.

"You don't have gas."

"Sorry?"

"In your cottage. You don't have gas."

"I know."

"Emily, is everything all right?"

"Yes. Excuse me. Sam needs to go to the ladies room."

Grantley looked at Miss Blunt with whom they were sharing a table. Two had been pulled together to accommodate six people. Sitting with them was Ian, his wife Sheila and their fourteen year-old daughter Becky. They were as puzzled as he when Emily left them.

She found Samantha waiting to be served at the bar. As usual Ron, Maggie and their staff were rushed off their feet. The Coaching Inn was packed with UFO hunters and locals. It was as if everyone in Kent had descended on them.

The only person not present was Delia. She had noticed a flat tyre on her camper van when she and Samantha left Meadow Cottage and stopped to change the wheel in preference to doing it in the morning. She intended to leave for London early and didn't want to start the day doing battle with a wheel brace.

"Come with me," Emily said, taking Samantha's arm.

"I'm next in line. I've been waiting ages."

"That's not our fault," Ron said, pulling a pint for a man wearing a UFO themed T-shirt. It had a picture of a flying saucer on the front and the words *'The thing about space is there's a lot of it'* printed on the back.

"I wasn't having a go," Samantha replied.

"I need to speak to you," Emily said, trying to manoeuvre her away.

"But I'm next."

"This is important."

"So is my drink. I've been here half an hour and haven't had one yet."

"You've got aliens from outer space to thank for that," Maggie said, rushing past with a glass of whisky.

"Right, Sam. What would you like?" Ron asked.

"She needs more time to think about it," Emily said, dragging her off to the ladies room.

He thought he heard Samantha call *White Russian* from a distance but it may have been *I'm going to kill you.*

"I wonder why Emily took Sam off to the ladies room like that," Ian said to Sheila.

She shrugged her shoulders. "Maybe she didn't want to go on her own."

"I think you should check on them. Make sure everything is all right."

This sudden interest in Emily and Samantha's toiletry habits worried her. There were some things a vicar shouldn't have concerned himself with, his wife too for that matter.

"I'm not going into the ladies to spy on them. I'll get arrested," she said.

"You don't have to do that. Just go in and ask if everything is okay."

They were still debating it when Emily returned five minutes later.

Samantha rejoined the throng of people laying siege to the bar in the hope that Ron had heard her request and she wouldn't have to wait three months to be served but the more he thought about it the more it had sounded like a death threat and she found herself back at square one.

Emily sat beside Grantley.

"Is everything all right?" he asked.

"Yes. Are you enjoying yourself?"

"I'm having a wonderful time. Pity the pub is so crowded though," he added, casting around the room.

Miss Blunt tutted behind her sherry glass. This was what she had warned against all along. "It is like the village is not our own anymore. Outsiders interfering in local affairs and events. I said it would happen."

"I wonder how long they will stay for," Sheila said.

"Until this ridiculous story has run its course and they find something better to do with their time," Miss Blunt answered.

"Don't you believe in the UFOs, Miss Blunt?" Becky asked.

"My dear Rebecca, the only things flying above our heads are the birds that God in his wisdom put in the sky and aeroplanes that man in his stupidity put there to pollute it. There is as much chance of us being visited by aliens as there is of me becoming the first woman to set foot on the moon."

Ian smiled. "I agree, but it doesn't stop this one from stargazing out of her bedroom window every night when she should be asleep," he said, tipping his thumb at his daughter.

"I don't look every night," she stated in her defence.

"The next time you do, Rebecca, pay less thought to UFOs and appreciate what *is* above us."

Ian looked at Miss Blunt sincerely and nodded. "Well said."

Grantley considered the people waiting to be served at the bar and turned his thoughts to what should have been a less frantic village event. "I hear there is a fête coming up soon. It's a week tomorrow, isn't it?"

"Yes, that's right. The 17th," Emily replied.

"What are they like?"

"The same as fêtes everywhere; bring and buy stalls, coconut shies, home-made wine and jam. We set up a marquee on the green."

"Always supposing we can clear it of the cars, caravans and tents that have taken up residence there," Miss Blunt said.

Emily hadn't thought of that and looked concerned. "Oh yes. What are we going to do if they're still here?"

"Employ the services of the R.A.F. I have never held with carpet-bombing but it would be one way to remove them."

The statement was out of character for Miss Blunt and laughter went around the table.

"We'll have to find somewhere for that marquee," Ian said. "Rumour has it Mrs Jenkins has made a hundred pots of jam this year. We might have to move the fête to a larger county."

Emily looked at Harry. He was quiet and played no part in the conversation. Normally he would have chipped in with comments designed to put those who could see and hear him on the spot. He liked to see their reaction and how they got out of the awkward situations he created in his desire to create mischief but this evening he was a spectator, a silent, withdrawn figure who stood at a distance from them.

He was dismayed that Grantley was sitting at Emily's table. In his opinion he had no right to be there. He wasn't a local like the others, he wasn't a part of Emily's wider social circle. He was a man not to be trusted who was up to something.

Harry would have preferred him to have sat in his lounge at home, better yet the fast lane on the M1, but it was obvious he would have spent the evening in Emily's company and he resigned himself to it. Candice would have sat where Grantley was if she had been alive. That made his presence all the more unpalatable.

He missed her. She should have been there.

A moment later he left to commence his rounds. He didn't tell Emily, Ian and Samantha he was going. He just went.

*

Harry checked every room in the cottages he was safeguarding. He did so without prying. He was there to protect homes, not to intrude in personal lives. There was no sign of the burglars but it was early yet. He expected them to make their move later, after dark when the village was at its most vulnerable.

During his return to Meadow Cottage he saw the wheel on Delia's camper van had been changed. She wasn't there and he assumed she was on her way to the Coaching Inn. He didn't know he had missed her by a matter of seconds.

He went to the attic room in the hope that Candice might have come home. She hadn't. He stared at his dartboard on the wall and recalled the day she bought it for him soon after she moved in, how they had words over the fact that she had forgotten to buy darts to go with it which made owning one a pointless exercise.

What would he have done without her if she didn't come back? Who would have laughed at his silliness? Who would have told him to shut the hell up when proved wrong about something? Who would have taken delight in seeing him proved wrong? Who would have loved him like she did?

He heard a sound from Samantha's bedroom.

The door was closed. She always left it closed.

Harry walked through it and looked around the room from the foot of her bed.

"Candice? Are you here?"

"She was never here," a voice said.

Harry didn't recognize it. It was that of a woman but it was unfamiliar. He couldn't tell if it was in the room or inside his head. "Who are you?"

"That's not important."

"Are you the force controlling Candice?"

The voice laughed.

"Show yourself," Harry demanded.

"All in good time, Mr Black. All in good time."

"I want an answer."

There was no response. Whatever it was, it had gone.

*

Harry returned to the Coaching Inn. He saw Emily look at him as he approached the table. "Nothing to report. There's no sign of them yet. Where is Ian?"

"Ian has been in the garden a long time," she said to Sheila. "I know he wanted to get some air but I hope he hasn't gone to China for it."

"He's probably chatting to someone. You know what he's like when he gets started," Sheila replied.

Harry smiled. "Effortless."

Emily smiled too as he went outside.

It was a nice evening and many people had chosen to sit in the beer garden, most of them smokers. Ian didn't smoke but had gone outside to stretch his legs and find a respite from a pub that was becoming increasingly busy. It occurred to him that it was more peaceful in the garden and they could have celebrated Emily's birthday out there instead of the crowded and noisy interior.

"Nothing from the burglars yet," Harry said, standing beside him.

"Nothing at all?" Ian asked.

"You sound disappointed."

"You said I was going to be burgled tonight."

"And you will be. Good things come to those who wait."

Ian sighed and pulled on his drink.

"Something happened at Meadow Cottage while I was there. I heard a voice," Harry told him.

"A voice?"

"It was a woman but it wasn't Candice. At least I don't think it was."

Ian looked around the garden to ensure they had privacy. It wouldn't have done for his parishioners to see him talk to himself. "What did it say?"

"It said Candice was never here. I asked if I was speaking to the force that is controlling her and it laughed. When I demanded an answer it said *'All in good time, Mr Black.'*"

"It said your name?"

"Yes. It knew who I was. Then it stopped. I didn't hear anything else."

"What is going on?" Ian asked, perplexed.

"I wish I knew. Hopefully Delia can shed some light on it. Where is she?"

It dawned on Ian that he hadn't seen her.

"I don't know. I don't think she's arrived yet."

"She changed the wheel on the van and Meadow

Cottage is a five minute walk away. She should have been here by now," Harry said.

"Don't tell me she's missing too?"

"I hope not. Losing a ghost is bad enough. If we start misplacing mortals we'll really be in trouble."

They saw Samantha stride towards them. When she arrived she took a packet of cigarettes from her bag.

"What are you doing?" Ian asked. "You don't smoke."

"It's all the stress. I've started again. I bought a pack of twenty this morning."

"Sam, you've never smoked," Harry said.

"I did when I was at school. Don't tell mum and dad. They won't like it."

"We won't have to tell them. They'll smell it on your clothing," Ian told her.

Samantha took a tin of deodorant from her bag too. "My secret weapon. A quick spray of this over my blouse and no one is any the wiser."

Harry let out a deep sigh. He was not impressed. "I have to say, Sam, I'm very disappointed in you."

"Oh shut the hell up."

Samantha had responded like Candice on purpose but in the moment of doing so was swept by doubt and wondered if she had acted wisely. She didn't know how Harry would have taken it and looked at him anxiously.

His expression gave nothing away. Then he burst into laughter.

"Blow some of that smoke in my direction. I haven't had a cigarette since I was fifteen," he said.

Ian pointed at the packet in her hand. "Can I have one?" He met their stunned faces with a plausible reason for wanting a cigarette and a confession. "I'm going to be burgled tonight and I haven't had a fag since I was twelve."

A moment later he and Samantha were coughing like hardened forty-a-day smokers.

"I've really missed this," Ian said, turning blue.

*

"... And the policeman said 'Yes, I do, but only on Thursdays.'"

Everyone laughed at Grantley's joke, except Miss Blunt who didn't get it. Humour remained a stranger to her.

Grantley eased his chair away from the table and stood up. "If you ladies will excuse me, duty calls."

He manoeuvred his way through the packed bar en route to the toilet.

"Mum, what did the policeman do with his truncheon on Thursdays?" Becky asked, not understanding the joke either.

Bearing in mind it hadn't been suitable for young ears, that was probably just as well.

"I'll tell you when you're older," her mother replied.

'The speed birthdays come around here, that will be in five minutes,' Emily recalled Candice saying to Melanie when she asked a similar question the previous year. The memory of it made her smile.

"Everything okay, Emily?" Sheila asked, realising she had slipped away.

"I was thinking about Candice. My birthday last year was the last time we were all together." She looked around the room. It was crowded and bursting at the seams but they had some great times there.

"Do you remember Halloween a few months after she came to the village and that revealing dress she wore?" Sheila asked.

"I remember how she kept popping out of it," Emily replied. "It's a good job the paparazzi weren't around. They would still be selling the pictures now. Then there was the Nativity play. What an evening that was."

"Candice played the Virgin Mary," Sheila recalled. "The birth scene was horrific. I've never seen an audience grimace like that. Some of them passed out."

Emily remembered how nervous Candice had been about acting in a small village play and paid tribute to her professionalism. "She was petrified about doing it but rose to the occasion superbly. The moment she stepped on stage she became a different woman. It was a privilege to see her at work, doing what she did best."

Reminiscing took its toll and she began to cry. No one knew she had more cause to miss Candice now, almost a year after her death.

Sheila moved to Emily's side of the table to console her. "It's all right, Emily. It's good to remember her but you mustn't upset yourself. Not today. Candice would want you to enjoy this evening."

"Yes, you're right of course. I'm just being silly," she replied, patting her hand.

"You're not being silly at all."

Emily's distress fuelled the grief that Miss Blunt kept hidden and she went out to the beer garden to be alone with her thoughts.

Ian saw her and stubbed out his cigarette. He could tell she was upset. "Excuse me," he said to Harry and Samantha.

He went to join her.

"I hope I'm not intruding," Ian said on arrival.

Miss Blunt didn't answer.

"Are you all right?"

"Sheila and Emily were talking about Candice." She looked at the sky. It was the same one she had told Becky to appreciate but to her it had lost its appeal. The heavens were cold and lonely and the stars shone only half as bright. "So much pain, Father. Why does there have to be so much pain?"

"I gathered yesterday at the riding school that all isn't well with you. You haven't come to terms with your loss. I can help you, Prudence."

"I am in no need of it."

"Yes, you are. You don't have to grieve in private. Candice was your friend. It's only right that you would mourn her passing but you can gain strength by expressing your grief to others. It's not something to do alone, Prudence. When we lose someone we love our pain shouldn't be hidden away in a room. It has to be let out."

Miss Blunt abandoned the faded stars in their lonely heaven and bowed her head as she confided the secrets of her life now. "I cry every night. During the day I can busy myself to take my mind off it but I cannot do anything about the nights. That is when it is worse for me. The night is my tormentor."

"Then let me help you. May I call on you tomorrow?"

"Yes."

Ian took her hand. *"In darkness I walk alone but in light I find salvation. In light my Lord is of comfort to me and takes the darkness away.'* It will be light soon, Prudence. The Lord will not leave you in the shadows of despair."

Harry and Samantha watched as they embraced.

*

The bar was becoming more crowded by the minute. Wherever Sheila looked it was standing room only.

"Is it me or is it getting busier in here?" she asked.

"Perhaps we should try the garden?" Emily suggested.

"There may not be any tables available," Sheila replied.

Miss Blunt returned.

"We were thinking of going out to the garden. Did you see any free tables?" Emily asked her.

Miss Blunt was of the opinion they would have been better off staying inside and stated the fact with her special brand of disapproval. "Most of these people have a connection with the outdoors. If we go to the garden we will be tripping over telescopes, inflatable aliens and goodness knows what else."

Becky laughed. "Oh Miss Blunt, you're so funny."

"It was not my intention to be amusing," she said, raising her eyebrow.

This prompted Becky to laugh more.

Sheila turned her head away to hide her amusement. A loud cheer from across the room focused her attention. "It's getting rowdy too," she remarked.

"I think we should go outside," Emily repeated.

"There are no tables," Miss Blunt said, finally answering her question. "Some only have two people sitting at them but they are all taken."

"Dad's coming back," Becky said, pointing at Ian as he approached.

Sheila tapped her hand without looking at her. "I've

told you before about pointing."

Always one to favour the dramatic, Becky nursed her hand in the other and mumbled.

"You hurt me doing that."

Sheila laughed.

Another loud cheer went up as Ian retook his seat.

"Thank you," he said in a manner to acknowledge applause. "Really, it was nothing. Sitting down is a skill I was born with."

It was typical of him to have milked the moment.

The noise was an accompaniment to a drinking competition that was taking place not far from the Copeland's table.

Emily watched Samantha rejoin her family but her attention settled on Melanie. She looked uncomfortable and had pulled her chair close to her father. Another cheer rose and she hunched her shoulders trying to be small.

"That's it. We're going outside," Emily said.

"There is nowhere to sit," Miss Blunt insisted, wishing she didn't have to repeat herself.

She sucked on her lemon as Ron appeared beside them.

"I'm sorry, it's getting a bit loud in here," he said. "Would you rather sit in the garden?"

"We were just discussing that but there are no free tables," Emily replied.

He was a man determined and looked at her assuredly. "This is your night and there bloody well will be. Give me five minutes."

Maggie had conveyed the same message to the Copeland's.

Sheila sniffed the air and looked at her husband. "You've been smoking!"

Martin sniffed the air and looked at his eldest daughter. "You've been smoking!"

"I only had one," Ian said.

"I only had one," Samantha said.

"I had two and they were very nice," Harry said.

"What sort of example is that to set to your daughter?" Sheila demanded of Ian.

"What sort of example is that to set to Melanie?" Martin demanded of Samantha.

This deodorant is rubbish, she thought.

That deodorant is rubbish, Ian thought.

It got worse for him when Sheila smelt what was lurking beneath the smoke.

"Are you wearing *Surrender to the Night?*"

*

They relocated to the beer garden a few minutes later. Ron told people outside that a private party had arrived and tables had been reserved for them. One took a dim view of having to move and argued that reserved signs should have been placed on them but the expression he met told him not to pursue it and he beat a hasty retreat. Ron re-arranged the tables to allow Emily's party to sit together.

Grantley was still in the toilet. Like the rest of the pub it was crowded and doing ones duty took longer than usual. Ron told Emily he would inform him of their whereabouts. He and Maggie were apologetic and gave them free drinks. They were sorry the celebration had been marred by crowds and noise and went out of their way to make amends. Emily assured them no harm had been done and she was having the best of evenings but they knew she was being economical with the truth.

Delia arrived soon after and fought her way to the bar to seek directions. "Can you tell me where I might find Emily Braithwaite's party? I could look for them but it might take hours and I'm late as it is."

Maggie smiled. "They're in the garden. Just go through the doors over there."

Delia looked in the direction of her outstretched hand. She wasn't sure what she was pointing at. "There are doors over there?"

"Yes. You can't see them because 50,000 UFO watchers are standing in the way but they are there. Do you want to take a drink with you? If you go out and come back for one it could be years before you're served."

"Good idea. May I have a white wine please?"

Maggie poured it for her and refused to accept payment. The free drink policy for Emily's party applied to all no matter how late they were.

As Delia made her way across the room she saw Grantley emerge from the toilet.

"Professor!" she called, waving to him.

Ron had seen him too. "Norman, they're in the garden."

Grantley ignored Ron and looked for the other person who had called but saw no one he recognized in the packed room.

Ron assumed he hadn't heard him above the noise and called again. "Norman. Emily and the others are in the garden."

Grantley looked at him and gave the thumbs up. "Thank you, Ron."

"Professor!" Delia said, finally reaching him.

There was no hiding his surprise. For an assured man he was completely thrown by this unexpected meeting.

"Delia. What are you doing here?"

"I've been invited to a birthday celebration. A woman called Emily."

"You know Emily Braithwaite?"

"We met a few days ago. It's a long story I'm afraid. But what are you doing here? I was going to London tomorrow in the hope of seeing you."

"You wanted to see me?"

"Yes, on a matter of great urgency." Delia leaned closer to him to avoid being overheard, not that there was much danger of it given the circumstances. "There is something jolly strange going on in this village." She realised her mistake and raised her hand to her lips. "Oops. I shouldn't have said it was here."

Grantley's mind was spinning. There were too many people around for him to think clearly. He would have taken her to the garden but couldn't risk being seen with her. Not until he had found out what was happening.

An air of confidence returned and he took her arm.

"My dear, Delia. Let's find somewhere quieter to talk."

"The garden is just through there," she said, pointing to the double doors now in view.

"Perhaps the street would be better. There are tables out there. We could make ourselves comfortable."

"There are tables in the garden," she said, pointing to the doors again. "And we're a lot closer to the rear of the building than we are to the front."

Grantley's only option was to steamroll her into doing what he wanted. "Yes, the front would be ideal. Come along."

He led her to the entrance.

The time it took to reach the street worked to his advantage. He was able to compose himself and deal with his surprise. Grantley hadn't expected to meet someone in the village who knew him. Delia's presence threatened the smooth-running of his plans. He didn't know her well but she always struck him as being a decent sort, a good egg as she would have put it. He liked her but she was in the wrong place at the wrong time. It may have been necessary to smash the egg in order for his plans to proceed.

"Well, Delia, I really am delighted to see you. How long has it been?" he asked, inviting her to sit down.

"Oh, it must be three, perhaps four years," she replied.

"As long as that? How easy it is to fall out of touch with friends and colleagues that one has great admiration for."

"It's jolly nice of you to say so, Professor."

There was a long pause.

"I feel the same way of course," Delia blurted. She felt embarrassed and smiled nervously. "I wouldn't want you to think I wasn't going to return your compliment."

Grantley smiled too. "Quite so. Now, what brings you to Cloverdale St Mary? You said something strange is happening here."

Delia regretted what had been an unguarded moment and creased her chin. The promise of confidentiality had fallen at the first hurdle. "Yes, that was rather careless of me. I was asked not to divulge the location."

"I see. What can you divulge?"

"Well, there is a ghost here and something most odd is happening to her... him... it."

"I take it you were not meant to divulge that either."

Delia sighed. "No."

"What is happening to, her?"

"Professor, please don't tell anyone it's a her and her is here... I mean, she is here. I did give my word."

"You have my assurance that anything you tell me will be treated in the strictest confidence, Delia."

Hearing this was a huge weight off her mind and she relaxed. When she recounted her story it was with her usual gusto and enthusiasm.

"It really is jolly exciting. Quite a challenge in fact. I believe this ghost is being controlled. Some unknown force is influencing her, exerting its power over her. She disappears against her will and remembers nothing of it when she returns. She doesn't know where she goes, what happens or how long she is away. She's missing at the moment. In addition to that other spirits are communicating through her."

Grantley considered what he had learnt thus far. He hesitated for just the right length of time to create the illusion that he was working it out, answering questions in his mind that he already had answers to.

"I gather from what you have told me that this ghost enjoys the company of mortals. I can see no other way that she could be described as missing. Am I correct in making this assumption?"

"Yes, you are."

"More than one mortal?"

"Three."

"And they all live in this village."

"Yes."

"I take it the ghost we are talking about is that of Candice Freeman."

Delia was astonished that he had made the connection and wasn't sure how to answer. She needed Grantley's help but had promised to keep Candice's identity a secret and couldn't allow that runner to fall at the second hurdle. "I'm afraid I can't say. Sorry."

It was time for Grantley to influence the living as well as the dead. He had decided what to do about the unexpected complication that was Delia Truebody. It was simply a case of getting the packaging right.

"I know Candice Freeman is the ghost in question because that is what brought *me* to the village. I've known of her existence for several months, since the day of her funeral in fact. I don't possess the psychic gift but many of my friends do. One of them told me that when he watched a news report of the funeral on TV he saw her in attendance."

"Gosh," Delia gasped.

"When I heard this I felt it was my duty to investigate. I've been researching the death of Candice Freeman ever since. A short time ago I discovered what you have discovered. You're right, Delia. Something is trying to gain control of her, something evil from another dimension. What it is and what it wants of Miss Freeman I don't know but I came to Cloverdale St Mary in order to find out. I'm renting a cottage here."

"I see."

"It was of the utmost importance that the residents of the village didn't know who I was or my reason for being here. It may have hampered my efforts to help her so I told them I was a retired doctor by the name of Norman Grantley. They are unaware that I'm a college professor engaged in paranormal research. Until we can identify what this force is and find a way to stop it I must maintain my cover story."

Delia was engrossed in what he was telling her and nodded. "Yes, yes of course. I fully understand."

"That's why I wanted to speak to you here and not in the garden. If they discover that you and I know each other it would interfere with my work and Miss Freeman may be lost to us forever."

"Fear not, Professor, I won't say a word. Are you close to making a breakthrough?"

"I have made progress but there is still much to do."

"Do you know where Candice is?"

"Only that she is trapped in that other dimension. She is, no doubt, trying to come back to her friends, but the force holding her is strong and she may not be able to." He smiled and held Delia's hand. "Her chances are greatly improved now she has two of us fighting her corner. I am confident that with your help I can save her."

"I hope so, Professor. I will do everything I can to assist you."

"I know I can rely on you, Delia." Grantley looked at his watch. "I've been away from the others for quite a while. They will be wondering where I am. I would like to speak to you about this in more detail but now isn't the time. Do you know Falworth?"

"The town not far from here? Yes. I had lunch there the other day."

"There is a pub called the Millstream. Do you think you would be able to find it?"

"Easily. That was where I had lunch."

"Splendid. They serve an excellent breakfast. Perhaps we can meet there tomorrow and work out our next move? Shall we say nine o'clock?"

"Yes. Just one thing though. I was meant to be going to London tomorrow to see you. What excuse can I give for not doing so?"

He thought about it for a moment. "Have you been trying to contact me?"

"Every hour on the hour. You really must invest in a new mobile phone, Professor."

"Tell them you tried again on your way here and spoke to me. You explained the situation and I agreed to look into it. I said I would call you back in a day or so. That will serve a dual-purpose. Not only does it make your trip to London unnecessary, it will give us more time to work in."

"Good thinking."

Grantley stood up. "It's agreed then. I must return to the others. Wait a few minutes and follow me in. Remember, when you join us you don't know me. I will be introduced to you as Norman."

"Yes, Pro... Norman."

He forced a smile that appeared to be genuine and went inside.

*

"I was about to send out a search party," Emily said when Grantley arrived at their table.

"Sorry, got chatting to Ron and Maggie. I ordered a round of drinks. They're arranging for them to be brought out to us – if they can get through."

"I can remember a time when this pub used to be quiet on Friday nights," Samantha said, raising her glass to her lips.

"I can remember a time when you didn't smoke,"

Martin told her.

"Smoking is bad for you, isn't it, daddy?" Melanie said, taking delight in her older sister being found out.

"Yes, it is. You wouldn't do something like that, would you?"

"No. I don't do bad things."

Apart from smacking other kids in the mouth, Janet thought.

Samantha said nothing as she hid behind her wine but her expression as she looked at Melanie was one of *I'll get you for that.*

Ian wore a similar face as he hid behind his beer.

Melanie smiled and sipped her lemonade loudly through a straw.

"I'm going to do my rounds," Harry announced. "With any luck you're being burgled as we speak."

That made Ian feel a lot better.

No sooner had he gone, Delia arrived.

"Where have you been? It doesn't take this long to change a wheel," Samantha said.

"Sorry. The jack isn't very good and I had to find something to wedge under the axle. Then I got absolutely filthy and had to change my clothes. Motor mechanics has never been my strong point."

Samantha realised she was wearing a different dress to the one she had chosen at the start of the evening and thought no more of it.

Delia sat down and was introduced to everyone.

"It's very nice to meet you," Grantley said, leaning across the table to shake her hand.

Miss Blunt was less courteous when she offered her greeting. "Have you trespassed anywhere today?"

Emily was puzzled. "What do you mean by that?"

"Miss Truebody and I met yesterday at the riding

school."

Delia looked embarrassed and glanced around the table. She didn't know Miss Blunt was a friend of Emily's. She would have thought twice about attending if she had. "I'm sorry, Miss Blunt. I didn't mean to intrude."

"Well, what is done is done," Miss Blunt replied, seemingly ready to put the incident behind her. "As long as there is no repetition of what happened."

"Oh no, it won't happen again. I can assure you of that," Delia said.

"Then we can consider the matter closed."

Those with no knowledge of what had taken place at the riding school looked at one another blankly but no one took it further.

"Are you a UFO hunter?" Sheila asked.

"No, I'm just passing through. Thought I would hop in the camper van and drive around for a few days," Delia replied.

"Are you staying in Cloverdale St Mary long?" Janet asked her.

Delia glanced at Grantley. It was subtle and went unnoticed by the others. "I might stay for a week or so. See how the mood takes me."

"Mummy, may I look at the fish?" Melanie asked.

"Yes, but don't be gone too long."

Melanie spun on her chair and ran to a fish pond at the far end of the garden.

"Don't lean over the fence," Janet called after her.

"I won't."

Maggie and Ron added the water feature to the beer garden six months previously. A lot of families went there, many with small children, so a fence had been built around it as a safety precaution.

Samantha had been waiting for an opportunity to speak to Melanie in private after hearing what she said to Emily. It had surprised both women and required explanation. "I think I'll take a look too," she said, standing up.

"As long as you don't have a crafty cigarette while you're there," Martin told her.

She rolled her eyes at him. "I'm not going to smoke around Mel."

"You shouldn't smoke at all," Janet said.

Samantha didn't see the point in debating it further and left to join Melanie.

Emily watched her go.

They talked for five minutes. From a distance Melanie appeared to be comfortable and at ease with the conversation. She listened carefully and answered Samantha's questions with a confidence that came naturally. She seemed settled and assured, undaunted by what she was telling her.

Emily watched with interest. She wasn't sure how to gauge Samantha's expression as she walked back to their table. It gave nothing away, no hint of what had passed between them.

Samantha re-took her seat but Emily's curiosity got the better of her. She couldn't sit there for the rest of the evening wondering about it. She had to know what Melanie said.

"If you'll excuse us. Sam needs to go to the ladies room again," she announced.

Samantha was as surprised as anyone to hear this but smiled politely and followed Emily when she went inside.

Grantley looked at Martin dumbfounded. "How old is Samantha?" he asked.

"Twenty-one," he replied.

There was a queue for the ladies room and as neither of them wanted to use it for conventional reasons they went out to the street. Sitting at the table that Delia and Grantley had used, Samantha recounted what she had learnt.

Melanie said Candice had spoken to her the night before. She told her she was sorry for going away but there was no need to be sad because she was coming home. Everything would be like it was. She would live in Meadow Cottage and Melanie could visit whenever she wanted. They would go horse riding together and have fun like they used to. When they finished talking Candice turned Jo Jo on a tight rein and they galloped towards a setting sun with hair and mane of shimmering gold. Faster and faster they went and soon they were flying high above the clouds. That was when Samantha realised Melanie had been dreaming. It was wishful thinking that had manifested itself into something real while she slept. It was a little girl's desperate hope that she would see her best friend again.

*

Harry stood in the lounge of the vicarage. Like Ian, he was disappointed that it hadn't been burgled yet but it was still early and he was confident they would have made their move sooner or later. He couldn't see them missing an opportunity like this. Tonight had easy pickings written all over it.

His next port of call was Emily's cottage. That too was burglar free. He looked at George's picture on the wall but didn't linger. He knew Emily well but the picture of her husband was a testament to private lives that he had no right to pry into.

Grantley entered his thoughts and he wondered what George would have made of him. Would he have been jealous or would he have given Emily his blessing, wanting her to be happy? Harry didn't know and went to Meadow Cottage.

There he looked at another picture. It was one of Candice that Samantha had framed and hung in the kitchen, a still from a film made in 2014, a comedy called *Leaving Jack Spencer.* Her character, Julia Spencer - who was plotting to leave her husband by killing him - stood in a kitchen holding a baking tray that was on fire. The expression on her face was one of panic. Samantha liked it because it summed up *her* culinary skills. Like Julia, she was a dreadful cook. Most of her meals came ready-made from the microwave. The toast she ate in the mornings while being late for work was invariably burnt.

Harry smiled at the picture and returned to the Coaching Inn.

*

The rest of the evening passed in a relaxed and jovial manner. Harry continued to make his rounds every half an hour but at no point did he see a burglar. He couldn't believe he had been wrong in thinking they would have struck that night. It was perfect. What more could they have asked for? A key under the doormat and a lorry in which to drive away with their ill-gotten gains? The problem with burglars these days, he thought, was that they were unreliable.

Delia got on well with everyone present. Miss Blunt was sometimes blunt when she spoke to her but she was like that with everyone and in a private moment Emily told her not to take it personally.

Most of all Delia enjoyed talking to Melanie and Becky. She was single and didn't have children but she knew how to interact with them at their level and all three hit it off immediately. Melanie especially warmed to her. This became clear when she took her hand and dragged her away to look at the fish.

By 11:00 p.m. the pub had become less crowded and when the air took a chill to it they went back inside. The drinking competition had come to an abrupt end some time before when a table was overturned and Ron invited the contestants to leave. This was done by punching one of them when he aimed a punch at him and suggesting to his friends that they carried their fallen comrade outside. For Maggie it was Greece all over again.

The ufologists had left to begin their nightly vigil at Cross Drummond and many of the thrill-seekers had gone too, so Emily and her party were able to rearrange more furniture and continued to sit together.

Ron appeared with a bottle of champagne and wished Emily, not for the first time, a happy birthday.

"You're not going to open that, are you?" Ian asked him.

"How else are we going to drink it?" he replied.

Maggie joined them wearing a crash helmet and a bullet-proof vest. "Have you uncorked it yet?"

Ron sighed. "Why do you people assume the worse when I open a bottle of champagne?"

"Because in your hands it's a lethal weapon," Ian told him.

"Dad, I want to go home now," Becky said, shifting uneasily in her chair.

"It's all right. Trust in the Lord, he will protect you. But to be on the safe side hide under the table," Ian replied.

Ron rose above these negative comments and attended to the uncorking. It exploded from the bottle and ricocheted off three walls before blasting through the roof, narrowly avoiding a jumbo jet bound for Saudi Arabia.

He stood drenched in champagne and said what he usually said on these occasions. "I'll go and change my shirt."

Maggie fetched a replacement bottle from the bar. "While you're doing that I'll open this one."

"Is it safe to come out now?" Becky asked from under the table.

"Yes," her father replied.

She re-took her seat.

Maggie poured the champagne and when Ron returned in a dry shirt everyone raised their glasses to the guest of honour.

"Thank you," Emily said. "You shouldn't have gone to so much trouble for me."

"I can't think of anyone more deserving. Happy birthday," Maggie replied.

Emily raised her glass in gratitude but wished Candice had been there. She was glad to be surrounded by friends old and new, they had made the evening special for her, but she couldn't help feeling sad.

Come back to us, Candice. You have to come back to us.

Twenty

Grantley met Delia for breakfast at the Millstream on Saturday morning and convinced her that all would be well. The force controlling Candice would be defeated and life would return to normal. Delia had no idea that he was the one controlling her and for many life would never be the same again.

His plans were nearing completion. Grantley stood on the brink of greatness. He couldn't allow Delia to interfere in his work now he was so close to achieving his goal. All he had to do was make her think their intentions were the same. A successful outcome was guaranteed if she believed the only way of saving Candice was to do as he said. He would feed her snippets of information at times of his choosing, enough to keep her fooled and prevent her from asking awkward questions.

Grantley was surprised the vicarage hadn't been burgled as instructed. He expected to see the police in the village when he woke but there was no sign of them. A smile and a wave from Ian when he saw him across the street was proof that something had gone wrong. He put it to the back of his mind over breakfast as he had to focus on the matter in hand but when he got home he called Baker for an explanation. His reason for not robbing the vicarage was laughable given his talent for burglary and would have amused Grantley had he been in a laughing mood. The van wouldn't start.

Baker and Tate had been set to go. An unoccupied house awaited them and they had all the time in the world to carry out their task but a faulty alternator put paid to that and they spent a frustrating evening watching TV in Baker's flat in Falworth. They considered using the car but it was too small to have suited their needs. That aside it would have been risky. It was registered to Baker and would have been easily traced back to him. The van was stolen and carried false number plates.

Grantley agreed with Baker's decision to err on the side of caution while ruing the lost opportunity. He stood to gain nothing from the burglaries, it wasn't what motivated him, but they were important to his plans.

They were a diversion, a means for him to prepare for his day of triumph safe from the gaze of public scrutiny. Moving into a small village wasn't like moving into a city or a town. A newcomer had eyes on them constantly and faced questions from residents wanting to know something about them. Miss Blunt's self-invitation to tea and butterfly buns the day after he arrived was a prime example of that. Grantley needed to direct their attention elsewhere. What better than a spate of burglaries? While the locals were focused on the threat to their homes who would have paid an interest in him?

It had worked well. Grantley had been able to integrate himself with the village on his terms and without too many questions asked. He allowed Emily to become close to him but that was out of necessity. He didn't have feelings for her. The truth was he didn't like her much. He needed to befriend someone inside Candice's social circle, an ace to keep up his sleeve should something have gone wrong. If the situation demanded he could have gained valuable information from her, not regarding Candice but about Harry Black.

Grantley hadn't known of Harry's existence before he arrived in the village. He didn't know that Emily, Samantha and Ian knew of Candice. He only found out when he took control of her. Under questioning, Candice told him everything he needed to know. Mortals presented no threat to him. People could be lied to and were easily manipulated but a second ghost was another matter. Grantley was able to control one but couldn't exert his influence over two. Harry was the one element in the coming together of his plans that gave him cause for concern.

He didn't have control over that van either.

Baker told him it was being repaired. He was due to pick it up later that afternoon. Grantley thought about it long and hard. There hadn't been a burglary in six days and an air of confidence was returning to the village. Some residents had convinced themselves the burglars had moved on and the threat was over. It was time for another but not the vicarage, the Coaching Inn, Pine Trees or Meadow Cottage. They remained prime targets that would only be hit when Grantley gave the order to do so. He instructed Baker to select a property of his choice, a random theft to re-install uncertainty and keep people on their toes. The burglary would be committed on Monday night.

Baker was eager to add to his awards haul and argued that the vicarage should have been done next but Grantley refused. He agreed that one of the prime targets needed to be burgled soon but they had to choose their moment carefully. He gave permission for the vicarage to be robbed the following Saturday. It was the day of the fête and again the vicar and his family would have been out for much of the time.

*

It was the worst weekend Harry had known. The two days following Emily's birthday passed slowly, not with enjoyment and purpose but with a sense of loss and foreboding. Candice was gone and hope was fading. When they left the Coaching Inn on Friday evening Delia told him and Samantha that she had spoken to the Professor and he promised to get back to her. Emily and Ian were informed the next day but it did nothing to lift the gloom in the lives of friends who missed Candice and were desperate for her to return.

Now, on Monday afternoon, Harry spent much of his time roaming the hills beyond Cross Drummond. It was where Candice had been last seen. Maybe she would go there again. She didn't. He returned to Meadow Cottage and found Delia typing notes on her laptop. She was transcribing them from a paranormal journal.

"Anything?" she asked him.

"No. The other day you mentioned holding a séance. Do you think that would help?"

Delia closed her laptop and leaned back on the sofa. There was a possibility it might have but she suggested it before she knew Grantley was in the village. Holding a séance now might have interfered with his efforts to bring Candice back. She was reluctant to do anything without first seeking his advice. "I don't know. It might help but there are no guarantees."

"We have to try something, Delia. Candice has been gone three days. If she could have pushed through this barrier you spoke of she would have done so by now. She needs our help to do it."

"Well," Delia hedged.

"Have you ever performed a séance?"

"Yes, but with no success I'm afraid."

"But you know how it's done."

"Yes."

"Then let's try. We owe it to Candice to at least try."

Delia rethought her position. Harry was desperate. With each day that went by he felt more powerless, more inadequate, more lost without her. A heart that couldn't beat was broken. Delia didn't have time to seek Grantley's permission. Harry needed an answer and she made a snap decision.

"Okay, I'll do it. Can you arrange for Emily and Ian to come over this evening?"

"Yes."

"Tell them to be here for 8:30. Samantha will need to be present too."

Harry nodded. He left to let them know what was happening.

*

Maggie had no reason to apologize to Brian and Neil but she did so out of courtesy. She had made the situation clear to them when they checked into the Coaching Inn seven days previously and they knew what to expect but the time had come to change their sleeping arrangements and she felt bad about uprooting one of them.

"I'm afraid you'll have to vacate your room by nine o'clock tomorrow morning. The couple who reserved it will be here at ten and we need an hour to turn it around," she told Neil.

"Couldn't he move in with Rafe?" Brian asked.

He didn't mind his colleague bunking down with him, they had shared rooms in the past, but Neil could snore for queen and country. If it had been made an Olympic event he would have won gold.

"His room only has a single bed," Maggie replied.

"I'm not sleeping with Rafe," Neil protested in a raised, panicked voice. "I want to sleep with you."

"Why don't you say that louder?" Brian complained, seeing a bar full of strangers look in their direction.

He realised he was standing with his hand on his hip and quickly removed it.

"I did say at the time of your arrival that Neil might have to share with you," Maggie told him.

"Yes, and I understand completely," Brian relented with a heavy sigh. "Is there somewhere in the village where I can buy earplugs?"

"That won't do you any good," Ron said, eavesdropping from behind the bar. "Maggie and I sleep in the next county and we can hear him from there."

"I don't snore that much," Neil snapped.

"We had to repair the roof on Friday."

"That was because you blasted a champagne cork through it," Maggie said, looking at her husband sharply.

She was trying to soften the blow of relocating one of her guests and didn't appreciate Ron's tell-it-how-it-was honesty. Her eyes said *'shouldn't you be somewhere else?'*

"I think I should be somewhere else," he said, walking away.

"So you're okay with vacating the room by nine o'clock then?" Maggie asked Neil.

"Sunderland," Brian said from nowhere. "There are some nice pubs there."

"There are some nice ones on Pluto too," Ron said, walking past while on his way to somewhere else.

The look in Maggie's eyes changed to *'when you get there don't feel the need to hurry back.'*

She was surprised the ufologists were still there. Neil had encountered what he believed to be aliens on two occasions but the others had seen nothing. They went out every night and watched the skies from key positions around the village, only to return at dawn none the wiser to what was allegedly happening there. If the picture of the UFO that appeared in the newspapers had been genuine the aliens must have had some kind of cloaking device because no one had seen hide nor hair of it since.

Many of the thrill-seekers had gone home. Only the family from Bristol, the couple in their converted ambulance and the biker from Wales remained. Most left on Sunday morning, the others during the afternoon. It was like the closing of the Glastonbury Festival; a mass exodus after one hell of a party. It meant the locals could enjoy the peace and quiet of their pub again and would have space on the green to erect the marquee for the fête on Saturday. Miss Blunt was delighted that life was returning to normal but Bill and Susan had never had it so good and missed the increase in custom.

Brian was loathed to admit it but he was convinced the UFO story was a hoax. Siobhan too who didn't believe in them anyway. She only joined the team to be with Karen. Where she went Siobhan went, usually with her hand in Karen's back pocket.

"How much longer will you be staying?" Maggie asked him. "Not that I'm trying to get rid of you," she quickly added.

"I would like to stay till the end of the week. If there are no sightings over the next few days we'll have to file it under 'unexplained' and return to London," Brian replied.

"That would be a shame. You've put a lot of work into it," Maggie said, trying to sound interested.

Brian sighed again. "It's our lot in life I'm afraid. We

put the hours in and work tremendously hard but more often than not we go home empty-handed."

"With any luck there will be a full-scale invasion before you leave," she said, this time trying to sound encouraging.

"I hope so, Maggie. I really do hope so."

She smiled out of politeness and went upstairs to begin sound-proofing their room.

*

"It's not a good time for me. I'm not sure I can get away," Samantha said on the phone in her office at the riding stables. "No, I'm not saying I don't want to go. It's just a bit difficult at the moment."

She was studying the plans for the stables extension as she spoke and looked up when one of her colleagues entered the room.

Roy Daniels placed a brown folder on her desk and mouthed 'feed log sheets.' Samantha had asked for them earlier.

"I want to celebrate Charlotte getting her decree absolute like everyone else but I don't think I can do it by jetting off to Paris for the weekend," she said.

Daniels flapped his arms and left the office.

Samantha smiled. "Sorry, what was that?... Okay, the Eurostar. Anyway, it's our village fête on Saturday." She listened for a moment and laughed. "No, I'm not running the coconut shy this year but my presence will be expected. How long are you going for?... Yeah, that sounds good. I would love to come, Xanthe, but I really don't know if it's possible. I'll have to think about it before

I commit to anything... I'm not being dramatic, I just need to give it some thought.... Okay. I'll call you tomorrow... What?" She laughed again. "Only if I have to. Give my love to Steve. I'll speak to you tomorrow. Bye."

Samantha hung up the phone and considered the weekend to come. She enjoyed the village fêtes but a failure to attend wouldn't have meant the end of the world. She would rather have been in Paris with her friends but how could she when Candice was missing and Harry needed her?

She thought about the séance planned for later that evening and hoped something good would have come from it.

Twenty-one

Samantha drew the dining room curtains at 9:00 p.m. It was still light outside but a séance was better conducted in the dark and Delia asked for them to be closed. Everyone was present and waited as she made her final preparations.

"Perhaps it would be better if that potted plant was put over there," she said, pointing across the room.

Samantha thought it wouldn't have mattered where the plant was but moved it because she knew nothing about this sort of thing and it may have been important.

Emily and Ian looked nervous. They didn't know what to expect either and wondered what the evening held in store. Ian, especially, felt uncomfortable about attending a séance. The Church had guidelines for situations such as this and his presence put him in breach of them but Candice was his friend and he wasn't about to turn his back on her. He just hoped his Bishop wouldn't have got to hear about it.

Harry stood silently by the door.

"Okay, I think we're ready to begin," Delia said, looking around the room. She gestured to the dining table. "If you would all sit down please."

"Do you want me to be seated?" Harry asked.

"That won't be necessary."

Not for the first time since Candice disappeared, he felt unable to help in any way.

Delia sat at the head of the table and the others took up their positions; Emily and Ian sitting to the left and right of her and Samantha at the other end.

"We need to hold hands," Delia told them.

They held hands and she closed her eyes in a moment of preparedness.

"Has anyone seen my mascara?" Candice asked, strolling into the room.

To their knowledge it was the first time a spirit had manifested itself at a séance in advance of an invitation being extended.

Candice looked at their stunned faces and wondered what was going on. "Why are you sitting in the dark? Are we saving money on lighting?"

Harry went to meet her. "Thank God you're back."

"Back?" she asked, puzzled.

"Can you remember where you've been?"

She tried to hide her bemusement and pointed to the ceiling. "I've been in the attic room with you discussing how to catch the burglars."

It was clear from her response that she had no memory of disappearing at all.

"Candice, we had that conversation three days ago," Harry told her.

"Three days ago?" She looked at the others and realised something was wrong. Very wrong. "It happened again, didn't it?"

"Yes."

"And I've been gone three days?"

Harry didn't answer.

Candice too was silent. The last thing she remembered was agreeing to keep an eye on the vicarage, Pine Trees and Meadow Cottage during Emily's birthday celebration at the Coaching Inn. For that to have been three days previously weighed heavily on her mind but her thoughts were divided when she pointed across the room. "That plant needs to go over there."

"Sit down," Samantha said, giving up her chair for

her.

Candice sat without further comment. Her eyes stared into emptiness.

"It's okay. You're safe with us now."

"For how long, Sam? It's been three days. What is happening to me?"

Samantha recalled the evening she broke the news of her father's affair and how Candice wished she could have hugged her. Now she felt that way. She wanted to reassure her that everything would be all right but how could reassurance have been given when the cause of the problem was unknown?

"Try to remember, Candice. Can you think of anything that might be of help to us?" Delia asked.

"All I remember is being upstairs talking to Harry and then I walked in here."

"There must be something."

"What do you want me to say, Delia? I can't fucking remember," Candice snapped. She regretted being short with her and apologized. "I'm sorry. I didn't mean to jump down your throat."

"It's all right. I appreciate how difficult this must be for you."

"How can I lose three days and know nothing about it?"

"It must be the drink," Harry told her. "John Lennon lost eighteen months when he went on a bender."

Candice knew what he was doing and smiled. It wasn't a hug but reassurance could be offered in other ways.

Ian rose from the table. "Delia has a theory about that but lets go to the lounge and discuss it there." He turned to Samantha. "I don't mean to be critical but your dining room chairs aren't very comfortable."

"Don't blame me, I didn't buy them. She did," Samantha replied, pointing at Candice.

There was that smile again, warm and appreciative in the company of friends who meant the world to her.

They went to the lounge.

*

"What's your theory?" Candice asked Delia as she sat on the sofa beside Emily.

"I believe that some kind of force is taking control of you. You're not completely under its influence but it's growing stronger all the time and soon you might be."

"That's encouraging. What do you think it is?"

"Something evil."

Candice looked at the others. It was clear from their worried expressions that they had spoken about this in her absence. She was the only one with no prior knowledge of it. "You mean I'm gonna turn into a monster or something?"

"I'm sure it wouldn't be anything like that," Emily said.

"I would sit someplace else if I were you. You might catch something horrible if you get too close to me." Candice had answered light-heartedly but the more she thought about it the more concerned she became. "My God, what if you do? I might be contagious."

"I don't think that is likely," Delia told her.

"I could be carrying the plague for all you know." She looked at Harry. "Have we got any paint?"

"Why?"

"We need to put a sign on the front door to keep people away."

"We're stepping into the realms of fantasy now," he told her.

Candice didn't share his optimism and fell silent.

"The Professor shares my view that something is trying to take you over," Delia said.

"You've spoken to him?" Candice asked.

"Yes, on Friday evening."

"What did he say?"

Delia hesitated over her reply. She didn't like lying to people that she had got to know well and regarded as friends. She wished she could have been honest with them. "He was surprised when I told him about it but said he would do everything in his power to help. He's getting back to me in a few days."

"Let's hope I'm still here in a few days," Candice said ruefully. "Did you tell the Professor it was me experiencing these problems?"

"No."

"You needn't worry about that, Candice. We can rely on Delia's discretion," Ian said.

"Yeah, of course. Thank you, Delia."

The show of confidence made her feel worse.

"What do we do now?" Harry asked.

Delia sighed and hunched her shoulders. The question of what to do next wasn't for them to answer. That, and Candice's fate, lay in the hands of another. "All we can do is wait and hope for the best. I'm sure the Professor will have something for us soon."

"And if I'm taken away again?"

"You must be strong, Candice. Don't allow the force to exert its influence over you fully. I cannot stress this enough. You must retain your free will and identity. While you have that you have a measure of control. You can escape from whatever it is that is keeping you prisoner and find your way back to us. It will be difficult, the force is powerful, but if you resist it won't be able to hold you against your wishes."

"If only I knew what it was. I could fight the damn thing if I knew what it was."

"You're missing the point, Candice. When you're under it's influence you *know* what it is. You may not know what it wants of you but you are aware of it. That is when you have to be strong, when you're in its presence."

Delia made it sound easy. The reality of course was anything but.

"I'll try," Candice said.

Emily read the doubt in her voice and smiled to encourage her. "I know you can do it, my dear. You're Candice Freeman and no one gets the better of her."

"I'm sorry I wasn't around for your birthday."

"You're here now. That's all that matters."

Emily dabbed away a tear with her handkerchief.

"Don't cry, Em. Please don't cry."

"I didn't think I would see you again."

Now it was Candice who smiled to encourage her.

"Are you kidding? I'm Candice Freeman and nothing keeps me away from the people I love."

Emily grinned and was rescued.

Candice turned to Delia. "What about the spirit of the little girl that spoke through me? Did it happen again the last time I was taken away?"

"Yes, but it wasn't her. It was someone else," she replied.

"Could it have been the force?"

"It's possible but I don't think so. When you're under its influence rogue spirits are drawn to you. You become a vessel, an outlet through which they can communicate with others. On the two occasions it happened you disappeared moments later. At that point you ceased to be an outlet and they moved on, wandering between the two planes, not in this world or the next."

"So you think it's unrelated?"

"Yes. I can't see why the force would want their presence. It was something that happened by chance, a by-product of plans already set in motion. You're the one it wants. When it comes for you it opens a window of opportunity but when it has you that window closes and the spirits are driven out."

"Two's company, three's a crowd," Candice said thoughtfully.

"Something like that."

"So we wait for the Professor to make contact and hope nothing happens in the meantime," Harry said.

"Yes, Mr Green. That's all we *can* do."

"We could run through the introductions again," he sighed.

"I'm sorry?"

"Never mind."

Candice put aside the mystery of her disappearance and asked to be brought up-to-speed with what happened during Emily's birthday celebrations. The way she remembered it that was the night they were going to catch the burglars. "What happened at the vicarage while I was gone?"

"Nothing," Harry replied.

"I thought the burglars were gonna rob it?"

"That's what we thought but I'm glad to say there was

no sign of them," Ian told her.

Candice recalled Harry's courtroom assessment of what they were up against and where the thieves were likely to have struck next. As far as she was concerned the discussion had taken place just a few minutes previously so it was fresh in her memory. "You said the vicarage was the most likely target because Ian, Sheila and Becky would be at the Coaching Inn. The burglars would go for a family home if they knew the family was out."

He shrugged his shoulders. "I was wrong."

"Did they burgle anyone else?"

"No."

"No one at all?"

"You don't have to sound disappointed," Ian said.

"I thought you would have had it all wrapped up by now. It was three days ago. What have you people been doing in my absence?"

"Worrying about you mostly," Samantha said.

Candice smiled. "Oh Sam, that's so sweet." The smile disappeared faster than she had and was replaced by a look of disapproval. "In the meantime we've still got burglars in the village and homes under threat. I turn my back for five minutes and everything falls down."

"It's not my fault the vicarage wasn't burgled," Harry snapped in his defence.

"M.O.C."

Ian laughed. It was nice to see them sparring again. "Welcome home, Candice. We've missed you."

*

Emily and Ian left at 9:30. Delia went to bed early but Candice, Harry and Samantha talked for a while.

The conversation returned to the burglaries and what could have been done to stop them. Harry was convinced the vicarage would be burgled next and left at eleven o'clock to scout around the village. From there he went to Emily's to commence his nightly vigil. He was reluctant to go. No one knew if Candice would have disappeared again and he wanted to stay with her but he had given Emily his word and Candice would have made him leave if he went back on it.

"Are you okay?" she asked Samantha, following an unusually long silence between them.

"Yeah. I'm just glad to have you back."

"No, that's not it. You have something on your mind. Is it your mom and dad?"

Samantha wasn't surprised Candice had seen through her. Despite having problems of her own it was typical that she would have put others first. "No, they're getting on really well. They went to the Coaching Inn on Friday and had a good night. It was like old times. You wouldn't have thought anything had happened."

"Is Martin still sleeping in your room?"

"Yeah, but I don't know for how much longer. They still have a way to go but I think they'll be all right. It's looking promising."

"I'm glad to hear it, Sam. So if that's not bothering you, what is?"

"It's nothing really."

"Um, hello. Candice Freeman, remember? Nothin' gets the better of her."

Samantha smiled. "Some friends of mine are going to Paris this weekend and invited me along."

"That is so cool. I love Paris. Walks along the Seine, lunch in the Eiffel Tower, throwing up on the metro after too many daiquiris. When do you go?"

"I'm not. I told Xanthe I couldn't get away."

"Are you kiddin' me? This is Paris we're talking about. You have to go."

"It's only a weekend. I can go some other time."

Candice put two and two together and hit four in the blink of an eye. "You mean when things are better for me."

"My place is here, Candice. You and Harry need me." Samantha began to cry. "And I need you. I couldn't bear it if I went away and you weren't here when I got back... What if I never saw you again?"

As before, Candice wished she could have held her. It was what friends did in times of distress, when they were upset and needed consoling, when everything seemed lost and a hug would have made it better.

"I know where you're coming from, Sam, but you can't put your life on hold for me. You're twenty-one years old, your whole life is ahead of you. The good times don't last long. You need to grasp them while you can. Go to Paris with your friends. Don't worry about me, I'll be here when you get back. I promise."

"It doesn't seem right."

"That you'll be having a great time in Paris while some force is screwing with me? No, it isn't, you bitch."

Samantha laughed.

"That's more like it. Life is for living, Sam. Go out there and grab it by the throat. If you're going on a girls weekend find a guy and grab it by the balls. You don't have to earn it, it's yours by right. It's everything you want it to be and more."

Samantha hesitated. The worst case scenario refused to leave her thoughts. How could she have been anything *but* concerned after recent events? "If I go you will be here when I come home, won't you?"

"Yeah, because this is where I want to be. I wanna be with you and Harry and no damn force is gonna get in the way of that. So you're going to Paris, okay?"

"Okay."

"The Notre Dame line. That's a good one to throw up on."

"I know... I've thrown up on it before."

The relief of Candice's return collided with three days of worry and Samantha wept.

Twenty-two

Harry was not impressed. Cloverdale St Mary had woken to news of another burglary. A young couple had been robbed overnight. No harm came to Phil and Jackie Llewellyn but they were left shaken by the experience and were being interviewed by the police as Harry took Samantha to task over the breakfast table.

"I don't believe what I'm hearing. Another house has been burgled and you're going to Paris for the weekend? It's hardly a good time to leave your home unattended, is it?"

"It won't be unattended. Delia and I will be here," Candice said in Samantha's defence. "It's been a difficult couple of weeks and Sam deserves a break. Paris is a great opportunity to get away from it all."

"Leaving the burglars to *walk* away with it all," Harry pointed out. "Why are you going?"

Samantha looked at him anxiously. She felt like a child having to explain a mischievous act to an angry parent. "A friend I used to work with got divorced, her decree absolute has just come through. She and another friend are going to Paris to celebrate. They invited me along."

Delia dug her spoon into her cereal bowl and spoke without raising her head. Breakfast was the most important meal of the day and deserved her full attention but she felt compelled to comment on Samantha's choice of words. "I wouldn't have thought the breakdown of a marriage was something to celebrate."

"It is in this case. They hated each other," she replied.

Harry felt the timing couldn't have been worse. There was too much going on at home to go gallivanting off to France. The situation regarding Candice and the burglaries called for solidarity, a united front against enemies unknown. Aside from that it was the village fête on Saturday and Samantha should have been there to support it. It would have been better to cancel and go some other time.

"I think you should reschedule," he said.

Candice wouldn't hear of it and assumed the role of travel director. "I'm not gonna let you bully Sam into staying when she wants to go."

"It might be better if I did stay at home, especially with the burglars striking again," Samantha said, her doubts returning.

"We've discussed this. You're going to Paris and that's final," Candice told her.

"You can't make me go."

"Do you wanna put money on that? I'll drive you to the airport if necessary."

"We're going by Eurostar."

"Then I'll drive you to St Pancras. I'll drive the train too if it gets you out of the country."

"It's nice to feel wanted," Samantha muttered.

Harry looked at the clock on the wall. It was just after 9:00 a.m. and Samantha was late for work again. She was meant to start at eight o'clock but she and Candice had talked into the early hours of the morning and Samantha overslept. If she didn't leave now she would have set a new record for being late. Her personal best was 9:47 and she was destined to beat that hands down.

"We'll discuss this later," he said.

"There's nothing *to* discuss," Candice replied. She

looked at Samantha and outlined her plans for that evening. "When you get home from work I'll help you to pack."

"I'm not packing yet. We don't go till Friday."

"It pays to be prepared."

Harry recalled Candice in life and what she was like on departure days. The term *headless chicken* came to mind. For someone who travelled the world in pursuit of her career it was amazing she ever left the house. He had never known anyone to get in such a panic about going on a journey. Her passport came out six days before she was due to leave and she spent every waking moment thereafter fretting about where she had put it. On one occasion Candice turned the cottage upside down trying to find it, only to realise she had it in her hand all the time.

"You're a fine one to talk about travel arrangements. When you went to Japan you almost had to be sedated," he told her.

"You have to be sure everything is accounted for. The entire trip might be ruined if you forget something," she insisted.

"M.O.C. Sam, go to work. Delia, phone the Professor to see if he has any news. Candice... do whatever it is you do at this time of day."

"I could start packing for you if you show me what clothes you're gonna take," she said to Samantha.

"If you agree to that you need your head examined," Harry announced.

Samantha smiled awkwardly and went to work.

"I'll get your passport ready," Candice called after her.

*

Maggie watched the car pull up outside the Coaching Inn and went to greet her guests. She hadn't seen them since Candice's funeral. They had an open invitation to visit and stay for as long as they wanted but grief and the pressure of work made it impossible. Until now.

Brenda Taylor embraced Maggie as her husband fetched their luggage from the back of the car. "Hello, Maggie. It's good to see you."

"You too. It's been too long."

"I'm sorry we haven't come down before." Brenda held Maggie's hands and looked beyond her to the pub. She had fond memories of it. "I wasn't sure if I could."

Maggie understood and nodded. "I know. Hello, Mike," she said, extending her welcome to Brenda's husband.

He put the cases down and embraced her too. "Hi, Maggie. How are you?"

"I'm fine. Did you have a good journey?"

"Yeah, clear roads all the way. The last traffic we saw was in London." Mike looked around from his stationary position. The village was as he remembered it, with one or two exceptions. "Why is there a caravan and an old ambulance on the green?"

Maggie smiled. "You should have seen it last week. You couldn't move for them. They're UFO watchers."

"Oh yeah, we read about that. Cloverdale St Mary was being invaded."

"We were invaded all right but not by aliens. I've never seen the place so busy."

Brenda had walked a short distance ahead of them and stood just outside the entrance to the pub. It was a warm day but she felt cold and hugged her arms. She bowed her head and began to cry.

"It's okay, Brenda," Maggie said, going to her.

"I didn't mean to do this," she wept.

"It's a difficult time. Anniversaries always are."

"I miss her so much."

Maggie put her arm around Brenda's shoulder and led her inside. Mike followed with the suitcases.

Candice and Harry watched them enter.

"She'll be all right," Harry said.

Candice didn't answer. Seeing her friend hurt so deeply got in the way of words.

She wished she could have gone to her as Maggie had done, to have reassured her and made the pain go away. It was within her power to have done so but it would have been wrong of Candice to intervene. As hard as it was, people had to experience grief in order to appreciate life. They had to mourn in order to find happiness. They had to cry in order to love.

There were no short-cuts to living.

*

Brenda was Candice's agent. She had been for ten years. During that time a bond formed between them that made them the best of friends.

Brenda was opposed to Candice leaving London. She thought swapping the city for a small village miles from nowhere was a mistake. *'It won't take long for the novelty to wear off'* she had told her but Candice settled into country life well and never regretted her decision to move. When Brenda saw how happy and content she was she supported her decision. The distance between them had no effect on their friendship. If anything they became closer.

Brenda was devastated when Candice died. At the time of her death she and Mike were separated. He had one affair too many and their marriage collapsed but they continued to see one another on a daily basis through work. When Candice died they were reunited in grief and had been together ever since. Their relationship now was built on love and trust. There would be no going back to Mike's womanising days. It took the death of someone close to him to make him realise how short life was, for him to appreciate what he had and to treat Brenda with the respect she deserved. He realised, for the first time, that his world would have come to an end if she wasn't a part of it.

They had gone to the village to attend Candice's memorial service and were staying for two nights. Mike had to return to London for a meeting on Thursday but he wanted Brenda to stay longer. She had a full workload and had been doing too much, mostly by her own design to take her mind off Candice's death. He wanted Brenda to stop immersing herself in work as a distraction and be among people who felt their loss the way she did. Perhaps then she would have coped better.

At 1:00 p.m. they met Emily and Miss Blunt for lunch. Ian was meant to be present too but he was unusually late. Candice and Harry stood nearby.

"How is Samantha settling into Meadow Cottage?" Mike asked, tucking into the largest ploughman's he had ever seen.

"Very well. She loves it there," Emily replied.

"It's good that you rented to someone Candice knew. She would have approved."

"Yes, I'm sure she would have."

Brenda nodded out of politeness. She was glad someone known to them was renting the cottage, it was better than a stranger taking possession of it, but she regarded Samantha as a trespasser.

She didn't mean to. Brenda liked her. On the few occasions they had met they got on well but Meadow Cottage wasn't Samantha's home. Candice should have been living there. She should have grown old in a house she loved. She should have lived and died within its walls, not in the mangled wreckage of an airliner that crashed in a field outside Connecticut. That was no place for her. She should have been here now having lunch with them and doing what Candice Freeman did best.

Living life to the full.

"Tell me more about these burglaries," Mike said, changing the subject. "How many have there been?"

"Six," Miss Blunt replied.

"My God. As many as that?"

"Yes, and I fear there will be more. I cannot see the thieves moving on, not while the police are doing so little to apprehend them."

"They must be protecting the village surely," Mike said.

"That has been left mainly to the residents. We have set up a neighbourhood watch scheme and organized night patrols but still the burglars are able to strike whenever they have a mind to. I wish I could see an end to it."

"Prudence has been burgled too," Emily told him.

Mike was appalled to hear it. Miss Blunt in full battle cry scared the hell out of him but he respected her and was genuinely saddened.

"Oh, Miss Blunt. I'm so sorry. Did they take much?"

"The usual things people steal when they invade the homes of others."

"Did they take Candice's Oscar?" Brenda asked.

Miss Blunt bowed her head in shame. She couldn't bring herself to look at her. "Yes, I regret to say they did. The loss of the Academy Award pains me more than anything else. Not because of its value but because Candice entrusted it into my care. I let her down in allowing it to be stolen."

Brenda held her hand. "You mustn't blame yourself, Prudence. It wasn't your fault. You had no way of knowing something like that was going to happen."

"It does not make it easier."

"It should. You're not responsible in any way."

That was the reaction Mike wanted to see and hear; Brenda sharing in other people's sorrow and not consumed by her own.

Her response would have been different if the theft had happened anywhere else. She would have blamed the owner for not taking better care of the Oscar, for not putting it somewhere safe to make it difficult for the burglars to find, but in Cloverdale St Mary, among people who loved Candice and knew her well, that judgement never entered her thoughts. Miss Blunt was wrongly accusing herself of negligence and Brenda wouldn't stand for it.

"Did you have it insured?" she asked.

Miss Blunt was almost too embarrassed to answer. The value of the Oscar was unimportant, it was what it represented that made her loss hard to bear. "Yes, it was insured but I would not dream of registering a claim. It was bequeathed to me. It is not my place to seek financial gain from its theft."

"Candice would," Brenda said, smiling.

Candice smiled too. "Damn right. It stopped being mine when I gave it to you, Pru. File a claim."

"It stopped being hers when she gave it to you. File a claim," Brenda said.

Candice felt uneasy and looked at Harry. "How did she do that?"

He was taking no chances after what happened with Delia when she saw them on the village green. "Wave."

Candice waved at her.

Brenda showed no reaction to it and they breathed a sigh of relief.

"Oh, look what the cat dragged in," Harry said, turning his attention elsewhere.

"I'm sorry I'm late," the vicar apologized.

Mike smiled and shook his hand. "Hello, Ian. It's good to see you again."

"It's good to see you, Mike. Hello, Brenda."

"Hello, Ian." He was clean-shaven the last time they met and she complimented him on a new, rugged look. "The beard suits you."

"Thank you, Brenda. Sheila hates it."

"Me too," Candice said.

Ian glanced at her.

"I didn't say anything before 'cos I wanted to spare your feelings but it makes you look ten years older."

"It makes you look older though," Brenda said.

"How is she doing that?" Candice asked Harry.

They both waved this time but Brenda saw nothing. It was simply a case of great minds thinking alike.

Ian sat down and looked at Maggie when she appeared at their table. "You like my beard, don't you?"

"Yes, it takes years off you," she replied.

"We don't have anything to worry about there," Harry said to Candice.

Ian placed his lunch order and Maggie left them to pass it to Ron in the kitchen.

"What time is the service tomorrow?" Brenda asked him.

"Midday. A lot of people are taking time off work or extended lunch breaks in order to attend. I'm expecting a large turn out."

"As it should be," Mike said. "Have the reporters and TV people arrived yet?"

"No, I expect they'll be here first thing in the morning." Ian paused and recalled a heated phone conversation with one of the TV companies two days previously. It was one of the rare occasions he had been uncivil towards someone. "A news crew from Canada wanted to film the service but I refused permission. It's a private gathering for the village and close friends to pay their respects. I can't stop them from setting up on the green but there will be no filming inside the church."

Brenda and Mike nodded in agreement.

"How are you these days?" Ian asked him. "No more health scares?"

Mike grinned. "No. I decided one heart attack is enough for me. I've been following doctors orders and looking after myself. I have to say I feel a lot better for it. I should have adopted a healthier lifestyle years ago."

Candice recalled that awful night in November 2015 when she arrived home from a firework display to find Harry sitting at her desk in the lounge. Brenda had called and left a message. Mike had been taken ill in a restaurant and admitted to hospital. She sounded frantic on the phone. She didn't know what to do and was going out of her mind with worry. Candice drove to London immediately and spent a few days with them while he recovered. It was the start of Brenda and Mike's reconciliation, a path back to a marriage that both had thought to be broken beyond repair.

"I hear there's a new face in the village," Brenda said, looking around the table.

"Yes, Norman Grantley. He arrived two weeks ago," Miss Blunt replied.

"What's he like?"

Ian grinned. "You should ask Emily that question. They spend a lot of time together."

"More's the pity," Harry muttered.

Brenda smiled knowingly and teased her. "Been showing him the ropes, have you?"

The question had *Candice Freeman* written all over it.

Emily shifted uncomfortably in her chair. She still found being put on-the-spot embarrassing. "Norman is a very..."

"Nice man," that disapproving voice interjected.

"... welcome addition to the community. He said he might pop in later."

"Oh good," Harry said, in no way trying to sound enthusiastic.

"What does he do?" Brenda asked.

"He gets on my wick mostly." Harry noted the unappreciative glance from Emily and raised his hands in apology. "Sorry. The floor is yours."

"He was a doctor in London. He saw Cloverdale St Mary on TV when Candice passed away and thought it would be a nice place to spend his retirement."

"He's got a big one, hasn't he, Em?" Candice joined in.

Ian laughed.

"What is amusing you, Father?" Miss Blunt asked.

"This should be good," Harry said, looking forward to his response.

"Um, I was thinking about a joke he told when we were here celebrating Emily's birthday. He's a very..."

"Nice man?" Harry prompted.

"... humorous chap."

"You were outside in the garden when Norman told that joke," Emily said, unwittingly making it more difficult for him.

Ian had plucked his answer from thin air. He was unaware that Grantley had told a joke and had to think fast. "Oh, yes. I remember now. He told me the next day."

Harry was impressed. For a man of God Ian was an excellent liar. He had missed his vocation. He should have been a politician.

Mike was always on the look out for a funny story. It helped to break the ice with new clients and he was keen to add it to his repertoire. "What was it about?"

Ian didn't have a clue and smiled awkwardly. "It's not really suitable for female company. I'll tell you later."

"Should you be listening to jokes of that sort?" Brenda asked him.

"I couldn't stop him from telling it."

Miss Blunt remembered the joke well but the punchline continued to puzzle her. It was a mystery on a par with the Sphinx and why aliens should have wanted to invade the village. "I could not see anything remotely funny about it. It was never fully explained what the policeman did with his truncheon on Thursdays."

Mike roared with laughter. "Oh, I know that one. It's very good."

Brenda rolled her eyes. It was like being out with a

kid.

At least it got Ian off the hook.

"Are you staying in the village long?" Miss Blunt asked.

"Just for the service I'm afraid. We have to get back to London," Brenda replied.

Mike put aside his amusement over policemen and what they did with government-issued equipment on their days off and pointed his fork at her. "I have to get back to London. You could stay for a few days."

"I have work commitments too," Brenda said.

"I know, and that's all you've been doing lately. I went down that road and had a heart attack for my trouble. You need to relax and take it easy. Being here is the perfect opportunity to take a break."

"Why don't you stay?" Ian said to her. "It's our village fête on Saturday. You haven't come to one yet."

"It would be nice but I have to go back. I have a pile of contracts on my desk that need signing and scripts to send out."

"That's why you have an assistant," Mike persisted.

Brenda didn't answer and a lull in the conversation followed. She looked around the room and realised little had changed over the past year. It was the same now as it was then; a good reason for swapping the city for the countryside and moving out of the fast lane. Her eyes found Edmund in his glass case at the end of the bar. She recalled a time when he had been removed from it. It was during the house-warming party Candice had thrown soon after moving into Meadow Cottage.

In the week leading up to it Brenda asked if any men would have been present, preferably rich ones who owned most of Wiltshire and were looking for a woman to lavish their money on. Candice said there would be and one in particular was dying to meet her. He was a local man, an actor who was at the top of his game and in great demand. Some said his performances were a little wooden but he was good-looking and word had it he was dynamite in bed. When Brenda arrived she found Edmund propped on the sofa with a bunch of flowers resting on his lap and wearing his best bow tie.

Emily knew what she was thinking and held her hand when she bowed her head. "It's good to remember her."

"Remember her, Emily? Candice is never out of my thoughts."

Brenda's tears came easily and she escaped to the garden to compose herself.

"Do you want me to talk to her?" Ian asked Mike.

"Later perhaps. She needs to be on her own for now."

Ian abided by his wishes, knowing that Brenda wasn't alone.

Candice had followed her out.

Twenty-three

"How long has Brenda been this way?"

Mike looked at Candice's grave and felt a depth of sorrow the like of which he had never known before. The last time he saw her she was alive and vibrant, the way many had seen her since in her films and TV appearances. Now she was a corpse decaying in a box under ground. It was late-afternoon and he and Ian were alone in the churchyard.

"Since it happened. Brenda has gone through the grieving process in two ways, both of them wrong. When Candice died she began to drink. She was getting through a bottle of vodka a day. Then the drinking stopped and she threw herself into work. That's how it's been for the past four months. She's rarely at home, she spends all her time at the office. When she is at home she works from there. I'm worried, Ian. She's working herself into an early grave and I can't get her to stop."

"Has she been here today?"

"No. She couldn't bring herself to visit the grave. Coming back to the village was always going to be difficult for her, this would be a step too far. I'm dreading tomorrow. I don't know how she's going to get through it."

Ian remembered Brenda at the funeral, the explosion of grief when the coffin was lowered into the earth, the broken-hearted, inconsolable woman who had to be helped away from the graveside when the service was concluded. He had witnessed grief before, up-close and sometimes too personal, but never had he seen it like that. The day Candice Freeman died Brenda Taylor died too.

"Has she been back to Meadow Cottage?" he asked.

Mike was surprised by the question. "No."

"I think she should. Brenda hasn't come to terms with her loss, you don't need me to tell you that. The way to do it isn't through drink or work but through remembrance under the guidance of our Lord. The service tomorrow will help but a church is no place to say goodbye to a friend. That should be done in familiar surroundings where the deceased lived, laughed and cried. Where the bereaved feels close to them."

"Do you think it would do any good?"

"It wouldn't do any harm. Let me speak to Samantha. I'm sure she would be happy for Brenda to visit."

"Should I go with her?"

"It would be better if it was just Brenda." Ian smiled and placed his hand on his shoulder. "I know you're doing everything you can to support her, Mike, but she needs to do this on her own. Saying goodbye in these circumstances is better done in private. If you let me arrange it with Sam I'll ask that she leaves her alone for a while."

"Okay. I'll put it to Brenda when I get back. Thank you, Ian."

"I'm here to help. I'll do whatever I can."

"Will you pray with me?"

Ian nodded.

He and Mike stood before Candice's grave, heads-bowed, and prayed for the dead and the living.

*

"Paris, you say."

"Yes. She wasn't going to go at first but now she's really looking forward to it."

"How delightful. It's always been one of my favourite cities. More tea?"

"Yes, thank you, Norman."

Grantley poured a fresh cup for Emily in the lounge of Brook Cottage while mulling over the worst news he could have heard. Samantha was going to Paris with friends on the very day he planned to abduct her.

Research, months of preparation, equipment tried and tested. Grantley stood on the verge of achieving something remarkable, a feat so challenging lesser men would have crumbled at the mere thought of it, but now his plans were threatened by the one thing he had failed to legislate for; three girls going to Paris on a boozy weekend with the intention of getting laid. This wouldn't do. It wouldn't do at all.

"Are you looking forward to the fête on Saturday?" Emily asked.

"Sorry? Oh yes, very much."

I would rather be kidnapping Samantha, he thought.

"I hope we have nice weather for it."

"Yes. What time is Samantha leaving on Friday?"

"Three o'clock. She's taking the afternoon off work. One of her friends is picking her up from home. She's taking Monday off too. They don't get back till seven in the evening."

That gave him a window of opportunity. How to open it was the question. He couldn't snatch her from work, it would have been too risky.

As perplexing as Grantley's problem was it did present him with an unexpected bonus. If he abducted

Samantha when she came home from work she wouldn't have been reported as missing until late Monday evening. No one would have been alerted to her disappearance over the course of the weekend. Why should they? She was in Paris. That worked to his advantage. Samantha would be held prisoner for five days before he killed her. The longer her abduction went unknown the better.

The problem of what to do about her travelling companions was easy to solve. He would force Samantha to call one of them, saying she couldn't go after all. She would only have been on the phone a short time, not long enough for them to hear the fear in her voice or arouse suspicion. A knife held to her throat would have ensured that she said only what he told her to say.

"Are you donating anything to the bring-and-buy stall?" Emily asked him.

"I expect I can look something out. I have a set of kitchen knives I never use. It's a pity Sam will miss the fête."

"Yes, it's a shame in that respect but look at where she'll be instead. I envy her going there at this time of year."

Grantley's basement wasn't a nice place to go at any time of year, it was cold, damp and dark, but while people enjoyed the fête just a short walk from where his cottage stood it was where Samantha would be. Her last days on earth would be lonely and terrifying, locked in a dungeon that would become her tomb.

In order to achieve greatness one had to perform torturous acts.

*

Emily had gone to Brook Cottage to ask Grantley if he was going to attend Candice's memorial service. When he told her he was they agreed to go together. The service was also a topic of conversation in the attic room of Meadow Cottage later that evening.

"I wish people wouldn't go to so much trouble for me," Candice said.

"Your first anniversary isn't going to go unnoticed. It was always going to be marked in some way," Harry replied.

"I guess. It's Brenda I'm worried about. I thought she was getting over it. You should have seen her in the beer garden, Harry. She was so upset."

Harry didn't answer. He let the silence speak.

Candice knew that Brenda had struggled to cope with her death. She was a regular visitor to her and Mike's home in London. She saw the vodka bottle come out during those first few weeks and despaired at what Brenda was doing to herself. She watched her cry in her drunkenness, sobbing over a photograph album while putting her fingers to pictures of her and Candice that were cold and dead. If only they could have come to life. She longed for things to be the way they were.

Eventually the drinking stopped. Mike didn't know why but Candice did. She was in the car with her the day it happened.

Brenda was still hung over from the night before and almost knocked down a pensioner as he crossed the street. The brakes screamed and Brenda screamed. The car came to a halt touching the old man's legs. He looked petrified and she realised what she had become; a menace to herself and others, a wreck. A sorry excuse for a human being who was letting grief destroy her life.

Candice thought she was over the worst of it. Brenda

went back to work and was more like her old self. What Candice didn't know was that work had become the new vodka, small measures at first that turned into doubles and triples. Over recent months Brenda had done everything to extremes. She got to the office early. She left late at night. She took files home and worked into the small hours of the morning. She even went in on Saturdays and Sundays until Mike put his foot down and made her stop.

Hearing him speak of it in the Coaching Inn and seeing how upset she was made Candice realise that this was Brenda's life now. It wouldn't have gotten any better. She would have carried on that way unless Candice did something.

"I'm gonna make my presence known to her. Let her know I'm okay."

"Is that wise?" Harry asked.

"I don't know, but I have to do something. I watched her fall apart before. I'm not gonna do it again."

"You're not looking at the whole picture, Candice."

"What do you mean?"

Harry hesitated. He wasn't sure how to answer. The worst case scenario was anchored in his thoughts.

"Let's say you make your presence known to Brenda and she's the better for it. What will happen if you're taken away and don't come back? She would lose you all over again. Do you want to put her through that?"

Candice didn't answer.

"I know how much she means to you and seeing her upset can't be easy but now isn't the time to act rashly. In wanting to help you could do more harm than good. I'm not saying it should never happen, just that it shouldn't happen now. We need to understand what is going on with you first. Then we can help Brenda."

He was right of course.

"Okay," Candice said. "But when this is over I'm gonna do it. I want Bren to know I'm still here."

"What about Prudence and Maggie?"

Candice was puzzled. "What about them?"

"I've seen the way you look at them. You miss not being able to talk to them, don't you?"

"I miss that with a lot of people."

"Yes, but with Prudence and Maggie especially. Ron too. It saddens you that you can't share things with them, that your friendships had to end. You've never really come to terms with it."

Candice conceded the point because it wasn't worth debating. Losing friends and loved ones was what death was all about. No one said it was easy. "Yeah, I would like our friendships to continue but what can I do? I can't walk into their homes and say *Hi, guys. Put the kettle on and let's have a catch up.*"

"It's what you're proposing to do with Brenda."

She hated it when he did that.

"The situation with Brenda is different. She needs me. Pru and Maggie don't."

"You're wrong. I've seen the way they look at *you.*"

Candice was stunned and feared the worst. His comment could only have meant one thing. "What?"

"Your picture in the Coaching Inn. Every time they go to that table by the fireplace they look at it. I see a longing in their eyes, a sense of loss that consumes them. They miss you as much as Brenda does. The difference is they hide it better."

Candice was relieved that she had misunderstood. Now she was just confused. "Harry, I wanna be sure I've got this right. A few minutes ago you told me it would be wrong to make my presence known to Brenda. Now you're saying I should go on the six o'clock news and tell everybody. You know the importance of keeping our existence a secret. The more people who know about it, the more chance there is of everyone finding out."

Harry sighed. She had missed the point.

"We know we can trust them. Don't make the mistake I made with Ian. I thought it was better he didn't know about me so I kept my distance, then one day he saw me anyway. It wasn't of my doing, it just happened, but when it did I thought of all that lost time. We could have been two friends enjoying each other's company but instead I stayed at a distance and simply wished for it. That was wrong of me. I should have made myself known to him."

"Do you think I should?"

"When the time is right to make your existence known to Brenda maybe you should tell Maggie and Prudence too. Where is it written that ghosts can't have friends?"

Candice was intrigued by what he *hadn't* said. "There's more to it. What's going on inside that head of yours?"

"The bottom line?"

He had chosen the American vernacular so she responded in her native tongue.

"Lay it on me, babe."

Harry spoke with a passion and intensity that surprised her, small measures at first that turned into doubles and triples as he confided his true feelings.

"I don't know what is happening to you and it scares me. I can only stand by and watch while something takes control of you and threatens to wreck everything we have together. That I can't help you is tearing me to pieces.

I've come to appreciate the true value of friendship. It's not something that has to end with death. Emily, Ian and Sam are proof of that. If it's genuine it can go on beyond the grave. The more friends we have the stronger we are and no fucking force, whatever it is, can change that."

"My God, Harry."

"I love you, Candice, and I would do anything to keep you safe, but I don't know how."

"Is that why you've been with me constantly today?"

"I'm terrified of losing you, that you'll be taken away again. Not that I would be able to stop it from happening."

Candice saw the fears and frailties that lay hidden beneath his surface, the insecurity that lay hidden inside everyone. Dead or alive, the doubt monster didn't discriminate. It tore chunks out of the uncertain and the assured.

"Don't sell yourself short, Harry. I know we have Emily, Ian and Sam's support, and Delia is doing everything she can, but you're the one I feel safe with. I crossed an ocean to find you but you found me. You saved me when I was lost and couldn't get home. You'll save me again. I know you will because no one else can. I loved you in life and I love you in death. And you're right. No force is gonna change it."

"So you don't think I'm pathetic?"

Candice was astonished by the question. "How could I think that? You're wonderful."

It was the best description of love Harry had ever heard.

"It's getting late. You should go to Emily's."

"I'll check in with you every hour on the hour," he said.

Candice smiled. "To make sure I'm still here?"

Harry didn't. "Yeah."

She saw concern in his eyes, a fear that the doubt monster wouldn't allow him to conquer, and the smile left her face. "Okay."

*

Harry checked the vicarage before he went to Emily's. Ian had grown accustomed to seeing him lurking in the garden and nodded through the lounge window as he drew the curtains. When Sheila asked why he was nodding he said he had a headache and was exercising his neck to alleviate it. That was when she made him take paracetamol.

If you go to bed with a headache you wake with one and that's no way to start the day, she told him.

Harry left to continue his rounds.

It was just after midnight when he saw them, two figures hiding in the bushes as he walked to Pine Trees Cottage to begin his vigil. His sombre mood lifted at the thought of what was about to happen.

I'm going to catch a couple of burglars.

The importance of the occasion was not lost on him. The acclaim. The thanks. The gifts of appreciation that would have been lavished on him for saving the village from more robberies and hardship. Then it occurred to him that he was dead and none of those rewards would have been forthcoming.

At least he would have had the satisfaction of knowing he had saved the day. That in itself was adequate reward. It would have given him bragging rights over Candice for years to come. A part of him wished the village would have been burgled more often. He was wonderful, Candice had said so. If he had a cape and wore his underpants over his trousers he would have been perfect.

Harry slipped into stealth mode and crept up on the burglars silently. Being a ghost he had no reason to do this but he felt the situation called for it. When he arrived at their hiding place he realised things were not as they seemed.

"It's my turn to wear the costume tonight," said one spotty teenager to another.

"No it isn't. You wore it last time."

"We've only done it once."

"Yeah, and you wore the costume. So it's my turn."

"Shhh. He's coming."

Harry looked over his shoulder and saw Neil walk towards them. He watched, unimpressed, as one of the youths donned an alien mask.

"See if you can make him pee himself this time," his friend said.

Harry despaired. What should have been burglars was two idiotic locals playing a prank on the ufologists. It was time for number twelve to make an appearance.

"You like scaring people, do you?" he said, looming before them.

One youth fainted. The other peed *himself* and ran screaming into the night.

"Let that be a lesson to you," Harry called after him. "If you're going to play silly buggers make sure there are no ghosts in the vicinity."

Neil walked by a moment later none the wiser to what had happened.

*

Grantley looked at Candice's grave in the churchyard. It was half past one in the morning and no one was around. The night patrols were out as usual but the consecrated ground behind the church didn't warrant protection. They had no reason to go there. They were guarding against burglars, not people who entertained ghoulish thoughts. Grantley had taken to going for late night walks and visited the grave often. He felt nothing for the body lying in it.

He wasn't a fan of Candice Freeman. He had no interest in actors or the roles they played for a public that demanded to be entertained. The last time he went to a cinema was twenty years ago and he only went then because he couldn't get out of it. His TV viewing didn't extend beyond the news and documentaries. He would have died of boredom if he had to sit through car chases or doctors involved in love triangles that became more complicated with each passing episode. Yawn, yawn.

For him real life was more important. How to preserve it. How to take it to the next level. How to end it. He was surprised by how long it had taken his wife to die when he killed her. Six minutes was a long time in anyone's book. Samantha would die quicker, of that he was certain. His first murder had been ill-timed and clumsy. He had rushed it and hadn't been properly prepared. It was different now. Grantley had learned from his mistakes. He knew what he was doing.

He formed a mental picture of Candice lying in her coffin. It didn't matter that she had been a famous actress loved and respected the world over. What she did in life was irrelevant. It was what she did next that mattered.

A new picture replaced the old; Samantha held prisoner in his basement, pulling at the restraints in a desperate attempt to free herself, terrified eyes staring at the knife as the ghost of Candice Freeman drew closer.

Twenty-four

As expected the media arrived in Cloverdale St Mary early. The village green was packed with reporters and film crews setting up. The memorial service for Candice may have been a private affair but that it was taking place had become global news.

Candice watched from a distance. This time the cameras held no interest for her. Her thoughts were on the service and the effect it may have had on her friends. She appreciated the gesture of remembrance but wanted it to be over.

"Are you okay?" Harry asked, standing beside her.

She forced a smile. "Yeah. I saw Brenda and Mike when they were taking breakfast. She seems better this morning."

"I spoke to Ian earlier. He and Mike are keen for Brenda to visit Meadow Cottage. Ian thinks it might help her. He's going to talk to Sam about it after the service."

"Do you think Bren will go?"

"I don't know. I hope she does. It could be what she needs, to see the place again and put her thoughts in order."

"Closure."

"That's the idea. Whether it turns out that way is for Brenda to decide."

"I guess it always was."

Harry saw Delia walk towards them. He wondered what colour she would have confused him with and drew a heavy sigh. Over breakfast in Meadow Cottage he had been Bronze, Silver and Gold.

Candice knew what he was thinking and this time

smiled genuinely. "My money is on Magnolia."

"Hello, Candice. Mr Lavender."

"Black, Delia. My name is Black. Think the opposite of white and that's what I am. It's like someone being punched black and blue. If you remember half of that phrase you'll get my name right."

"Of course, Mr Blue."

"I give up."

"Have you heard from the Professor?" Candice asked.

"Yes, and it's jolly good news. He bought a new phone."

"That is good news," Harry said, trying to sound upbeat and cheerful.

Candice was less thrilled. She had hoped for something related to her situation. "When he spoke to you on it did he say anything about me?"

"I'm afraid that isn't so good," Delia replied. "All his attempts at cracking the case thus far have proved unsuccessful but do not despair. There is hope. On Monday he's going to speak to Mr Kienholtzer."

"Kienholtzer?" Harry asked.

"He's very big in Germany." Delia allowed herself to drift away from the conversation and looked thoughtful. "At seven feet tall he's big in any country. He has a devil of a job buying clothes. They have to be made-to-measure."

"Delia..."

"Even his socks."

"Yes, that's very interesting but who is he?" Harry was able to finish.

"Who?"

"Kienholtzer."

She answered in a manner to suggest he should have known. "He's head of Paranormal Research at Leipzig University. Did I not tell you that?"

"No, you didn't," he replied.

"Goodness, how remiss of me. He and the Professor have worked together in the past on a whole range of subjects spanning the paranormal field. With two such brilliant minds working on our behalf I'm confident we will make the breakthrough in a matter of days."

"That sounds promising," Candice said, nodding her approval.

Harry was disappointed that the Professor alone had failed to solve their problem and they were no further ahead than they were a week ago. "Yes, and the Professor has a new phone. All we need now is a pair of socks for Kienholtzer and the day will have gotten off to the perfect start," he said sarcastically.

Delia rose above his negative response, mainly because she had a question to ask Candice and hadn't been listening to him. "Would it be all right if I attended your memorial service today? I know I'm a stranger to the village and have no right to ask but I would like to pay my respects."

"That's really kind of you, Delia. I would love you to attend," Candice replied.

"Thank you very much. It's awfully decent of you."

"Don't stand there talking to yourself, you stupid cow. Get out of the way," a man barked as he pushed past her.

He worked for a TV company and was striding towards his van. Candice and Harry didn't like his attitude and joined forces to do something about it.

As he approached a water dispenser Harry lifted a cable off the ground. The man tripped over it and fell down. Candice turned on the tap, giving him a good soaking.

Having taught him a lesson in manners, she returned to Delia.

"That's what happens when people mess with our friends," she said.

"I think I should finish him off with number twelve," Harry growled, standing over him.

"Maybe we should leave it the way it is," Candice suggested.

"It worked on the pranksters last night. I've never seen anyone run so fast."

It was the first Candice had heard of it and she looked at him questionably.

"Pranksters?"

"Yes. The UFO sightings remain unexplained but I've solved the mystery of the aliens that have been seen around the village. It was a couple of teenagers. They were taking it in turns to dress up as one. I saw them last night and scared them off. While I'm standing here can I at least stick the boot in?" he asked, staring at the man again.

"That would be a no," Candice told him.

Delia looked at her watch. She had things to do. If she was going to attend the memorial service she had to prepare for it. "I'd better be going. I need to select something to wear for this afternoon." She turned to walk away but stopped and looked back at them. "It was jolly nice of you to beat up that dreadful man for me. And for calling me a friend."

She wiped away a tear as she left.

"What do you make of that?" Harry asked, rejoining Candice.

"I know she can't get your name right and sometimes

she's a bit over-zealous but our Delia is okay."

Harry looked at the man drenched in water. He was sitting in a puddle. "We make a good team you and I. If you ever changed your views on haunting we could cut a path of mayhem clear across Kent and the home counties."

"And Kansas and Missouri and Oklahoma," Candice replied in a fine Warren Beatty impersonation.

"What?"

She smiled. "Come on, Clyde. I wanna see what they're doing in the church."

*

Miss Blunt refused to be interviewed for *USA Today* as she left the Church of St Mary when the service had been concluded. She didn't appreciate having a microphone thrust in her face, nor did she welcome the question '*Did you know Candice Freeman well? It must be a terrible loss.*' She left the reporter in no doubt that she considered him to be a buffoon and marched to her cottage.

"What did you think of the service today?" he asked Maggie when she left with Ron soon after.

"Not now," she said.

She could barely speak. She was close to tears.

Ron cut him a hard glance and took her back to the Coaching Inn. Brenda and Mike followed. They ignored the reporter when the question was asked of them.

The service had gone well and Brenda remained composed throughout. Only once did she dab away a tear, when Ian read a tribute sent by the actor Trent

Cartwright. He had been invited but filming commitments in Washington meant he was unable to attend. The singer Beth Hammond was another reluctant absentee. She was on tour in China but she too paid tribute in a live satellite link. Shanghai was seven hours ahead of the UK, it was 7:30 in the evening there and she was on stage, but she interrupted her concert to take part. Her words moved everyone present, as did her performance of the ballad *Lost Without You*, a song she had written for Candice after her death.

Ian wanted the service to be a celebration of Candice's life and that was how it transpired. There were hymns and readings, heads bowed in prayer, but the overriding feeling was one of love and respect, gratitude in memory of a woman who had the world at her feet and could have lived anywhere but chose to live with them. In doing so she had enriched their lives. Maggie found it hard to control her emotions, Miss Blunt too, but there was no breaking down or displays of grief as Candice had feared.

"What is your one lasting memory of Candice Freeman?"

"She didn't ask irritating questions," Janet replied as she left the church with Martin, Samantha and Melanie.

The reporter gave up at this point.

He drew his hand across his throat in a signal to cut camera and let his microphone hand drop to his side. It was like trying to get blood out of a stone. Then he saw Emily and Grantley being interviewed by a Spanish TV crew and gave serious thought to changing his profession. His father wanted him to be a milkman.

He considered becoming a high-speed vicar when Ian rushed past him in pursuit of Samantha as she walked to her car.

"Sam, do you have a moment?" he called.

She turned to look at him.

Janet had already left for home but Martin was taking Melanie back to school and kissed Samantha on the cheek as he said goodbye.

"Have a great time in Paris. Be safe," he told her.

"I will. I'll see you next week. Bye, Mel."

"Bye."

Melanie wasn't interested in Samantha's travel plans. She didn't even look at her as she waited in Martin's car, her attention was focused on her mobile phone. What was more important? Her sister going to boring old France or texting her friends to tell them about the service she had attended? Yeah, no contest.

Samantha walked back a short way to meet Ian.

"I know you have to get back to work but I have a favour to ask," he said.

"Okay."

"Mike and I are worried about Brenda. She isn't coping with Candice's death. I think it might help if she visited Meadow Cottage. It would give her an opportunity to reflect in surroundings that she and Candice knew well. It might allow her to move on."

Samantha nodded. She thought it was a good idea. "Yes, of course. I don't have a problem with that."

"The thing is it would have to be this evening. I'm sorry to throw this on you at short notice but they're going back to London tomorrow."

That was a problem.

"I'm going out this evening. It's Sally's last day at work. She's on maternity leave from tomorrow so we're going out for drinks."

"Should Sally be drinking in her condition?"

Samantha smiled. "She'll be on orange juice."

"I'm glad to hear it."

"Brenda can still come over. Delia will be there. If Brenda wants some time on her own she can make herself scarce."

"You're sure it's no trouble? I don't want to inconvenience you."

"It's no inconvenience. I like Brenda and I'm sorry to hear things aren't going well for her. I'm happy to help in any way I can."

"Thank you, Sam."

"It may sound an odd question but does she know what's going on? If Brenda thought we were conspiring to help her she would regard it as charity and have nothing to do with it. You know how stubborn she is."

Ian knew it only too well. Brenda had a proud streak that made her confident and as hard as nails but in this instance it wasn't an issue.

Mike had told her straight that she couldn't carry on as she was and visiting Meadow Cottage would be the first step in reclaiming her life. Brenda recalled a frightened pensioner standing in front of her car and too many days and nights spent throwing herself into work. She agreed, at last, that something had to be done. For the first time since Candice's death she acknowledged that she needed help to come to terms with it.

"She knows it's not a casual visit," Ian said. "Mike was honest and open with her when they talked. I think Brenda will find it difficult but hopefully she'll be better for it."

"Then it's agreed. Shall we say eight o'clock?"

"Yes. I'll let them know."

"I'll check with Delia but I'm sure she doesn't have

anything planned for this evening."

"Okay. Thanks again, Sam."

Samantha embraced him and kissed his cheek. "It was a beautiful service, Ian. You got the balance just right."

"Thank you. I think Candice liked it. She kept giving me the thumbs-up from the aisle."

Samantha laughed and walked to her car.

Ian returned to the church.

No sooner had her key found the ignition, Samantha was again prevented from leaving. If she had been delayed much longer she would have been late for work twice in one day. That *would* have been a record.

"Samantha, may I have a word?"

"Of course, Norman," she said, smiling at Grantley through her open window.

"Would it be possible for me to visit the stables tomorrow? I know you said you're always open to visitors but I thought I should check with you first. I don't want to turn up unannounced when you might be busy."

"No, tomorrow would be fine. Feel free to come along whenever you want."

"Thank you. I'll stop by in the afternoon."

"I'll look forward to seeing you. Don't forget, training and a shovel can be provided," she added, switching on her engine.

"I think I'll leave that side of things to the professionals," he replied, grinning. "Enjoy the rest of your day."

"You too. Bye."

Grantley watched her drive away and crossed an important item off his things-to-do list. He needed to know Samantha's schedule prior to her abduction on

Friday. What time would she get home from work? What time was her friend picking her up? Would Delia be there? He would have to think of a way to get her out of the house if she was.

He couldn't snatch Samantha when she finished work. A kidnapping carried out on a quiet country road miles from nowhere appealed to him but he would have been left with the problem of what to do with her car. In order to further the illusion that she was in Paris it had to be garaged at home. Presumably she would have packed a case or an overnight bag. That would have to be removed. There could be nothing left at the cottage to suggest that she hadn't gone to France as planned.

A visit to the stables followed by a pleasant chat over a cup of tea would have answered all those questions. Just as importantly it would have provided him with a reason for calling on her the next day.

The moment of his triumph was almost upon him.

Have a pleasant afternoon, Samantha. There are so few left ahead of you.

*

Brenda arrived at Meadow Cottage on the stroke of eight o'clock. She was met by a smiling Delia who stood aside in the doorway to let her in.

"Hello. You must be Brenda."

"Yes. Delia?"

"That's right, Delia Truebody." She shook her hand so vigorously it was a wonder it didn't come off. "I'm jolly pleased to meet you. Tea?"

"That would be nice. Thank you."

She followed Delia to the kitchen.

It was the first time Brenda had been back to Meadow Cottage since she and Mike sorted through Candice's belongings a week after her death. Emily and Miss Blunt helped them in their task, a duty they never expected to have to perform. Brenda felt like a criminal going through her things, a snooper reading personal documents and making an inventory of possessions. It didn't seem right. It was Candice's home, her life, everything that made her who she was. Now it was in the hands of others who were there for one reason and one reason only; to catalogue that life and put it into storage until her estate had been settled.

"Samantha asked me to convey her apologies for not being here to meet you," Delia told Brenda as she switched on the kettle. "She said she would catch up with you the next time you're in the village."

Brenda nodded.

"You were Miss Freeman's agent, weren't you?"

"Yes."

"I'm very sorry for your loss."

It seemed an odd thing to say a year after Candice's death but Brenda took it for what it was; genuine sympathy from a caring woman.

"Thank you. Are you staying as a house guest for long?" she asked.

"About a week or so. It's rather hard to tell really."

"How do you know Samantha?"

"We met by chance in the village. I arrived at the same time as the UFO watchers but I'm not one of them. I'm just driving around. See where the road leads me sort of thing. Samantha and I got talking and she offered to put me up for a while."

That seemed odd too. Samantha was kind and

considerate to others but wasn't given to taking strangers in off the street. Brenda assumed that when they got talking they hit it off immediately. She could see no other reason for it.

"Where do you live?"

"When I'm not in the van I live in Reading," Delia replied. "Milk and sugar?"

"Milk please. No sugar."

"Good for you. I'm trying to cut down on that myself," she said, preparing the cups. "It must be awfully exciting being a theatrical agent, working with such talented people."

Brenda smiled. "It has its moments. Some of them only think they're talented. What do you do?"

Delia didn't want to confide that she was a paranormal investigator in search of ghosts and snatched the first thing that came to mind. She tried to appear enthusiastic but in her eagerness to hide the truth she made it sound like the most boring job known to man. "I work in an office selling paint."

"That sounds... colourful," Brenda replied weakly.

"I get lots of free samples. My kitchen looks like a rainbow with a headache. It's one of the reasons I leave it so often to go on the road."

Brenda didn't know what to do with that.

"Your tea."

"Thank you," she said, taking it from her.

"I'm going to pop out to the garden. Perhaps you would like to make yourself comfortable in the lounge?"

It was an awkward attempt at raising the subject of why Brenda had gone there and Delia hunched her shoulders nervously.

Brenda smiled again to put her at ease. "Yes, I think

I will. Thank you, Delia."

"Give me a shout if you need me for anything."

She went outside.

Brenda returned to the lounge. She put her cup and saucer on the coffee table and stood in the centre of a room that was cosy and familiar. Samantha had redecorated and most of the furniture was new but Brenda saw beyond the changes and remembered Meadow Cottage as it was the first time she had seen it. It was the day Candice moved in. Brenda had promised to help with the move but arrived late and most of the heavy work was done by the time she got there.

'Did everything go okay with the removal firm?'

'They broke my guitar. The one you bought for me in Canada," Candice had lied.

'What! That guitar cost five hundred dollars.'

'You told me it cost a thousand.'

'Oh, did I?'

'Yeah, you went to great lengths to tell me. Usually when we had to settle the cheque in restaurants.'

Brenda looked at the guitar on its stand in the corner of the room. Candice played it well but Samantha played it better and more often.

'Have you had lunch yet?'

'No, I've been busy.'

'Let's go to the pub.'

'Bren, this place looks like a storage facility. I ain't got time for lunch.'

'Haven't. I haven't got time for lunch. Better yet, have not.'

Brenda was a stickler for the correct use of the English language. Candice was an American who adapted it to suit her needs. Why say 'have not' when 'ain't' meant the same thing and tripped off the tongue easier? It was like people who said 'aluminium' instead of 'aluminum.' What was all that about?

'I could find another agent you know.'

'Yes, but would she buy you lunch and help to unpack your boxes afterwards?'

'You're buying?'

'Well, depending on what you have. That guitar cost a thousand dollars.'

'You said it cost five hundred.'

'Stop laying traps for me. Do you want lunch or not?'

Brenda strummed the guitar strings with her forefinger as she stood over it. She smiled. It was a happy memory.

One not so good took its place when she looked at Samantha's answering machine on the sideboard. It stood where Candice's desk had once been.

'Candice... Mike's had a heart attack. He's in Victoria General... I don't know what to do.'

Candice did. She drove to London immediately and stayed at Brenda's side during the worst three days of her life. When Mike was well enough to travel she insisted that they stayed with her in Cloverdale St Mary. It was only for a weekend but the fresh air and change of scenery did him the world of good.

Brenda went upstairs and stood outside the attic room door. Her thoughts turned once more to the day Candice moved in.

She had come across a box containing books that Candice intended to store in the attic. By now it was late evening and they were relaxing over a drink but Brenda got it into her head that the box should have been taken up there and then and nagged Candice to seize the moment. Reluctantly she agreed and they carried it upstairs. It was the heaviest thing either woman had ever lifted and when they got there they dropped the box to the floor and rested against the wall like their lives depended on it.

'You'll thank me for this when it's done,' Candice had said, mocking Brenda's words of wisdom prior to leaving the lounge.

'Don't give me a lecture... I think I've snapped something.'

'You wouldn't have anything left to snap if I had the strength to get my hands on you. You're meant to bring wine and flowers to a new house, not suffering and misery. You should be locked up.'

'You should get a lift. Come on, we've done the hardest part. Let's take it inside. When you've opened the door grab an end.'

'What I need to grab is an oxygen mask.'

Candice turned the doorknob but it wouldn't open. Unknown to them, the ghost of Harry Black was standing on the other side preventing them from gaining entry. They abandoned their efforts and Candice took the box in by herself the next day.

Brenda turned the doorknob to go in but it wouldn't open. Unknown to her, the ghost of Harry black was standing on the other side.

She went downstairs and returned to the lounge where she sat on the sofa with her cup of tea.

"I miss you," she said to the empty room.

"And I miss you, Bren."

Candice was sitting in the armchair opposite her.

Brenda reacted calmly to the sound of her voice. She wasn't shocked or disturbed by it. She was convinced it was inside her head. "How am I meant to carry on without you? You were my best friend."

"I will be again. When the time is right I'll come back to you. I promise."

"Do you remember how I was opposed to your

coming here?"

"You said the novelty would wear off in six months."

Brenda looked around the room again. It was still Candice's home. It always would be. "I was wrong. Moving to Cloverdale St Mary was the best thing you ever did. I see that now. The friends you made here, the way you were accepted, the way you accepted them. You didn't have to work at it. It happened easily because you were special. The world will never know another like you."

Candice appreciated the compliment but was under no illusions. She wouldn't have achieved the success she enjoyed by her efforts alone. It took people as gifted as her to make it possible. It took Brenda and her unshakable faith in her. "I have you to thank for that. You saw me through some difficult times, you kept me sane when it would have been easier to have lost control and gone crazy. I would have been just another hopeful actor struggling to pay the rent if it wasn't for you."

"Are you happy?"

"Yeah, I'm very happy. I'm with Harry now. You haven't met him but you will some day. When mom died she told me there is always love. It was the last thing she said to me. She was right. Some of it stays behind but the rest you take with you. That's how it is with Harry and me." She smiled and corrected herself. "Harry and I. It's the way it is with you and Mike. It doesn't matter what we achieve in life. We can have it all and be the saddest person in the world. When the credits roll at the end it doesn't mean a thing. It's love that counts. The way I love you and you love me. That's what keeps our two worlds joined. It's what keeps us together."

"They held a memorial service for you today. That's why Mike and I are here. You would have liked it."

"I'm glad you guys came."

"And now it's time to move on. I would do it if I knew how."

She began to cry.

"You know how to, Bren. You've always known."

Brenda composed herself. This was no place to shed tears, not in a house that had offered Candice a new start and would do the same for her.

Recollections good and bad drifted in and out of her thoughts and she found a glimmer of hope in each one. Grief was still her Master, it would be for a long time to come, but in the lounge of Meadow Cottage it didn't hurt so much. A raging pain became less savage and she was able to see beyond it.

She talked with Candice without realising it for a further twenty minutes.

Twenty-five

Grantley arrived at the stables at 2:00 p.m. Samantha gave him a guided tour that was nearing an end as they watched Jo Jo graze in the back paddock.

"That's a fine looking animal. Who does it belong to?" he asked.

"She belonged to Candice. She's Mel's now."

Grantley raised his eyebrow in surprise. Jo Jo was a strong, powerful horse. Melanie was a schoolgirl, slight in build and not as strong. He wondered how she would have been able to manage her.

"Melanie can control a horse of that size?"

Samantha smiled. "Mel is an experienced rider. She was practically born in the saddle. She only started to ride her recently. Despite her experience we wanted to be sure she was ready to handle a horse of Jo Jo's strength. She's doing really well. A bond has developed between them. Now it's time to take it to the next level."

"Mutual trust between horse and rider must be very important."

"It's the key to everything. Without trust on both sides there is no relationship. If there is no relationship there is no bond."

"It becomes a team effort."

"That's right. Mel has two horses. The other is Misty, a fourteen-hand Welsh cob. We were concerned when we learnt Candice had bequeathed Jo Jo to her. We thought Mel might have devoted all her attention to her new mount and spent less time with Misty but we had no reason to worry. It's that bond you see. Once you have it it can't be broken. She loves them both equally. Truth be told, Misty has never had it so good."

"You're very proud of Melanie. I can hear it in your voice."

"She can be a right pain sometimes."

Grantley laughed. "Show me a younger sibling who isn't."

"Yeah, I suppose so. Have you enjoyed the tour?"

"Every moment of it. Thank you for taking the time to show me around. And not once did you threaten me with a shovel."

"I'll do that on your next visit, Norman. Would you like a cup of tea? I have a kettle in my office."

"Refreshments too. I will definitely come here more often, shovels or no shovels."

They left the back paddock and returned to the yard.

As they crossed it to Samantha's office Miss Blunt approached them. She held an envelope aloft in her left hand, rather like Neville Chamberlain proclaiming peace in our time.

"Samantha, I have correspondence for you. It was delivered to the school in error," she said.

"The postman is always doing that," Samantha told Grantley. "Thank you," she said, taking it from Miss Blunt when she arrived.

"Good afternoon, Norman. I did not expect to find you here."

"I expressed an interest in seeing the stables. Samantha kindly offered to show me around."

"What do you think of them?" Miss Blunt asked.

"I'm impressed. The horses are content and well looked after and the stables themselves are spotless. Take a look around this yard. There isn't so much as a broom out of place. That's a sign of good management."

Samantha grinned at the compliment. "Thank you."

Miss Blunt nodded favourably. It was nice to receive positive feedback. "I am glad you have enjoyed your visit. Perhaps you would care to see the school while you are here?"

"Would that be possible?"

"I see no reason why not. Unless you are in a hurry to leave of course."

"No, far from it. I was about to have tea with Samantha. Maybe I can stop by afterwards."

"By all means. I will see you there."

Miss Blunt bid them farewell and returned to the school.

"You're having an equestrian day," Samantha said as she led him inside her office. She gestured to a sofa in the corner of the room. "Please, make yourself comfortable."

"Thank you," he replied, sitting down. "Yes, it's a new experience for me. As I said before I don't know the first thing about horses but that's something I'm eager to change now I live in a village where they form a part of everyday life. You don't get many of them in Harley Street," he added, grinning.

"I imagine not. Milk and sugar?" Samantha asked, attending to the tea.

"Just sugar please."

"Are you thinking of buying a horse?"

Grantley smiled. "I'm a bit long in the tooth to take up horse riding."

"You're never too old to learn, Norman. A lot of people turn to it in their retirement years. The oldest person we have on our books is seventy-eight. She comes twice a week and hacks for an hour. She says it keeps her young."

"Maybe there is something to be said for it."

"Speak to Miss Blunt or myself if you want advise on the subject. We'll be more than happy to help."

"I'll bear that in mind."

Samantha gave Grantley his tea and sat beside him. She had no way of knowing this time tomorrow their roles would have been reversed. She would be the guest but the hospitality shown to her would not have been so kind.

"I hear you're off to Paris this weekend," he said.

"Yes. A friend of mine recently got divorced. It was a messy one I'm afraid. She wanted to get away for a couple of days and invited me along."

"How many of you are going?"

"Just three of us."

"It's not an invasion then."

Samantha laughed. "No, although the locals might think it is. My friends can be a bit loud when they're in party mode."

"I hope you have a wonderful time. It's a shame you'll miss the fête on Saturday though."

"Yeah, that is a pity. It will be the first one I haven't attended."

"What time do you leave tomorrow?"

"Xanthe is picking me up at three. I'm working in the morning but I'll be home just after midday. Then we go to Canningwell to collect Charlotte and from there to London to get the Eurostar."

"Which of those is the divorcee?"

"Charlotte. She and her husband were only married two years. In all honesty they shouldn't have got married at all." Samantha sighed and recalled how she and her friends had tried to talk her out of it. "It wasn't a match made in heaven. I'm surprised they stayed together as long as they did."

"Doomed from the start?"

"Something like that."

"Aren't you worried about leaving Meadow Cottage unattended in light of the burglaries?"

"It should be all right. Delia will be there."

"Oh yes, I forgot about your house guest. She seems like a nice woman."

"Yeah, she is. I've got used to having her around the place."

"Is she staying with you much longer?"

"Another week or so."

"I'm glad to know the cottage will be in safe hands while you're away. Will she be there to see you off?"

"I expect so. She's usually there at that time of day."

Grantley's questions had been answered. Now he could finalise his plans for Samantha's abduction.

He had to get Delia out of the house before Xanthe arrived but that wouldn't have presented a problem. He would tell her he had been contacted by someone who claimed they could help to solve the puzzle of Candice's disappearances and send her to Falworth on a wild goose chase. While Delia waited to meet them Grantley could make his move. The three-hour window of opportunity gave him all the time he needed.

He also knew what to do about Harry. He couldn't be at the cottage either. Sending a ghost on a fool's errand wasn't an option but there were other ways to ensure his absence. Grantley had an ace up his sleeve when Candice was under his control. Removing Harry from the scene of the crime would have been simplicity in itself.

Samantha didn't see Grantley stare at her wrist as

she raised her cup to her lips. She had no idea what he was thinking.

Such delicate skin. How easily it will bruise.

He imagined the iron shackles securing her hands and feet, the chains that would make escape impossible, but she wouldn't die in them. Samantha would meet her death in what had been inside the wooden crate on the day he moved into Brook Cottage.

*

Brenda had decided to stay in Cloverdale St Mary for a few more days. Visiting Meadow Cottage had been good for her and she wanted to attend the fête. It would have been the first one Candice had attended too. The year she moved to the village it was held early. She arrived two weeks later. The next one took place a month after her death but she and Harry were in Tahiti and missed it.

Mike had returned to London earlier that morning and said he would go back to the village to take Brenda home on Sunday but she wouldn't hear of it and insisted on getting the train. Miss Blunt offered to drive her to the station and Mike left Brenda in safe and trusted hands. The change in her was already noticeable and he felt confident that a few more days spent relaxing in Cloverdale St Mary would have been the best thing for her.

Candice was glad she was staying too.

"Have you finished packing for Sam yet?" Harry asked her as they roamed the fields beyond Cross Drummond. It was one of their favourite places to go walking.

Candice grinned. "I'm not packing for her."

"How many times are you going to say her passport is on the coffee table? The last count was two hundred and five."

"I don't want her to forget it."

"You've pointed to it so often she'll probably take the table by mistake."

"It's beautiful here, isn't it?" she said, changing the subject.

"I know a better field not far from here. It has cows in it."

"I'm not gonna look at cows."

"You make me look at horses."

"That's different."

"How is it different?"

Candice sighed. "Do you know of many cows that can gallop and jump over fences?"

"I know of one that jumped over the moon. I would like to see a horse do that."

Candice rolled her eyes. Harry in cow mode was difficult to have a conversation with. "What time is it?"

"Half past cow."

She laughed. "Be serious."

"My watch stopped when my heart did so I'm not sure but I think it's about six o'clock. Why? Are you late for an appointment?"

"Bren is having dinner with Emily and Norman at seven. I wanna watch them eat."

"Nor-man," Harry said in a child-like voice. "Personally I would like to see him choke."

"Come on, Harry. That's a bit strong, even for you."

"Why does everyone like him?"

"Why do you dislike him?"

"I asked my question first."

Candice couldn't give a specific reason. There was just something about Grantley that made him likeable. "I dunno. He's nice."

"So was Hitler when he wasn't invading Poland."

"You're comparing Norman Grantley to Adolf Hitler?"

"I'm not sure what I'm comparing him too. He's up to something. I can feel it in my bones."

"You ain't got bones."

"Haven't got bones. Better yet, have not. Don't forget, Brenda is in the village."

Candice laughed again.

"It's good to see you so relaxed," Harry said.

"Where did that come from?"

"Things haven't been easy for you. It's been a worrying time."

"It hasn't been easy for you either."

"No, but I'm not the one being threatened by some unknown force. You're handling it really well. You dealt with the memorial service well too. You weren't exactly looking forward to it, were you?"

"It went better than I expected. Ian did a great job. That reminds me, I haven't thanked him yet. I'll swing by later."

"Make it supper time. You can watch him eat too."

"Are you coming to the Coaching Inn with me this evening?"

"Yes, I'll come. Maybe Grantley will slip up and give himself away. Then you can tell me I was right all along and beg my forgiveness."

"You do know that will never happen, don't you?"

"A gracious ghost admits when they're wrong."

"Who said I was gracious? Come on, let's head back. I like to watch Ron fold the napkins too."

*

"What is that supposed to be?"

"It's what we in the trade call a dinner napkin," Ron said to Maggie as she inspected his handiwork.

"You were meant to fold them, not demonstrate your origami skills. It looks like a whippet impaled on a metal spike."

"It looks like a kangaroo to me," Candice told Harry.

"It's a cow," he replied confidently.

Maggie looked at Brenda, Emily and Grantley in turn and apologized. "I'm sorry. I'll fetch napkins that you can actually use."

"That can be used," Ron protested.

"Yes, as a sign to keep dogs away from sharp objects."

"My talents are wasted here," he mumbled, following Maggie as she left their table.

"So, Brenda, are you looking forward to the fête on Saturday?" Grantley asked.

"Yes, I am. I'm not really a summer fête person but Emily has told me so much about the ones here I thought it would be nice to stay for it."

"It will be my first one too," he said.

"Have you looked out anything for the bring and buy stalls?" Emily asked him.

"I went through my record collection and selected a few LPs I don't play anymore. Mainly classical. Easy listening, that sort of thing. They might fetch a couple of pounds."

"That's good of you," Brenda said. "How many are there?"

"Eighty-six."

Emily almost choked on her Minsk. "That's more than I have in my *entire* collection."

Grantley smiled. Her reaction amused him. "I have a lot of records but I listen to CDs mostly. People say vinyl sounds better but I disagree. The slightest scratch ruins the listening experience. As someone who is clumsy with records, CDs are much better."

"Where does the money raised go?" Brenda asked Emily.

"A hospice in Falworth. We support it every year."

"An excellent cause," Grantley said, raising his glass. "Let's hope the weather holds fair and the fête is a huge success."

"I'll drink to that," Brenda said, joining in with the impromptu toast.

"I feel sick - and it's not Ron's cow-on-a-spike that's doing it," Harry muttered so Emily wouldn't hear.

"Behave," Candice told him. "Em, ask Brenda if she sees anything of David Kitrow these days. Tell her I mentioned him to you one time. He bought something that isn't usually for sale at bring and buy stalls."

"Do you see anything of David Kitrow?"

Brenda laughed. "David? My God. What made you ask about him?"

"Candice once told me he bought something unusual at a bring and buy stall."

"What was it?" Grantley asked.

Emily didn't know but made a good job of deflecting. "I'm sure Brenda could tell the story better than I."

Brenda smiled and shook her head. What happened to David Kitrow was several years previously. She had quite forgotten about it.

"David went to a fête in Camden one Saturday. He was perusing the bring and buy stalls but nothing of interest caught his eye, except a woman who was running one of them. He gave her a five pound note and asked her to marry him. They went on a date on the Sunday and got married on the Monday."

"Good heavens," Grantley said. "Are they still together?"

"Yeah. The last I heard they had four kids and were living in Waltham-on-Thames."

"It just goes to show, there are some happy endings."

"He's not going to propose another toast, is he?" Harry whispered.

"I see there are still some UFO watchers in the village," Grantley said by way of changing the subject. "The ambulance has gone but the family from Bristol and the man in the tent are still on the green."

"They will have to move by tomorrow afternoon. That's when most of the stalls are being set up. Ian is erecting the marquee too," Emily announced.

"Let's hope he does it better than the year before last," Harry said. "It fell down twice. The second time Prudence was inside. They had to dig her out."

"What time are they setting up?" Grantley asked.

"About two o'clock I think."

This was something Grantley hadn't considered in his abduction plans. Samantha's arrival at Brook Cottage would have gone undetected. She would be in the boot of his car which he intended to drive straight into his garage. There was a connecting door between it and the kitchen so no one would have seen him take her inside but he didn't like the idea of so many people being nearby at the time. His cottage was practically on the green, too close for comfort if something had gone wrong. Setting up at 2:00 p.m. cut an hour off his window of opportunity. Erring on the side of caution, he decided to abduct Samantha at one o'clock.

Harry saw that Grantley's thoughts had travelled elsewhere and wondered why. It wasn't like him to drift away into private moments but he was drawn back to the conversation when Emily spoke again.

"The ufologists are still here too."

They looked at them in conversation at their usual table by the window.

"At least they won't be hindered by the pranksters now," she added.

"Pranksters?" Grantley asked.

"Yes, didn't you hear? The aliens that were seen around the village was a prank staged by a couple of teenagers. One of the night patrols discovered them. One had fainted in bushes and the other was found wandering in a daze mumbling *'make the horrible thing go away.'* He was holding an alien mask."

Harry whistled nonchalantly and looked at the ceiling.

"What the hell did you do?" Candice asked him.

"I told you. I used number twelve on them."

"You didn't tell me one lost consciousness and the other suffered a mental breakdown."

"He who lives by the sword dies by the sword."

"You scared the crap out of them. One is in a

vegetative state."

"I think you might be over-reacting just a tad."

"Tell that to the kid who's on medication for the rest of his life. Because of you all he has to look forward to is being turned every two hours."

"Candice, it must be said that on occasion you are prone to exaggeration."

"I never exaggerate. I've told you that a billion times."

"I stand by what I did," Harry insisted.

"Which is more than can be said for those kids. They'll be lucky if they ever stand up again. This is why I'm anti fur."

"Pardon me?"

"I mean anti hunting."

"It still needs work."

"Anti haunting."

"That's the one."

Now Candice had started to ramble, she decided it would have been a good time to shut up.

"Have either of you seen strange lights in the sky?" Brenda asked.

"I can't say I have," Emily answered.

"Me neither. The whole thing is a hoax if you ask me," Grantley told Brenda.

"It would make a great film," she replied. "A small village community invaded by aliens from another world. Candice would have been perfect for the lead; the heroine who does battle with them and saves the day."

"You didn't think of that, did you?" Harry said to her.

"Em, tell Brenda to get a script to me by Wednesday and I'll read it."

Emily would have found it difficult to pass on that

message and elected not to.

"There might be a slight problem with you going for a role like that," Harry pointed out.

"What, you don't think I could play a heroine who saves the world?"

"You could if you were alive."

Candice clenched her fists and snarled in frustration. "Dammit. I keep forgetting that."

"Never mind, dear. I'll remember for you."

It was the first time Harry had called Candice 'dear.' The look of disapproval he received in return suggested it might have been better to not do it again.

*

They stayed till one o'clock in the morning. Harry didn't return to Meadow Cottage when they left. He went straight to Emily's. It wasn't a lock-in in the true sense of the word but the police would have regarded it as such. Not that they were seen in the village at that time of night. There were too many burglars around.

Maggie and Ron tilled up at midnight and joined them for drinks. Brenda went to bed after one of the best evenings she could remember. It was strange. Sometimes she felt Candice was there, playing a part in the conversation and joking with them, doing what she used to do before death called her name and evenings like this came to an abrupt end.

She thought of an airliner lying in a field in Connecticut but Candice wasn't in the wreckage. She was in Cloverdale St Mary. She was where she was meant to be. In the memory and hearts of people who loved her.

One such person was Samantha. She slept, unaware that Candice was watching her in her trance-like state.

In the basement of Brook Cottage Grantley made the final preparations for her arrival. He was ready. Candice was ready. Samantha was ready.

Tomorrow, he thought. *It begins tomorrow.*

Tomorrow would be the longest day of Samantha's life, a life that meant nothing to a man driven to extraordinary lengths in pursuit of his goal.

Twenty-six

Melanie woke to sunlight and birdsong outside her window. At three o'clock that morning she had been woken by a nightmare.

She was hysterical, screaming in the darkness of her room as she watched her sister die. She didn't know it was Samantha, she didn't know where it was happening. All she knew was that she felt the woman's final gasps for air catch in her throat and her lungs were set to explode as she launched forward in bed.

Janet and Martin were alerted to the disturbance and went to her room immediately. They tried to comfort and settle her but she was too frightened by the experience to acknowledge their presence. She howled and wept, heart pounding in fear and desperation until exhaustion took her and she fell sobbing into her father's arms. Melanie had nightmares before but never like this.

*

"I don't believe it. You're actually going to be on time," Harry said, looking at Samantha across the breakfast table. "This is one for the diary."

"I'm not late for work that often."

Her response astonished him.

"How many days do you work over the course of a week?" he asked.

"Five."

"How many days were you late last week?"

"Five."

"Why are we having this conversation?"

"Is the answer five?"

Candice smiled. "Are you still on for finishing at midday?"

"Yes," Samantha replied.

"That's when she'll be late," Harry said. "Not going *to* work but coming home from it. She'll probably wander in at ten to six."

"I'm an excellent timekeeper," Samantha insisted.

"What! You can't... you don't... you wouldn't...."

If his voice had gotten any higher his ears would have popped.

"Harry, only dogs can hear you now," Candice said.

"I don't believe the audacity of this woman. You're so late if you were put on a three day week you'd only get in for two of them."

"As much as I would like to debate this, Harry, I have to go."

"That would be Mr Black to you."

"Who is Mr Black?" Delia asked from behind her cereal bowl.

Candice laughed. She loved breakfast time at Meadow Cottage.

"And mow the lawn!" Harry called after Samantha as she left, determined to have the last word.

"What are your plans for today?" Candice asked Delia.

"I'm going to find a man."

Harry frowned. He wasn't opposed to Delia embarking on a relationship that may have led to lifelong happiness but the timing could have been better. "Shouldn't you be trying to help Candice?"

"I never needed help in that department," she boasted.

"I think I might be on to something," Delia told them. "I've been researching the Paranormal Archives online. In August last year a medium by the name of Alex Crosby claimed to have been contacted by a spirit in distress. He was jolly shaken by the experience. The spirit told him she was being influenced by something unknown to her. She felt it wanted to gain control of her in some way. The spirit appeared to him several times, each time more distressed, then it stopped. He hasn't seen her since."

"What is familiar about this picture?" Candice said thoughtfully.

"I don't have a phone number for Crosby but I'm going to dig around in the hope of finding one. The similarities between that case and yours are too strong to ignore. I really need to speak with him."

"Have you told the Professor about this?" Harry asked.

"Not yet. I made the discovery last night. It was too late to call him but I'll let him know asap."

"Keep us posted," Harry said.

"Absolutely. What are you doing today?"

"We're going to Norwich," Candice replied.

It was the first Harry had heard of it.

"Are we?"

"We're gonna track down that couple who reported seeing the lights over Cross Drummond and solve the UFO mystery."

Harry liked the idea of turning detective but thought Candice had chosen the wrong way to go about it. "I can't see them helping us much. In order to get to the bottom of it we need to find whoever sent that picture to the newspapers."

"I think it was them. They planned the whole thing while they were here on their camping holiday. First they claim to have seen strange lights in the sky. A few days later they produce a photograph to back it up. Call it a gut feeling but I'd bet my last Benjamin Franklin that's what happened."

Delia was puzzled. Her command of the North American language was poor. "Benjamin Franklin?"

"His picture is on the hundred dollar bill," Harry enlightened her.

"Oh."

Candice had given it a lot of thought and was sure she was right. She wasn't a believer in coincidence. The chances of the report and the photograph coming from different sources within a few days of each other were slim to non-existent.

"You caught the local pranksters - by using methods I'd rather not dwell on – and now it's time to catch the ones who started it all," she told Harry. "We'll have this thing put to bed by this evening."

"We'll need to do it by three o'clock if were going to see Samantha off."

She looked at him tiredly. "Yeah, like it will take hours for us to get to and from Norwich."

"When we find these people can I use number twelve to get a confession out of them?"

"No."

"Number fourteen?"

"No."

"What about number ninety-six?"

Candice was horrified. "The last time you used that one the guy threw himself under a train. They never did find his head."

It was at this point that Delia decided she had eaten enough cereal.

*

"I'm glad you phoned, Professor. I have something to tell you."

"Later, Delia. This is important," Grantley said from the lounge of Brook Cottage. "There has been a development that requires our immediate attention."

"Gosh, it sounds quite urgent. What is it?"

"I received an anonymous call earlier this morning from a woman who claims to be able to help us. She said she knows what is happening to the ghost of Candice Freeman."

"She mentioned Candice by name?"

"Yes. It took me completely by surprise. Are you aware of anyone else who knows of her existence?"

"No, Professor. Only the people I told you about."

Grantley paused to create the illusion of a man deep in thought. "Fascinating. However, we have much to do. This woman has asked to meet with me. She's going to be at the Millstream at one o'clock this afternoon. The problem is I can't make it. I have a call scheduled for that time with Lance Cunningham at the Institute for Psychical Research in New York. I think he may be of help to us too. I need you to go to Falworth to meet her on my behalf. Will you do that for me?"

"Yes. Yes, of course. How will I recognize her?"

"She said she'll be in the beer garden. She'll be

wearing a *Back to Basics* T-shirt. It's a pop group I'm given to understand."

"Yes. They're awfully good."

"I bow to your greater knowledge of popular music." Grantley made no attempt to hide the condescending tone in his voice. "She'll be sitting by the door in the wall that allows access to the main road. The fact that she knows the lay-out of the garden leads me to think she's a local woman."

"Yes, I see what you mean."

"Find out all you can and call me the moment you get back. This could be the breakthrough we've been waiting for."

"I do hope so, Professor. Should I mention this to Candice?"

"It can't do any harm. It may go some way to offering reassurance that something is being done to assist her. Of course, you won't be able to mention me in any of this. You'll have to say she contacted you."

"Yes, quite. Are you sure you want me to call after I've met with her? It might be better if I came to your cottage and told you what she said in person."

"I don't know if I'll be here. I may have to go out after I've spoken to Cunningham. Probably better to phone me."

"Okay."

"Thank you, Delia. I'll speak to you later."

Grantley ended the call.

Delia realised she hadn't told him *her* news but it didn't matter now. She wouldn't have needed to find Alex Crosby if the mystery woman was in a position to help. She thought of Candice and Harry somewhere in Norwich and wished they were at home. Grantley was right. It *was* an important development and they should have known about it.

*

The newspaper journalist leaned back in his chair exasperated. He didn't like computers. He was old school and hankered for the distant days at the start of his career when he banged out proof on a typewriter. Now it was email, page formatting and copy and paste. *Computers rule the world* they said but he failed to see how this one could have ruled anything when it kept going potty every time he touched the keyboard.

"What is wrong with this thing?" he cried to his colleagues in the office. "Whenever I press a key it goes back to that damn UFO story."

"Yes, a story I'm trying to read," Harry said, using the down arrow to scroll through it.

"Does it give a name and address?" Candice asked, trying to press the up arrow.

"That's what I'm looking for. Leave it alone," he told her, gesturing to slap her hand away.

The journalist sat forward at his desk and pressed return for the fifth time.

"Do you mind?" Harry snapped, pressing back space.

"Dammit! This thing is going out the window if it doesn't do what I want."

Striking the side of the monitor with his hand was never going to help.

"Aha! The source's name and address," Harry announced with gusto. "Do you have a pen?" he asked

Candice.

"Do you have a pen?" she asked the journalist.

"Does anyone have a pen?" he asked his colleagues. "It would be quicker for me to write about Mrs Boggins' bloody cat being stuck up a tree."

"I think we'll have to memorise it," Candice told Harry.

"Duly noted," he confirmed.

Harry turned off the PC and he and Candice left.

"I don't believe it," the journalist moaned. "Now it's shut down completely."

"Mrs Boggins doesn't have a cat," a disinterested voice said from the next desk.

*

The house in Fairfield Avenue wasn't what Candice and Harry had expected. The front garden was immaculate and the back looked like it had won several awards. The landscaping was the best they had seen for a property of this size.

The house itself was detached and had been recently painted. A double garage stood beside it. A flower trough had been fixed to the wall beneath the lounge window and more plants hung in baskets around the front door. It was picture-perfect suburbia. Candice considered selling Meadow Cottage and making them an offer.

"Shall we?" Harry said, gesturing towards it.

Candice put aside her reluctance to snoop around people's homes and followed him when he went in.

The house was empty and they explored it room by room. Candice didn't like the kitchen, it wasn't up to the standard of what they had seen thus far, but the lounge was light and spacious and the master bedroom was one to die for. She loved the drapes. They went so well with the carpet.

Harry found what they were looking for in a small room at the end of the landing. It was home to a desk, a computer and more pictures of flying Frisbees than he could have shaken a stick at. They covered an entire wall. The hoaxers had made many attempts at getting their photographic evidence just right.

"Bingo," he said when Candice joined him. "You got it spot on. Tell the press how you saw strange lights in the sky, wait a few days and then send a picture of Rover's favourite toy dressed up to look like a UFO."

"Have you seen the bathroom? It's amazing in there. Where can I get a shower like that?"

"I think this is more important than their bathroom."

"My shower unit is crap. I never liked it from the day it was installed."

"Look, Frisbees," Harry said, pointing at the wall in an effort to focus her attention.

"I know. Do you think they're covering a damp patch? There has to be something wrong with this house. It's too good."

"You said you didn't like the kitchen."

"I changed my mind. I think it's pretty cool now. I want one like it."

Harry opened his mouth to answer but Candice strode past him to the window on the other side of the room.

"Wow, look at that blind. It's fantastic."

It was like investigating a hoax with an interior designer.

"If you can tear yourself away from the décor for a moment, what are we going to do about this?" he asked.

"The first thing we need to do is find out where they shopped for this stuff."

They heard the front door open.

"Come, Watson. The game is afoot," Harry said, going outside.

Candice wanted to take the blind with her but she couldn't get it down.

They found Ruth Winters in the kitchen unpacking groceries. Candice looked over her shoulder as she put a carton of milk in the fridge.

"Oh, that's nice. Harry, look at the shelf space they've got in this bad boy," she said, waving her hand at him.

He would have killed her if she wasn't dead.

Winters put away the last of her purchases and sat at the kitchen table. A letter lay upon it which she unfolded but didn't read. She was more interested in the cheque stapled to the back. A magazine had paid her and her husband £3,000 for their story of how they saw UFOs in the skies over Cloverdale St Mary. The anonymous hoaxers were about to go public and take their scam to the next level.

Harry was appalled. "They're making some serious money out of this."

"What was that?" Candice asked as she inspected their washing machine.

"Some magazine has paid them £3,000 for their story."

Candice wondered what they would have spent it on. They didn't need a new washing machine that was for sure. It was state-of-the-art. "This baby has ten settings for auto-rinse and twelve spin speeds. Do you believe that?"

"I'll buy you one tomorrow," he said with a heavy sigh.

Candice managed to drag herself away and joined him at the table. The change in her was immediate.

"Harry."

"I'm moving in with Emily permanently if you say you want a table like this one."

"Something's wrong. I can't... I can't stay."

Harry realised what was happening. Candice was beginning to fade. He could see through her.

"Calling me... Master... is calling."

"You have to fight it, Candice. Resist it."

"Must... go..."

She disappeared completely.

Harry returned to Meadow Cottage but she wasn't there. He went to the village. There was no sign of her. He looked everywhere, frantic with worry. Finally, he went to the hills beyond Cross Drummond, the one and only place she had been seen when she disappeared before.

"CAN-DICE!"

His anguished cry carried away on the breeze in one of their favourite places and he knew he was alone.

*

Samantha arrived home at 12:35. An emergency at the stables had delayed her departure. One of the horses had been taken ill and she had to wait for the vet to arrive. It was nothing serious and she left soon after.

She garaged her car and went indoors, not knowing she had missed Harry by a matter of minutes. She called to Delia but received no reply. Her house guest had gone out. Samantha thought nothing of it and went upstairs to take a shower. She looked at her suitcase on the bed and stood it on the floor beside the wardrobe. She would unpack it later.

Samantha was one of those people who spent an eternity in the shower and by the time she finished and dressed it was five to one.

She returned to the lounge and flipped through the TV guide in the hope of finding something to watch that evening. *Killing Asia* was on again but it wouldn't have been her preferred choice. Finding nothing else of interest, she went to the kitchen to boil the kettle for a cup of tea. While she waited she phoned Janet to let her know there had been a change to her plans but the doorbell rang and she abandoned the call before it connected.

"Hello, Norman," she said, surprised to see him.

"Hello, Samantha. I'm sorry to bother you like this, I know you have things to do before you leave for Paris, but there is something I would like to speak to you about. I won't detain you long."

"It's okay, I'm in no rush. Paris is off," she replied, standing aside in the doorway to let him in.

"You're not going?"

"No. Xanthe called me at work this morning. Charlotte fell off a bus yesterday and broke her leg. It's not much fun going away in a plaster cast."

"Oh dear, that's dreadful news. Is she all right?"

"She's a bit down but she'll be okay. As I had a half day's holiday booked I decided to take it anyway. I've not long got in."

"Seems a shame to waste it."

"That's what I thought. I was making tea. Would you like a cup?"

"Yes, thank you."

He followed her to the kitchen.

"When do you think you'll be going now?" he asked her.

"Charlotte will be in the cast for six weeks. Some time after that I suppose."

"I'm sorry your trip had to be cancelled. You were so looking forward to it."

"At least I'll be here for the fête."

"Quite so. Every cloud as they say. Martin and Janet will be pleased about that. Young Melanie too."

"I haven't told them yet. I haven't told anyone. It was hectic at work this morning, I haven't had a chance. I was about to call mum when you arrived."

"Oh, I'm sorry."

Samantha smiled. "It's all right. I'll call her later."

The silver lining in Grantley's cloud equated to solid gold. It was perfect for him. He wouldn't have to force Samantha to call her friends to pull out of the trip and everyone else would have been under the impression she had gone.

They took their tea to the lounge.

"What did you want to speak to me about?" she asked.

"I can't tell you how impressed I was by the stables yesterday. I didn't realise how important it is to the local community. That being the case I would like to make a small donation. You do accept donations?"

"Yes. Yes, we do."

"I would consider it a privilege to contribute. I was thinking of £5,000."

Samantha gulped over her teacup. "Five thousand? Norman, I couldn't accept that much. Usually a donation is a couple of hundred pounds, if that."

He smiled. "Money is not an issue for me. One doesn't practice in Harley Street for as long as I did without reaping certain rewards."

Samantha was stunned. The last donation the stables received was made by a schoolgirl from Chalborough who saved up her pocket money and gave £20. "It's very generous of you. I don't know what to say."

"You could say yes."

"I think I could with a bit of practice." She smiled too. "Yes. Thank you, Norman. Thank you very much."

He took out his wallet and handed her a cheque. "At the risk of being presumptuous, I made this out before I came."

Samantha shook her head in astonishment. Hearing him say the amount was one thing, seeing it written in black and white was another. "I don't believe it. Are you sure you really want to do this?"

"I'm positive – and now it's in your hand it's yours. No going back."

"Thank you, Norman. Miss Blunt will be over the moon when she hears of this."

Grantley bridged his fingers under his chin. He had another surprise in store for her. "On that point I would rather my name wasn't mentioned."

"You want to remain anonymous?"

"I've only been in the village a couple of weeks. I don't want people to think the new man is throwing his money around. They might think I was trying to buy acceptance."

"I'm sure no one would think that."

"No doubt I'm judging my fellow residents unfairly but I would rather it was kept just between us."

Samantha understood his concerns but his generosity prompted her to make a confession, one she found embarrassing. "I would have to tell Miss Blunt I'm afraid. I'm not good at maths and she helps me with the bookkeeping. She would want to know where the money has come from."

"I see. Well, I'm sure Prudence can keep a secret. I would appreciate it if you didn't mention it to anyone else though."

"Of course. It will just be the three of us."

"Thank you."

Grantley sipped his tea and pulled a face that was designed to be troubled but not ungrateful.

"Is everything okay?" Samantha asked.

"Um, yes."

"Is something wrong with your tea?"

"It would benefit from another spoonful of sugar perhaps but really, it's all right."

Samantha stood and took his cup. "Norman, you've just given me £5,000. The least I can do is make the tea to your liking. I'll just be a moment."

"Very well. Thank you, Samantha," he replied smiling.

She went to the kitchen.

Grantley took a small bottle from his jacket pocket and unscrewed the cap. He poured a clear, odourless liquid into her cup and stirred it with the spoon nestling in the saucer.

"Is that better?" Samantha asked on her return.

He took a sip and nodded. "Ah yes. Thank you."

Samantha re-took her seat on the sofa and joked with

him. "I don't know. Someone comes to your home with an open chequebook and demands more sugar in their tea. What is wrong with the world?"

Grantley laughed.

Samantha sipped her tea and looked at him appreciatively. His donation would have made a huge difference to a business that was thriving but still had to keep an eye on costs. Who didn't these days? "I really appreciate your support. The stables extension is a major outlay and this will be a big help. Thank you."

"Not at all. I'm sure the money will be put to good use. What are your plans for this evening now you're not going away?"

"A quiet night in watching TV I think. What about you?"

She took longer sips of tea while he answered.

"I'm meeting Emily for a drink in the Coaching Inn. That will be two nights on the trot I've been to the pub. I'll have to be careful. I could get a reputation for being a drunkard."

Samantha grinned.

"It was nice to meet Brenda last night. I hardly know her but I'm glad she's staying in the village a bit longer."

"Yes, me too."

"Do you know her well?"

"Not very. Only through her visits really. And what Candice told me... about her."

She rubbed her forehead with her hand.

"She strikes me as being a very outgoing woman. Strong-minded too. I get the impression she isn't slow in stating an opinion."

Samantha's eyelids grew heavy. She had to concentrate on what she was saying. "Yes. She can be out... spoken."

"She reminds me of a patient once in my care. A delightful lady but unshakable in her views. It was around the time of the EU referendum. I voted to stay in but she was committed to the leave camp. She spent an hour trying to convince me that leaving was the best thing for the country. It put me behind schedule for the rest of the day. Had to cancel my four o'clock appointment."

Samantha could barely keep her eyes open. She swayed and gripped the arm of the sofa to stop herself from toppling over. "I'm sorry... I feel... tired."

"That would be the drug I put in your tea."

"Dwug?"

"Yes, when you went to the kitchen. It's one of the faster-acting sedatives. I expect you to lose consciousness any moment."

"I don't... under... under..."

"Stand? No, I'm sure you don't. Far better to relax and let it take effect. It's best not to fight these things."

The lounge faded in a dark blur and Samantha tried to stand up. Speckles of light stabbed her fading vision. Her head spun. A ringing sensation went through her ears. Her legs buckled and she fell back on the sofa.

"Why... have you... done this?"

He smiled. "I want *something* for my money, Samantha."

She lost consciousness.

Grantley laid her on the sofa and lifted her eyelids to make sure she was fully under. She was. Now he could go to work.

He put on a pair of surgical gloves and retrieved the cheque from the coffee table. Returning it to his wallet, he left the lounge and went upstairs to her bedroom.

As expected, Samantha had packed a suitcase. He took it outside and stood it on the landing. Next he went to the bathroom. Toiletries were needed in the mornings and she wouldn't have packed them until she came home from work. He took a plastic bag from his jacket pocket and removed what he thought she would have taken with her. Some didn't need to be removed but he left nothing to chance.

Grantley returned to the landing and took the case downstairs. He stood it in the hallway. Her keys were on the table and he dropped them in the bag. From there he went to the lounge and took the teacups back to the kitchen. He washed and dried them and put them away. He saw her mobile phone on the worktop where she had left it and put it in the bag too.

Returning to the lounge, he cast around it carefully. Samantha's passport was on the coffee table and that too was deposited in the bag. When he was satisfied he had left nothing to suggest that she hadn't gone to Paris he proceeded to the next phase.

Meadow Cottage was distant from other houses, an out-of-the-way property that stood isolated on Meadow Lane, but he couldn't run the risk of being seen when he put Samantha in the boot of his car. A dog walker could have gone by, someone on horseback, anyone. Damn horses. He hated them.

Grantley went outside and turned his car around, reversing it close to the front door. He opened the boot and returned to the lounge to fetch his victim.

The drug he had used guaranteed unconsciousness for at least three hours, more than enough time for him to do what had to be done. It wasn't simply a case of abducting Samantha. She had to be prepared and confined in the restraints. Grantley needed her to be unconscious throughout.

He picked her up and carried her to the front door where he stopped to make sure the coast was clear. He saw no one and placed her in the boot. Next he fetched Samantha's suitcase and the carrier bag. The boot hadn't been designed for transporting bodies and Grantley had to tuck her in a foetal position to make space. The bag presented no problem and was tossed in. It fell beside her head.

Grantley returned to the cottage for a final look around. He checked upstairs and down. Everything was in order. Delia would have returned from Falworth before Samantha was due to leave at three o'clock but her car was in the garage and her passport and suitcase were gone. Delia would have assumed she had left earlier than planned and thought no more of it. Job done.

All Grantley had to do now was kill her.

Twenty-seven

Delia returned to Meadow Cottage at ten to three. She waited at the Millstream till half past two, thinking the woman she was there to meet had been delayed. When she failed to show up she called Grantley. It went to voicemail.

Delia saw that Samantha's passport was no longer on the coffee table and went upstairs to check her bedroom. Her suitcase was gone too and she assumed, as Grantley expected, that she had left earlier than planned. Delia regretted that she had missed her, she wanted to wish her well for the weekend, but the meeting with the mystery woman was important and she had no choice but to wait for her.

She made a cup of coffee and called Grantley again. This time he answered.

He listened to her account of the no-show and sounded surprised and disappointed, at a loss to understand why a woman who had gone to so much trouble to arrange a meeting would have chosen not to attend it. She must have been genuine. She mentioned Candice by name. Why wouldn't she have shown up? Grantley was so convincing in his performance he almost had himself believing his lies.

Delia told him about Alex Crosby and he agreed it would have been worth pursuing. She was to devote all her attention to finding and talking to him. If the mystery woman called again he would let her know.

But I wouldn't hold your breath, Grantley thought when the call ended.

*

Delia had grown accustomed to Candice and Harry popping up when she least expected it. They usually arrived together in the same part of the room but when they appeared in the lounge at 3:30 they stood at opposite ends of the sofa either side of her and she wondered if she had been caught in a pincer movement.

"Hello," she said, looking at them in turn.

Harry stared at Candice. "Where have you been?"

She was as surprised to see him as he was to see her. "Norwich. Where have *you* been?"

"I've been looking for you."

"Did you look in Norwich?"

"You left Norwich."

"I know. I left it to look for you."

"How has your day been?" Delia asked, playing neck tennis again.

Harry joined Candice on her side of the sofa. That suited Delia perfectly. She wouldn't have to work so hard regarding her head movements when she spoke to them now.

"The force took control of you," he said.

As before, Candice had no memory of it. She sat on the arm of the sofa and stared into empty space.

"Oh."

"It happened again?" Delia asked.

"Apparently," Candice muttered.

Delia looked at Harry. She was eager to know more. "Was it like the other times?"

"No."

"How was it different?"

"Candice seemed to know what was happening."

"Candice is here. Don't talk about me as if I fucking wasn't," she snapped.

"I'm sorry," Harry said.

Candice walked to the fireplace and leaned her shoulder against the wall beside it. She had allowed herself to be drawn into a false sense of security. Nothing had happened over recent days. She thought the threat was past. "No, I'm sorry. I didn't mean to sound off at you. I wasn't expecting it."

"You thought it was over," Delia said.

"Yeah. Dumb or what?"

"You're not dumb," Harry told her.

"I'm not as safe as I thought I was either."

Harry had known that all along. It was not knowing why and coming to terms with it that he found hard.

"What happened in Norwich?" Delia asked.

Candice gestured to the floor to let Harry know she was happy for him to speak on her behalf.

"We got the name and address of the couple who reported seeing the UFO and went to their house. It is a hoax. We saw evidence of it. Soon after we arrived the woman came home. She had a cheque for £3,000. A magazine has bought their story. Candice was standing on the other side of the room but when she joined me she began to fade." He looked at her. "I could see through you."

"Did I say anything?"

"You said something was wrong and you couldn't stay. Your Master was calling you."

"My Master?"

"Yeah. I told you to fight it, to resist, but you said you had to go. Then you disappeared."

"Did it happen suddenly like the last time Candice was taken?" Delia asked.

"No. She just faded away."

"How long did it take? Be precise if you can. It may be important."

"From start to finish, no more than ten seconds. It was sudden in that respect, that it came from nowhere, but not the actual disappearance. That was gradual."

"And no other spirits spoke through her?"

"No. Do you have any idea where you went?" he asked Candice.

"The way I saw it I didn't go anywhere. I was checking out their washing machine and then I was alone in the kitchen. I thought *you* disappeared. I came here to look for you and walked into all this. Again."

"The woman wasn't there?" Delia asked.

Candice hadn't thought of that. "No," she said, thinking about it now.

Harry glanced at the clock on the wall. "She may have gone out again. You disappeared three hours ago."

Candice closed her eyes. It was less worrying than going missing for three days but she drew little comfort from it. In her time frame she and Harry had been standing in that kitchen just two minutes previously.

"It doesn't make sense," Delia said. "Why was this time different from the others?"

"What do you mean?" Harry asked.

"Candice knew she was going. You were aware that someone or something had summoned you. In the past you hadn't known. Other spirits spoke through you yet this time they didn't. It's almost as if you were taken away for another reason, that instead of wanting to have control over you the force was using you for something."

"That's an encouraging thought," Candice said. "Have there been any bank robberies over the past three hours?"

"Now I know why you have all that cash stashed under your mattress," Harry replied.

Candice appreciated his light-hearted response and grinned.

"Did you have any luck tracking down Crosby?" he asked Delia.

"No. I haven't made a start on that yet. I've been following up a lead."

"What sort of lead?"

"After you left for Norwich I received a phone call from a woman. She didn't tell me her name. She said she knew what was happening to Candice. She asked me to meet her at the Millstream at one o'clock."

"What did she say?" Candice asked.

"It was a waste of time I'm afraid. She didn't show up. I waited an hour and a half and came back here."

"What time did you come home?" Harry asked.

"Ten to three."

"At least one of us was here to see Samantha off."

"She had already gone. Her friend must have come early. Her passport wasn't on the table so I looked in her bedroom. Her suitcase was gone too." Delia realised her actions may have been frowned upon and explained her reasons for going into a private room. "I wasn't snooping. I didn't know if she was here or not."

"That's okay. We would have done the same," Candice said.

Delia seemed relieved to hear it.

Harry faded from view.

He left without saying anything. For one horrible

moment they thought the force had power over him too but he returned a moment later none the worse for his exit.

"Her car's in the garage," he announced.

"Don't do that," Delia said, breathing a sigh of relief.

Candice imagined the fun weekend Samantha was destined to have in Paris and turned her thoughts to how to ruin it for others. Three thousand pounds for a fake story was taking a prank too far. "What are we gonna do about the UFO hoaxers? They stand to make some big money out of this. That's why they live in the best house on the block. The way they scam people they can afford to."

Harry had an answer to that problem at least. A great many things remained out of their control but how to bring to account a couple of con artists with a taste for the luxurious wasn't one of them. "Delia, if I gave you a name and address how would you feel about making an anonymous phone call to the police?"

"It would be my pleasure, Mr Violet."

Harry sighed. If he hadn't been a ghost he would have lost the will to live.

*

Samantha woke to a dimly-lit room. Two fluorescent lights hung from the ceiling but only the one nearest her was on.

She was standing against a wall, her arms raised above her head. She tried to move them but couldn't. She looked up and saw she had been confined in wrist irons. They were connected to a chain that passed through a metal ring ten inches above her hands. The chain trailed off to her right and was secured on a hook driven into the base of the wall.

She felt cold and shivered. When she became fully awake she realised she was dressed in just her underwear. There could have been only one reason for her to be held captive in such a way and panic took her.

Samantha pulled against the restraints and felt them dig into her skin. She grimaced, tugging as hard as she could. She tried to move her feet to get leverage but her ankles were in irons too forcing her legs apart. Desperation surged through her. She continued her efforts to break free until the pain from the restraints cutting into her wrists became too much and she was forced to stop.

Samantha tried to compose herself and looked at her surroundings. Dark corners that concealed every threat imaginable met her frightened eyes. The air was damp and musty. It caught in the back of her throat as she took short, sharp breaths. Cobwebs had taken hold everywhere, one just a few inches from her left arm. She was scared of spiders and seeing one so close to her made her shudder.

On the other side of the room directly opposite her stood a long table with something resting on it. She didn't know what it was. It was covered by a dustsheet. The sheet also covered something standing on the floor beside it. To the right of the table was a wooden staircase.

To her left was a smaller table. A water jug and a glass rested on it, her watch and jewellery too. Her suitcase stood underneath. An old radiator that hadn't worked in years was fixed to the wall to her right. Beside it was a plastic bucket. These were the only features in a room that would be home from now on.

Samantha bowed her head to look at herself, fearing what may have been in store for her. She wore skimpy underwear. Her bra was revealing and her briefs lay low on her hips. It was designed for dates and nights on the town, not a basement that doubled as a dungeon. Under normal circumstances she wouldn't have thought twice about using it for general wear, like today she often did, but these circumstances were anything but normal and anxiety welled up inside her like a beast trying to break out.

She hadn't seen Grantley enter the basement. He had watched her reaction to being confined from the shadows at the top of the stairs.

"I'm glad to see you have given up your struggle," he announced, descending the staircase. "There really is no point. Your confinement is secure."

His eyes settled on her breasts when he stood in front of her.

Samantha tried to pull her knees together to close her legs but she was at full stretch and the irons around her ankles made movement impossible. It was like being lashed to a vertical rack. Her fear hammered. She was petrified and defenceless. "Where are my clothes? What is this place?"

"All you need to know is that you are my prisoner and will remain so until my work is finished. You will be given water to drink but no food. You will do as I say at all times. Non-compliance will be punished. Do you understand?"

Samantha didn't answer. She was too afraid.

Grantley slapped her face. "I asked you a question, you stupid bitch."

The pain stung her cheek and she wept.

He struck her again when she failed to respond.

"This falls into the category of non-compliance and it will not be tolerated. When I ask you a question you will answer. Do you understand?"

"Yes," she cried.

"Good. Don't make me do that again."

"Why did you bring me here?... What are you going to do to me?"

Grantley understood her concern but showed no sympathy towards her. Stories of young women held against their will in places not dissimilar to this were often in the news but their abductors were driven by lust and sexual perversion. He had turned kidnapper for reasons that were altogether different.

"I have no interest in you sexually. You're an attractive woman but you are not here as a plaything for my amusement."

"Why did you take off my clothes?"

"I undressed you because it's important that the air circulates around your body. You will be here for a number of days and your skin must be allowed to breathe prior to the event. To afford you privacy I didn't take off your bra and panties but they too will be removed in due course. In order for the event to proceed you must be naked."

His statement reinforced what Samantha dreaded. Grantley may not have been interested in her in a sexual sense but some might. The possibilities were too horrendous to contemplate. Would others come to this place to rape and abuse her? Would her ordeal be photographed or filmed and made available to websites that catered for sick and perverted minds? The thought of it made her stomach churn.

"No... please."

"I know you will find it embarrassing but you have no say in what happens to you so there is no point in discussing it further. The important thing is that the event proceeds according to schedule."

"What event?... Why are you doing this to me?"

"You will be silent now. Do not speak again until you're spoken to."

"Don't make me stay like this... let me get dressed," she pleaded.

Grantley slapped her face, harder than before, and Samantha screamed with pain.

"Non-compliance. How many times do I have to hit you before you get it into your head that I won't stand for it?"

"Please... don't hurt me."

"Hurt you?"

He seized her chin and pressed her head tight against the wall.

Samantha pulled at the restraints, shaking with fear.

"This room is underground. That makes it soundproof. I can do whatever I want to you without fear of being discovered. I could rip off your toe and fingernails one by one and no one would hear you scream. I could shove a hot poker up your twat and no one would know. I can hurt you in ways you wouldn't have thought possible and no one would be any the wiser. You will remain as you are. You will not make demands of me. You will do as you are fucking well told. DO YOU UNDERSTAND?"

The venom in his voice made her shudder.

"Yes," she wept.

"Do you want me to do those things to you?"

"No."

"Do you want me to cut out your tongue so you can't speak at all?"

"No... please..."

"Do you want me to stick needles in your eyes?"

"No... dear God... please don't..."

"I will strip you naked now and do all those things if you defy me. I don't expect us to have this conversation again. Is that clear?"

"Yes..."

He released her.

Samantha turned her cheek to her arm and cried uncontrollably.

Grantley rose above her distress. It meant nothing to him. That Samantha had feelings and was afraid never entered the thoughts of a man who became a sadistic tyrant in the prison he had created beneath his home. She was there for a reason, a purpose, and that outweighed everything else.

A beautiful slim body met his eyes. He was in no doubt that he had chosen his victim wisely. Samantha's figure drew wolf whistles from men and stirred envy in other women; unblemished skin, good sized breasts and long shapely legs. Exercise and a healthy diet had served her well. Hers was a body to be proud of.

One thing not to his liking was that she had a tattoo, three stars drawn in a curved line below her navel, but that could be removed later. It was a minor detail that didn't matter in the overall scheme of things. The finishing touches could be applied afterwards, slight alterations that would have made an ideal body perfect.

The tattoo was partly hidden by her briefs. He wanted an unobstructed view and pulled them down.

Samantha shook catching her breath. They were made of delicate lace. It wouldn't have taken much to have ripped them off her.

"I don't understand why people decorate their bodies," he said disapprovingly. "You have excellent skin. Why spoil it by defacing yourself?"

"It's just a tattoo," she sobbed.

"It will have to be removed. What is acceptable to you is not to me. However, we can deal with that later."

Grantley inspected her genitalia. He was glad she shaved. He thought poorly of women who didn't.

Samantha tensed in fear of what he might have done next but his examination didn't go beyond the visual. He stood back to get an overview. Her briefs remained around her knees leaving her exposed to him. He had no intention of pulling them up. It didn't appear on his list of priorities. So much for affording her privacy.

He felt like an explorer on the verge of making a great discovery, a man whose work would be held in the highest regard by his piers. Grantley was destined to go down in history as a genius years ahead of his time. In contrast, Samantha felt like breeding stock that was bought and sold at a slave market.

"The tattoo aside, you meet my requirements perfectly. I couldn't have wished for better," he said.

"Please, let me go... I won't tell anyone, I promise."

Grantley knew she wouldn't. How could she have said anything when soon she would be dead?

He walked to the foot of the stairs leading out of the basement. The first phase of his plan had gone well. His prisoner was confined with no hope of detection or rescue. Her death was assured. He would succeed in achieving what he had set out to accomplish because no one could stop him.

"We will continue our chat later. It really is a pity about that tattoo. It will definitely have to go."

He climbed the stairs and turned off the light when he reached the top, locking the door behind him.

Samantha hung her head and cried, frightened, half naked and alone in the darkness.

Twenty-eight

Ian returned from the bar in the Coaching Inn and set down two glasses, a lager for himself and a Chardonnay for Brenda.

"Thank you," she said, turning the glass on the table they were sharing. "I didn't say at the time but it was a wonderful service on Wednesday."

"I'm glad it was well received. Did it help?"

Brenda smiled. It had helped in more ways than Ian could have imagined. "Yes, it did. That and going to Meadow Cottage. Delia allowed me privacy, she let me do my own thing. I thought that was nice of her."

"She's an understanding woman."

"Yeah, she is. It was funny. I sat in the lounge with a cup of tea and Candice and I talked. I could hear her in my head. It was like she was there."

Candice looked at the ceiling and whistled.

Harry was more interested in Emily and Grantley who were drinking at their usual table by the fireplace.

"What did she say to you?" Ian asked.

"She told me to stop being a silly cow and to get on with life." Brenda smiled again. "Typical Candice. She was a great leveller."

"Yes, that she was. Do you think you can? Get on with life."

"I know I owe it to her to try. That's what friends do for one another. I won't forget what you did for me either. Thank you, Ian."

"It's all part of the service, Brenda."

They both knew it was more than that.

"Has he got his hand on her knee?" Harry asked from nowhere.

"What?" Candice said.

"Grantley. What is he doing under that table?"

"His hands are in clear view."

Harry tutted and shook his head.

"What can I expect to see at this fête tomorrow?" Brenda asked Ian, changing the subject.

"The usual things. Coconut shies, fun and games, stalls selling home-made jam."

"Collapsing marquees," Harry added.

Ian ignored him.

"Are you sure the marquee is safe? It looks a bit lop-sided," Brenda commented.

Harry felt vindicated and pointed at him. "Ha!"

"Brenda, marquees and I have an understanding. I erect them and they stay erected."

"Except for those that succumb to poor workmanship and the laws of gravity," Harry told him.

"I bow to your experience in these matters," Brenda said.

"Bow by all means but don't go inside," Harry advised, convinced that nothing but disaster lay in store.

Brenda sipped her wine and returned the glass to the table. It was her third and she planned to have an early night but the company was good and she was enjoying herself. That meant only one thing. Another lock-in.

"Miss Blunt mentioned home-made jam yesterday. Something about a local woman who makes it?"

"Yes, Mrs Jenkins," Ian replied. "She is a jam-making legend in this part of the world. She's made jam to sell at the fête for years but recently her productivity has gone into overdrive. The year before last she made fifty jars.

Last year she made seventy-five. Tomorrow there is a real chance that she'll break the hundred barrier."

"Does she sell them all?"

"Yes, it's become a cottage industry. She's very gifted in the art of jam-making. Last year Sheila bought ten jars. I was still eating the stuff at Christmas."

"Do I detect a hint of non-enthusiasm?"

"I can't stand it. I've never been a fan of jam. *A Town Called Malice* was good though."

Brenda laughed. "What do you do at the fête? Aside from erecting the marquee to an excellent standard."

"He coordinates the rescue effort when it falls down," Harry said.

"I coordinate... I run the *bowl out our best batsman* stall," Ian corrected himself.

"What's that?"

"I have the privilege to be Captain of the village cricket team and every year our star batsman pits his skill against the public who are invited to bowl him out in three balls or less. 50p a ball, get him if you can."

Cloverdale St Mary's cricket team was another bone of contention as far as Harry was concerned. Bowling out their star batsman wouldn't have been difficult. His name was Ron Jones and the last time he made contact with a cricket ball was in 1986.

"May the gods preserve us," he muttered.

"Ron is very good," Ian said through gritted teeth.

"The Ron here?" Brenda asked, pointing over her shoulder at the bar.

"Yes. He's a genius with a cricket bat."

"A genius? The last time we played Falworth in a fifty overs match he held it upside down. He got a duck," Harry reminded him.

"He's very good with wildfowl too," Ian said.

Harry looked to Candice in the hope that she might have supported his claim that Ron was the worst cricketer to have ever walked to the crease. Why he bothered to venture onto the pitch baffled him. The way he played he could have saved himself the time and effort and been declared out in the pavilion. It occurred to him that she had taken no part in the conversation and he looked at her anxiously.

"Are you all right?"

Candice smiled. "Yeah, I'm fine. I'm just happy to see Bren being a part of this."

"Me too," Ian said in an unguarded moment.

"Me too what?" Brenda asked.

"Um, me too is also good with a cricket bat," he struggled in reply.

"That has to be the worst recovery in history," Harry told him.

Ian was of the same opinion but made his response worse by trying to make it sound normal. "You good perchance with bat too as well, are you?"

Brenda had to work at it but she got the gist. "I don't play cricket."

"Ron doesn't either and he's our star batsman," Harry said.

What Ian needed was a distraction and one came to hand when Grantley appeared beside their table.

"Forgive the intrusion, but Emily and I wondered if you would care to join us. It seems odd sitting at separate tables – unless your conversation is private of course," he said.

Ian and Brenda looked at one another and nodded.

"Yes, we would love to join you," Brenda replied.

"May I voice an objection?" Harry asked.

"Splendid. I'll tell Emily the good news."

A moment later they had relocated to the table by the fireplace.

"Norman asked me about the picture of Candice," Emily said to Brenda, pointing to it on the wall. "Do you know what film it's from? I can't recall seeing it in any of the ones I've seen."

"It's a promo shot for Hell Captures the Brave," Candice said.

"It's from On Distant Shores," Brenda replied.

"No, Bren. It's Hell Captures the Brave."

"Actually, I think I remember it now," Emily said, studying the picture at length. "Are you sure it's that one? It might be Hell Captures the Brave."

"No, it's definitely On Distant Shores. She said the sense of togetherness on the set was the best she had ever known."

That wasn't how Candice remembered it.

"Are you kiddin' me? It was shot on location in the wilds of Canada in the dead of winter. We spent all our time in a wooden hut. No one spoke to each other for three months. I hated it. I couldn't even send out for pizza. Hell Captures the Brave on the other hand was one long party. We had a great time making that movie."

"She always said On Distant Shores was one long party. She had a great time making that film," Brenda told the others.

"How much as she had to drink?" Candice asked Ian. "On Distant shores was as much fun as having all your teeth pulled out by a drunken dentist on New Year's Eve."

"Someone told me you were allowed access to one of her films while it was in production," Grantley said to

Emily.

She recalled her day at Elstree Studios fondly. It had been a privilege to see someone so talented at work. "Yes. It was the last film Candice made, Killing Asia. She arranged set passes for Maggie and I."

Candice smiled proudly. "It's become a modern-day classic."

Harry yawned.

"It must have been a wonderful experience," Grantley said.

"It was. I was terrified to begin with. I thought I would cough or something while they were filming a scene and ruin it but Candice put me at ease. She said if anything happened and the director took me to task over it she would have him fired." Emily grinned. "She was always saying things like that."

"I meant it too. I've had more directors replaced than you've had hot dinners," Candice told her.

"What was she like on set?" Grantley asked.

"Totally professional. In between takes she was Candice, laughing and joking around, but the moment the cameras rolled she became the character she was portraying. I know that's what actors do but she did it effortlessly, like it was the most natural thing in the world. She knew it was time to go to work and put everything into it. When the cameras stopped she was Candice again.

"There was only one occasion when she didn't speak to anyone between takes. She wasn't happy about the scene. Something bothered her and she sat quietly by herself working it out. She didn't have a script in front of her, she was doing it in her head. Maggie and I were in tears when they filmed it. She did it so well the crew applauded at the end. They knew they had witnessed something special. That's when I realised how talented she was. Candice deserved the awards and accolades she received, the recognition that comes with success. She earned it because she was the best there was." Emily looked her in the eye and paid her the ultimate compliment. "She was Candice Freeman."

Candice smiled again. "Thank you, Em."

"I'll drink to that," Brenda said, raising her glass.

The others did the same and an impromptu toast followed.

"I thought Killing Asia was rubbish," Harry said.

"Only because I didn't take my clothes off," Candice replied.

"There could have been one shower scene. People wash in Asia, it happens all the time. That film is not a true reflection of daily life during the Vietnam War."

"Have you considered seeking professional help?" Candice asked him.

Grantley looked at his watch and changed the subject, turning the conversation to absent friends. "I wonder what Samantha is doing in Paris?"

"Having the time of her life I expect," Emily said.

"It's such a vibrant city. Has she been there before?"

"Yes, she's been a few times," Ian replied.

"She will know all the good places to visit then," Grantley said. "It's a shame she's not here for the fête though."

"I'll buy her a pot of jam for when she gets back."

Brenda looked at Ian and grinned.

"A hundred and fifty," Emily announced.

"Sorry?" Ian asked.

"I hear Mrs Jenkins has made a hundred and fifty jars this year."

The vicar sighed. He would have been up to his neck in jam for the rest of his life if he didn't hide Sheila's purse.

"I hope our kitchen cupboards can take the weight," he said.

"I imagine tomorrow will be a long day for you," Grantley said to him.

"Yes. I'll be there from start to finish."

"What time *does* it start?"

"Nine o'clock. Most of the stalls will close around five in the afternoon but the marquee will be open till gone midnight for food and drinks."

"Always supposing it stays up that long," said a voice yet to be convinced of its stability.

Ian was stunned. He thought he could have relied on Emily for support at least. "Are you saying my marquee isn't safe?"

"It does have a tendency to fall down," she replied.

Harry laughed. "You tell him, Emily."

"It fell down once. It was subsidence," Ian claimed.

"How can a marquee be subject to subsidence?" Harry asked.

"Moles," Ian said.

Brenda wondered if she had heard him right and looked puzzled. "Pardon me?"

"That's why it subsided. They got on the green with their little spades and dug around it. Moles are very devious creatures."

"And you say I need help," Harry said to Candice.

*

It wasn't a lock-in. The evening came to an end at ten o'clock and Brenda had her early night after all.

Grantley walked Emily home and kissed her goodnight at her gate, much to Harry's dismay as he watched from the doorstep. It was only a peck on the cheek but to Harry it signalled a deepening of their relationship and that made him feel uncomfortable. He wanted Emily to be happy but was of the opinion that she could have done better. He didn't know why he was suspicious of Grantley. The village newcomer had done nothing to warrant it, he was pleasant and courteous and had been accepted by all, but Harry had a feeling about him that he found impossible to dismiss.

Love and mistrust. It wasn't the best of combinations.

Grantley made a cup of tea when he got home and decided to have an early night too. It had been a long day and another lay in store tomorrow. He could have done without the village fête. Home-made jam and bowling out star batsmen would have been fun at any other time but not when he had important work to do. That work had to come first but his presence at the fête was expected and he had no choice but to attend. In that respect he had been accepted *too* well.

He took his tea to the basement.

A rush of fear surged through Samantha when the light came on and Grantley descended the stairs. She remembered how he had been violent towards her, the things he said he would do if she didn't obey him. He had demonstrated a willingness to hurt her without hesitation and the thought of enduring further pain tied knots in her stomach. Samantha was more than afraid. She was petrified.

Grantley put his teacup on the table and stood in front of her. He was surprised to see bruising on her face. He didn't think he had hit her that hard but Samantha bruised easily. She only had to knock her leg on the coffee table at home and would carry the mark for days. Her skin was important and he didn't want to damage it but he wasn't overly concerned. Bruises had a habit of fading.

He dismissed it and came to the point in addressing the reason for his presence. Not that he had to explain his actions to her. She was there to die. Why stand on ceremony or make polite small talk?

"Do you need to pee?"

She was too scared to answer.

Grantley sighed. "Non-compliance. I thought I made myself clear on that point."

He slapped her.

Samantha cried and pulled against the wrist irons. The sound of the chain rattling above her head rang in her ears.

"I asked you a question. You've been here for several hours and at some point you will have to pee. Do you need to do so now?"

"Yes..."

"There would have been no reason for me to hit you had you said that to begin with."

He struck her twice more to underline his authority.

Samantha grimaced and shook, begging him to stop. She didn't know how much more she could take. "Please... please don't hurt me..."

Grantley slapped her again. "I will do to you what I choose."

And again.

"When I ask a question you will not keep me waiting for an answer."

And again.

"You will respond immediately."
And again.
"Is that understood?"

Samantha tasted blood on her lips. It was almost impossible to speak through the pain surging through her but she had no choice. "Yes..."

"You will comply in future?"
And again.
"Yes..."

"You will do whatever I demand of you?"
And again.
"Yes..."

"You know your rightful place?"
And again.
"Pleeeease... please stop... I'm sorry..."
"Answer the question."
And again.
"Yes... I know my place..."
"I'm glad we understand each other."
And again.

Grantley looked at the blood snaking down her chin. The cut to her upper lip had been caused by a ring he wore. "Don't make me angry, Samantha. Incurring my wrath is not something I would recommend. If there is a next time I'll cut off your fingers with a pair of secateurs and stuff them down your throat. Is that clear?"

"Yes."

She knew he would. Her abductor wasn't given to making idle threats.

Grantley released the chain from the hook in the base of the wall. He let out the slack and lowered her to a squatting position. The relief at being able to move her arms and shoulders was immense.

He fetched the bucket from the other side of the room and placed it under her. "Do what you have to do."

The thought of it filled her with shame and embarrassment.

Now her arms had been lowered Samantha was able to reach between her legs and pulled the bucket closer.

Grantley stood in close attendance and watched. That he wouldn't allow privacy drove her to new depths of despair and she bowed her head sobbing.

Fear had taken command of a body that struggled to perform its natural functions and she found it difficult to urinate. It would have been hard for Samantha had Grantley turned his back or left the room. Knowing her jailer was standing over her made it worse but finally she managed it.

Being scrutinized while performing such a personal task was degrading but that was what Grantley wanted. She had to feel worthless, humiliated, a wreck of a human being whose only purpose was to obey him and pee into a bucket.

When she was finished he took it away.

"Please, may I pull up my briefs?"

"You may."

Samantha attended to it. She couldn't lift them over her buttocks as she was unable to move her hands behind her back but succeeded in pulling them up at the front. That at least gave her some privacy.

"Can I stay like this?" she asked. "My arms hurt."

"No."

He pulled on the chain and returned her to a standing position. Samantha cried in pain as her arms lifted above her head. Grantley secured the chain on the hook and left the basement without saying another word.

The lights went out.

The door was locked.
Samantha wept.
"Please help me... Someone help me..."

Twenty-nine

"Three hundred and sixty-five? Who can eat that much jam?"

Ian had to be supported as Sheila as led him away from Mrs Jenkins' stall. He was in shock.

"You could have a jar every day of the year if I bought them all," she said.

"I forbid you to go anywhere near that stall. I'm in favour of supporting charity but a line has to be drawn. What is that woman trying to do? Take over the world with jam? She must be stopped."

"Ian, I can't help thinking you're over-reacting. Let's go to Bill and Susan's stall. They're selling jam sandwiches."

"I want a divorce."

Sheila laughed and hugged his arm. "Okay, I'll buy you an ice cream instead."

It was a beautiful day. The sun was shining and the sound of people enjoying themselves carried on the air. It was 1:00 p.m. and the village fête was in full swing.

Martin and Janet were in conversation with Miss Blunt as Melanie waited at the ice cream van for her chocolate sundae. They would never have guessed that in the basement of a cottage twenty metres from where they stood their eldest daughter was confined in chains. They didn't know the agony she was going through, that she had passed a long and terrifying night praying they would find her.

In the cold darkness that surrounded Samantha something had scurried over her foot at four o'clock that morning. She hadn't considered that there may have been rats in the basement but she did now. She imagined a plague of them converging on her in search of food and biting her feet, running along the chain and biting her hands. Running down her arms and biting her face. In truth there was only one but she had no way of knowing that. One fear was as strong as ten thousand. Desperation didn't do mathematics.

"Hello, Melanie. Are you having a good time?" Sheila asked when she arrived at the ice cream van with Ian.

"Yes thank you."

"This is better than going to Paris any day of the week," Ian said.

"Who is in Paris?" Melanie asked him.

"Your sister," he replied. "You know, the tall woman with blonde hair."

Melanie was more interested in the treat she had just received. "Oh, her. Thank you," she said to the ice cream man.

Sheila smiled. "Aren't you excited about Sam being in France?"

Melanie had to think about it. She loved Samantha but she got on her nerves sometimes, especially when the ten year-old did something wrong and she reprimanded her. On those occasions she didn't like her at all. "I suppose it's all right. Especially if she brings something back for me."

Ian laughed. "That's right, Mel. Life is all about priorities."

She didn't know what he meant by that and went skipping off to join her parents.

"That young lady is growing up fast," Sheila said.

"Yes, she is. Where's my ice cream? I want a cone with two flakes."

"It's a pity we can't all do the same," Sheila muttered,

taking out her purse.

Janet watched Melanie approach and smiled fondly. Things were better between her and Martin now and Melanie was happier because of it. They still had a long way to go and trust had yet to be re-established. Like forgiveness, it took time, but they were going in the right direction and the future seemed brighter.

"Did you get what you wanted?" she asked on her return.

"Yes. Mummy, may I go on the swings?"

The play area was distant from where they were standing and Janet didn't like the thought of Melanie going off on her own. Cloverdale St Mary may have been a small village with a strong community spirit but the safety of the young could never be taken for granted. Not every face on the green was familiar. In a world of deception, hatred and violence it didn't pay to take chances.

"I'll come with you."

"I can go by myself," Melanie sulked, not wanting to be treated like a child.

"I know you can but I want to go on the swings too." Janet grinned and nudged her arm. "Come on, I'll race you."

Melanie laughed and took off like a rocket, leaving Janet in her wake.

Miss Blunt nodded favourably as she watched them go. "What it is to be young and carefree."

"Yes," Martin said, watching too. "The innocence of youth doesn't last long, does it?" he added sombrely.

"Sometimes that innocence is taken away too soon."

He knew what Miss Blunt was referring to and searched her eyes when he looked at her, expecting to meet disapproval. He didn't see it.

"I am not judging you, Martin. You are a valued friend and I hold you in the highest regard. I am glad that you and Janet are working through your difficulties."

"Thank you, Prudence. I know I acted irresponsibly and I'm grateful to have been given a second chance. I look at Jan and the kids and think how could I have been so stupid to risk throwing all that away? It's true what they say. You don't appreciate what you have until you're in danger of losing it. I'll never put them or myself through that again."

"You have learnt a valuable lesson. A foolish man will turn his back on things that are important to him but a wise man will turn again and admit to his mistakes. Janet loves you and you love her. In the end that is what matters."

Martin appreciated what Miss Blunt had said and smiled. "Thank you for not condemning me."

She grinned and made a veiled reference to the Miss Blunt of old, the Miss Blunt she still was to those less deserving. "I, Martin? Condemn? How could you think me capable of such a thing?"

*

Candice was enjoying her first village fête. She had always been a strong believer in community and liked to see people come together. It didn't happen in London, L.A. or New York. Big cities were not the cold, impersonal places they had once been but they couldn't rival days like this. There was something special about a village green, of locals enjoying what they normally took for granted, and Candice loved being a part of it. She wasn't going to let a thing called death stand in the way of having fun.

For many the day would be long. Those running stalls had set up early. Some would stay open till six. There was plenty to see and do. There were attractions and competitions, a whole range of activities designed to make people part with their money in support of their chosen charity. It was a combination of fête and fairground with rides and stalls taking up every inch of available space. In the centre of it all stood the marquee which hadn't fallen down yet and provided a safe haven for those who wanted to escape from the noise and mayhem and enjoy a refreshing drink in peace and quiet.

Entertainment had been arranged for later in the evening. Ian had booked a group from Falworth who went by the name of *Some Bloke Called Bert*. They had performed at the fête before and were very good. Brenda and Grantley assumed the worst when they heard the name, thinking their ears would have been blasted by a combination of punk and heavy metal, but they were relieved to hear their music was easy listening and not overly offensive. It would see them through to the early hours of the morning when people would go home to start planning next year's event.

For the Coaching Inn it was a normal day. Maggie and Ron would be kept busy with the entire village camped on their doorstep but wouldn't reap the rewards from having so many customers in a financial sense. Twenty-five per cent of their takings would be donated to the hospice. They would have liked to have done more but had overheads to consider. The same was true of Susan. She had moved her tearoom business outside and would give ten per cent of her takings to the charity.

Maggie had drawn up a rota to allow the Coaching Inn staff to take regular breaks so they could enjoy the fête too. At one point it broke down and they were all outside at the same time. Happy hour took on a completely different meaning.

'If this rota is going to work we have to read the bloody thing,' Maggie told her re-assembled troops as she pointed to it behind the bar.

Candice and Harry watched Rafe walk by with a pot of jam that he clearly didn't want and turned their attention back to the coconut shy. Every time Ted Cooper set them up they knocked them down. He had more fun being burgled.

Candice saw the latest one fall and punched the air in celebration. "That's five-four to me." A thought occurred to her and she looked at Harry puzzled. "Shouldn't we be throwing stuff at these?"

"Balls," he said.

"I was only asking."

"We should be throwing balls at them."

"Oh. But they're hard to pick up."

"I know. That's why it's easier to push them off. Five-all," he said, watching his coconut fall to the ground.

"It's not testing our throwing skills though. Six-five."

"No, but it's testing our pushing skills. Six-all."

"Why won't these damn things stay up?" Ted said, bending to retrieve the last coconut to have fallen.

Ron was waiting to play the game in a more conventional way and tapped his watch. "Hurry up, Ted. I have to pad up in three hours."

He was more worried about being spotted by Maggie as he was in breach of the rota again and shouldn't have been out there.

"Seven-six," Candice said.

"They won't stay on the posts," Ted protested.

"Seven-all."

"This one is staying up if it kills me."

"Eight-seven."

By the time the score reached twenty-all Ted's back was in two. He couldn't bend to retrieve the coconuts anymore and sought assistance from a first-aider. Ron gave up waiting and tried his luck at the *Test Your Strength* machine but couldn't lift the mallet. Candice and Harry called it a draw and looked for somewhere else to cause havoc.

They saw Brenda walk by with a pot of jam that she clearly didn't want and eavesdropped on her conversation with Bill and Susan when she stopped to chat.

"I see you've been buying jam," Susan said.

Brenda gazed in the direction of Mrs Jenkins' stall as if in a trance. She was bewildered. How she had come to be in possession of something she never ate was a mystery to her. "I don't even like jam. I only stopped to say hello."

"Mrs Jenkins can be very persuasive," Bill said. "I saw one of the UFO chaps with a jar just now."

Brenda nodded. "Yes, Rafe. He made the mistake of asking her for the right time. That will teach him for not winding his watch."

"I thought the ufologists would have left by now. The family from Bristol are still here too," Susan remarked.

"They're leaving after the fête. I don't know about the ufologists. I assume they're staying a bit longer," Bill said.

"Have either of you seen strange lights in the sky?" Brenda asked them.

"No, not a thing," Susan replied.

"And nor will you," Harry said.

What he and Candice knew but they didn't was that

following Delia's phone call to the police the previous afternoon the hoaxers had been charged with receiving money by fraudulent means and taken into custody. No more flying Frisbees for them. They would have to rethink a planned holiday to Mexico on their ill-gotten gains too.

"Are you enjoying the fête?" Susan asked Brenda.

"Yes, I am. To be honest it's better than I expected. I didn't think so much would be going on."

"We usually push the boat out. It's a small village but this is one of the largest fêtes in the area," Bill told her.

"You've certainly done yourselves proud. I'm already making plans to come back next year."

Susan smiled. She read between the lines and found something she hadn't expected to be there. "It sounds like we have a convert on our hands. Are you thinking of swapping London for village life?"

Candice scoffed at the idea. Brenda was a confirmed city girl, always had been, always would be. The air wasn't worth taking into her lungs if it didn't have petrol fumes in it. "No way," she said confidently.

"I'm considering it," Brenda replied. "I know Mike would like to get out of London."

Candice was stunned. "My God. The last party animal has fallen."

"Would you like to live here?" Bill asked.

"Yeah, I think I would. We're not planning to retire, that's a few years away yet, but we need to slow down and start taking things easier. Mike's heart attack was proof of that."

Bill nodded.

"I think a village like this would suit us well."

"You and Mike would be more than welcome," Susan

said.

For Candice it was the best news she could have heard.

Samantha was a good friend and Candice loved being with her but if she had known Brenda felt this way she would have left Meadow Cottage to her and not Emily. She and Mike could have moved in whenever they had a mind to. It would have been perfect. There was no question of asking Samantha to leave in order for Emily to sell the cottage, it was her home and she was welcome to stay for as long as she wanted, but it was an opportunity lost in terms of continuing her friendship with Brenda.

"I'll let you know if anything becomes available," she said.

Harry advised caution. He didn't want to see Candice get ahead of herself. "I wouldn't rush off to the estate agent's just yet. She's only thinking about it."

"I know, but if Bren and Mike lived here it would be so cool."

Bill had one eye on the future too; the near future as opposed to the distant. It was nice to see so many residents out and about enjoying themselves but that could have brought problems later.

"I hope the burglars don't pay anyone a visit tonight. A lot of homes will be left unattended till the early hours of the morning. It would be the perfect time for them to strike."

"I hadn't thought of that," Candice admitted.

Harry had but didn't comment.

"I spoke to Prudence earlier. She told me the night patrols are going out as usual," Susan said. "I wish the police would hurry up and catch them."

"I can't think of anything worse than thieves breaking into your home," Brenda replied. "I'm sorry you and Bill were burgled too. It must have been awful."

"Yes, but everyone rallied around and helped us. That's the nice thing about living in a village like this. People pull together in times of crisis," Bill said.

"Did they take much?"

"It was mostly electrical; the TV, stereo, laptops, that sort of thing. Fortunately they didn't come upstairs. They only took what was in the lounge. What I found surprising was they didn't go after the day's takings. That was locked in a safe that we have in our bedroom. We would have lost a lot more if they *had* come upstairs so in that respect we were lucky. We didn't even know they were in the house."

"How long will the insurance claim take?" Brenda asked.

"Months probably. Our insurers have made an initial payment so we've been able to replace the essentials but the rest could take some time."

"Let's hope they settle it sooner rather than later. I'll let you get on. You have cream teas to sell."

"Can we tempt you with anything?" Susan asked.

"I'm going to wander around for a while but I'll be back. I hear your cakes are to die for and I'm not leaving this village until I've tried several."

Susan laughed. "Okay. It was nice talking to you."

"You too."

Brenda left them to browse the stalls.

"What are we gonna do about the burglars?" Candice asked Harry. "Bill's right. Today has got '*Come and rob me*' written all over it."

"We can do what I did on Emily's birthday. While everyone was at the Coaching Inn I did the rounds every half an hour. With two of us doing it we can cover more ground." He shook his head, recalling a lot of effort on his part that had brought no reward. "I still don't understand why nothing happened that night."

"Maybe they were waiting for a better opportunity - and it doesn't get much better than this. The green is crowded now. You won't be able to move out here after dark when the music kicks in."

"That's why we have to remain vigilant at all times."

"What are you like with a rifle?" she asked.

"You don't want to shoot the burglars, do you?"

"No, I wanna shoot some metal ducks."

Candice led him to a stall that catered for that sort of thing.

As they turned to leave Delia walked by with a pot of jam that she clearly didn't want.

*

Delia was on her way to the Coaching Inn to have lunch. When she arrived she saw Emily sitting at her table by the fireplace. Grantley was at the bar ordering drinks.

"Hello, Pro..." She stopped abruptly and corrected herself. "Norman. How are you today?"

"I'm very well, Delia. Are you enjoying the fête?"

"Yes, I think it's going jolly well."

"Emily and I were about to have lunch. Perhaps you would care to join us?"

"I wouldn't want to intrude."

"It would be no intrusion."

Delia looked at Emily and received a pleasant smile in return. "In that case, yes. I would love to join you."

Grantley bought her a drink and they sat down.

"Have you heard anything from Samantha?" Delia asked Emily.

"No, but I wasn't expecting to."

"She said she would call me when she got there but hasn't yet." She smiled and paused over her drink. "Too busy having a great time I expect."

Grantley didn't know Samantha had intended to call. How would he? He wondered if she had made a similar arrangement with her parents but didn't consider it to have been a problem. Like Delia, they would have assumed she was busy or it had slipped her mind. Who thought of home when they were in Paris?

The subject was dropped when Maggie appeared at the table to take their food orders.

"Have you decided what to have?" she asked.

Grantley handed her the menus that he and Emily had studied upon arrival. "Yes. Emily and I will have the fish board sharer please."

"Okay. Delia?"

Delia hadn't looked at the menu but there would have been little point in her doing so. She wasn't adventurous with food and always went for the simple option. "I'll have the cheese burger."

"Would you like the standard or the special?"

"What is the difference between the two?"

"The special is a half-pounder and comes with onion rings and a free house in Malibu."

"I'll have that then. Thank you."

"No problem."

"I meant to ask you, Maggie. What time does Ron take up his bowling challenge?" Grantley asked.

"Four o'clock. I expect it to be over by five past."

Emily recalled his performance the previous year against Falworth and thought she had been over-generous in her estimate.

"I might send down a couple of fast ones myself."

Maggie was horrified. Grantley was twenty-five years older than Ron but in better shape. A delivery in excess of a snail's pace may have led to serious consequences. "Don't bowl too fast. You'll kill him."

Emily grinned and rose from the table to go to the ladies room. "Excuse me."

Always the gentleman, Grantley stood too.

Maggie was impressed. She recalled the one and only time Ron had stood for her when she left a room. He had cramp in his right foot and shot off the sofa like a rocket being launched into space.

She left to take their orders to the kitchen.

Grantley re-took his seat and used this moment alone with Delia to discuss private matters. He wasn't in the least bit interested in what she was doing but had to make it look like she was engaged in work of great importance. Now his prisoner had been installed in Brook Cottage he had to keep Delia occupied and at arm's length. He couldn't allow himself to be distracted by trivial issues. There was too much at stake.

"Are you any closer to locating Crosby?"

"I'm afraid not. He's a very difficult man to track down."

"Keep trying. It is imperative that we speak with him."

"I'll do my best. What about you? Did the woman I was supposed to meet in Falworth call again?"

"No, I've not heard from her since." Grantley rubbed his chin and put his acting skills to work again. "I'm completely baffled by that. She mentioned Candice by name. She must know what is going on but who is she?

And why didn't she show up for the meeting?"

"It really is most perplexing," Delia said.

"Our one chance of making a breakthrough and it comes to nothing."

"How did you get on with Mr Cunningham in New York?"

"Not good I'm afraid. He said he couldn't help."

"Oh dear. Let's hope you have more success with Mr Kienholtzer when you speak to him on Monday."

"I regret to say it's bad news on that front too. He's had to go to Zurich on urgent business. I won't be able to speak with him for another week."

That was the last thing Delia wanted to hear in light of recent events. Her trusted friend didn't know it but they were running out of time.

"Professor, we may not have another week. Candice disappeared again yesterday."

"Yesterday?"

"She was only gone three hours but this time she knew what was happening. I think the force almost has her completely under its control. My fear is the next time she disappears she won't be able to come back."

"That is a cause for concern. You said she knew what was happening. In what way did she know?"

"She knew she was being taken. On previous occasions she was unaware. She said *'My Master is calling me.'* Then she was gone."

"Her Master?"

"That was what she said. We must do something, Professor. I think Candice is in terrible danger."

Grantley saw concern in her eyes and responded as any good actor would have. He was a gifted manipulator of people. Use them and throw them away was his motto in life. It had served him well. "Try not to worry, Delia. I'm sure we can get to the bottom of this and save her."

"I do hope so. She has come to mean rather a lot to me."

A door to their left opened and Emily returned from the ladies room.

"We'll talk again later. Do everything you can to locate Crosby. I can't stress how important that is."

"Yes, Professor."

An excellent lunch followed. As a cricketer Ron was a disaster waiting to happen but as a chef he was one of the best in the business. There was nothing he couldn't do in the kitchen. The meals they had chosen were basic, the sort of food he could have prepared in his sleep, but even burgers and a smoked fish board of mackerel, trout and salmon demanded respect and he did it better than anyone Maggie knew. She couldn't cook at all. Before they married she made a meal for him which she presented in a romantic ambiance, candles on the table, flowers, the whole works. When Ron got out of hospital he said if he ever saw her with a saucepan again he would kill her.

Grantley and Delia held up their side of the conversation without allowing secret ambitions and fears to betray them. To Grantley it came naturally. Delia had to work at it but although she found it difficult at no point did Emily suspect something was wrong. She was unaware that Candice had disappeared again. It wasn't a conscious decision to keep it from her. Candice and Harry simply hadn't spoken to Emily since it happened. Harry would bring her up-to-date when he commenced his vigil at her cottage that night.

After lunch they left the Coaching Inn together and looked around several stalls before Delia took leave of them. When they parted company they saw Ian walk by with a pot of jam that he clearly didn't want.

*

"Are we going out again tonight?"

Brian met Siobhan's question with a shrug of his shoulders. He couldn't see the point. In the six days they had been in the village they hadn't come within shouting distance of a UFO. Why should tonight have been any different? Despite this he felt they still had work to do and made a snap decision.

"Yes, I think we should."

"There's a live band on later," Neil protested.

"What is more important?" Brian put to him in a manner to underline his authority. "Making contact with an alien species or listening to a group that call themselves *Some Bloke Called Bert?*"

"They might sing Agadoo."

"All the more reason to miss it," Siobhan muttered.

Standing beside her, Karen had slipped into a dreamy smile.

"Can you push your hand inside my right pocket now?" she asked.

Her girlfriend duly obliged.

"H'mm, nice."

Rafe frowned at his estranged wife swaying on the point of ecstasy. The truth was he was jealous. If he could have satisfied her the way Siobhan did they might have still been together. It galled him to know she had succeeded where he had failed, not that he had tried that often. The more he thought about it the more he realised the phrase *not tonight, darling, I've got a headache* had been his undoing.

"I think Brian is right. We'll kick ourselves if we don't go out tonight and miss something," he said.

"Oh... yummy."

"Will you pay attention?" Rafe snapped.

Neil had been told the aliens he thought he had seen were a couple of pranksters out to scare him and was glad they had been caught, but he remained nervous and would rather have done his UFO watching from the front row of a concert with a drink in his hand. If this group was as good as people said they might have performed the Birdie Song too.

"We don't have to go out into the fields. We can see the sky from here. All we have to do is look up," he told his colleagues.

"We can't set up our equipment here. There will be too many people around. It might get damaged," Brian said.

"It doesn't work half the time anyway," Neil muttered.

As far as Brian was concerned the decision had been made and he saw no point in debating it further. They were in Cloverdale St Mary to conduct important scientific research and some bloke called Bert couldn't have been allowed to stand in the way of it.

"We're going out at ten o'clock and that's final," he told Neil. "In the meantime it's a lovely day and I suggest we enjoy the fête."

"Well said," Siobhan agreed. "Um, does anyone want this pot of jam?" she asked, holding it aloft in her free hand.

The others held up theirs.

*

At five to four Ron marched across the green in his whites with his cricket bat tucked under his arm. If he had been playing in a match he would have marched back to whence he came any moment but as this was a charity event he felt confident that his time spent at the crease would have been longer than usual.

Ian watched him approach and began the task of drumming up business. "Roll up, roll up. It's the moment you've all been waiting for, a chance to bowl out our star batsman in three balls. 50p each. Test your skill against the best in the village."

Even Maggie was surprised to hear this.

"Who's he talking about?" she asked Emily.

"Your husband."

"Oh. I thought Ian had got someone else to do it."

Harry shared her sense of impending doom and shook his head as Ron arrived at the crease. "This is going to be embarrassing to watch."

"Don't be so negative. He might hit one," Candice said.

The expression on Harry's face told her he didn't think there was much chance of that happening.

Melanie stepped up first. She liked cricket and she liked Ron but this was sport and friendship counted for nothing once the ball was in her hand.

He looked at her and smiled as he stabbed the ground with his bat. "Don't worry, Mel. I won't hit all of them for six."

Her first ball took out his middle stump. Her second smacked into off-leg. Her third blasted everything out of the ground and sent the bails flying into the next county.

"Just warming up," Ron said, head-bowed as he practised the strokes he should have played.

Melanie was having so much fun she bought three more balls.

Out, out, out.

"I think there's something wrong with this bat," Ron said, examining it.

"Yeah, it's in the hands of someone who can't play cricket," Harry announced.

"Are you still warming up?" Emily asked.

Ron looked at her assuredly. He was an ace batsman and knew what he was doing. "You have to ease yourself into these things, Emily, get a feel for the wicket."

"Can I buy another three?" Melanie asked Ian.

"No, go away," Ron snapped.

Ian smiled and escorted her back to Martin and Janet. "Maybe later. Let's give someone else a go first. Besides, you wouldn't want to see a grown man cry, would you?"

Melanie received praise and congratulations from her parents and taunted Ron by waving a five pound note at him. She was sugar and spice, all things nice, but her eyes said *I'm out to get you.*

Ron gulped and felt decidedly uncomfortable.

Grantley stepped up next.

Out, out, out.

*

Over the next hour the entire village bowled Ron out. Even Emily succeeded in getting him out despite the fact that she had never held a cricket ball in her life and bowled her deliveries underarm. Her final ball slipped from her hand and rolled along the ground but still he was out. The ball didn't make contact with the stumps. Ron did that himself with his bat when he danced around the crease in readiness to give it a good whack. It became apparent to everyone watching that he was rubbish at golf too.

Harry looked ahead to Cloverdale St Mary's annual cricket match with the team from Falworth and saw nothing but doom and gloom on the horizon. The sad truth was Ian was right. Ron was the best batsman they had. It went some way to explaining why they got massacred every year.

"That was the worst display of batting I've ever seen," he told Candice.

"Don't be so hard on him. He's warming up," she said in Ron's defence.

"Candice, it's finished."

She raised her eyebrow. "He's not still warming up?"

"No, the challenge is over."

"But he didn't hit anything."

Harry sighed. "I know. That's *why* it was the worst display of batting I've ever seen."

Candice shrugged her shoulders and looked on the positive side. "Well, he may not have impressed the England selectors but he's raised money for charity. I take my hat off to him for that."

"Yeah, that's the most important thing today," Harry conceded.

It was just after 5:00 p.m. and most of the stalls were closing. Some were still doing a brisk trade and would stay open till six.

Mrs Jenkins' stall was one that had closed and Ian

was curious to see Sheila walk towards him carrying a large cardboard box.

"What have you got in there?" he asked her.

"I bought some jam. I got it this morning but Mrs Jenkins put it aside for me."

A feeling of dread rose from the pit of his stomach. The last time he saw a box as big as that it had their new stereo inside it.

"How many did you buy?"

"Thirty jars."

"Thirty! On Monday morning I'm starting divorce proceedings."

"Okay. We'll fight over Becky and the CDs but you can have custody of the jam. I detest the stuff."

"Then why did you buy so much of it?"

"It's for charity."

"That you want to support it is very commendable but not if it means it will take up every inch of cupboard space in our kitchen. We might have to sell up and buy a bigger house."

Sheila began to wilt under the weight. "Can you take this home before we call the estate agent? It's a bit heavy."

When Ian took it from her he almost fell down.

"This isn't over," he said.

"Mrs Jenkins is going to make marmalade too next year."

"This is definitely not over."

Ian staggered to the vicarage. It looked like he was drunk. He considered getting that way later. It was preferable to over-dosing on a food mountain of strawberry jam. It would have been higher than Everest if they spooned it out.

Sheila watched him go indoors and was joined by Bill and Susan. Bill was holding a pot of jam that he clearly didn't want.

"Would you like to have this?" he asked, offering it to her.

"That's very kind of you. We always have room for jam," Sheila said, accepting it. "How did you do today?"

"We haven't counted up yet but I think we've done all right. We've been quite busy," Susan told her.

"Thank you for putting so much effort into it. I'm sure the hospice will be delighted."

"It's a worthwhile cause. The work they do is outstanding," Bill said. "I see some stalls are still open," he added, looking around the green.

"Yes. I think they'll be done by half past five, six at the latest. Then we can start the evening do," Sheila replied. She turned and looked at Becky when she appeared beside her. "What have you got there?"

"I'm not sure," she said, studying the LP in her hands. "It's by someone called Mozart. I got it for you and dad."

"For us?"

"You don't think I would buy classical music for myself, do you?"

Sheila grinned. Going by the racket that emanated from her daughter's bedroom that wasn't likely at all. "Thank you, Becky. That's very sweet of you."

"I got you a pot of jam too."

"Ah, just what we needed," she said, taking it from her.

"Where is dad?"

"He popped home for a moment." Sheila looked across the green to see if he was on his way back. "I don't know what he's doing in there. He might be rearranging the kitchen cupboards."

Becky didn't know what she meant by that.

"I'm going home myself so I'll tell him to get a move on," she said.

"Why are you going home?"

"I want to buy some T-shirts but I've run out of money. Ten pounds will be enough," she added, looking at her mother in hope.

Sheila knew how to read her thoughts and grinned again. "Take it from my other purse in the sideboard."

"Thanks, mum."

Becky returned to the vicarage.

"She's tuned in, isn't she?" Bill said smiling.

"Yes, that she is. We get a second-hand LP and a pot of jam and she gets ten pounds to spend on clothes."

No sooner had Becky gone indoors she ran out again, screaming and in tears.

"HE'S DEAD... MUM... DAD'S DEAD!"

*

Ian insisted on walking to the ambulance. He had a bad cut to the back of his head and should have been on a stretcher but he didn't want to alarm Sheila and Becky any more than they were. He wouldn't have gone to hospital but as he had suffered a head injury the paramedics advised him to. He had to be examined thoroughly. It wasn't surprising Becky had assumed the worst. She found him lying unconscious in a pool of blood.

Sheila and Becky went with him to the hospital.

Sheila left her spare key with Miss Blunt. It was an irrational thought given what had happened but she wanted to be sure the house was properly locked and secured in her absence. Miss Blunt was calm and dependable in a crisis and assured her she would take care of it.

A large crowd had gathered outside the vicarage and watched as the ambulance drove away. Candice and Harry were in the lounge. A police forensics team dusted for fingerprints as the investigation into this latest burglary began.

People were stunned that the thieves would have struck in broad daylight but the fête provided the perfect distraction and their task couldn't have been easier. They had removed a fence panel in the back garden and drove their van up to the kitchen door. With no one to disturb them they had all the time in the world to search the house and take what they wanted. They went through it systematically room by room.

Baker and Tate were about to leave when Ian returned home. He entered the lounge to find Baker taking Sheila's purse from the sideboard. Before he could do anything Tate appeared behind him and knocked him out. He didn't use a baseball bat. Ian was felled with the element of surprise and brute strength. When he regained consciousness Sheila was kneeling beside him holding his hand and Bill was on the phone to the police. Becky was being comforted by Susan on the sofa.

Harry looked at the blood on the carpet and held himself responsible for what had happened to his friend. "This is my fault. I should have been here."

"You had no way of knowing. We thought they would strike at night, not during the day," Candice said.

"Look at this place. Everything is gone. They've lost

it all."

"Ian is gonna be okay. That's the important thing."

It was of course but Harry was too angry to acknowledge it. He looked at the shelf on which Candice's Golden Globe for her performance in *The Eternity Child* had once stood.

"I'll get those bastards and when I do..." He stopped. Candice wouldn't have wanted to hear what he was capable of.

She encouraged him to leave. "Come on, let's go outside."

Emily watched them walk along the path but couldn't say anything because too many people were present. She had never seen Harry look so mad. He didn't speak as he walked past her. Candice didn't speak either. She met her eyes with an expression that suggested a storm was coming.

"This is a terrible business," Grantley said.

Secretly he was impressed. He had given permission for the vicarage to be burgled but thought Baker would have done it after dark. The man was more courageous than he had given him credit for. Maybe he had misjudged him?

"Do you want to go home, Emily? This must be very distressing for you."

"Yes, I think I will."

"I'll escort you."

"No, it's okay. Thank you anyway."

"Are you coming out again later?"

"Ian and Sheila would want the evening party to go ahead. They put a lot of work into making today possible. I'll be there."

Grantley smiled. "Then so shall I." He looked at his

watch. "It's ten to six now. Shall I meet you in the marquee at seven?"

"Yes, that sounds good."

"Try not to worry. I'm sure Ian will be all right."

He kissed her and they parted company.

*

Samantha tensed as Grantley descended the stairs into the basement. It was a reflex action born of fear. The nice, courteous man who had made such a good impression on everyone in the village terrified her now. He wouldn't stay long. He wanted to shower and change before he went out again.

Grantley walked to the table on which the water jug and glass stood. "You should take a drink. It's been several hours since your last one."

He filled the glass and held it to her lips.

Samantha's throat was dry and she was glad of the opportunity to drink but he increased the angle of the glass faster than she could swallow and she had to gulp in order to keep up with him. Even when the water filled her mouth and she began to cough and splutter he continued to raise it.

When the glass was empty he returned it to the table.

Samantha looked at the other table across the room. She had no idea what was concealed beneath the dustsheet. What it hid was on a need-to-know basis and she didn't need to know.

"May I have something to eat?" she asked.

"I told you. You will be given water to drink but no food."

"Please, I'm hungry."

"You should have gone to the fête today. There was plenty of food on offer there. When I go back for the evening party I'll ask them to prepare a doggy-bag for you."

Grantley laughed at his hilarious joke, he should have been a comedian, but unknown to him he had made his first mistake.

Samantha assumed she was held prisoner in some secret, isolated place far from home but realised that wasn't the case. If Grantley had attended the fête he wouldn't have travelled any great distance to have given her water prior to going back. Home was closer than she thought. She was in the village. She was in *his* home. Knowing this gave her a slender thread of hope. If there were people around someone might have come.

Please God, let them come. I beg you, let someone come.

"Were you meant to call anyone when you got to Paris?" he asked her.

"I said I would phone Delia."

"Anyone else?"

"No."

"You weren't going to call your parents?"

"No. I don't when I go away."

"So why would you call Delia?"

"I don't know. I just said I would."

"I should have been made aware of that."

Grantley punched her in the stomach.

Samantha couldn't absorb the blow with the wall at her back and the air exploded from her lungs, her winded body convulsing as she struggled to breathe. She spat mucus from her nose and pulled at the restraints, trying to lift herself off the floor as the hammer impact drove through her. She fought to pull air into her mouth, crying, gasping, desperate to regain control of a body under attack.

"I hope you're not keeping anything else from me?"

Pain and tears prevented her from answering.

He punched her again.

Samantha coughed and choked. She twisted her hips in a desperate attempt to force her lungs to work. She had to draw in air. She had to breathe. She had to save herself before she succumbed to asphyxiation.

Grantley slapped her face. "I don't expect to have to repeat myself."

"No... ple... ple... please..."

"If you keep anything from me the punishment will be severe. Do you understand?"

"Ca... can't... breat..."

He slapped her a second time. "ANSWER ME, YOU FUCKING BITCH!"

And a third.

"Ye... yes..."

She twisted her hips as before, eyes fixed on a ceiling that was distant and pulling away from her. It was as if the oxygen had been sucked out of the room.

Grantley watched Samantha fight to recapture her breath, her ribs almost bursting through her skin as she shook. Every nerve in her body screamed in agony. She thought she was going to die but slowly her breathing returned to normal. Her pain lingered but at least she could breathe.

Grantley reacted calmly to her distress and showed not a hint of concern. That she was suffering was unimportant. He would have taken her to the gates of hell and beyond in order to make a point.

"You'd better pee again. I won't be back till late."

He unhooked the chain and let out the slack. Samantha slid down the wall to her squatting position.

She found no respite from her pain as she settled on her haunches. Her back, arms and shoulders ached and her legs were stiff. Her stomach hurt and her face was sore from assaults past and present. Prisoners at the time of the Spanish Inquisition would have received better treatment.

The bucket was slid under her.

"Get on with it. I'm in a hurry," she was told.

Samantha pulled her briefs aside.

Grantley knelt in front of her and she hung her head in embarrassment, weeping as she urinated.

"Why are you doing this to me?... I never did you any harm... I'm a good girl... I never did you any harm..."

He didn't answer. He watched her urinate without saying a word.

When Samantha had relieved herself Grantley returned her to a standing position. He left the basement immediately afterwards.

In darkness once more, trembling with fear, that slender thread of hope was gone.

"I'm a good girl... Daddy... please help me..."

How the good suffered at the hands of the bad.

*

It was a decent turn out for the evening party but the burglary at the vicarage had taken the edge of what had been a perfect day. Many people didn't attend because of it, thinking the thieves may have struck again, but those who returned to the green were determined not to let the scum of the earth get the better of them. How else could thieves have been described? What better description for people who invaded the homes of others?

Some Bloke Called Bert were better than Grantley and Brenda had expected. It was the first time Candice had seen the group too and she was equally impressed, although her interest was focused on the lead singer as opposed to the band as a whole. She thought he was rugged and good-looking. He could sing as well.

Harry had calmed down after the attack on Ian and failed to see what the attraction was. Every time he looked at Candice she wore a dreamy smile. "There is more than one person on that stage," he told her.

"What?"

She couldn't tear her eyes away from him. If she had drooled any more Harry would have given her a bib.

"He's only a mortal. You've seen them before."

Candice applauded as the Adonis from Falworth brought the song they were performing to a close. "Come on, Harry. You have to admit he's pretty cool. Well, drop-dead gorgeous to be precise."

"Look at his shoulders. He's got dandruff."

"There's nothing wrong with his hair. It's perfect for running your fingers through."

"And he's got a crooked nose."

"He's got the best ass I've ever seen. What's on the flip side of it looks pretty good in those jeans too."

"Disgusting," Harry muttered.

"Do I detect a hint of jealousy in your voice?"

Harry scoffed at the idea. "Me? Jealous of him? You're having a laugh."

"I can see why you would feel intimidated. He's

young, handsome, has a body that no woman in her right mind would kick out of bed..."

"What do you mean, intimidated? I could knock spots off him. I can hold a tune better too."

"I've heard you sing. You sound like a neutered cat."

"I do not."

"When you sang along with the radio the other day you sounded like Pyewacket did when I had his bits chopped off." Candice paused and rubbed her chin. "I don't think he's ever forgiven me for that."

Damn right I haven't, the cat thought as he marched through the crowd.

He had gone there to lodge an official complaint. Some bloke called Bert was scaring the mice away.

"Did you used to sing in the shower?" Candice asked.

"All the time."

"Be grateful I didn't know you then. You wouldn't have liked where I would have put the soap."

"Tosh," came Harry's considered reply.

"There's one other advantage he has over you," she went on.

"What could he possibly do that I can't?"

"A girl could listen to his heartbeat when she lays her head on his chest."

"Apart from that."

Candice laughed.

He was about to argue further but she shushed him silent when the next song began. For the next four minutes it was like he didn't exist. A nuclear bomb could have fallen on the village and Candice would have been the last one to notice.

The party on the green gathered momentum and a good time was had by all. The Coaching Inn was deserted which allowed Maggie, Ron and their staff to join in. People danced and sang but Ian, Sheila and Becky should have been there too and their absence was felt by many. Ian and Sheila had worked hard to make this day possible. That they were not there to enjoy the finale was a bitter pill to swallow.

Harry left every half an hour to check Pine Trees and Meadow Cottage. He kept an eye on the Coaching Inn too which was technically still open for business even though no one was there. In-house security was provided courtesy of the rota that Maggie had drawn up but it was still prone to breaking down and it was better to be safe than sorry.

Candice played no part in doing the rounds. She was too busy enjoying herself. She ogled the lead singer – who had been prized into his jeans with a shoe horn – and danced with Brenda and Maggie without their realising it. Emily couldn't recall a time when she had seen her so relaxed, certainly not over the past few weeks. Everyone entered into the spirit of things but the best was yet to come.

At midnight a taxi pulled up outside the Coaching Inn and a bandaged Reverend Ian alighted with Sheila and Becky.

The lead singer saw them and announced their return over his microphone. The green erupted in applause as they walked to the stage beside the marquee which was still standing. In that respect it was like Ian and his family. There was no power on earth that would have brought it down.

Such was the response to their arrival, Ian felt compelled to say a few words.

"Don't worry, I'm not going to sing," he said, unclipping the microphone from its stand. "I just want to say the doctors have given me a clean bill of health.

Tomorrow Sheila and I will sort out our insurance claim but tonight is about the hospice which will benefit from your remarkable support so let's keep this party going."

"Can I stay up late tonight, dad?" his daughter called.

"It's late now. Of course you can, Beck's."

Ian had never heard applause like it. Everyone rose to a man.

He twirled his finger in the air as a signal for the band to re-start but nothing happened. For one horrible moment he thought they were going home but his fears were dispelled by the drummer who was the leader of the band and followed him off-stage.

"We're happy to go on for as long as you want. In addition to that we're waiving our fee. I've spoken to the boys and we want you to give it to the charity."

"I don't know what to say. Thank you," Ian replied.

"Don't thank me, you're the one who put all the work into this. I'm sorry about what happened. I hope the police catch them and you get your stuff back."

"Thank you, Bert."

"No, I'm Fred. The chap on bass is Bert."

The drummer re-took his place on stage and nodded to his band mates.

Bert counted them in for the next number and they performed one of the best covers of Sally Pressberger's *Give Me a Reason to Believe* that Candice had ever heard.

In a basement dark and forgotten, Samantha too heard music but it may have been her imagination.

The rat biting her foot was not.

Thirty

Ian held his Sunday morning service as usual. God would have forgiven him for not doing so under the circumstances but Ian wouldn't have forgiven himself and was determined it would proceed. Jesus Christ had given his life for the good of man. The least Ian could have done was give an hour of his time for the good of his parishioners.

He and his family found it difficult to settle in a home that had been stripped bare at the hands of thieves who dispensed loss and misery to the good and decent. Becky seemed to have taken the burglary in her stride but it became too much for her at four o'clock in the morning when she woke from a troubled sleep. Awareness opened the door to shock and she cried in her room. Ian and Sheila were alerted to her distress and sat up with her. For all of them the day started then.

The task of returning the green to normal began before the service took place and carried on long after. The marquee was taken down and put in storage for another year, the stalls, bunting and side attractions too which were kept in garages and garden sheds dispersed throughout the village.

When the clear up was over all that remained was a solitary pot of jam standing on the spot where 364 of its compatriots had found homes to go to. Why no one wanted this one was a mystery. It was a nice little pot of jam, it could have made someone very happy. That it didn't have a cupboard to live in and a round of toast to befriend was sad but no one took pity on it in its solitude and it was left to contemplate the unfairness of life and what might have been. The only passer-by to show an interest was Pyewacket who would have had it for a snack if he could have got the damn thing open.

Oh well, that's what birds are for, he thought, moving on.

Brenda went home after lunch. Miss Blunt drove her to the train station in Falworth and told her not to be a stranger. Brenda agreed that she and Mike had allowed too much time to pass since their last visit and they would return to Cloverdale St Mary soon. Candice accompanied them as they walked to the car but didn't go to Falworth. She wasn't good at train station goodbyes in life. In death they were better avoided.

Candice's mood was subdued when she returned to Meadow Cottage. She began to miss Brenda the moment she left but cheered up when Harry reminded her that they were attending a birthday party for one of their friends in the afterlife later that afternoon. Delia was surprised to hear that ghosts celebrated birthdays, she assumed they had no interest in cake and party-poppers, but in reality the opposite was true. It was hard to imagine a conga-line of drunken ghosts dancing through the village but Harry assured her it happened on a regular basis. They let their hair down at New Year too.

Today's celebration was special. The ghost in question was a native American who went by the name of Sam Two Coats. He was prone to feeling the cold and wore more than the average North American Indian. He would have been a hundred and sixty-eight years old if Custer hadn't shot him at the Battle of the Little Bighorn.

Harry was looking forward to going out but was worried about leaving the house unattended. Delia often went for long walks and what happened during the fête made him feel uneasy. Now the vicarage had been burgled he was convinced Meadow Cottage would be targeted next and advised caution. It was no longer a case of being vigilant after dark. Whether it was day or night was irrelevant as far as the thieves were concerned. They had proved they were capable of striking at any time.

Unknown to Harry, in Falworth the burglars were discussing that very point.

*

Baker was angry. He had been angry since three o'clock the previous afternoon when he learnt that Samantha had gone to Paris for the weekend. Grantley should have told him. They were allowing a gilt-edged opportunity to slip through their fingers.

"Why didn't he say anything? We could have done Meadow Cottage on Friday night," he told Tate as he paced the lounge in his rented flat.

His associate was more interested in the Golden Globe that had come with their latest haul. It wasn't true what they said. All that glittered *was* gold.

"He must have his reasons," he answered.

"Grantley isn't the one planning the burglaries, I am. If a house is unoccupied I should know about it. Why is he making us wait for the big one? It doesn't make sense. Freeman and Copeland were close friends. That cottage will be packed with expensive stuff that we should have acquired long ago. It should have been the first one we did, not the fucking last."

"What do you propose to do about it?"

"We're gonna do it tonight. Copeland isn't due back until tomorrow evening. We can walk in unchallenged and clean the place out."

Tate was in favour of the idea, he had developed a fondness for awards, but he was cautious too. "Grantley won't like it."

"Fuck Grantley. He wanted these burglaries to act as a diversion for something *he's* working on and that's what I'm giving him. Who I hit and when I hit them is none of his concern. He's not the one climbing in and out of fucking windows at three o'clock in the morning. We do Meadow Cottage tonight."

"It sounds good on paper but it might lead to a stronger police presence in the village. That could make robbing Pine Trees and the pub more difficult."

"We won't lose anything by it if it does. There will be enough in Meadow Cottage to compensate for what we might have to turn our backs on elsewhere. If the place is swarming with police afterwards we can take a break for a while and come back for the other two when things have calmed down."

Tate nodded. He didn't mind playing a waiting game with regard to meeting their schedule. The way things stood they had enough to retire on now. "Okay, tonight it is." He looked at their previous hauls taking up every inch of available space in the flat. Everything they had stolen up to now was there. It looked like a warehouse. "When are we going to start fencing this lot?"

"When we've done the last job. If it becomes too difficult after tonight we'll leave tomorrow. I know a man up north who can find buyers for the Candice Freeman stuff. That's where the real money is. The rest is crap. We can get rid of that ourselves in some pubs I know."

"I thought we would have fenced it in London."

"It's too close to home. The more distance we put between ourselves and this village the better. London is the first place they'll look for us."

Tate bowed to his experience. For him burglary was a new entry on his CV. He was a small-time thief, a mugger who snatched handbags from little old ladies, a man who watched someone on their mobile phone in a pub and relieved them of it when they left. If it hadn't been for Baker he would have been scoring twenty or thirty pounds a day. He wouldn't have been sitting on a sofa with a Golden Globe in his hands.

Baker was more adapt at burglary. Before he became a yard hand at the equestrian centre – a job he took with the intention of robbing it – he made a good living from breaking and entering. It enabled him to drive a nice car and take two foreign holidays a year but it was never enough to buy a place of his own and live in a manner to which he wanted to become accustomed. No, to which he felt he had a right.

The moment he heard Candice Freeman was involved in the equestrian centre he knew that was where he had to be in order to set himself up for life. If he had played his cards right he could have walked away with enough money to have bought property and taken four foreign holidays a year but instead he lost his temper and kicked a horse, getting himself fired by Miss Blunt who saw him do it.

In an act of revenge he returned to the riding school soon after his dismissal and set fire to one of the stables. He was apprehended by a security guard and detained until the police arrived. Candice got there soon after and proved that her temper was just as volatile by trying to rip Baker's head off his shoulders. It was only Miss Blunt's intervention that prevented her from being arrested too.

Baker threw a brick through Candice's lounge window in a further act of revenge before he went to trial. He did revenge well. It was his way of paying her back for showing him disrespect when the burglar turned arsonist and was caught in the act.

Baker treated himself to a night on the town when Candice died. While others mourned her passing he celebrated it. He hated her. He hated Miss Blunt. He hated Cloverdale St Mary because it represented everything he wanted but couldn't have. While he carried out community service as punishment for his crime it occurred to him that if he had done an honest day's work he could have realised his ambitions. But work? Nathan Baker? Surely not. That was what fools and horses did.

Now, looking at possessions once owned by those he detested, he set his sights on the ultimate prize.

"We'll do Meadow Cottage at 2:00 a.m."

*

Delia enjoyed having the cottage to herself. Not for the first time, she considered the trust that had been shown in her.

With Samantha away and Harry and Candice out she could have done whatever she wanted but they didn't think twice about leaving Meadow Cottage in her care because they knew she could be relied upon. She had never found that sort of acceptance anywhere else. She was a loner and didn't have friends. To have been accepted by people who hardly knew her made her feel liked and a part of things for the first time in her life.

She had spent the afternoon trying to locate Crosby and at 4:00 p.m. made a breakthrough. It wasn't what she had hoped for.

Delia called Grantley but there was no answer. It didn't go to voicemail, the phone just kept ringing. He was in the basement attending to other business. She went to the kitchen to make a cup of tea but found she had used the last of the milk. Delia was adaptable and could turn her hand to most things but drinking black tea wasn't one of them and she decided to take a stroll into the village to get some. While she was there she would call on Grantley in person. Brook Cottage was only a short distance from Bill and Susan's shop.

*

"Hello, Ian. How are you feeling?"

Delia had met the vicar on her way to Bill and Susan's. It was the first time she had seen him since he was taken to hospital. She wasn't one for live music and left the party on the green before his return.

"I'm fine, Delia. Thank you," he replied.

"I'm awfully sorry about what happened. Are your wife and daughter all right?"

"Yes. Becky didn't pass a good night but she's okay now." He saw genuine concern in her eyes and smiled in appreciation. "It's very kind of you to ask after them."

"I wish I could do more. It was jolly unfair what they did to you. I hope the police catch them soon. There is only one place for people like that, behind bars."

"I couldn't agree more."

"Have you forgiven them?" she asked from nowhere.

Ian smiled again, this time in amusement. The clergy abided by the code of Christ and advocated turning the other cheek. That was all well and good but it did present an attacker with a second target. Why hit someone in the face once when they could have done it twice?

"No. If I get my hands on them I'll wring their sodding necks," he said.

Delia laughed. "Good for you. It may not be the acceptable way to administer justice but should the opportunity arise I'll hold your coat."

Ian laughed too. "What brings you into the village this afternoon?"

"An absence of milk in Samantha's fridge. She left me with a full carton but I do drink rather a lot of tea. I'm on my way to replenish our stocks. Where are you off to?"

"I'm visiting the Preston's. Albert was discharged from hospital this morning."

"That was the fifth burglary, wasn't it? The chap with the fractured skull?"

"Yes. He's responded well to treatment and the doctors said he could go home. When I spoke to him on the phone earlier he was laughing and joking. He sounded like his usual self. I said I would pop in to see him."

Delia was impressed. Here stood a kind and compassionate man. Ian had suffered at the hands of the burglars too, the carpet in his lounge wore his blood, yet he was prepared to devote time to someone less fortunate than himself. For everyone bad in the world there was someone good. What it needed was more people like the Reverend Ian Dawson.

"That is jolly decent of you. I haven't met Mr and Mrs Preston but please give them my best wishes."

"I will, Delia."

Ian's thoughts were the same when they parted company. The world could have done with more people like her too.

Delia went to buy her milk.

*

Grantley had spent three hours in the basement. He took a dining room chair with him for comfort and used his time well. He wrote notes about Samantha and filmed her with a camcorder. Later he would print photographs from the footage he had shot.

For his prisoner it was another example of how Grantley had total control over her and was capable of anything. It reinforced Samantha's fears that he had social media in mind but his motives were private. He wanted to keep a record of her incarceration for future reference. He planned to write a book about it.

At no time had he spoken to her.

He was loading his washing machine in the kitchen when the doorbell rang. He glanced at the basement door as he walked along the hall but didn't lessen his stride. Down there in the darkness Samantha waited quietly. She visualized the camcorder on the chair he had left behind and dreaded his return. She was still in her underwear but Grantley had made it clear that it too would be removed prior to the event he had spoken of. What sort of film would he have made then and to what end?

"Delia," he said, hiding his surprise at seeing her. "How nice of you to visit."

"I hope you don't mind my calling on you unannounced, Professor, but I have news. I thought I should tell you straightaway."

"In that case you'd better come in." He stood aside in

the doorway to allow her access. "The lounge is just through here," he said, gesturing to his left.

Grantley followed her to the living room, parting another glance at the basement door as they exited the hallway. He hoped he was right about the basement being soundproof. He had tested it by playing music in the lounge at a high volume and going downstairs to listen. He could barely hear it so it was safe to assume sound wouldn't have travelled well in the opposite direction. That was the theory. Now it was time to put it into practice. Delia had been his first visitor since he abducted Samantha.

"I was about to make some tea. Would you care for a cup?" he asked.

Delia smiled and made a show of the milk she had bought. "I came prepared for that eventuality."

Grantley was unimpressed by the joke. He grinned out of needing to offer a response and took it from her. "Let me put that in the fridge for you. We wouldn't want it to go off."

"Thank you, Professor."

"Please, make yourself comfortable. I'll just be a moment."

He left the room and made sure he closed the door behind him.

Delia sat on the sofa and cast her eyes around a lounge that was impressive. She was under the impression he had rented the cottage and thought how fortunate he was to have found something so good. Interior designers and estate agents often spoke of the wow factor and this room had it in abundance. The furniture was the best money could buy and expensive paintings adorned the walls. The TV and DVD player were state-of-the-art and the stereo Baker had criticised wouldn't have looked out of place in a sheikh's palace. If the burglars robbed this house they would have made a fortune.

Grantley hadn't gone to the kitchen. His concerns had gotten the better of him and he made a quick dash to the basement. Samantha was terrified by his return and trembled fearing the worst but he only stayed long enough to cover her mouth with duct tape. It was better to be safe than sorry.

"Don't say a word. If you make a sound I'll kill you."

In his haste to return upstairs, he forgot to lock the door.

"Your tea," he said to Delia, returning soon after.

"Thank you. You have a beautiful home. Did it come furnished?"

"No. Everything here belongs to me."

"It really is fabulous," she said, looking around the room again. "How long are you renting it for?"

"Just a few months."

"I don't expect you'll want to give it up. It's such a nice village, isn't it?"

"Yes," he replied, smiling falsely.

Grantley disliked Cloverdale St Mary and couldn't wait to leave. He intended to move back to London when his work was finished. Villages like this were for people devoid of ambition. They made jam and erected marquees, they chatted with no sense of purpose over garden gates and walked their dogs across fields that should have been tarmacked and turned into roads. They settled for the boring and mundane because they didn't have the drive to do anything else. It wasn't for him. He would return to London a revered and respected man and reap the rewards of his brilliance.

"What did you want to tell me?" he asked.

"It's not good news I'm afraid. Alex Crosby is dead."

"Dead?"

"Yes. I read his obituary this afternoon. He died in a car crash last year, just before Christmas."

"How sad for his family."

"And for us. He was the only person we knew of who has come across this type of situation before. His insight could have proved invaluable."

"Indeed so. Is there any way of gaining access to his work?"

"Not that I can see. I've searched everywhere but can't find any additional information to what we already have. It's a jolly bad stroke of luck."

"Worse for him I think, Delia," Grantley said, frowning.

"Sorry? Oh yes. Yes, of course."

She sipped her tea to hide her embarrassment at sounding selfish over Crosby's demise.

"The question is where do we go from here?" Grantley said. "We'll be back to square one if Kienholtzer is of no help to us when I speak to him next week."

"I know. That's what worries me."

"Where is Candice now?"

"She's attending a birthday party."

"A birthday party?"

"It's one of her friends from the afterlife. He was a very nice chap apparently but General Custer didn't think so. He shot him."

This was one of those moments when Grantley felt his life had left him behind and he elected not to comment.

"What are we going to do if she disappears again?"

"Try not to worry, Delia. I'm sure Harry won't allow it to happen."

The moment the words left his mouth Grantley knew he had made a huge mistake.

Delia looked at him curiously. "How do you know about him?"

He bridged his fingers under his chin, resigned to his unguarded moment and what would have to be done in order to repair the damage.

"Yes, that was careless of me, wasn't it? The only way I could have known of Mr Black's existence would be if Candice Freeman had told me about him. For her to have done so we must have spent time in each other's company."

The penny dropped like an anvil crashing through the floor.

Delia stood up. Her mind was overloaded with questions that she had no answers to in her moment of realisation. That Grantley was the force controlling Candice had become obvious but this wasn't the time to debate how and why. She had to get out. She knew what a dangerous position this had put her in and tried to deflect from it.

"I'd better be going. I've been gone a long time and Candice will be worried."

"Miss Freeman is at a birthday party. Presumably Mr Black is there too, helping to blow up the balloons."

The change in Grantley's manner did not go unnoticed. He had been warm and welcoming. Now he was cold and sinister.

"May I have my milk?" she asked.

Grantley laughed. Found out he may have been but she continued to be a source of amusement to him. "My dear Delia. We have arrived at a watershed moment and you concern yourself with milk. Did anyone see you come here?"

"Yes. Father Ian. He walked me to your door."

"I think not. I saw the vicar a short while ago when I took some rubbish out to the bin. He was walking in the opposite direction. He may have passed the time of day with you but he didn't walk you to my door."

"I told Bill Pearce I was coming here. I said the milk was for you."

"I don't drink milk. Pearce is aware of that." Grantley stood too. "Are we going to do this the easy way or the hard way?"

"Do what?" she asked, trying to look and sound innocent.

Grantley sighed. His plans had suffered an unexpected setback and he wasn't in the mood to play games. Desperate times called for desperate measures. "The hard way it is."

He punched Delia in the face and she fell back on the sofa unconscious.

*

Grantley had much to do after taking his second prisoner. It was a complication he could have done without.

He carried Delia down to the basement and tied her to the radiator. Samantha watched him bind her hands and feet. In her fear and confusion she thought she was dead but the notion soon left her. Why would Grantley have tied a dead body? There was another reason for taking Delia captive and Samantha drew the wrong conclusions. Two women held prisoner in a basement, there to be raped and abused and forced to rape each other. The sick and perverted online would never have had it so good.

When Grantley finished he returned to his first victim. There was no need for the duct tape now and he pulled it from Samantha's mouth.

"I thought you might like some company," he said.

Samantha shuddered. She tensed with fright every time he went near her. "Why? Why are you doing this?"

He looked deep into her eyes. Where he saw fear she saw cold, callous disregard, a torturer who thought nothing of the pain and misery he inflicted, an executioner who would soon have his prize. "Because I can."

Grantley exited the basement. This time he locked the door but the light was left on.

He didn't want Delia to regain consciousness in the dark. He wanted her to see Samantha in chains. He wanted her to be in no doubt of his authority, the power he held over the innocent and the lengths to which he was prepared to go in order to exercise it. He wanted her to be afraid too.

He returned to the lounge to work out what to do next. Delia couldn't have simply disappeared. She knew people in the village who would have missed her. The problem wasn't what to do about her, he could have kept her in the basement for as long as he wanted. The problem was her van parked outside Meadow Cottage.

If it wasn't there they would have thought she had left. It would have been strange but not unheard of. People who drove camper vans had a habit of coming and going. Delia would have been one more traveller who stopped for a while and moved on to pastures new. She didn't have to explain her actions to anyone. In that respect she could have simply disappeared but to avoid arousing suspicion that van had to go.

How? That was the question now. Delia had walked to the village. She didn't have the keys on her. Grantley had gone through her pockets and found the key to Meadow Cottage and some loose change but nothing else. So how would he have moved it? He couldn't hot-wire an engine to save his life.

It occurred to him that if he did have the keys he would have been confronted with another problem. What if someone saw him while he was taking it? He didn't want to be arrested for car theft when he stood on the verge of global recognition. That wouldn't have looked good on his list of achievements at all.

How do I move that van? he pondered as he relaxed in his armchair. The answer, when it came to him, was obvious. *Mr Baker. I wonder if you would like to make a hundred pounds for a little job on the side?*

Of course he would have.

Baker wouldn't have needed the keys. He hot-wired his first car at the age of ten.

*

For a man who knew the importance of planning, Grantley's mistakes were mounting up. First he alerted Samantha to where she was being held prisoner, then he confessed to Delia that he was the force behind Candice's disappearances by mentioning Harry. He was unaware of his latest blunder. Had he realised, it would have made the removal of the camper van unnecessary. It was now hidden in woods adjacent to a nearby quarry, for all the good that would have done.

Grantley had failed to take into consideration that Delia was a house guest and wasn't living in the van. Her possessions were inside Meadow Cottage; her mobile phone, wallet, laptop. Her clothes hung in the wardrobe in the spare room and her toiletries stood on a shelf in the bathroom. Her keys were there but that would have been easily explained. They were a spare set and she had forgotten to take them with her. Everyone knew what a scatterbrain Delia could be.

For Samantha's abduction Grantley had been thorough. He went through the cottage with a fine-tooth comb to create the illusion that she had gone to Paris. He overlooked nothing. Even washing up their teacups and putting them away had been planned in advance, he didn't want it known that she had a visitor before she left, but when it came to Delia that attention to detail was missing.

As far as Grantley was concerned his problems started and ended with that camper van. He hadn't thought of the little things and because of it he missed the big things; like a mobile phone that Delia was rarely seen without and clothes she would never have left behind. People had gone to the gallows for less.

"I wonder where she is?" Candice said after she and Harry had conducted a search of the house and garden.

Harry was still wearing a party hat. "Sam Two Coats loved his present. Buying him a plastic bow and arrow set with those little suction pads on the end was a great idea."

"Delia," Candice repeated. "Where do you think she is?"

"Maybe she felt like going for a drive."

"She can't have. Her keys are on the hallway table."

"She took a stroll into the village then."

"Yeah, and pulled the van behind her on the end of a piece of string."

Harry frowned. "Sarcasm is the lowest form of wit."

"I know. That's why I like it so much. Come on, Harry. You have to admit it's pretty strange. Delia didn't say she was going out and her van is gone when the only means of starting it is still here."

"Do you suspect foul play?"

"You're not gonna do your Old Bailey thing again, are you?"

Harry took off his hat and dropped it on the sofa. That Candice was suspicious made him suspicious and he began to take it seriously. "Maybe she went for a walk and the van has been stolen. We're not immune to car theft."

"That's a possibility," she agreed.

"I'll take a look around the village. You stay here in case she comes back."

"Okay."

He began to fade away, only to return when Candice called to him.

"Harry, do you think she's all right?"

"There has to be a logical explanation for this. I'm sure it's nothing to be alarmed about."

"Yeah," she replied, unconvinced.

"Don't worry. We'll find her."

Thirty-one

Delia regained consciousness. It took a moment for her head to clear, for the gravity of the situation to take hold in her thoughts, but when it did she was shocked by what she saw. Nothing could have prepared her for the sight that met her eyes.

"Samantha?"

"Thank God you're awake."

Delia tried to stand but couldn't. Her hands were tied to the top of the radiator and her feet were lashed to the bottom. She succeeded in pulling herself to a sitting position but that was all she could manage.

"What is this place?" she asked.

"I don't know. I think it's Grantley's basement."

"Have you been here all the time?"

"He came to the cottage when I got home from work on Friday. He drugged me and brought me here. What day is it? I lose track of the days."

"It's Sunday."

Samantha was surprised. She had been in the basement for fifty-one hours. It just seemed longer.

A damned existence hammered inside her head, the violence, the humiliation, the thought of more brutal treatment to come. Now Grantley had two prisoners. The thought of her and Delia forced to watch one another suffer was too hard to endure and she retreated to the silence that up to now had been her only companion.

Delia didn't know what was happening or why. She had gone to Brook Cottage to tell a respected colleague important news and became trapped in a nightmare beyond all reasoning. It was hard for her to accept that

Grantley was responsible for Candice's disappearances. That he had kidnapped Samantha was unbelievable. Seeing her confined in just her underwear made her fear the worst and she hesitated over her next question.

"Why did he take off your clothes?"

"He said my skin has to breathe. He told me I was here for some kind of event but didn't say what. He's going to take off my underwear too. Whatever the event is he said I have to be naked."

"Has he touched you?"

"No. He looks at me." She turned her head to draw attention to the chair and the camcorder resting on it. "He sits on that chair. He filmed me and wrote something in a writing pad. If I don't answer when he speaks... he hits me."

Delia looked at the bruise on her cheek. Another the size of a fist scarred her stomach. She couldn't begin to imagine what Samantha must have been going through. "Try not to worry. We'll get out of here. I promise."

"I don't know why he's doing this... Why is he doing this?"

The pain of mental and physical abuse was etched on a face that couldn't take anymore and Samantha closed her eyes, turning her cheek to her arm. It was as if she was trying to blot out the agony that had been forced upon her, desperate to hide from a phantom that hid in the darkness and brought nothing but suffering when it stepped into the light. Savage, relentless suffering.

Delia pulled at the rope tying her hands but it was no use. She might as well have been in chains too. Her confinement was as secure as Samantha's. She tugged at the radiator in an attempt to dislodge it from the wall but old radiators were built to last and this one wasn't going to budge.

She looked at Samantha sobbing on the other side of the room and wondered what sort of animal Grantley had become. She thought she knew him. She thought she could trust him. She thought he was the last of the true gentlemen.

How wrong she was.

*

It was yet to be confirmed officially but there was no doubt in the minds of a select few who didn't need to be told the obvious. Delia was missing.

Harry had spoken to Ian in the village and was informed he had seen her around 4:15 but nothing had been seen of her since then. Harry asked him to speak to people he was unable to approach in the hope they may have known something but the vicar drew a blank. Emily asked around too but received the same response. Now, with the time approaching eleven o'clock in the evening, Harry and Candice had genuine cause to be concerned.

Ian had called the police. They took details; name, age, address, what she was wearing, where she was last seen. They asked if Delia was taking medication and if Ian knew of anyone that she might have gone to visit. The information he provided would be circulated around other police forces within forty-eight hours but the officer he had spoken to didn't seem concerned. That her camper van was missing and her belongings were still in Meadow Cottage led him to an obvious conclusion. Delia had more than one set of keys and had gone for a drive. She would be back in no time at all.

Harry and Candice knew that wasn't the case. Emily and Ian too. They had got to know Delia well and she wouldn't have left the village without telling anyone. She made a point of announcing when she was going to bed and that was only upstairs. That she would have taken off without saying a word was not like her. There was more to her disappearance than met the eye.

"Do you think it has something to do with the force? Could it have gained control of her too?" Candice asked Harry.

He looked through the lounge window, willing a camper van to come into view. "I don't know. I suppose it's possible. If it can influence the dead why not the living?"

"It might not be a supernatural thing," she said, reconsidering. "Maybe it's this guy Crosby? Delia might have found him. Perhaps he took her for some reason."

Candice was clutching at straws and knew it.

Harry knew it too. "When we left this afternoon she didn't know where he was. It's not likely she would have found him and he was close enough to the village to come here and abduct her. Even if he did how do you explain the van? He would have used his car. He wouldn't have taken the camper."

"He would if he arrived on foot."

Harry didn't answer. The look was enough.

"You're right. I'm talking out of my butt."

"You're worried and for good reason. I am too."

Candice looked at Delia's wallet and laptop on the coffee table. Her mobile phone was connected to its charger on the sideboard. Her cardigan lay in the armchair where she had discarded it the previous day. She wasn't the tidiest person in the world.

Everything Candice saw suggested that Delia would

have walked into the room any moment but she knew it wasn't going to happen.

"Where the hell is she?" she said.

*

"Are you sure she's away?"

Tate leaned over the steering wheel of the van to get a closer look at the cottage in Meadow Lane. It was in darkness but many houses were at two o'clock in the morning. He wanted to know what to expect before he broke in.

Baker unfastened his seatbelt. It was a legal requirement to wear one and he was, after all, a law-abiding citizen. "Copeland's on the pull in Paris. She's probably drunk and being fucked senseless as we speak."

"What about the woman who's staying with her? The one you nicked the van from?"

"She's not here either. Grantley told me she's staying with a mate in Canningwell."

"Why didn't she take the camper with her?"

"How the fuck should I know? He didn't give me chapter and verse. All he said was that she was away and he wanted the van gone. I don't ask questions for a hundred quid cash in hand."

Baker could tell by Tate's expression that he wasn't convinced. His philosophy was to err on the side of caution but this burglary didn't warrant concern. The baseball bats beside their seats wouldn't be needed tonight.

"Don't worry about it. I overheard some bloke talking about Copeland at the fête yesterday. He said she's coming home tomorrow evening. Aside from that I gave the place the once over when I came for the camper van. There was no one around because it's unoccupied. Come on, let's do this."

The bloke was Samantha's father. Martin had told Brenda how he missed her when she went away, even for the shortest of times.

Baker and Tate alighted the van.

Entry was gained through the front door with the use of a crowbar. As the property was isolated they didn't have to do subtle.

"I hope they're gonna pay for that," Candice said, inspecting the damage to it.

Harry watched them enter the lounge. "They'll pay all right."

He followed them in.

Candice joined him a moment later. She had gone to fetch Harry from Emily's the moment she saw the van pull up. It was unlikely to have been a couple of nuns asking for directions at that time of night. It was only now that she got a good look at them and snapped her fingers as she watched Baker unplug the TV.

"Wait a minute. I know that guy."

"I said there was a chance you might have," Harry replied.

"I don't mean in a social sense. That son of a bitch is Nathan Baker."

"Of course he is. Who is Nathan Baker?"

"He was the guy at the riding school that Pru fired for attacking Flame Girl."

Harry felt compelled to sit down but stood again when Tate emptied a sideboard drawer on the sofa to go through its contents. "Sorry, didn't mean to get in your way. Who is Flame Girl?"

"The horse that Baker attacked."

"And suddenly everything becomes clear," Harry said, clasping his hands.

"I've told you this before. Baker was fired for kicking Flame Girl. In an act of revenge he snuck back to the riding school and set fire to her stable. Pete Warren caught him and called the cops and the fire brigade. When I got there Baker and I had a slight disagreement..."

Harry stopped her at this point. "Would you mind clarifying that please? The Oscar is on a shelf over there," he told Tate as he walked past.

"Okay, when I got there I tried to kill Baker 'cos he's a little shit who was messing with my horses. He was arrested, I was too until Pru got me off on a legal technicality, and ten days later he threw a brick through my lounge window."

"Did you have a slight disagreement about that too? The diamonds and tiaras are in the third drawer on the right," he told Tate when he returned to the sideboard.

"I was working out what to do about it when the plane I was on made an unexpected landing. Nose-first. I don't know what pissed me off more; the fact that I couldn't get Baker or they were about to serve breakfast when we came down."

Candice stood aside as her nemesis carried the TV out to the van. "Shouldn't we be doing something about this?"

"I was thinking of number twelve followed by eighteen and thirty-four," Harry replied. "Maybe a slight dash of ninety-six too," he added in afterthought.

"If you do that they'll run screaming from the building

never to be seen again," Candice told him. "I know you wanna make them suffer after what they did to Ian and the others but our best option is to call the cops."

"What about number twenty-seven? That only induces a minor heart attack."

"No."

"It's nothing more than a mild bout of indigestion."

"No."

"Trapped wind?"

"No."

"I'll tell Emily to call the police," Harry conceded.

Not for the first time that day, Candice called him back as he faded from view.

"Make sure she tells them it's a robbery in progress. They need to arrive quietly. They won't catch anyone if they hit the blues and twos and let them know they're coming."

Harry had thought of that. "Anything else?" he asked tiredly.

"Yeah. Where do we keep our best silver? These guys couldn't find a grand piano on a football field."

*

While Harry instructed Emily on what to say to the police Candice shadowed the burglars as they went through Meadow Cottage room by room.

She watched every move Baker made. He hated her but Candice hated him more. She never thought she would have taken a grudge to the grave, a dislike of people was a mortal trait better left behind, but hers was alive and flourishing. She watered it every day, spoke to it in soft, reassuring tones and played it the 1812 Overture. It responded well to Chuck Berry too. Now it was more than a grudge. Seeing Baker trespass in her home, it had grown into a hundred foot tall English oak.

He entered Samantha's bedroom and looked through her wardrobe. When he closed the door Candice allowed her reflection to be seen in the mirror.

Baker caught his breath and spun around but nothing was there. His eyes darted to the window sill where a Newton's Cradle clicked into motion. The metal spheres kept perfect pace but his heart began to beat so fast he thought it would have leapt from his chest. On the wall a framed print by Mathias Zachary tilted, as if moved out of position by an unseen hand. When the wardrobe door creaked open again Baker made a speedy exit.

"Look what I found," a smiling Tate said when he rejoined him in the lounge. He was clutching the Oscar awarded to Candice for her portrayal of Chrissie Banks in the Helen Cooper film *On Distant Shores.* "Two down, one to go. It's a pity the fourth one isn't in the village."

Baker was unsettled. This was the job he had wanted to do from the outset. Now he was there he couldn't get out fast enough. "Let's bag this stuff up and get it in the van. I'll take the stereo while you make a start."

"Okay."

"There's a valuable lawnmower in the garden shed," a helpful voice pointed out.

"We would have to pay them to take that away," Candice said, standing beside Harry on his return. "Are the cops coming?"

"They're in the pub at the moment but said they'll send someone as soon as they run out of best bitter."

"Quietly I hope."

"It depends on how many whisky chasers they have. I see they found your Oscar."

"Yeah. I shouldn't have got it really. Meryl was a stronger nominee than I was. She did some really good stuff that year."

"What, Meryl as in Meryl..."

"Bogsworthy. That's right."

Candice grinned. Harry was a huge fan of Meryl Streep.

"I'm going to see how much room they have left in the van. I hope they can fit it all in," he said.

The way the cottage was being emptied Candice had doubts about that.

Some of what was being stolen had belonged to her; the stereo, guitar and the Twin Towers print that hung on the wall above the fireplace, but most of it was Samantha's. They were possessions she had worked hard for, things that stamped her personality on Meadow Cottage and made it her own.

That they were being taken was a travesty, even if the thieves were going to be caught red-handed and everything would be returned to its rightful place. They had no right to be there. Aside from murder and rape, the violation of ones home was the worst crime Candice could imagine.

She thought of how terrible it must have been for the other residents of the village who had been burgled with no hope of having their possessions returned to them. She and Harry treated this intrusion with calm disregard because nothing was going to come of it. For Prudence, Ian, Sheila and the others it was different.

They had been robbed of everything. In some cases they had been viciously attacked by the people Candice was now watching. It meant nothing to Baker and Tate, they didn't care, but she and Harry did. The burglaries had to end somewhere and she was glad they were destined to end here. Harry and Candice wouldn't have got the credit for it but that didn't matter. As always the community came first and after tonight Cloverdale St Mary would have been a safe place in which to live again.

"They've taken my Santa on a moped," Harry said, returning to the lounge.

If he had been capable of shedding tears he would have bawled his eyes out.

Candice looked at him nonplussed. She couldn't understand why its loss would have had such a crushing effect on him. "That crap Christmas decoration you made me buy?"

"Yeah."

"Pyewacket knocked it off the shelf and broke it. Santa couldn't have ridden the bike anyway. He didn't have a head."

"That's not the point. He was special."

"He was made of plastic."

Harry's lower lip quivered. For a moment Candice thought he *was* going to cry. If he did she could have made a fortune selling the story to the paranormal journals.

"It was special because it was a gift from you."

Candice hadn't expected to hear that and mellowed towards him. The sadness in his eyes mirrored the love and affection in hers. "Oh Harry. That's so sweet."

"I didn't say anything at the time but it really meant a lot to me."

Moment over.

"Grow a pair, will 'ya? Where the hell are the cops?"

"They're on their way," Harry snapped.

"By the time they get here there will be nothing left. They took the coffee table out ten minutes ago."

"Burglars don't steal furniture. They go for small things they can sell in pubs."

Candice pointed to the floor in front of her. "Do you see that big empty space? It's where the sofa used to be."

Harry came to the conclusion she may have been right when Baker and Tate banged their way downstairs carrying Samantha's bed.

"Maybe I should get Emily to call them again," he said.

They heard a loud commotion from the hallway.

The words *'you're under arrest'* were lost to the sound of a scuffle as Baker and Tate fought against police officers trying to restrain them. Somewhere between *'you have the right to remain silent'* and *'get off my bloody foot'* Baker broke free and ran to the lounge. He closed the door and pushed his weight against it as the police hammered on the other side.

"Number twelve?" Harry asked Candice.

She shrugged her shoulders. "It can't do any harm now."

A blood-curdling scream pierced the air and Baker did something regrettable in his trousers.

Shaking in fear and desperation, he grappled with the doorknob. He opened the door at the third attempt and stumbled out of the room, falling into the long arms of the law who had no hesitation in handcuffing him.

"That's what you get for standing on my foot," one of the policemen said.

Candice and Harry ventured into the hallway and watched as he and Tate were taken outside and led to a patrol car. For the second time that night, she saw someone she recognized.

"Hey, that's the cop who arrested me at the riding school."

"I think we should hold these reunions more often," Harry replied.

Knowing the burglars were in custody, Candice returned to the lounge to see what they had left behind. It didn't take long. Another five minutes and they would have stolen the wallpaper. She went to the attic room and found that was even worse. The term *barren wasteland* came to mind. The only thing to have escaped their attention was Harry's dartboard. It would have given him cause for celebration had they not taken the darts.

Candice recalled the day she moved into Meadow Cottage and the conversation she had with Brenda when she arrived to help her. She said it looked like a storage facility. Now it looked like a shop that had gone into liquidation and closed its doors to a non-buying public. It wouldn't have been that way for long. The police had no reason to take the stolen items into evidence and would return everything once their reports had been filed but Candice couldn't help feeling sad. She felt sorry for Samantha too who would walk into all this when she returned from Paris tomorrow evening.

What a homecoming.

Harry stood outside on the drive. He hadn't finished with Baker and Tate yet. He saw they had been left unattended in the police car while officers chatted nearby and seized his opportunity with eager hands.

"Good evening, gentlemen. How was your day?" he asked, turning in the driver's seat to face them.

The officers heard a lot of screaming and saw the car rock from side to side but had no idea what was causing it.

"That's not number twelve," Candice said to herself as she watched from the attic room window. "More like ninety-six."

Thirty-two

That the burglars had been apprehended came as a relief to everyone in Cloverdale St Mary and people looked forward to getting back to normal. No more night patrols. No more having to look out for suspicious characters. No more fearing the worst at three o'clock in the morning after being woken by the slightest sound. Normality had a reassuring feel to it and was welcomed like an old friend returning home after a long time away.

How the police became aware of the burglary at Meadow Cottage remained a mystery. The rumour mill, for so long a dependable source of information relating to village matters, was divided on that point. Some said they received an anonymous tip-off alerting them to a crime in progress. Others claimed a late-night dog walker had called them. Someone suggested a bright star had appeared in the sky over Meadow Cottage drawing attention to their presence. Ian pointed out that was the birth of Jesus Christ and as far as the Church was concerned there was no connection between that event and this.

One person who didn't greet the news well was Grantley. He wasn't happy that Baker had gone against his wishes by attempting to burgle a cottage that was out of bounds. That the damn fool had been caught was proof that he should have followed orders and waited until he was told to do so.

Grantley was confident that he wouldn't have been implicated in the crimes. He and Baker had an agreement. In the event of their capture Grantley would pay for a top lawyer to represent them, discreetly of course. It was in their best interests to say nothing and keep the mastermind behind the burglaries out of it.

On reflection Grantley decided it didn't really matter now. Baker and Tate had served their purpose. Everything was in place in his basement prison and he wasn't in need of diversions anymore. His victim was ready, as were the chemicals that would kill her. They had needed time to settle and that process was now complete.

He could have killed Samantha whenever he chose but it wouldn't happen today. Today would have been like any other. He would place the bucket under her when she needed to pee. He would write notes that would eventually turn into his book. He would slap and punch her if he felt so inclined and make her final hours on earth a misery. The actual killing could wait. It was what motivated and drove him, what he had worked hard for all these years, but why rush it when he was enjoying himself so much?

He would rather Delia had not been present to witness Samantha's death but in some ways it was a good thing. It gave Grantley an opportunity to show how gifted he was to an audience, however small it may have been. She would have to be killed too but her exit wouldn't have been as grand as Samantha's.

Samantha would die in a manner befitting someone chosen for greatness. Not for her a quiet whimper as life ebbed away. There would be no gentle release from her pain. She would go terrified and desperate, kicking and screaming, struggling to the very end, and what an end it promised to be. Grantley intended to film it so he could watch her final moments over and over again. What better way to spend a cold winter evening than to relax in front of the TV watching a frightened young woman plead for mercy as she died? A glass of wine, a bowl of nibbles and TV worth staying in for. It was his idea of heaven.

Who needed soap operas when the dramas he created were far superior?

Delia was a different matter. Someone who blundered in unexpectedly and threatened to ruin his plans didn't warrant a glorious exit. She would be found dead at the wheel of her camper van at the bottom of Bennett Quarry. The alcohol in her bloodstream and the empty bottle of Scotland's finest on the passenger seat would have made a good advertisement warning against the dangers of drink driving. Who would have thought it of her? Silly Delia. Nice Delia. Not a friend in the world Delia.

Dead Delia.

*

That the burglars had been caught wasn't the only good news in the village on this warm and sunny morning. The local and national newspapers carried headlines that came as a relief to many and made Miss Blunt feel totally vindicated.

She dropped her copy of the Falworth Daily News on the table beside her cup and saucer in Susan's tearoom and looked at Emily in a manner to suggest the world should have listened to her in the first place.

"I am glad to see this ridiculous UFO story has been laid to rest. I find it inconceivable that such nonsense has been allowed to go on for so long. Aliens from outer space indeed. Anyone with a modicum of common-sense must have realised it was a hoax."

"I thought there might have been something in it," Emily replied.

"I rest my case."

"It would be exciting though, wouldn't it? If we had definite proof that there was life on other planets."

"If there is I can only hope they are more sensible than the life on this one. Hoaxers claim to have seen lights in the sky over Cross Drummond and mass hysteria ensues. They turned our green into a caravan site. I have never seen anything like it. If aliens did visit earth they would think us to be quite mad. Not to mention hopeless at parking."

Emily had a copy of the paper too and put it aside as Miss Blunt had done. "I suppose the ufologists will leave now."

"And good riddance too."

"Don't be like that, Prudence. They're nice people."

Miss Blunt scoffed at the description. It wasn't how she saw them. "Nice people? They are not the sort we want here. The men are buffoons and the women engage in acts of public intimacy that are sordid and totally inappropriate. The way they carry on is disgusting." She pointed to the window. "There is not one squirrel left in the trees out there. They have frightened them all away."

"I didn't know we had squirrels," Emily confessed.

"We had a great many things before those so-called scientists arrived, not least a code of conduct for acceptable behaviour. This village is better off without them. The sooner they leave the happier I will be. I have neither the time nor the inclination to associate with people who are so foolish and uncouth."

"They do a lot of good work for the scientific community."

"How you can refer to it as work is beyond me. I

doubt if any of them has had a real job. It is a widely accepted fact that standing in a field in the dead of night with a pair of binoculars is not regarded as a profession. People have been locked up for less."

"Astronomers stand in fields at night and they don't get locked up," Emily ventured.

"More is the pity," Miss Blunt snorted.

"Well, I shall miss them when they've gone. Especially young Neil. He's such a nice boy."

"He is a twit."

"I like Brian too."

"An imbecile."

"And Rafe."

"A complete and utter clot."

"Karen and Siobhan?"

Miss Blunt didn't qualify that with an answer at all.

*

In the Coaching Inn Miss Blunt's favourite people had packed their bags and were in the process of settling their bills.

"I'll put it on my card. We can square up when we get back to London," Brian said, taking his credit card from his wallet.

"That's a good reason for us to go to the Lake District," Siobhan told Karen.

Miss Blunt wouldn't have liked where she had her left hand.

"H'mm... yummy snuggle buns."

"Quite," Brian said, turning his attention back to

Maggie behind the bar.

"I'm sorry things didn't work out for you," she said as she printed off an itemised invoice. "I imagine you get a lot of hoaxes."

Brian sighed. Sadly it went with the job. In fact in his experience it *was* the job. "I'm afraid so. Still, it gets us out of the office."

"I know it didn't turn out the way you would have liked but I hope you enjoyed your stay with us."

"We couldn't have wished for better. The rooms are excellent and I've never eaten so well. I would have no hesitation in recommending your establishment to others."

"Thank you," Maggie replied.

She gave him the invoice.

Brian read it and nodded favourably. Not only had the Coaching Inn been a nice place to visit it was cheaper than he expected. He had forgotten about the 10% discount for an extended stay. "That's splendid. Thank you very much."

Maggie turned the card reader towards him and he entered his details.

Rafe and Neil had been loading their equipment in the cars and returned with exciting news. The disappointment that had been Cloverdale St Mary was about to be forgotten in light of a new investigation.

"There are reports of a crashed UFO in Scunthorpe. We just heard it on the radio," Rafe announced. "I think we should go there immediately."

"I want to go to the Lake District," Siobhan said.

"They don't have any crashed UFOs there."

"No, but they have lakes." She looked at Karen and undressed her with her eyes. "We could go skinny-dipping."

"Yummy, yummy... Ouch! I wish you wouldn't do that so hard sometimes."

"Where did they say it came down?" Brian asked.

"On an allotment adjacent to Fools Road," Neil answered.

Maggie didn't think that sounded encouraging at all.

Brian did. He couldn't get out of the door fast enough. "To Scunthorpe!" he cried, leading his troops forward. "Thank you, Maggie, can't stop, work to be done," his voice carried as he dashed outside.

Siobhan picked up the invoice and receipt that Brian had left behind in his haste to leave and followed her colleagues head-bowed. "Here we go again."

Maggie lifted her eyes to the ceiling, her thoughts turning to the five guest rooms that were now empty upstairs. "I think it's time the Loch Ness Monster was spotted in Cloverdale St Mary," she said to herself.

*

Baker wasn't saying anything. Neither was Tate. They were being questioned by the police separately but it was Baker's interview that Harry had chosen to sit in on. He was curious to know what the ex-yard hand/arsonist/brick-throwing burglar had to say for himself now he had been caught.

The police knew their names but nothing more than that. Baker had rented his flat from a private landlord under a false identity. They would learn the address eventually and recover the stolen property in storage there but Falworth was a large town with many private landlords, not all of them registered. It would have taken time.

"We don't seem to be getting very far, do we?" DS Paula Drysdale said.

Baker didn't answer. He let his smirk speak for him.

"You think this is funny, do you?"

Nothing.

"Leave him alone with me for five minutes," Harry said. "I'll make him talk."

Drysdale took a photograph of Albert Preston from a brown folder and placed it on the table. Baker showed no emotion when he lowered his eyes to the bruised and battered face staring up at him from his hospital bed.

"That's grievous bodily harm. In addition to the burglaries it will put you away for a long time. Would you care to make a statement, Mr Baker?"

No, he would not.

DI Alec Newton was in danger of losing his patience and looked at their suspect sharply. He was a hardened copper of twenty years experience and didn't like the game Baker was playing. It was an easy get out for those with something to hide. *'You have the right to remain silent'* had no place in a police caution. It should have been changed to *'I have the right to kick your head in if you don't stop wasting my time.'*

"Let's not beat around the bush," he said. "You were apprehended at the scene of the crime and resisted arrest. We have you banged to rights for the Meadow Lane burglary. All we need from you is a statement regarding the other burglaries in Cloverdale St Mary that you're not connected too but we know you committed. When we have that statement we can get on with the rest of our lives. Wouldn't that be nice?"

Baker examined his fingernails.

"I'll get a response out of him," Harry offered again.

"Interview terminated at 9:42," Newton said, switching off the tape machine. He stood up and walked to the door. "We'll let you rest your voice for a while. You've talked so much you must be quite hoarse."

"A cup of tea would be nice," Baker replied.

"I'll see what I can arrange for you," Newton said through gritted teeth.

"Has my solicitor arrived yet?"

"No, not yet."

"Be a good chap and let me know when she does."

Newton and Drysdale left the room.

"I'll have his fucking balls in a sling," Newton said, marching down the corridor.

He would have had them long ago if it had been left to Harry.

*

Grantley went to the basement to check on his prisoners at 10:00 a.m. It was the first time he had done so since Delia regained consciousness. She watched without comment as he descended the stairs.

"How are my two favourite ladies today?" he asked when he reached the bottom.

Neither answered.

"Cat got your tongue, Delia?"

He swung his foot and kicked her.

She grimaced and yelped with pain.

"We have rules here that must be obeyed. One rule is that you speak when you are spoken to. Did you pass a pleasant night?"

Delia wasn't sure how to answer. Her night had been far from pleasant but she didn't want to anger him by complaining. The bruising to Samantha's face and body proved he was not a man to antagonise.

"It was all right."

"I'm sorry if you find the floor uncomfortable but your visit took me by surprise and I didn't have time to prepare the en-suite. You're not meant to be here. However, now you are I'm sure we'll make the best of it. It may interest you to know that people in the village have been asking after you. The general consensus is that you have broadened your horizons and moved on but some are concerned for your well being. You've obviously made a good impression. Well done you."

His false compliment left her cold.

"What are you going to do to us?" she asked.

"That is for me to know and you to find out."

Grantley left her and stood in front of Samantha.

Her incarceration was taking its toll. She was tired. She was hungry. She was almost out of her mind with fear.

"Do you need to pee?" he asked her.

"Yes."

Grantley unhooked the chain from the wall and let out the slack. Samantha dropped to her squatting position.

She placed her hands between her legs in readiness to do what the situation demanded. It was second nature to her now, a procedure she followed without thinking about it. It was how the damned and fearful went to the toilet. She waited for him to slide the bucket under her and pulled her briefs to one side.

Delia couldn't watch. The only decent response to what was unfolding was to avert her eyes. "This is barbaric," she protested.

"We all have bodily functions to perform. It's nothing to be ashamed of," Grantley told her. "Do you need to pee too?"

"No."

"You will at some point. When you do you'll find the facilities to be more than adequate."

Delia was disgusted. He took callousness to new heights.

The sound of urine striking the bucket made her despair. Then she heard something else, a heavy thump that came soon after.

"Oh, a number two as well," Grantley said, pulling the bucket away. He turned his nose up and held it at arm's length. "We are making progress."

Samantha hung her head in embarrassment and cried. That she was forced to relieve herself in such a degrading manner may have been acceptable to him but to a normal person it was torture.

Her tears began as gentle sobbing, almost unheard by the good that was Delia and the evil that was Grantley, but it grew louder as she succumbed to the wretchedness that was her life now. Within moments she had broken down completely, a victim of a monster who masqueraded as a man and left suffering and misery in his wake.

Delia felt for her. Never had she known such cruelty.

Grantley returned her to a standing position and left the basement to empty and clean the bucket. It wasn't for their benefit, more his own. He didn't want it to smell while he worked down there. He closed and locked the door but again the light was left on. Grantley wasn't being considerate to his prisoners in allowing them to have light. He wanted them to see the brutal and desperate position they were in.

"I'm so sorry," Delia said from across the room.

Samantha didn't answer. She felt too ashamed. She turned her head away and cried into her arm.

"We will get out of here, I promise. I know it's hard for you, Sam, but don't lose hope. Don't let him take that away from you."

Samantha knew Delia was right. They had to be strong if they were going to survive this ordeal but it was easier said than done for a woman who was forced to piss and shit in a bucket in the presence of others.

*

"Did the cops say when we can have our stuff back?" Candice asked Harry in the lounge of Meadow Cottage.

"I did ask but they wouldn't tell me."

"I hate seeing the place so empty."

"I blame you for this."

Candice raised her eyebrows in astonishment. "Why?"

"They wouldn't have removed so much if you had let me use number twelve on them sooner. They would have been too busy melting."

"That's not my fault. If anything it's yours for allowing me to keep you under my thumb."

Harry was outraged. "I am not under your thumb!"

"I let you wriggle out sometimes but let's face it, it doesn't happen often."

"I wear the trousers in this house."

"You might wanna zip them up."

"What?"

He examined himself.

"Ha, made you look."

As the self-proclaimed head of the household Harry rose above this silliness and allowed Candice to enjoy her playful moment in the name of love and affection. He would make her pay for it later.

"At least we have a front door that works now," he said.

"Yeah. It was good of Ron to help out like that. It's just as well he had the number for an emergency service."

"And that Ian asked him for it. We couldn't have."

"True."

Harry looked in the direction of the window. Candice knew his thoughts because she was thinking the same. There should have been a camper van parked outside on the drive.

"Has Ian heard anything from the police?"

He noticed how Candice changed her choice of words. In lighter moments they were cops. When a situation was more serious they became the police.

"Not yet."

An uneasy silence followed.

Harry didn't want to dwell on the negative. They had no way of knowing what had become of Delia but their instincts told them to expect bad news. A lot could have happened to a missing person in the first twenty-four hours and it was almost that now. For her to have been gone overnight made a tense situation worse.

"What time is Sam due back this evening?" he asked, changing the subject.

"Around seven. It might be better if she stayed with Martin and Janet tonight." Candice looked around the room again. "There isn't much for her here."

This time Harry knew her thoughts. She was still thinking about Delia.

"Try not to worry. We'll find her."

*

The police returned the stolen items at midday. Ian and Ron acted as Samantha's representatives and saw the delivery in. Candice and Harry were surprised by how quickly it happened. The wheels of justice turned slowly and they thought her possessions would have been antiques by the time they got them back.

"That needs to go on the shelf over there," Candice said to Ian as he took her Oscar from a box.

"I know," he whispered.

"What do you know?" Ron asked.

He may have been rubbish at cricket and golf but the man had superhuman hearing.

"I know how much Sam will appreciate our help in getting the cottage straightened out."

Harry applauded. "Oh, good save."

"Thank you."

"You don't have to thank me, Ian. I'm just glad to do whatever I can," Ron said, assuming he had been talking to him.

"Yes, quite."

"What time does she get back?" Ron asked.

"Seven o'clock," Candice answered. "Why do people keep asking that? Did no one pay attention to what she said before she left?"

"Half past six," Ian replied in mischief.

Candice poked her tongue at him. "The Oscar goes on the top shelf not the bottom. It's symbolic. It signifies that I was at the top of my profession when the world was robbed of a truly great talent."

"While we're doing this why don't we put the TV on that wall?" Ian suggested, pointing across the room. "I always thought it would look better over there."

"You put that TV back where it was," Candice said.

"It's not for us to start rearranging the furniture," Ron pointed out.

"Sam will thank us when it's done."

"No she won't. She'll hate it," Candice protested.

"What you mean is you'll hate it," Harry told her.

"I put the TV on that wall the day I moved in and there it stays," she insisted.

Ian stood in the centre of the room and rubbed his chin. The creative juices were flowing and he had become a man on a mission. "I think the sofa over there, the sideboard over here and the stereo beside the window."

Candice looked at Harry in desperation. "Number twelve, now. This maniac must be stopped."

"Beside the window would be the best place for the stereo," Harry agreed. "Better yet, the dustbin taking into account the rubbish Samantha listens to. We've got it back but with any luck the police will have kept the CDs."

"A lot of what she plays used to be mine."

Harry whistled in the air.

"Are you saying you don't like my taste in music?"

"Yes."

"Let's put it back the way it was," Ron said. "If Sam wants to move things around it should be her decision."

"We're missing a great opportunity," Ian insisted.

"You'll be missin' your teeth if you mess with this stuff," Candice told him.

Ian grinned and brought her torment to an end. Everything he said had been designed to get her going. It was his way of paying Candice back for telling him where Oscar lived and acting like a foreman.

When everything had been unpacked and returned to its proper place he and Ron left. Ian nodded at Candice and Harry as he closed the front door. His eyes said it was over. Thank you. Thank you for all you did and for being such good friends.

Candice and Harry returned to the lounge. It was good to see it back to normal but it wasn't where she wanted to be, not while there were more pressing issues to address. Possessions were nice to have, they turned a house into a home and brought a sense of belonging, but people in need were more important.

"Let's go look for Delia."

*

Janet went into Falworth once a week. She did her grocery shopping there. Village shops provided the essentials but were limited in what they stocked and Melanie's favourite brand of fish fingers could only be found in town.

She was on her way home but as she walked to her car she saw a familiar face on the high street.

"Hello, Xanthe. I thought you weren't getting back till later this evening," she said, stopping to chat with Samantha's ex-workmate.

"Hi, Mrs Copeland. Back from where?"

Janet smiled. "France must have been exhausting if you can't remember it."

Xanthe was puzzled. She hadn't given Paris a second thought since their trip was cancelled. "France?"

"Yes. You know, that big patch of land between Spain and Germany."

"We didn't go."

Now it was Janet who was puzzled. She smiled again, this time curiously.

"What do you mean, you didn't go?"

"Didn't Sam tell you? Charlotte broke her leg the night before we were due to leave. She fell off a bus. The trip was cancelled."

"Cancelled?"

"Yeah. We're rearranging it for some other time. I don't know what Sam has done but I took today off anyway. That's why I'm not in work."

Gone was curiosity. In its place was a look of concern.

Janet hadn't been to the village that morning. She was unaware that Meadow Cottage had been broken into and the police found it to be unoccupied when they arrived. If she *had* known alarm bells would have rang sooner.

"No one has seen Sam since Friday," she said.

"She went to the fête surely?"

"No. We assumed she was in Paris."

Xanthe was at a loss to explain it. Samantha loved the village fêtes, she enjoyed spending time with her family. The moment their plans changed she announced her decision to attend it as usual. Xanthe couldn't understand why she hadn't.

"I don't know what to tell you, Mrs Copeland. When I called her at work on Friday morning Sam told me she was going. She joked about it. She said she would buy a pot of jam from that lady who makes them to give to Charlotte as a get-well present."

"No, Xanthe. She wasn't there."

"Maybe she wasn't feeling well and spent a quiet weekend at home."

"She would have called to let me know Paris had fallen through. We haven't heard from her. No one has."

"She might have gone somewhere on her own. We were considering going to Brighton for a weekend a while ago. Perhaps she's gone there."

"Sam wouldn't do that. She would have told us if she changed her plans."

Janet wrung her hands anxiously. She didn't know what was happening but a feeling of dread rose in her stomach. Every worst-case scenario stampeded through her mind. A mother's intuition told her something was wrong. "It's not like Sam to not get in touch. She would have called me if she was at home or had gone somewhere else."

Xanthe shared her concern, it wasn't like Samantha at all, but she tried to reassure her. "I'm sure it's nothing to worry about, Mrs Copeland."

"Will you come to the police station with me?"

"I don't expect anything bad has happened. Have you tried calling her?"

"No, I had no reason to. I thought she was with you."

"I think we should try calling Sam before we involve the police. I'll call her mobile. You ring the stables."

They took out their mobile phones.

Xanthe's call didn't connect because there was

nothing to connect to. Mobile phones could be tracked and Grantley had taken no chances. He smashed it with a hammer after garaging his car. It was the first thing he did upon his return to Brook Cottage. While it was in working order it posed a threat. Disposing of it was vital.

"Hello, Roy. It's Janet. Can I speak to Samantha please?" She listened to his response and the feeling of dread became all-consuming. It swept over her like a tidal wave. "Thank you." She closed the call and held the phone limply at her side. "She's not at work."

"Try her at home."

Janet called the landline but it went to her answering machine. Samantha always turned it off when she was at home but forgot to on Friday. That it was on should have been encouraging but she wasn't at work and Janet was positive she wouldn't have gone somewhere else for the weekend without telling anyone.

"Please come to the police station with me," she said.

The anxious mother was almost in tears.

Xanthe picked up her shopping bag from the pavement. It was clear Janet was worried and Xanthe had no intention of turning down her request but she didn't want to act hastily. They couldn't report a missing person while other avenues remained open to them. "I think we should go to Meadow Cottage first."

"Sam isn't there," Janet insisted.

"We can't be certain about that, Mrs Copeland. Sam might have been out of the room when you called, she could have been upstairs or in the garden. We can't go to the police if nothing is wrong. I expect she's at home safe and well."

"Do you think so?"

"I'm sure of it. There must be a simple explanation for why she hasn't been in touch. If Sam isn't there we'll go to the police. I'll come with you, I promise, but we have to try Meadow Cottage first."

She was right of course. The police wouldn't have launched an investigation into someone not answering their phone.

Xanthe called Charlotte as they walked to Janet's car in the hope she may have heard from Samantha. She hadn't.

*

In an interview room at Falworth police station Nathan Baker was given news he did not want to hear.

"We know why your solicitor hasn't shown up," DI Newton said, entering. "She was involved in a car accident in London this morning. Her injuries aren't serious but she's been admitted to hospital. She'll be there for a few days."

Baker stared through him. Isabelle Richmond was the best money could buy. Grantley had no hesitation in giving him her number. She was to the legal profession what Candice Freeman had been to the acting one. She was an up and coming star who commanded a courtroom and won more cases than anyone of her age and experience. To hear she was unavailable came as a blow.

"Do you have anyone else in mind or would you like me to appoint legal representation for you?" Newton asked.

"Um..."

"Perhaps you would like another cup of tea while you mull it over? Maybe a slice of cake as well."

Baker saw the glee in Newton's eyes. Now the big-hitter from London was out of the picture he could have appointed the first legal-aid novice available to him. What had been plain sailing for Baker upon his arrest was now a problem and Newton delighted in it.

"I don't know anyone else."

"Oh dear. What an unfortunate position to be in. Still, I'm sure I can find someone to assist you." Newton opened the door but didn't leave straightaway. He paused in the entrance to savour the moment. "And when I do we can stop fucking around and get down to business. Two sugars, wasn't it?"

*

The lock on the front door to Meadow Cottage didn't need changing when it was repaired and Janet gained access with her spare key. She had rung the bell but received no answer. When she and Xanthe went inside they made their way to the lounge.

"Sam?" Janet called. "Where are you?"

"I'll check the kitchen and dining room. You look upstairs," Xanthe said.

A thorough search of the cottage and garden failed to locate her.

Janet and Xanthe stood perplexed when they returned to the lounge. Not a thing was out of place, it was as they had come to expect from someone as neat and tidy as Samantha, yet to Janet it didn't feel right. There was nothing to suggest that her daughter hadn't gone away for a couple of days and was soon to return but the emptiness surrounding Janet convinced her something was wrong. It didn't feel temporary. Samantha's absence felt permanent. Cold and irreversibly permanent. It reached out to Janet through the silence like a monster about to strike and filled her with dread.

Samantha wasn't coming home.

Janet ran from the room and went upstairs again. When she returned she was crying. She had remembered something that Samantha kept in a drawer in her beside table. Finding it there confirmed her worst fears.

"Something's happened to her, Xanthe... She didn't change her wallet." She gave it to her in a hand that wouldn't stop shaking. "It's her travel wallet. I bought it for her the first time she went overseas... She always takes it with her."

Xanthe recognized it immediately. She had seen it on past trips. She opened it and found euros inside.

"Even if she had gone somewhere else for the weekend, Brighton or anywhere, she would have taken that wallet. I know it's silly but she would have."

It wasn't silly at all. During a holiday with Xanthe and Charlotte in Egypt two years previously Samantha thought she had lost it and flew into a panic, not because of the money and cards it contained but because it was a gift from her mother and was her lucky wallet. Xanthe didn't know why Samantha called it that, it had never taken a bullet and saved her life, but it was typical of her to have christened it in such a way. It was like her lucky underwear, the sort she wore for dates and nights on the town.

"Please, Xanthe. Come to the police station with me."

It was the most tenuous of discoveries but it changed

everything. Samantha was in trouble and Xanthe knew it.
"Give me your keys. I'll drive."

Thirty-three

Candice sat on the sofa. She was stunned by news that was sweeping through the village like wildfire. Everyone was talking about it but gossip didn't bring answers to questions that were many and confusing. "She didn't go to Paris? Then where is she?"

"We don't know," Ian replied. "Janet has informed the police. Samantha has been listed as missing. They're treating her disappearance seriously. They think someone may have abducted her."

"This can't be happening," Candice said.

Ian and Emily had arrived at Meadow Cottage thinking that Candice and Harry would have known about it. That they didn't was surprising and Ian brought them up to speed with the situation so far.

"The police have already been here. They sent a forensics team and searched the cottage. You must have been out."

"We were looking for Delia. We left soon after you and Ron," Candice answered.

She didn't mind the police searching the cottage. They had been respectful in their work and left few signs of having done so. Only now did she notice the smudge of fingerprint powder on the coffee table.

"How are Jan and Martin taking it?" she asked. "They must be going out of their minds with worry."

Emily dabbed her eyes with a handkerchief. She looked at a picture of the Copeland family on the sideboard across the room. It had been taken by Maggie at the fête two years previously. They were all smiling but no one wore a bigger smile than Samantha. She was sitting on the grass outside the marquee with her arm around Melanie's shoulder while Janet and Martin stood behind them.

"I spoke to Janet in the village but only briefly. Martin was on his way home from work and she wanted to get back. The poor woman is in pieces."

She began to cry.

"It's all right, Emily. I'm sure the police will find her safe and well," Ian said, trying to be of comfort.

"What about Mel? Does she know?" Candice asked.

Ian shook his head. "I don't think so. As far as I know she's still at school."

"Yes, she is. They're going to tell her when she gets home," Emily said.

Harry had played no part in the discussion but did now as he stood by the fireplace. There was no hiding his concern but his thoughts were divided. People went missing all the time in a world without rules but not two from the same house within a few days of each other. There had to be a connection.

"First Delia, now Samantha. Something is seriously wrong here," he said.

"You think the disappearances are related?" Candice asked him.

"They must be. It's too much of a coincidence. I think it has something to do with this force or whatever it is."

"You didn't pay it any mind when we spoke about it last night," Candice said.

"That was before I knew Samantha was missing too. You're still under threat, we know that after what happened on Friday..." Harry stopped abruptly. "Friday," he repeated to himself, deep in thought.

"What about it?" Emily asked him.

Harry walked to the window. Curious eyes followed him there. "That was the last time any of us saw Sam. No one saw her when she got home from work. Candice and I were in Norwich and Delia was in Falworth waiting to meet someone who failed to show up."

"What's your point?" Ian asked.

Harry ignored him. He was still thinking, trying to piece together what little he knew. "Then Candice disappeared and I went looking for her. That delayed our arrival back here. It's almost as if someone or something wanted us to be out of the house at a certain time. Delia too." He looked at Candice, the pieces of his puzzle falling into place. "When we told Delia about your disappearance she said the force may have been using you for something. It was. It was using all of us. Samantha had to be here alone. She was taken from this cottage."

"You can't be sure of that," Ian said. "We don't know if Sam *has* been abducted. There could be a simple explanation for all this."

"When was the last time Samantha went off somewhere without telling anyone?" Harry asked him.

Ian didn't have to think about it. The answer was never. "Okay, let's work on the assumption that she has been abducted. It could have happened anywhere. She may have been taken on the road coming home from work."

"Her car's in the garage."

"It could have been put there later."

"Yes, it could have, but why risk abducting someone on the road if there's a chance of being seen when you can take them from the privacy of their home? This cottage is isolated. It would be easy to smuggle someone out undetected. No one is going to see it happen. Aside from that her suitcase and passport were gone. The kidnapper must have taken them to make it look like Sam had gone to Paris as planned. That could only have happened if she was abducted from this house."

Ian didn't answer. He was forced to concede the point.

It made sense to Candice too but she felt Harry was addressing an issue the police would have taken into consideration.

"I can see where you're coming from but no one has suggested that Sam *wasn't* taken from here. Like you said, her car's in the garage and everything points to that, but where does it lead us?"

"It leads us to the woman who didn't show up at the Millstream," Harry said. "If there was a plan to get Delia out of Meadow Cottage she may have had something to do with it. While Delia was in Falworth waiting to meet her she could have been here abducting Samantha. She might be responsible for Delia's disappearance as well. What better way to stop her from talking than to kidnap her too?"

"You think a woman may be behind this?" Ian asked.

"It's possible. Now is not the time to be sexist."

Ian knew Harry wasn't accusing him of being so and retreated to silence to mull over what he had said.

Candice had already decided that Harry was right. "The police need to know about this."

"What do we do in the meantime?" Emily asked.

Harry looked at the picture too. He had never seen a family so happy, a family that had been torn apart by the cruellest of acts.

The evil people did was savage and brutal. It meant nothing to those who dealt in pain and suffering but it did to those who had to endure the consequences of their actions. It ruined lives. It screamed injustice in a world that pleaded for tolerance. It broke hearts and wrecked dreams. It took what was good and destroyed it because evil was the corner stone in the evolution of mankind and had shaped the human race.

"We do everything we can to find them," Harry said.

*

Grantley was in conversation with Ian on his doorstep. It was 5:00 p.m. and the vicar was talking to as many people in the village as possible in the hope of learning something that may have been of help to the police.

"What a terrible thing to have happened," Grantley said. "Samantha is such a nice girl. Martin and Janet must be frantic with worry. I can't begin to imagine what they must be going through."

"Yes. The police are with them now. They sent a forensics team to Meadow Cottage earlier. It's been searched from top to bottom."

"Did they find anything that might offer a clue to her whereabouts?"

"Not that I know of."

Grantley stood aside in the doorway and repeated an offer he had made to Ian upon his arrival. "Are you sure you won't come in? You look in need of a drink."

"Thank you, Norman, but I won't stop. I don't mean to insult you by stating the obvious but if you hear anything, however insignificant it may appear to be, please inform the police. We must do all we can to return Samantha safely to her family."

"Yes, of course. If there is anything I can do, anything at all, let me know. Tell Martin and Janet I'm thinking of them, young Melanie too."

"I will. Thank you."

Ian went to the next cottage on his list.

Grantley closed his front door and returned to the basement. He didn't appreciate being called away from his work and punched Samantha simply because she was a convenient outlet for his irritation. That aside, he liked to see her cry.

The interruption dealt with and no longer an issue, Grantley busied himself with work once more. He thought it was nice to have a local celebrity staying in his house. Soon the name Samantha Copeland would have been known throughout the world. He finished writing the notes for his book and filmed her again, but unknown to his prisoner chained to the wall worse was to come.

In less than twenty-four hours Samantha would be dead.

*

"Sit down, Melanie. Your father and I need to speak to you," Janet said.

Melanie had been in the garden when the police came and was unaware of their visit. She didn't know they had asked for details of Samantha's movements in the days leading up to her disappearance. She didn't know they left with a photograph of her to assist with identification. She had no idea her parents were beside themselves with worry because they did their best to act normal and hid it from her.

Now, called to the lounge by a mother and father who suddenly appeared anxious, Melanie lowered herself onto the sofa slowly. She knew it was something serious. Their expressions couldn't have meant anything less.

"Have I done something wrong?" she asked.

"No, darling. You haven't done anything wrong," Martin said, sitting beside her.

"Is everything all right with you and mummy?"

"Yes, it's nothing like that," Janet assured her. "We want to talk to you about Samantha."

"What about Samantha?"

Janet didn't know where to begin. How could news of this sort be broken to someone so young? *Sometimes innocence is taken away too soon*, Miss Blunt told Martin at the fête. They couldn't allow this to be one of those times, when the ugly face of adulthood cast its shadow over a child's world.

"I don't want you to be scared, I'm sure it's nothing to worry about, but we don't know where Samantha is," she said.

"She's in France."

Martin held her hand. "No, Mel. Samantha didn't go to France."

"Where did she go?"

"We don't know. The police are looking for her."

"The police? Has *Samantha* done something wrong?"

Janet choked back tears that she was desperate not to shed in front of her. Innocence was a fragile thing. "No, she hasn't done anything wrong either. You're both good girls. We think she might have gone somewhere and can't find her way home. The police are looking for her so they can bring her back to us. Do you understand?"

Melanie looked at them in turn. Their eyes were dull and sad. In speaking to the police the fears they tried to keep secret had risen to the surface and they couldn't disguise them anymore. However much they wanted to they couldn't hide from their youngest daughter that they were terrified.

"I think so. Can I help to look for her? I know some of her favourite places where she might have gone."

"No, Mel. You can't look for her," Janet said.

"Samantha would look for me if I was lost."

It was more than Janet could bear. She stood and fled the room in tears.

The suddenness of her departure and the manner of it alerted Melanie to the seriousness of the situation. She felt afraid.

"Daddy?"

"It's all right, Mel. Listen to me carefully, this is very important. Your mother and I don't want you to look for Samantha by yourself. You mustn't go off on your own. Promise me you won't do that."

"But I might be able to find her."

"You must promise, Mel. Promise me you won't go off on your own."

"I promise."

Martin put his arm around her. He too was close to tears. It was all he could do to stop himself from falling apart.

Melanie instinctively cuddled into him. Whenever she was afraid the one place she felt safe was in the embrace of her father. He chased away the monsters when gentle dreams turned into nightmares. He stood up for her when she lacked the courage to defend herself. He calmed her in times of uncertainty with a reassuring smile and a simple I love you. He did those things for Samantha too. He did them for Janet. He did them because to Melanie he was the best dad in the whole world.

"If I wrote down Samantha's favourite places and gave it to the police they could look there," she said.

"That's a good idea. You make a list and I'll give it to them."

"Mummy told me not to be scared but I am."

"I know, Mel, but it's okay. Everything will be okay."

They sat silent with their thoughts, Melanie with her frightened eyes closed, Martin trying not to cry as he smoothed her hair.

Samantha hadn't lived in the family home in six months but her presence was everywhere. She was in the lounge, the kitchen, her bedroom. She was in the hallway repairing a table lamp that Melanie had contrived to break in a careless moment. She was in the loft with Martin, laughing as they sorted through old LPs that he felt too ashamed to play in the age of CDs and streaming. She was in the garden with Janet sipping lemonade on a warm summer afternoon. She wasn't being held somewhere against her wishes soon to die.

She was in their hearts.

*

Nathan Baker had confessed to his crimes. The solicitor who had been appointed to represent him advised against a wall of silence in favour of co-operation. Lionel Thorpe insisted it would have served him better in the long run and his client agreed, albeit reluctantly. Tate followed his advice too.

Baker told the police his address and officers were sent to search the flat. The moment they entered they were presented with all the evidence they needed to link the two men to the other burglaries that had taken place in Cloverdale St Mary. Everyone would get their possessions back but it would take time to list and catalogue it all. As a flat it was small and basic. As an Aladdin's cave it was a revelation.

The only thing Baker didn't confess to was his association with Grantley. Isabelle Richmond wouldn't have been in hospital for long and he could have enlisted her services before he went to trial. Thorpe was a temporary replacement who himself would be replaced but in order for that to happen Baker needed to keep Grantley sweet. If he told the police he was working for him Grantley would have been in need of Richmond's expertise himself and that would have led to a conflict of interest. For Baker she may have been the difference between eighteen months and five years. He didn't want to serve any prison time but the game was up and it wasn't hard to do the maths.

Baker made a full statement and was returned to his holding cell. The i's had been dotted and the t's crossed. He had been in this position before. He knew what would happen next and when it would happen. There were no surprises left for a man who had chosen a life of crime in preference to working for a living. Or so he thought. At 9:00 p.m. he was taken back to the interview room.

"What's this about? I've made my statement," he told a sombre looking DS Drysdale across the table.

"There is something else we think you may be able to help us with," she replied.

Baker turned to Thorpe but the solicitor appeared to be equally bemused by this unexpected recall.

"I'm sure my client will do everything he can to be of assistance."

DI Newton took a photograph from a folder and placed it in front of their suspect. He did it without looking at him. "Do you know this woman?"

Baker paid the picture of Samantha nothing more than a passing glance. He was more interested in the clock on the wall that showed no sign of a long and tiring day coming to an end. "No."

"You might want to actually look at it before committing to an answer," Newton suggested.

Baker sighed. His dislike of Newton was matched only by his contempt. He picked up the photograph and grinned, knowing his response would annoy him. "She's a bit of all right. Quite a looker in fact. It's not really my sort of picture though. Have you got one where she's flashing her tits?"

"That sort of talk will not help," Thorpe said, frowning.

Baker returned the photograph to the table. He sat back in his chair and folded his arms across his chest. "No, I don't know her."

"That's Samantha Copeland. You burgled her cottage last night," Drysdale said.

"I break into people's houses and nick their stuff. I don't pay much attention to what they look like."

"She's missing," the detective sergeant told him.

Baker didn't answer.

Newton took another photograph from the folder and laid it beside the one of Samantha. "What about her? Have you ever seen her before?"

"No."

"Her name is Delia Truebody. She was staying with Copeland as a house guest," Drysdale said.

"She's missing too," Newton added.

Baker turned his eyes to him without moving his head.

"Strange, isn't it?" Newton went on. "You burgle a cottage in the early hours of the morning and the two women who live there disappear without trace. How would you explain something like that?"

Baker didn't like where this was going. He looked at him coldly. "What are you asking me for? How should I know where they are?"

Newton picked up Samantha's picture and grinned as their suspect had done. "You're right. She is a bit tasty, isn't she? The other one's not bad either."

"I don't know where they are," Baker insisted.

"Take a look at this picture again," Newton said, turning it towards him. "Are you telling us you've never seen her before?"

"No. Never."

"That's odd."

"Why is it odd?"

"You worked with her at the Cross Drummond Equestrian Centre. I wouldn't have had you pegged as the sort of man who forgets a pretty face."

Drysdale dipped into the folder and produced a sheet of paper from which she read. "In 2016 you were employed there as a yard hand. You were caught mistreating one of the horses and dismissed. You returned to the premises soon after and set fire to a stable. You were arrested at the scene and sentenced to thirty hours of community service. There was also a fine of £50."

She placed the paper on the table with the photographs.

"Now, tell us again how you don't know Samantha Copeland," Newton said.

Baker conceded. He had no choice. "All right. I know her from the riding stables and I knew she lived in Meadow Cottage, but she's not a missing person. She's in Paris. She's coming back tonight." He pointed to the clock. "She's probably at home now."

"What leads you to think that?" Drysdale asked.

"I was at the village fête on Saturday and overheard someone talking about her. He said she had gone away for the weekend and was due back on Monday evening. That's why we burgled the cottage last night. I wanted to do it while the place was unoccupied."

"Unoccupied aside from her house guest," Newton pointed out.

"I don't know anything about Trueblood or whatever her name is. She wasn't there. I didn't know Copeland had a house guest until you told me."

Baker lied easily and well. He hadn't met Delia but knew she was staying at Meadow Cottage. He would have admitted it but still didn't want to implicate Grantley. It would have stretched plausibility to the extreme had he said he overheard a conversation about Delia too and learnt she was staying in Canningwell that night. He held the police in low regard but they weren't fools.

An accomplished liar he may have been but on this occasion no one was buying it.

"I don't think you're being completely honest with us, Mr Baker," Drysdale said.

"I'm telling you. Copeland is due home tonight and I don't know where the other one is."

"Samantha Copeland didn't go to Paris," Newton told him.

"What?"

"The trip was cancelled at the last minute. No one has seen her since she finished work on Friday afternoon. That makes her very much a missing person and I think you can shed some light on her whereabouts."

For the first time Baker looked afraid. Beads of perspiration appeared on his forehead. He wrung his hands anxiously. Samantha and Delia's disappearances was the one thing he was innocent of but he couldn't prove it.

"Let's be clear about this," Newton said. "We're not talking about a five stretch for burglary and GBH anymore. We're talking about kidnapping and that's life. Let me ask you again. What can you tell us regarding the whereabouts of Samantha Copeland and Delia Truebody?"

Baker's anxiety got the better of him and he snapped angrily. "I can't tell you anything about their whereabouts. You can't fucking stitch me up like this." He looked at Thorpe and demanded action. "Are you gonna let this go unchallenged? You're supposed to be representing me for fuck sake."

The solicitor directed his response to the investigating officers.

"In view of these new developments I would like to request a ten-minute break so I might confer with my client."

"By all means. Take all the time you need," Newton replied. "We'll resume in the morning. Interview suspended at 21:06."

He turned off the tape machine as Drysdale gathered up their paperwork and returned it to the folder.

Newton followed the DS to the door but turned to look at Baker before leaving. His suspect was wriggling like a worm on the end of a fishing hook and he loved it but what he loved more was gloating over the guilty when they didn't have a leg to stand on. "Oh, I have some more bad news I'm afraid. The tea machine has broken down."

Baker ignored his parting remark. He was too busy trying to make sense of a worsening situation.

How the hell did I get into this mess? Kidnapping? What the fuck is that about?

*

Candice couldn't stand the silence of Meadow Cottage any longer. She had to divert herself from the fears she harboured over Samantha and Delia. She had to be around people. She had to be in the presence of the living.

Harry didn't want her to go to the Coaching Inn. He thought, rightly as it transpired, that she would have found it more difficult there. Samantha had many friends in the village and everyone was concerned.

"I can't believe it," Maggie said to Ron behind the bar. "You hear about this sort of thing but never think it's going to happen to one of your own."

"Let's not get ahead of ourselves. I'm sure the police will find her."

"These things seldom end well." She began to cry. "This can't be happening to Samantha... not to Sam..."

"I'm sure Ron is right, Maggie. The police will get to the bottom of this and Samantha will be returned to us in no time at all."

"I hope so, Norman... I really hope so."

Ron nodded at Grantley in appreciation of his support and the abductor of innocent women returned to his table.

"There must be something we can do," Candice said, watching him sit alone.

"I wish I knew what it was," Harry replied.

Maggie's words repeated in his mind. *These things seldom end well.*

"What if we... I mean we could..." Candice didn't know *what* she was trying to suggest and surrendered to the fears that she had gone to the Coaching Inn to get away from. "I guess all we can do is wait on the police."

"Have you spoken to Emily?"

"Not since she and Ian came to see us."

"Then go and visit her now. Grantley is here and that means Emily is at home by herself. She needs company too at a time like this."

Candice looked around the room. It was silent and almost empty. An air of gloom hung over it, a sense of loss that held the village in an iron-like grip and wouldn't let go. The feeling of worse to come was everywhere.

"You're right. There's nothing we can do here. Are you coming?"

"I'll meet you there later. I want to see Ian first."

Candice was about to leave when the door opened.

"We came as soon as we heard," Brenda said, walking hurriedly towards the bar.

Mike followed her.

Maggie went out to meet them and the two women embraced.

"Have there been any developments?" Brenda asked.

"No. How did you hear about it?"

"We saw it on the news. I didn't pay much attention at first. It was just another story about a missing person but when I heard it was Samantha I was stunned. How are Janet and Martin coping?"

"I haven't seen them but they're not good."

"Of course not. It was a stupid question," Brenda berated herself. "Mike and I packed a bag and came straight here. Don't worry if you can't put us up. We'll sleep in the car if necessary. We just knew we had to come back."

"It's okay. All the rooms are free," Maggie replied. "If they hadn't been we would have found somewhere for you. Did they say anything about Delia on the news?"

"Delia?" Mike asked.

"She's missing too."

"What?"

"The police aren't treating her disappearance as seriously as Samantha's but no one has seen her in over twenty-four hours. Her camper van isn't at Meadow Cottage. The police think she may have moved on but all her things are still there. I know Emily and Ian are worried about her."

"No, they didn't mention her," Brenda said. "Who would leave a place without taking their belongings with them?"

"That's what we thought. The police have made door-to-door enquiries about Samantha but don't seem to be doing anything as far as Delia is concerned."

Mike couldn't believe what he was hearing. Alarm bells rang immediately. "Two women living at the same address go missing and the police don't think there's a connection? What the hell are they doing?"

Brenda read anger in his voice and tried to calm him. "I'm sure they're looking into it. The important thing is that we lend our support in whatever way we can."

"Yeah, of course," he replied.

"I'll show you to your room," Maggie said.

Candice watched them go upstairs. She hadn't expected to see Brenda and Mike again so soon and a thought occurred to her, one that was pleasing from a personal point of view. That they had returned to the village during a time of crisis led her to only one conclusion. They were ready to swap the city for a new way of life. Cloverdale St Mary would be home to them one day. Of that Candice was sure.

Thirty-four

Grantley woke early. He went to the basement at 5:00 a.m. The light was left on permanently now and his prisoners watched him descend the stairs in silence.

He had with him a pair of scissors which he placed on the table beside the water jug. He unhooked the chain from the base of the wall and let out some slack, enough to lower Samantha's hands to the top of her head. The relief she felt was immense.

"Is that better for your arms?" he asked, standing in front of her.

"Yes. Thank you."

Grantley wasn't being kind. He had lowered her hands to suit his own purposes. Soon he would unlock the restraints around her wrists to take her out of them and didn't want to stretch in order to do it. Everything he did was designed for his comfort not hers. He had a chair to sit on. She had a wall at her back. He had a bed to sleep in. She had relentless pain that kept her awake. He had a bathroom. She had a bucket. Kindness died at the discretion of those who didn't understand the meaning of the word.

"The time has come to take off your underwear," he said.

Samantha wept. She was petrified whenever he went near her, she lived in a permanent state of terror, but more than anything she had dreaded this moment. "No... please..."

He fetched the scissors from the table.

Grantley had decided to cut off Samantha's underwear because it would have been difficult to undress her with her back pressed to the wall. Her bra would have been hard to remove. He was awkward and clumsy with them at the best of times. He didn't want to fumble like a teenager trying to make out with his girlfriend on the back seat of his car. He would have looked like an amateur. He could have ripped it off her, her briefs too, but there was something vulgar about such a heavy-handed approach. It would have been better to cut it. It was clinical, controlled. More dignified.

Samantha shuddered when he lifted her bra straps and snipped them from her shoulders.

Delia was desperate for her and struggled against the rope tying her hands. "Get away from her. Leave her alone."

Grantley pointed with the scissors. "I would advise you to be silent. My work must be completed and there will be no interruptions."

Delia didn't protest further. The intent in his voice scared her.

Grantley cut Samantha's bra between the cups. She choked back tears when it opened at her chest. He pulled it from her and dropped it on the floor. She felt the scissors under her briefs and pleaded with him to let her keep them on. He cut them from her left hip first, then the right. Nothing more than a rag now, they too were tossed aside.

Samantha trembled and cried. She couldn't bear the thought of him looking at her and turned her face away.

Delia was disgusted by what she had witnessed. "What sort of animal are you?"

Grantley paid no attention to her. He put the scissors on the table and returned to Samantha. "I wish you didn't have that tattoo. It will definitely have to go."

He placed both hands on her breasts.

She tensed, terrified of what he might have done

next. "No... please don't..."

Grantley watched how they moved beneath his palms.

Samantha tugged at the restraints in a desperate attempt to distance herself from him but it was impossible. He pulled her nipples in the hope of arousing her but fear wouldn't allow it. What was pleasure to him was torture to her. He pressed his right hand between her legs and she howled, begging him to stop.

"LEAVE HER ALONE!" Delia screamed.

Grantley unzipped his trousers.

Samantha lowered her eyes. Seeing his erect penis, she cried in panic and desperation. The unthinkable was about to happen and she was powerless to stop it. "Oh God... please... not that... You said you wouldn't..."

"I lied. I think you and I should spend some quality time together."

"GET AWAY FROM HER... LEAVE HER ALONE," Delia screamed again.

The voice of dissent from across the room was ignored.

"No... don't... Please don't... Please..."

Samantha's words caught in her throat in the moment of penetration. She tried to scream but that too died on her lips.

Closed eyes couldn't block out what he was doing to her; clammy hands gripping her breasts and shoulders, the wall hard at her back as she jerked, the searing pain between her legs that swept through her entire body. All she could do was cry and grimace as her jailer condemned her to hell.

When Grantley finished he looked at her unrepentantly. There was no sympathy in his killer gaze.

It had always been his intention to rape her. He

could have stripped Samantha naked on day one and abused her whenever he had a mind to but the element of surprise appealed to him. He had assured her that he had no interest in her sexually, it wasn't the reason for her abduction, and she, in fear and ignorance, believed him. Seeing her violated and destroyed now added to his pleasure and made the wait worthwhile. What better way to torture ones prisoner than to lead them into a false sense of security?

"A nice, snug fit. Just the way I like it," he said, nodding approval. "I assume it was good for you too?"

Agony and anguish overwhelmed her and Samantha broke down.

"Of course, you're the emotional type. I'll take that as a yes."

Grantley zipped his trousers and walked to Delia. She had crossed the line in protesting and had to be made aware of it.

"Don't tell me what I can and cannot do. If you raise your voice to me again I'll cut out your tongue and feed it to the rats."

He kicked her as punishment for her disobedience. He did it with such force it was a wonder her ribs weren't broken.

Grantley fetched the camcorder from his chair and filmed Samantha. He was thorough in what he recorded.

Again she pulled at the restraints, trying to escape from another deplorable act. She begged him to stop but he continued with callous disregard. Who was she to plead for mercy? What right did she have to it? Her body wasn't hers. It hadn't been from the moment he drugged her tea in Meadow Cottage. It belonged to the Master and he took what he wanted. He would be denied nothing.

The filming at an end, Grantley left the basement. He would return later to rape Samantha a second time. Perhaps a third would follow. He hadn't decided yet. His final visit of the day would be to kill her.

Delia cried too. She was in pain from Grantley's violent assault but it wasn't the reason for her distress. Her tears were for her fellow captive.

She bowed her head in shame and self-recrimination as Samantha wept. Delia would have helped her if she could. She would have raised the alarm had there been some way of doing it. She held herself responsible for the torment Samantha was forced to endure and her sense of inadequacy became a burden too heavy to carry.

Delia couldn't bring herself to look at her naked and defenceless, abused by a kidnapper turned rapist who inflicted pain and misery in equal measure. It would have been wrong too. Someone had to give her privacy. Someone had to show this poor, inconsolable woman some respect. Someone had to care.

"I'm sorry, Sam... I'm so sorry."

*

Miss Blunt joined Emily at her table in Susan's tearoom and stared past her to the street outside their window. It was a normal street on a normal day. People went about their business as usual. Nothing in their manner and appearance suggested that anything was different about this Tuesday morning in Cloverdale St Mary but of course it was. People may not have shown it but today was very different.

"Have you heard any news?" Emily asked.

Miss Blunt stirred her tea. "No. I went to see Janet and Martin earlier to offer my support. The police have assured them they will be notified of any developments and a liaison officer is at the house but they have established nothing so far. A search of Cross Drummond is going to be conducted this morning."

A cold shiver ran down Emily's spine. Cross Drummond was large and dense. Like many woodland areas it was not easily accessible. It was the way nature intended it to be; wild and untamed. The thought of Samantha and Delia being there, perhaps waiting to be found in shallow graves, was too horrible to contemplate.

"Is Melanie in school?" she asked.

"They have kept her at home. The school has been very understanding. They said they can take all the time they need."

Miss Blunt paused and recalled how Janet was with her youngest daughter during her visit. She wouldn't let Melanie out of her sight. Even in their own home she insisted that she stayed by her side.

"Janet is finding it difficult to cope. She has not slept. I do not think Martin has either but he seems to be the stronger of the two. Janet is close to mental and physical collapse. I fear for her."

"Maybe their doctor could give her something."

"I suggested that to Martin as I was leaving. He said he would call him."

Emily stared at the street too. It was still picture-perfect but no longer the safe place it had been this time yesterday. It was like it harboured a secret, something dark and sinister that stalked the pretty cottages and well-kept gardens. Birdsong continued to carry on the breeze but now it sounded like a plea for help.

At Cross Drummond and in the fields adjacent to it, the search for Samantha and Delia was underway.

*

"Do you think they're here?" Candice asked.

Harry didn't know what to think as he watched police officers fan out across the field. Local residents helped in the search and he tried to sound positive in answering her question. "No. I'm sure it hasn't come to that."

Candice looked at Cross Drummond. It loomed large on the horizon. The search party made its way towards it. Others were already there, prodding the ground with sticks and looking for graves no one wanted to find. If Samantha and Delia were dead that was where they would be. It would have been almost impossible to have found a body there. If they had been hidden well enough they could have lain undiscovered for years.

Candice and Harry looked in the adjacent field.

*

Ian and Ron had joined the search and negotiated trees that towered high above their heads. They reached to a distant sky, sunlight breaking through the branches in bright patches of blue, but it did little to illuminate a landscape that was dark and eerie. Parts of Cross Drummond were picturesque, a nice place for picnics and courting couples, but that was on the outskirts, not in the interior. Here the withered and dead moss crackled underfoot and a dank, musty smell rose from the earth. It was silent. Deadly silent.

"Prudence told me that Brenda and Mike are back in the village," Ian said.

"Yeah. They arrived yesterday evening." Ron stopped to inspect a mound of leaves. It was nothing. The wind had blown them into their suspicious shape. His relief was evident. "They haven't said how long they're staying but it could be a while. They want to help in any way they can."

"Are they taking part in the search?"

"Yes."

"Not here I hope. We know this place. They could be lost for days."

"No, they're in the fields."

Ian pushed aside a low branch while concentrating on his footing. It was a surreal position to have been in. They were desperate to find Samantha and Delia but didn't want to find them there. To have done so would only have meant one outcome. It would have been the realisation of their worst fears.

"How is Maggie taking this?" he asked. "I heard she was very upset."

"She's trying to keep busy to take her mind off it. She wanted to join the search party but I told her not to for now. Maybe tomorrow if we have to resume. I think it will help that Brenda and Mike are here."

"Yes. I'm glad they're here too."

"I find it surprising that Grantley isn't out here searching," Ron said. He almost sounded accusing.

"He's not as young as he used to be and this is pretty hard work."

"Yeah, I suppose. An extra pair of hands would have

been nice though."

"Do not judge harshly those who would not judge you," Ian said, slipping into Sunday service mode.

"Is that from one of your sermons?"

"No, I made it up."

"Don't give up the day job."

The vicar grinned and they continued with their search.

Ian was prepared to stay out all day and into the night if necessary but Ron had less time at his disposal and would return to the village later in the morning. He didn't want to in light of some residents electing not to help but he had lunches to prepare at the Coaching Inn and would have to get back. The search for Samantha and Delia had seen an influx of people to the village and at some point they would want to be fed. He couldn't let Maggie loose in the kitchen. Cloverdale St Mary had enough problems.

*

"No... stop... Please stop... Oh God... please stop..."

*

Baker cast his solicitor a disdainful glance. The look he received in return told him he had no choice.

"Okay. I'll tell you everything I know," he said to Drysdale and Newton.

"The tape is running," Newton told him.

Baker knew it was.

"A couple of months ago I met a bloke in a pub in London. We got talking and he told me he was moving to Cloverdale St Mary. That captured my interest because I know the place well. He said he had things to do there and didn't want any unnecessary attention. You know what it's like when you move to a new place. People are curious, they watch you all the time, even more so in a small village.

"He told me that in order to do these things he needed some kind of diversion. Something to focus people's attention elsewhere. A spate of burglaries for example. While the residents were worrying about being robbed they wouldn't take any notice of him. He asked me if I would be up for it and I said yes but there were conditions. I could only burgle houses that he had already chosen as targets and in a sequence that had to be followed. He'd done his homework. This bloke knew what he was talking about.

"He said if I needed help with the break-ins I could get someone to assist me. That's when Tate came into it. I met him soon after and he agreed to come on board. The bloke in London gave me a list of houses that he wanted us to burgle and said he would pay the rent on a flat in Falworth. All I had to do was find one and tell him how much."

"Did he say why he wanted you to commit the burglaries?" Drysdale asked.

"No, he wouldn't go into details. I asked him but he said it was none of my business. My job was to commit the burglaries. What he was doing in Cloverdale St Mary was private and none of my concern."

"Go on," Newton said.

"We did the first job the day after he arrived in the village. The others quickly followed. He wanted us to move fast so we did. He told us to vandalize the church too. There was no profit or gain in it, just smash it up and smear cow shit all over the place. It stank like fuck when we left. I couldn't see the sense in doing it, there was no point, but I did the next day. Everyone was there helping to clean it up. Diversion you see? While the locals were busy with that they weren't watching him.

"On Saturday I went to the village fête. I met up with Tate and we burgled the vicarage later that afternoon. While I was there I heard someone say that Copeland had gone away for the weekend. She was in Paris and wasn't due back until Monday evening. I wasn't supposed to burgle Meadow Cottage till much later, it was the last house on the list, but with the place unoccupied it was the perfect time to do it. It would have been stupid to let the opportunity pass. It was there for the taking so I decided to break in during the early hours of Monday morning. Then something odd happened.

"On Sunday evening I got a call from the bloke that hired me saying he wanted a camper van removed from Copeland's drive. He said she had a house guest but she wasn't there. She was staying overnight with a friend in Canningwell. I didn't know someone else was living in the cottage. There was no mention of her during the conversation I overheard at the fête. I wasn't told why I had to nick the van, just that he wanted it gone. It's now hidden in woodland near Bennett Quarry.

"Me and Tate went back to Meadow Cottage a few hours later to commit the burglary. If I thought it *was* occupied I would have stuck to the schedule and did it last. I didn't know Copeland hadn't gone to Paris and was missing. I didn't know her house guest was missing. My job was to carry out a spate of burglaries and smash up a church, not to abduct anyone. I had nothing to do with their disappearances."

"And you didn't know about the camper van in advance," Drysdale said.

"How could I? That arrived in the village a week later when the UFO freaks showed up chasing little green men. Removing the van was a job on the side. A hundred quid for getting rid of it quick."

Drysdale and Newton looked at one another. At last they were getting somewhere.

"I think we need to speak to your employer," Newton said. "Name and address. Tell us where we can find this man."

"Norman Grantley. Brook Cottage."

Newton lifted his eyes to the clock on the wall. "Thank you, Mr Baker. Interview terminated at 13:58."

He and Drysdale left the room.

Thirty-five

Grantley returned to the basement at 2:00 p.m. He carried a large tray covered by a white tea towel. He said nothing as he placed it on his chair.

Samantha was crying. She knew she was going to die.

Grantley had raped and beaten her. He had degraded and humiliated her. He had taken what little hope she had and crushed it in hands that were accustomed to dispensing pain and terror. When he returned to the basement to rape her again he whispered a chilling threat in her ear.

'The next time I come it won't be between your legs. It will be to kill you.'

That time was now and a fear like Samantha had never known surged through her. It was relentless. Brutal. The most savage, agonizing fear imaginable.

"Please don't hurt me... I beg you... don't hurt me..."

"Beg all you like. If you want to waste your final moments pleading for something you can't have go ahead. It makes no difference to me."

There was no sympathy in Grantley's voice. No regret. Just the cold, detached tone of a man who knew what he wanted and would have it. From the moment Samantha was born it was inevitable that she would have met her death here, chained to his wall crying and abused. She had been put on earth to be used by him, to serve him and to die at a time of his choosing. It was the way it was meant to be so how could he have felt regret? How could a monster have felt anything?

"Please, Professor. Let us go," Delia said.

"While I stand on the verge of achieving my lifelong goal? I think not."

"What are you going to do to me?" Samantha wept.

It was a question she had asked many times before. On previous occasions he ignored her. Sometimes he struck her as punishment for daring to speak out. Either way an answer had not been forthcoming. Until now.

Grantley crossed the room to the larger table. He removed the dustsheet to reveal a perspex box.

'It's long enough to be a coffin,' Ian had remarked when he and Emily watched the removal men carry the wooden crate inside Brook Cottage. Unknown to them it was a coffin. A coffin for Samantha Copeland.

On the floor beside it was an oil drum containing the chemicals Grantley had mixed. A tube connected the drum to the lid of the box.

"I'm going to place you inside this box," he told her. "When the lid has been secured you will be immersed in a chemical contained in the drum. You will take it into your lungs and drown. It has been specially formulated to prevent rigor mortis from setting in. It will also ensure that your internal organs do not suffer any damage."

"Why?... Why are you doing this?" Samantha sobbed.

"I have selected you for greatness. In you the ghost of Candice Freeman will live again. I have the ability, the power, to bring her back to life. In order for this to happen her spirit must enter the body of a mortal. A host if you will. You are the vessel, the new form that Candice Freeman will take. No one would know it by looking at her. When they see her they will see you but when she speaks and does the things she did in life they will be left in no doubt that she has been reborn."

"You're mad," Delia gasped.

Grantley raised his eyebrow. "Mad, Delia? I think not. Brilliant perhaps but not mad. The ghost of Candice Freeman has been under my control since I arrived in this drab, tedious village. She disappeared at my command. Each time I brought her here. She has no knowledge of being in this room and can remember nothing of what happened because I didn't allow her to. In death I am her Master. In the moment of her rebirth I will be her Creator. Candice Freeman will live again. Of that there is no doubt."

Grantley realised by Delia's expression that she had misunderstood his motives and felt that further explanation was required. He didn't want her to form the wrong impression of him, that he was fascinated by the world of celebrity and lived for nothing else.

"It didn't have to be Freeman. I've never been interested in the acting profession and certainly didn't follow her career. I'm not one of those people who must know what the rich and famous are wearing this week or who they're sleeping with. The actual subject is irrelevant. It could have been anyone. It was proving it could be done, that was the important thing. Taking an idea and turning it into reality."

"How is it possible to do this?" Delia asked him.

Even now she refused to believe it.

"I won't bore you with the details. To be perfectly honest you have neither the aptitude or the intelligence to understand what I am about to achieve. I will say this. After years of research into this field, six months ago a book came into my possession. It contained a detailed analysis of what had to be done, a step-by-step guide to resurrection so to speak. Through my research I was able to fill in the blanks."

"What book?"

"The Palaranti *Book of the Dead*." Grantley smiled. "I can see you're impressed."

"Amazed would be a more accurate description," Delia said. "That book is a myth. Tales of an ancient people descended directly from God were born of legend and folklore. The Palaranti never existed."

"Didn't they? How else would I be able to control a ghost?"

Delia was too stunned to answer.

Samantha didn't understand what had passed between them. She knew nothing of ancient peoples descended from the gods. She didn't know about books that could bring the dead back to life. All she knew was that she was scared. She was about to die and was gripped by sheer terror.

"Please, let me go," she pleaded with him. "I won't tell anyone... I promise... Let me go home... I want to go home..."

She broke down.

"And soon you shall, but not as yourself. You will return to Meadow Cottage as the greatest actress who has ever lived. Of course, in order to achieve that we must summon the missing element."

Grantley walked to the chair and lifted the towel off the tray. On it rested the book of which he had spoken. It was large and leather-bound. A hypodermic syringe and a dagger lie beside it. Post-it notes had been applied to the pages he needed and he turned to the first one, reciting words in a language his prisoners had never heard before.

"Nouson ka-mass kilbry, inquan imeel. Quannus patray. Rist kuma. Rist kuma. Rist kuma, incanti."

Candice appeared in the centre of the room. She didn't look at Samantha or Delia. She stood as if in a trance, staring into nothingness.

"Do you acknowledge that I am your Creator?" Grantley asked her.

"Yes."

"Do you see?"

"Yes."

"Do you understand?"

"Yes."

"Are you ready for your re-birth?"

"Yes."

Not once did she divert her gaze.

Grantley set the book down and turned to the next highlighted page. He read for a moment to re-familiarise himself with the text. He couldn't leave anything to chance. He had to be word-perfect when it came to the next phase. When he was ready to proceed he picked up the hypodermic. He stood in front of Samantha and tapped it with his finger, raising it before her frightened eyes.

"This is similar to the drug I put in your tea. It will cause you to lose consciousness but only for a short time. When I take you out of the restraints you will no doubt try to resist. The drug in this syringe will prevent you from doing so. You will be conscious when you drown. I know you'll find it distressing but that's how it must be. The Palaranti had strict guidelines for that part of the procedure. You must be aware at the time of your death. My advice is to not fight it. Try to relax and let it happen."

"No... please don't... Don't do this to me," Samantha cried.

"Candice. For God's sake, help her," Delia called.

Candice stood in her trance, present but not there, knowing but unknowing. Dead but soon to be alive.

Grantley inserted the needle in Samantha's neck.

*

Harry was frantic. Candice was there one moment and gone the next. It was a pattern that was all too familiar.

He returned to the village and looked around from his stationary position on the green. She was nowhere to be seen. He saw Martin in conversation with Emily and felt for him. The agony on his face was clear even from a distance but Candice had become his priority and he returned to Meadow Cottage in the hope that she may have been there.

As he faded away a police car turned onto the high street.

Martin watched it approach and flagged it down. He didn't know if the officers were involved in the investigation or had gone to the village on other business but he was desperate for news and couldn't have allowed it to drive by without asking. Unknown to him, in delaying Newton and Drysdale he was placing his daughter in more danger.

*

The drug had yet to take effect. It was fast-acting but desperation and fear kept it at bay. Not that Grantley was impatient for Samantha to lose consciousness. He had things to do before that happened.

He called Candice to attendance and pointed to the

chair. "Do you see the dagger on the tray?"

"Yes."

"Pick it up."

She did as instructed.

"You know what to do."

Candice knew exactly. Her Master had taught her well during past visits to the basement. Her duties had been made clear. Now the time had come to perform them she would not be found wanting. He who demanded obedience would have it.

She turned and walked towards their prisoner, raising the dagger in her right hand.

"No, Candice... please," Samantha wept.

Her words went unheard by the ghost under Grantley's control.

Candice pressed the tip of the dagger to her skin.

Samantha grimaced as she drew a two-inch cut below her left breast. The wound stung and she shook as a new pain took hold of her. A similar cut was made to the right side of her body, this time above the breast. Samantha's blood dripped to her waist and she pulled at the restraints in a final desperate attempt to free herself.

Candice stood back and stared at her but her trance-like eyes saw nothing.

"Allow me to explain the reason for what has just happened," Grantley said to Delia. "The spirit of Candice Freeman will enter the host through the left incision. The Palaranti placed great importance on this as it's on the side of the heart. The spirit of the host will exit through the right incision. This is on the opposite side of the heart which the Palaranti considered to be evil. I don't know how much of this is symbolic or if they really believed it but it's what it says in the book so it's how we must proceed."

"What else does your book say?" she asked. "Does it use the term that any sane person would use to describe what you're doing? Committing murder?"

Grantley sighed. "You're not getting this at all, are you?"

"What you're proposing to do is totally absurd. You claim the spirit needs to enter the body of a mortal in order to achieve rebirth but Samantha will be dead. All you're doing is taking an innocent life."

He wished he didn't have to spell out what should have been obvious. This was his shining hour. Everything he had worked for was about to come to fruition. He didn't have time to explain the finer points of death and reincarnation to someone who had no understanding of it. "The spirit of Candice Freeman will enter the host when it's confined inside the box. The chemicals will be pumped in after. There would be no sense in the spirit entering the body when the host is dead. As you correctly stated, that would achieve nothing." He paused and looked at Delia tiredly. "Would you like me to untie you so you can take notes?"

"Yes, untie me. Someone has to stop you. You're a madman."

Grantley took exception to her attitude. He considered it lacking in respect and resolved to teach her a lesson but he wouldn't deliver it. That would be left to his servant. "Kill her."

Candice walked towards her.

Delia tugged at the rope tying her to the radiator as her executioner approached. She twisted her hands, trying to pull them through knots that wouldn't slacken, but it was hopeless. There was no escape before and there would be no escape now. Her death, like Samantha's, was assured.

Candice stood over her and raised the dagger above her head. She wouldn't need a second order to strike. Grantley had instructed her to kill and it would have been unnecessary to repeat the command. What her Master said she did.

She was unaware it was Delia she was about to stab. She hadn't known it was Samantha's blood she had spilt. Candice knew they were people but that was all. It wasn't necessary for her to know who they were or why she had been called upon to harm them.

On the verge of bringing the knife down, Grantley intervened.

"Stop. Come back to me and put the dagger on the tray."

Candice obeyed.

"You see, Delia? It would have been that simple. I decide who lives and who dies. I have the final word in what happens and when it will happen. You would do well to remember that before you insult me again."

"Please. You don't have to do this."

"Oh, but I do, Delia. And something must be done about you. You are going to die but I would rather it didn't happen here. You've become quite a nuisance, a complication I could have done without, but when your camper van goes over the edge of Bennett Quarry with you drunk at the wheel that complication will have been removed."

Delia didn't answer. There was no mistaking the certainty in his voice, the cold promise of what would be.

Grantley looked at Samantha. She had stopped crying. Her eyelids had grown heavy. She was losing consciousness.

He took a bunch of keys from his pocket and knelt to open the shackles securing her feet. When they were free he unlocked the wrist irons. Samantha fell away from the wall and dropped in his arms. He scooped up her legs and turned to carry her to the box. It was only now that he realised the lid was in place.

Grantley cursed his oversight. In his eagerness to proceed he had forgotten to take it off. It would have been too time-consuming to put Samantha back in the restraints while he attended to its removal so he laid her on the floor. Her head rolled when she felt the cold concrete against her skin.

He unfastened the clips that secured the lid and removed it. When he was ready to proceed he returned to her.

"Please, let her go," Delia said.

He offered nothing in reply.

Grantley was faced with the difficult task of lifting a dead-weight from ground level and took a moment to prepare himself. He pushed his hands under Samantha's back and legs in readiness to pick her up.

Samantha felt something trying to lift her and a thread of awareness returned. She opened her eyes.

She realised what was happening and somehow found the strength to move. It took every ounce of energy she possessed but she swung her right leg and kicked him. Her shin barely connected with Grantley's arm but it was enough to push him off balance. He tried to steady himself but fell and hit his head on the floor.

Delia knew at once that he was unconscious.

Samantha got to her feet. She looked at him but couldn't focus.

"Samantha. Are you all right?" Delia called.

Candice shook her head as if awoken from a deep sleep and looked around the basement. She didn't know where she was or why she was there. The last thing she remembered was being with Harry at Cross Drummond. In a mind struggling to recall, that had been just seconds previously.

"What's happening? Where are we?"

Delia realised Grantley had lost control over her the moment Samantha rendered him unconscious. She felt encouraged for the first time. "Candice, thank God. You must help Samantha."

"What's going on here?"

"There's no time to explain. Do as I say."

Samantha's vision blurred in and out of darkness but she saw the table on which her water stood. She staggered to it, almost knocking the glass and jug over when she planted both hands on it to support herself. She picked up the glass and threw the water in her face in a bid to shock her senses back to life.

Her head cleared but it was only a temporary respite. The drug was in her bloodstream and it would only have been a matter of time before she succumbed to it.

Candice watched in astonishment. She feared the worst when her friends disappeared, she thought she would never see them again. The last thing she expected was to find herself in the place where they were being held prisoner. That Samantha was naked alarmed and confused her all the more.

"Will someone tell me what the hell is going on?"

Samantha walked towards Delia. She couldn't see Candice. In her drug-induced state she didn't know she was there. She was unsteady on her feet. It was all she could do to lift them. The floor pulled at her legs as if she was wading through quick-sand. When she reached her she dropped to her knees. It was her intention to untie her.

"No, Sam, there isn't time," Delia said. "The drug is

taking effect and Grantley could regain consciousness any moment. Get out while you can. Raise the alarm."

Samantha swayed and almost toppled over. She pressed her hand to the ground to support herself.

"Go now, before it's too late. Candice, help her."

Candice reconciled herself to a situation beyond understanding. It was clear that Samantha and Delia were in danger and had to get out. The time for questions was later. "Come on, Sam. You have to get to the stairs," she told her.

Samantha still couldn't see her but heard her voice. "Can-dice?"

"I'm here, baby. You have to get out."

Samantha turned her head and looked at the stairs. They were moving, losing their shape and definition to eyes that couldn't see clearly. She stood up and walked towards them. The more she exerted herself, the faster the drug took control of her body.

It took all the strength she possessed to climb the stairs. Candice encouraged her and Delia willed them on, praying they wouldn't fail. Their lives depended on it. She looked at Grantley. He was still lying motionless on the floor.

When Samantha reached the top she slumped against the door to rest but it was the worst thing she could have done.

"Keep going," Candice said to her. "Don't stop, Sam. Keep going."

"Want to... sleep."

"No, you mustn't. You have to fetch help."

Samantha rallied and gripped the doorknob. Her hand slipped off it but she found it again and pushed the door open.

Natural light blinded her after being held prisoner in

the dimly-lit basement and she shielded her eyes as she lurched into the hallway. The front door was to her right. Beyond it was Cloverdale St Mary. Rescue. An end to the nightmare she had found herself trapped in when a good life turned bad.

She stumbled off-balance and leaned her shoulder against the wall. A distant voice sounded inside her head, almost unheard as her body approached shut-down. It was one of reason when everything else was confused and beyond her control.

Don't stop. Get help.

Samantha forced herself to go on. She could hardly keep her eyes open.

When she arrived at the door she fumbled with the lock.

"Open the door, Sam," Candice said.

"Can't... can't open... drawer."

She rested her head against it.

"Yes you can. Open the door."

Samantha closed her eyes and mumbled. "Let me... sleep."

She was moments away from losing consciousness.

Candice shouted at her to shock her back to awareness. "COME ON, COPELAND. DON'T FLAP AT IT, OPEN THE DOOR!"

Samantha lifted her head and tugged at the handle weakly. She couldn't see what she was doing. Her eyes wouldn't focus.

"You need to turn it, Sam. Turn it downwards and pull it towards you," Candice said.

"Turn.... and... full."

"Turn it downwards and pull," Candice repeated slowly.

Samantha's arms fell to her sides. She lifted her

hands again and found the handle at the third attempt.

"He's waking up," Delia called from the basement.

"Come on, Sam. You can do this."

Samantha turned the handle downwards. She barely had the strength to pull the door open but succeeded in doing so. It didn't occur to her that she had to move away in order to open it fully and it stopped against her toes.

"It won't open while you're so close to it. Take a step back."

"Rest... now."

"No, don't rest. Step backwards and keep pulling the door towards you."

Samantha did as Candice said.

It was almost open wide enough for her to pass through when she fell against it and pushed it closed.

"Sleep... want to... sleep."

"No, Sam. Open the door."

"Hurry. He's heading for the stairs," Delia warned them.

"OPEN THE FUCKING DOOR! DO IT NOW!"

The angry and impatient voice that came to Samantha pulled her back from the brink and her hands found the lock again. This time she was able to open the door fully and stumbled outside. The fresh air on her skin had a similar effect to that of the water and she rallied once more.

Samantha walked dazed and disorientated along the garden path to the gate. It was open. Grantley always closed it but the postman didn't conform to his high standards and never closed a gate he had passed through. For Samantha and Candice it was a blessing. The latch was stiff and difficult to operate at the best of times. Samantha would never have done it in her present state.

Candice encouraged her to go on.

Short steps took Samantha onto the pavement, shuffling feet she could barely lift. There she stopped, near to collapse. In the distance she saw the vague outline of people standing on and around the green. A car was parked twenty metres away, four people in conversation beside it, but she didn't know who they were.

"Keep going, Sam. You have to keep going."

She forced herself to move and staggered towards them, slowly, painfully, hardly moving at all.

DI Newton couldn't believe his eyes when he saw her approach. "What the fuck?"

Martin and Emily stood with their backs to the green. They didn't know what had prompted his surprise and turned around.

"Oh my God... SAMANTHA!" Martin shouted.

He, Newton and Drysdale ran to her. Emily followed.

Now on the green, Samantha fell to her hands and knees but managed to get up. She had heard her father's voice and was desperate to reach him. She began to cry. Somehow she found the strength to go on. She tried to run to him but her legs gave way beneath her and she fell again.

Knowing she was safe, Candice returned to the basement to assist Delia. She was relieved to find that Grantley had stirred only momentarily. He had reached the foot of the stairs where he too had fallen and lapsed back to unconsciousness.

Outside, Martin was first to arrive and caught Samantha as she dropped to her knees once more.

"Sam... Who did this to you?"

"Grant-ley... He got... Dewia..."

Martin pointed for Newton and Drysdale's benefit. "Over there!"

They ran to Brook Cottage.

Emily stared at Samantha lying bruised and bleeding in her father's arms and raised her hands to her face in horror. "Norman did this?"

Samantha lost consciousness.

Maggie arrived with a blanket. Ron had seen the drama unfold and alerted her to what was happening.

"She's dead," Martin wept.

He cradled her shoulders and rocked back and forth, inconsolable and broken, his world in ruins.

Maggie covered Samantha with the blanket and felt for a pulse. "No, Martin, she's not dead. She's been drugged."

Residents who witnessed what had taken place gathered around them. Others massed on the green when they became aware that something was happening. Everyone was shocked by the sight that greeted them.

In the Coaching Inn Ron called for an ambulance.

Thirty-six

Martin and Janet sat at Samantha's bedside for half an hour. They would have stayed longer but she needed to rest and they didn't want to over-tire her. The doctors insisted their visit had to be brief.

Melanie didn't accompany her parents to the hospital. She was at home being cared for by Miss Blunt. She wanted to go with them but Martin and Janet said it would have been better for her to visit the next day. They didn't want Melanie to see the agony etched on Samantha's face even now she was safe. The ordeal she had suffered was one of the worst imaginable. It was upsetting for them to see her so fragile and afraid. There was no telling how a child would have responded to it.

Samantha would be in hospital for three days. If all was well she would be discharged on her twenty-second birthday, not that she was in a frame of mind to have celebrated it. She was dehydrated and the doctors wanted to be sure the drugs Grantley had used were out of her system before they allowed her home. She had given a brief statement to the police but fatigue and distress lingered and she was forced to stop. Newton and Drysdale would speak to her again later.

She was in a private room. The busy coming and going of a general ward was no place in which to recover. Candice watched Martin and Janet leave and went in. Samantha smiled when she saw her. It was a little after 6:00 p.m.

"How are you feeling?"

"I'm okay."

Candice sat on the edge of her bed. She would have

held her hand if she could. She would have picked the loose strands of hair from her forehead to keep them away from her eyes. She would have given her life a thousand times over for things to have been different. Just like her parents would have done. Just like they had done.

The bruising to her face was proof, had it been needed, of the terrible things Grantley had done to her.

"Do you want me to leave?" Candice asked.

"No. Stay a while."

"I don't mean here. Do you want me to leave the village?"

Samantha was surprised by the question. There was no reason to ask it. "Why would you leave the village?"

Candice looked at her solemnly. Guilt was a heavy load to carry. It was a burden not made easier by death but made all the harder because of it. This wasn't the time to discuss what had happened but she felt they had to. It couldn't have waited until Samantha was discharged from hospital. It was too important.

"I'm responsible for this. Grantley came to Cloverdale St Mary for me, to put his crazy plan of bringing me back to life into effect. None of this would have happened to you if I hadn't been here. You would have been safe."

"You're wrong to think that way, Candice."

"Delia told me what I did, how I cut you with a dagger and would have killed her if Grantley hadn't stopped me."

"You didn't know what you were doing. He was controlling you."

"I know, but I figure I'm not the sort of friend you need to have around. It would be better if I left. I don't wanna cause you more hardship by staying. You've gone through enough already."

"I don't want you to go."

"Every time you look at me you'll think of that basement and what happened there. I can't do that to you, Sam."

Samantha understood now but disagreed with her reasoning. It wasn't Candice's fault that a stranger to the village had conspired with insane ideas to plunge lives into ruin. She was as much a victim as Samantha was. It wouldn't have been right for her to have shouldered the blame. To have done so would have been a victory for the madman who had caused so much pain and misery.

"I don't hold you responsible. What happened was beyond your control. You mustn't blame yourself, you didn't do anything wrong. Neither of us did. I want to go home. I want to be with you and Harry. The thought of seeing you and my family again kept me going. If you left what would I do without you?"

"You could mow the lawn."

Samantha smiled again but in one inseparable moment it turned to tears.

"I'm sorry, Sam. I didn't mean to upset you."

"He hurt me, Candice... He kept hurting me..."

Samantha broke down and Candice knew she was wrong to have considered leaving. She was her friend and no one had the right to force them apart. In good times and bad, friends stayed together.

*

Delia could barely keep her eyes open. A lack of sleep had caught up with her and was taking its toll.

She had been examined at the hospital but there was

no need to admit her. She hadn't been drugged and beaten. She hadn't been chained to a wall and forced to stand for days on end. She didn't have rat bites to her feet and ankles. All this and more had been put in her statement to the police. Now, reflecting in the lounge of Meadow Cottage, it was over. For her at least.

"You should go to bed. You need to rest," Ian said over his teacup.

"Not yet. I'll wait for Candice and Mr Grey to come home."

There was no point in correcting her.

Ian returned his cup to the saucer. When he spoke he did so without thinking. "If anyone had to be in that basement with Samantha I'm glad it was you." He realised what he had said and cringed with embarrassment. "Oh dear, that sounded awful, didn't it? I meant you're calm in a crisis. I'm sure Samantha was glad of your support, that you were there to help and encourage her."

Delia smiled to put him at ease. "It's all right. I know what you meant and I thank you for it, although I don't know how much help I was. I was scared witless most of the time."

"That's understandable given the circumstances."

Delia slipped away. The basement and how they suffered at Grantley's hands was vivid in her memory. It would be for the rest of her days but her thoughts now centred on Samantha. When Delia's nightmares stopped hers would go on. "The way he treated her. It was terrible. I thought I knew him but how wrong I was. I had no idea what sort of monster he had turned into. If I had everything could have been so different."

Ian knew what she was eluding to. Delia had told him, Harry and Candice how Grantley was the professor she had spoken of and how he fooled her into thinking he was helping them. What happened in the basement of Brook Cottage was bad enough but Delia carried the shame and guilt of having lied to them. She felt like a traitor because of it, an accomplice to a man who had killed before and thought nothing of doing so again.

"You have no reason to reproach yourself, Delia. Grantley had us all fooled in one way or another. He came here with evil intent but none of us could see it."

Ian too slipped away when he realised he was wrong in his assessment. Harry knew. He had known all along.

The silence that descended on the room lifted when Candice appeared.

"How is Samantha?" Delia asked.

"She's sleeping now. Is Harry back from the police station yet?"

"No," Ian replied. "How are you doing?"

"I've been better, Reverend."

That in itself was proof of it. Candice never addressed Ian by his clerical title.

She sat in the armchair opposite them and looked at the two cups on the coffee table. There should have been three.

"Have they said how long Sam will be in hospital?" Ian asked her.

"The doctors are thinking two or three days. They wanna be sure the drugs are out of her system before she comes home. They're getting plenty of fluids into her and have given her a tetanus shot for the rat bites. Then it's a case of building up her strength and trying to get back to some sense of normality."

Normality. The concept was foreign to them.

Delia looked around her borrowed lounge from the comfort of the sofa and apologized when she caught a yawn in her hands. Out on her feet she may have been but that was no excuse for bad manners. "I'm sorry. That was no reflection on the company."

Candice grinned. "You should go to bed. You've had a busy day, Toto."

"That's what I told her," Ian said.

"It's only ten to seven," Delia protested.

"When was the last time you slept?"

"Saturday."

"I rest my case."

"Candice, you are not packing me off to bed. If I want to be bullied I'll call my mother."

Delia hadn't meant to be humorous. She too had spoken without thinking but her disapproval delivered with a dead-pan face was amusing and Candice and Ian laughed. It lifted the gloom and for the first time they relaxed.

"I don't know if I've told you this, Delia, but you're one hell of a gal," Candice said.

"And you're one hell of a ghost," the recipient of her compliment replied.

"There's a lot of hell going around this room at the moment," Ian commented.

"That's okay. You're one hell of a vicar," Candice told him.

He smiled and picked up his teacup. "Thank you. Be sure to tell my bishop that."

Candice turned her thoughts to an eventful past two weeks and the mysteries and trials that were now over.

It would take time for Cloverdale St Mary to recover from aliens from outer space and the evil that men did but recover it would. Solidarity and the will to overcome rose above all challenges. It was about community and community was forever. It didn't weaken. It didn't break. It stood tall and strong against everything that was thrown at it and emerged victorious. It did what it said on the tin.

"I hope you're not thinking of leaving any time soon," she said to Delia.

"I have to go home eventually."

The reference to Delia going home made Ian realise how little they knew about her and he raised a question that up to now had gone unaddressed.

"What do you do for a living? I know you're a member of G.A.G.A. but I assume that doesn't pay the bills."

"The society pays when I go on field trips, they reimburse me for petrol and accommodation, but they have no need to. I don't have to worry about money. I'm rich."

"Really? How much?"

"Me personally or the whole family?"

Ian shook his head. "It doesn't make sense. Why would they pay someone like you to look for ghosts?"

"They're only ghosts if you look at them from the water."

Ian didn't know what Delia meant by that but Candice did. Their exchange could have been taken from *Jaws,* one of her favourite films. Scheider and Dreyfuss delivered the lines better but it was a good effort.

"Sam is gonna need all the support she can get when she comes home. I think that's something you can help with," she said.

Delia nodded. "Of course. I'll stay for as long as I'm needed."

"Thank you."

"That might be a while," Harry told them, appearing in

the room. "I've just come from the hospital. Sam suffered a panic attack. It was a bad one. She had to be sedated."

"Oh God," Candice said.

"She was calmer when I left. The sedative will ensure she has an undisturbed night."

No one spoke for a moment. Their thoughts were focused on an absent friend in a hospital bed far from home, driven to fear despite being safe, only able to sleep after more drugs had been pumped into her.

Delia began to cry.

Ian held her hand. There was no point in depriving herself of sleep. Nothing more could have been done that night. "Go to bed, Delia. Try to get some rest."

"I want to know what happened at the police station."

Harry stood by the fireplace. The news on that front was more encouraging.

"As far as the police are concerned Grantley is a raving lunatic. He confessed to everything, including the murder of his wife, but he told them he did it in the name of science and for the *'advancement of mankind.'* He went into a rant at one stage. He said he must be allowed to bring the ghost of Candice Freeman back to life in order to continue his work." He looked at her sitting in the armchair. "You were the prototype. He planned to resurrect ghosts all over the world if he succeeded in bringing you back from the dead. I considered putting my name on the waiting list."

"Why did he kill his wife?" she asked.

"It was during the experimental stage. He used her to test the chemicals."

"He put her in that box?"

"Yes. He had to know if the chemicals would preserve the body in the way he thought they would.

Three days later he removed her internal organs and found they had. He burnt her remains in a furnace."

"Son of a bitch," Candice muttered.

"What makes it all the more amazing is that he expected to achieve celebrity status through his crimes. He thinks he would have been regarded as a hero, a brilliant man respected by all. He planned to write a book about it. There would have been interviews and TV appearances, maybe even a film." He looked at Candice again. "You could have played yourself if Hollywood knocked on his door. It would have been your best performance yet."

She shook her head in disbelief.

"Grantley was in the process of buying Brook Cottage when he murdered his wife. He made an offer the moment it went on the market," Harry went on. "When he arrived in the village it was important he had privacy. A newcomer attracts attention and he couldn't allow that to happen. He had to prepare for Sam's abduction so he devised a plan to shift that attention elsewhere. He arranged for a spate of burglaries to take place. While we were focused on home security he was able to go about his work unnoticed."

"So he was behind the burglaries," Candice said.

"Yeah. Grantley didn't play a part in them directly but he made sure they happened. When that was in hand he proceeded to the next phase. It was the most important one of all. You had to be prepared for your journey back to mortality. It wasn't just a case of reciting words from the Book of the Dead. You had to be a willing participant. The only way he could do that was by gaining control of you."

"And so the disappearances began," she said.

"Every time you vanished he took you to the

basement. It became your classroom. You knew what was going to happen to Sam long before it did but only when he *allowed* you to know. When you were with us you were oblivious to what was going on. This afternoon when Grantley summoned you for the final time you were completely under his control. He could have sent you out to kill everyone in the village with that dagger and you would have done so without knowing anything about it."

Candice turned to Delia. Even now she struggled to understand. "How could a book give him the power to do this?"

Delia had composed herself. She was thinking calmly and rationally.

"The Palaranti Book of the Dead stands on a par with the Ark of the Covenant in terms of its archaeological worth. I didn't believe it existed. Very few did. The Palaranti were said to have been an ancient people descended directly from God. Scholars and philosophers have debated their existence for years but nothing was ever proven and their story passed into legend. Seeing Grantley in possession of the book today came as a huge shock. He has stumbled across a truly remarkable discovery. It would have brought him worldwide acclaim had he not chosen to use it for darker purposes."

"So while the book is still out there Grantley could take control of me again," Candice said, alarmed.

Delia shook her head. "No. He would have to be in possession of it."

"And there's no chance of that happening while he's in a prison cell," Harry added. "Or a padded one which is probably where he'll end up."

Candice lapsed into thought and recalled an occasion when Grantley summoned her without being in possession of the book. "What about the time he and

Emily went to London? He didn't have the book with him then but still had control over me. I was gone for three days."

"He photographed the parts he needed and saved them on his mobile phone," Harry told her. "When it was time to summon you he did it from the men's room. That threat is gone too. He won't have access to his phone in prison either."

Candice was more concerned about the men's room part of his answer. "He called me from the toilet?"

"That's technology for you," Ian said.

She wasn't impressed and pulled a face at him.

Harry encouraged Candice to be positive. It had been a worrying time for her and everyone but it was over and there would have been no going back. Books and mobile phones were no longer a cause for concern.

"You have nothing to worry about," he said. "I spent two hours listening to Grantley telling the police how ghosts are all around us and it's his mission to bring them back to life. If they could have put him in a straitjacket they would have done it there and then. He'll spend the rest of his days in prison or an institution for the criminally insane. The book will end up in a museum after years of research has been carried out on it. As for his phone, are we really going to make an issue of that?"

Delia agreed. "Mr Indigo is right. Grantley and the Book of the Dead will never see the light of day again."

"Black, Delia," Harry said with a heavy sigh.

"It's very kind of you to offer but I can't drink tea without milk. Anyway, I've just had a cup." She stood up. "I think I *will* go to bed."

Harry shook his head in defeat as Candice and Ian wished her goodnight.

Delia paused in the doorway and looked at them

before leaving. Heavy eyes above lips trying to smile was what they saw. "Thank you for being so kind to me. I didn't know what friendship was until I came here."

She left without saying another word.

"You're right about her," Ian said to Candice. "She is one hell of a gal."

The doorbell rang.

"I wonder who that is?" Harry said.

"It's too early for carol singers," Candice answered.

They looked at Ian.

"Do you want me to see who it is?"

"If it wouldn't be too much trouble," Harry replied.

Ian grinned and left the room.

"Hello, Brenda," he said, opening the front door. "I'm afraid Delia has gone to bed. It's been a difficult few days for her and she needs to rest."

"I haven't come to see Delia. I'm here to see Candice."

The vicar was stunned by her reply.

"Can I come in?"

Ian recovered his composure and stood aside in the entrance. "Yes, I'm sorry. You'd better come through."

Brenda went inside but stopped to allow Ian to enter the lounge first.

"You have a visitor," he said to Candice.

Brenda appeared beside him. Astonishment spread her face when she saw her sitting in the armchair. She caught her breath, hands shaking, but wasn't fearful. There was nothing to be afraid of. Candice was her friend and wouldn't have harmed her but seeing her came as a shock.

"My God, we didn't imagine it. You really are here."

Candice stood. "You can see me?"

"Yes. I saw you on the green this afternoon while we waited for the ambulance to arrive. Everyone saw you."

"Everyone?"

Candice looked at Harry. Her eyes said *what the hell do I do now?*

He was just as surprised and waved at Brenda in the hope of attracting her attention. She hadn't so much as glanced at him. "Hello. Second ghost in the room."

Brenda didn't acknowledge his presence.

"It's just you then," he said to Candice.

"Bren, can you see him too?" she asked, pointing to where he stood.

"Who?"

Candice looked at him again and pleaded for help. "Come on, Harry. Give me a hand with this."

He shrugged his shoulders and allowed himself to be seen. "Evening."

"Fucking hell!" Brenda gasped, backing away.

Now she was afraid.

"It's okay, Bren. He's with me," Candice reassured her.

Brenda's mind was spinning out of control. It was incredible to have been in the presence of one ghost. Two was nothing short of unbelievable. "With you?... he's with... What the fuck is going on?"

Candice nodded towards Ian. "Don't swear in front of a vicar, babe. They don't like that sort of stuff."

"It would be nice to have a tad less of it," Ian said.

"But... but... but..."

"No, when you turn the lawnmower on it goes phut, phut, phut," Harry corrected her.

"I need to sit down," Brenda announced.

"Good idea. Use the armchair," Candice replied.

"The sofa might be better," Harry suggested. He looked at Brenda kindly. "That way when you faint we can lay you out on it."

"Who the hell are you?" she snapped.

"I'm Harry Black. That is to say Black. Not pink, brown, yellow, orange or blue but Black."

"I think I've got that," Brenda said.

"Good. It is quite important."

The mind that was spinning gathered speed to the point that it threatened to depart Brenda's head. She sat in the armchair and turned to Ian in a daze.

"Is there any chance of getting a drink in this house?"

"Of course. What would you like? Tea? Coffee?"

"Whisky. No ice. In the biggest glass you've got."

Ian went to inspect the drinks cabinet. "We have Kahlúa," he told her.

"Close enough."

"Don't give her a glass. I think Brenda would be happier with the bottle," Harry said. "We have some antifreeze in the garage if you would like something stronger?"

Now Brenda was seated and there was no danger of her falling down Candice took control of the situation.

"Okay, let's take a moment to collect ourselves. Breathe in and breathe out," she said.

"Candice, I'm not having a baby," Brenda told her.

"It wouldn't be wise at your age."

"What's that supposed to mean?"

"By the time you put them through college you'd be a hundred and twenty-five."

"I'm not that old."

"I've seen your drivers licence. It's carved on a stone

553

tablet."

"Bitch," Brenda muttered.

Candice looked at Ian as he handed their unexpected guest her drink. "You might wanna cover your ears. This is so fucking great!" she said, a huge smile lighting her face.

It was clear that Candice was happy for Brenda to have known of her existence. They were sparring with one another like they had in life and she realised how much she had missed it, but it was equally clear that she hadn't taken into consideration the problems that would have arisen from being in the public eye again.

"It would be great if it wasn't for the fact that everyone in the village has seen you," Harry pointed out.

"Oh yeah. I let that one get past me." Candice considered those problems now and concern welled up inside her. "I'm gonna be on the ten o'clock news."

"It's just as well you feel comfortable around cameras," Harry said.

"It's not that I'm worried about. I don't have a thing to wear and the shops are closed. I wonder if I have time to do my hair," she added in afterthought.

"I can't help thinking we're straying from the point," Ian said. "If everyone in the village has seen you your secret is out. Something like this would go global. It changes everything, not just for you but for every other ghost."

"Yeah, but if I wore my hair up it would look really cool."

"I don't know. I prefer it down," Harry said.

Candice pushed it up with her hands. "You don't like it like this?" she asked, pouting her lips at him.

"Now you come to mention it..."

Ian cleared his throat by way of focusing their attention.

"Up or down, Ian is right. We have a major problem," Harry said, returning to more pressing matters. He looked at Brenda making short work of her drink. "Are you sure that everyone saw her?"

"Well, I can't say it was everyone but I know Maggie and Ron did. Prudence and Sheila too."

"Sheila knows?" Ian asked.

"Yes. She asked me to send you home."

He wasn't looking forward to telling her that he had known of Candice's existence for the past year.

"When Samantha was taken to hospital we went back to the pub and discussed it. I said I would come here to speak to you. They're waiting for me to report back to them."

Candice and Harry looked at each other without comment.

Brenda had become more at ease with the situation and relaxed. The Kahlúa helped but it was seeing Candice again that brought a smile to a face that had worn shock and amazement. "I can't believe I'm talking to you like this. You're a ghost. I didn't think they existed. How can such a thing be possible?"

"I didn't move on, Bren. I was lucky I guess. I loved too many people, you included. Most of all I loved this guy. Harry became my world in life and remains so in death. I don't know what I would do without him."

Brenda was puzzled. "You knew this man when you were alive? Why didn't you tell me about him?"

"That will take some explaining. I'll bring you up-to-speed later. Right now I have to figure out what to do next. It doesn't matter how many people have seen me. This is a small village and word will soon get around."

"I think there's a reason why they saw you," a voice came from the door.

"Delia, you're meant to be resting," Ian said.

"I heard you talking. It's nice to see you again, Brenda."

"You too. Are you okay?"

"Yes, thank you." She went in and sat down. "As you will have gathered, I'm aware of Candice's presence too."

"This village is full of surprises," Brenda replied.

Ian clarified for her benefit. "Delia is a paranormal investigator. She's been helping us to resolve some issues we've had recently."

"Grantley?"

"Yes," Delia said. "The full story will be made known when the police have completed their enquiries but he came to Cloverdale St Mary with the intention of bringing Candice back to life. In order to do so he needed a host body. He chose Samantha. That was why he kidnapped her."

"What did you mean just now?" Harry asked. "You said there was a reason why Candice has been seen."

"I think Grantley enjoyed a measure of success."

Delia directed the rest of what she had to say to Candice herself. "The transfer of your spirit into Samantha's body hadn't taken place but in controlling you Grantley brought you to a level of human existence. That was why Brenda and the others were able to see you. You became visible to those you loved, people who loved you. That enabled them to see you again. I don't think it applies to everyone in the village. It was just a select few."

"People I wanted to tell anyway," Candice pondered.

"It didn't last long but for a short while on that green

today you were alive, not in terms of flesh and blood but emotionally. It was enough to open a door which allowed that love to come through. Now it has closed again but what entered through that doorway is still here because it was present to begin with. Love reaches out to love and holds on irrespective of what obstacles are placed before it. It crashes through barriers because it is what it is. The most powerful force known to man."

Candice looked at Brenda. She was so glad to be able to talk to her. "Let's take this out to the garden. We have some catching up to do."

Brenda followed her out of the room. A moment later she returned for her glass. "I still need this," she told a grinning Ian.

*

Delia didn't wait for them to return. She went back to bed. She was asleep within a minute of her head resting on the pillow.

Candice and Brenda spoke privately for half an hour. Candice told her how Harry had haunted Meadow Cottage prior to her moving in and continued to do so thereafter. She told her how they fell in love, how he left because he didn't want her to waste her life on him. How, after she died, he came back to spend eternity with her.

Brenda was surprised to hear this. She had no idea what had happened because Candice protected their secret well. Knowing it now answered many questions. Little unexplained things that puzzled her at the time became clear in light of the disclosure that Candice had been sharing Meadow Cottage with a ghost. Now she was a ghost too and the future seemed brighter to a woman who thought it held no promise.

Candice asked if she and Mike would be interested in moving to Cloverdale St Mary and was glad to hear the answer was yes. Brenda and Mike had discussed it at length and would keep an eye on properties in the village. They didn't know when the opportunity would present itself but if something became available they would look into it. That may have happened sooner than expected and Candice pointed out something that Brenda hadn't considered. Grantley would have no use for Brook Cottage from a prison cell. She told her she would keep them informed of developments.

They returned to the lounge and Brenda left soon after.

Ian walked her back to the Coaching Inn where she advised Mike and the others of how the situation stood. They hung on Brenda's every word and welcomed the prospect of continuing their friendship with Candice, an association from beyond the grave. It was unbelievable. It was impossible. It defied all logical explanation. It was the most wonderful thing to have ever happened.

Maggie and Miss Blunt in particular looked forward to seeing her again. They remembered in private reflection when Candice had arrived in the village.

'DON'T SIT THERE!' Maggie had shouted at her the first time they met in the Coaching Inn.

'You Americans are all the same, woefully lacking in manners and respect,' Miss Blunt had attacked during a vetting process that did not go well. *'There will never be a place for the likes of you here.'*

Maggie had been abrupt with Candice out of panic because the stool she was about to sit on was unsafe. She apologized immediately and both women laughed about it over a drink. Miss Blunt delivered her broadside because she thought Candice was a bitch and didn't like her. That meeting didn't end in laughter. War had been declared and people ran to air raid shelters when the sirens sounded. How times had changed. No one expected a bond to form between them that even death couldn't break.

*

"I hope Delia is right and no one else in the village knows about you," Harry said as he stared through the lounge window.

Candice had done nothing to warrant it but he almost expected to see an angry mob march on Meadow Cottage shouting 'Drive the witch out!' They lived in the country. People had access to pitchforks.

"What she said made sense to me. I guess we'll know for sure over the next couple of days," she replied.

"We'll know by breakfast tomorrow. You're forgetting the village grapevine. That works faster than a speeding bullet."

Candice pointed to the ceiling and made a joke of it. "Is it a bird? Is it a plane? No, it's the jam lady talkin' over her garden gate."

Harry actually looked up.

"Have you decided what to do? About those who *do* know?" he asked.

The time for joking was past. Candice had reached a difficult decision but in some ways it was the easiest she had ever made.

"I'm gonna speak to them later this evening. I told Bren to get everyone together at the Coaching Inn for nine o'clock. I would like Martin, Janet and Mel to be there too. She's gonna call them."

Harry didn't think that was a good idea and advised caution. "Are you sure that's wise? The more people who know, the more chance there is of everyone finding out."

"Martin and Jan should be in the loop, especially after what happened to Sam. She's gonna find it hard to get back to normal when she's discharged from hospital. I want them to know I'll be here looking out for her."

Harry nodded. There was no doubting her good intentions. "Yes, I can see why you would want to do that but I have to question your judgement in wanting Mel to be present. She's just a child. Aside from the fact that she may be frightened she might let something slip to one of her friends. Children don't keep secrets, they get excited and blurt things out. If that happens you *will* be on the ten o'clock news."

Candice was aware of the dangers but felt it was a chance she had to take. "I can't keep it from her. Everyone else would know and Mel would be left out in the cold. It wouldn't be fair. As for being scared, I don't think she will. She might be anxious at first but that's something we can work through."

"You would be asking a ten year-old to cope with a situation that many adults would struggle with."

"She's a bright kid. She's got more about her than people give her credit for. I wouldn't want her to know if I thought she couldn't handle it. Sam would rather she knew too. It tears her apart that she can't tell her the truth. She hasn't said as much but I've seen it in her eyes, the way she looks at her when we're together. She feels bad because Mel can't share in what we have. It's time I put that right."

Harry remained sceptical but realised he had prompted a discussion about something that may not have been an issue. The question of whether Melanie should have been told of Candice's presence wasn't for them to address. That decision would be made by others. "Martin and Janet might not want her to know."

Candice had prepared for that possibility. She had thought everything through very carefully. "If that's the case I'll respect their wishes. Maybe in time I could persuade them, get them to look at it differently. Irrespective of how long it takes, I want her to know I'm here."

"It's very brave of you."

"No it's not. I'm doin' bricks in my underwear. Will you come with me?"

Harry smiled. "How can I say no when you look at me through those sad, doggy-brown eyes?"

"My eyes are blue."

"Oh yeah," he said, squinting to look at her. "I never noticed that before."

"Let me refresh my memory. You did swear undying love for me, right?"

"Of course I did. How long have you been blonde?"

A change of subject was called for.

"Have you seen Emily since Sam and Delia got rescued 'an stuff?" she asked. "I thought she would have come over this evening."

Gone was the jovial banter. In its place came a look of concern.

"I saw her after they were taken to hospital. She's not doing very well. I said I would stop by later."

"What do you mean, she's not doing very well?"

Harry wasn't surprised that Candice hadn't seen the

crisis behind the drama. She had been involved in what happened at Brook Cottage directly. It was understandable that she would have become side-tracked and had yet to consider the repercussions.

"I don't know if she loves Grantley but she thinks a lot of him. That he was capable of doing something like this has devastated her."

Candice was disgusted with herself. She saw the repercussions now. "My God, I didn't think. She must be going through hell."

"She told me she's leaving the village."

"What!"

"She said she doesn't know how to face people. She feels guilty by association. Having feelings for Grantley makes her as bad as he is."

"That's crap."

"It's the shock talking. I don't think she will leave Cloverdale St Mary for one moment, this is her home and always will be, but it will take a long time for her to recover from this."

For Candice to have considered leaving the village was one thing, for Emily to have spoken of it was quite another. She *was* Cloverdale St Mary. It was her and people like her that made the village special. Emily was sanity in a world gone mad. She was the calming voice that rose above the madness and made it normal again. She was the first person people turned to when they needed a friend.

"How can one man fuck up so many lives?" Candice said.

"Ian would speak of forgiveness, of showing tolerance and turning the other cheek, but I hate Grantley with a passion."

"You were right about him. We should have listened to you."

"I was wrong about him being an alien."

"Two out of three ain't bad. You said there was something sinister about that crate when he moved in and that he was involved in the burglaries. You had it nailed, Harry."

"Actually, it's two out of four. I thought he was a grave robber as well."

"It wouldn't surprise me if we found out he is. That man is capable of anything. The bottom line is you were on the money and we didn't take you seriously." Candice grinned. "It wasn't all M.O.C."

"I wasn't much help to you though. I should have done more."

"There was nothing more you *could* have done."

Harry didn't answer.

The crimes committed by Grantley left self-recrimination all around. Candice blamed herself for him being in the village. Emily blamed herself for falling in love. Harry blamed himself for not protecting Candice to better effect.

She knew it was a conversation they needed to have but didn't pursue it now. It would have to wait for another day.

"Don't waste time talking to me, go see Emily. I'll meet you in the Coaching Inn at nine. Try to get her to come too. She doesn't have to worry about facing us. We're her family."

"I'll put it to her but it might be too soon," Harry replied. "Where is this meeting taking place? I assume it won't be in the bar."

"Bren said Jill and Deborah are working this evening.

That will allow Maggie and Ron to get away for a while. I figure we can talk in their lounge or the garden."

"Okay. I'll see you at nine."

Harry faded from view.

Thirty-seven

Melanie sipped from a glass of lemonade in Maggie and Ron's private garden. She hadn't said a word since she and her parents arrived. Normally she would have played with Ron and Maggie's Labrador, Barney, but he was in a lazy mood lying a short distance away and she hadn't gone to say hello to him.

Martin and Janet felt it would have been better if Melanie didn't know about Candice but she overheard them talking after Brenda called. When she heard she had been seen in the village she wanted to know more. Martin tried to coax her into thinking she had misunderstood but Candice was right. Melanie *was* a bright kid. She soon realised that her dream had come true. Her best friend had kept her promise and come home.

Martin and Janet were stunned by what Brenda told them. They never believed in ghosts but hearing that Candice was in Cloverdale St Mary a year after her death forced them to accept the impossible. How Melanie would have responded to it was another matter. The silence she had retreated to since their arrival concerned them.

All those who saw Candice on the green that afternoon were present. Maggie and Ron had set out chairs on the patio where the Copeland's, Brenda, Mike, Sheila and Miss Blunt awaited the arrival of someone they had thought lost to them. Sheila appeared uneasy about what was going to take place and looked at Ian often.

Emily had chosen not to attend.

"Are you sure you're not mistaken about this?" Janet

asked Brenda.

"I know it's hard to believe but I've spoken to her this evening. She'll be here soon and you'll see for yourself."

Janet glanced at her daughter anxiously. She wished Becky had been present. She was older than Melanie and more confident but Ian and Sheila didn't want her to know what was happening. Not yet at least. Janet regretted their decision. Melanie may have found this easier had she been in the company of another child.

Miss Blunt recognized her misgivings, Martin's too, but she felt their fears were unfounded. It was impossible to know how Melanie would have reacted to seeing a ghost but she and Candice shared a special bond in life and it was unlikely she would have ran screaming into the night. This wasn't the stuff of nightmares. It was a reunion of friends. That aside, Miss Blunt wondered how she would have reacted herself.

Not a day went by when she didn't think of Candice, of how war turned to peace and together they made the equestrian centre a success. In the weeks and months after her death Miss Blunt would have given anything to have seen her again. Now she was going to but she had mixed feelings about it. Why hadn't Candice made her presence known to them sooner? Why did she allow them to mourn her passing when there was no need to? The good outweighed the bad but she couldn't help feeling that Candice could have saved a lot of people a lot of pain.

Maggie was of the same opinion but to a lesser extent. She just wanted Candice to be a part of her life again, a life that had been all the better for knowing her but lost some of its sparkle when she died. That was what bereavement did. It took away the gloss and left a dull undercoat in memory of what had been.

She saw her at the bottom of the garden and smiled.

"Candice!" Melanie called excitedly.

She jumped from her chair and ran to her. She paid no attention to the man standing at her side.

It was clear from Melanie's outstretched arms that she intended to embrace her but Candice couldn't allow the attempt to be made.

"No, Mel, you can't touch me," she said calmly.

"Why not? Don't you like me anymore?"

Candice smiled and went down on one knee in front of her. What she would have given to have held her hands. To have smoothed her hair. To have made contact in a physical sense. "Like you? I love you, sweetheart, but we can't touch each other."

"I don't understand," Melanie said.

It was the key moment and it had to be handled delicately.

"Listen to me, Mel. You know I wouldn't let anything bad happen to you, don't you? You know you can trust me."

"Yes."

"Okay. I'm gonna hold out my hand and I want you to press your finger on it. Do it slowly. I'm not gonna tell you what will happen 'cos you're a smart chick and you'll get it right away. Just remember, there's nothing to be scared of."

"Okay."

Candice held out her right hand, the palm facing up.

Melanie put her forefinger to it. It passed through into thin air and she gasped.

"It's all right, don't worry. Are you okay?"

"Y-yes."

Candice smiled again and held out both hands. "Okay, gimme ten low."

Melanie slapped thin air once more as her hands passed through hers.

"Gimme ten high."

The same result.

Melanie laughed at a game she had played many times before but not with this outcome.

"You see? I'm here but we can't touch one another. If you tried to hug me you'd go straight through and fall on your butt. That's no way for a smart chick to go, is it?"

"No," Melanie giggled.

"So we're cool?"

"Yes."

"Okay. Let's go talk to your mom and dad."

Melanie led her back to the others.

Harry was impressed. He had voiced concerns about Melanie seeing Candice in her ghostly form but in doing so failed to take into consideration the obvious. If something that might have frightened a child was made to look like a game they would have no reason to be afraid.

"That was very well done," he said to her.

She grinned at the compliment.

Mike stood when they arrived. He hadn't seen Candice on the green. Brenda left the search party at Cross Drummond at 1:00 p.m. but he stayed longer and was still there when Samantha made her escape. Seeing Candice now was how he saw her in life. It was as if she had stopped by to say hello, popping in for a cup of tea and a chat while she happened to be passing.

"You still know how to make an entrance," he told her.

"It was the first thing they taught me at drama school."

Martin stood too. He couldn't believe his eyes. "My God. It's true."

"Hi, Martin."

"It's incredible," he said, looking her up and down.

Candice examined herself. T-shirts and ripped jeans had always been her preferred choice of casual wear and she used the way she was dressed to joke and lighten the moment. "I was gonna change into something more elegant but the shops are closed. I didn't have time to do my hair either."

Martin was forced to sit down again.

Ron looked at the familiar face standing beside her. "Hello, Harry. Long time no see."

"Hello, Ron."

"Brenda told us you were at Meadow Cottage too but didn't say why. Where do you come into all this?"

"It's a long story. If this was a book it would be a sequel."

Candice frowned and looked at them in turn. "Excuse me. I know you guys wanna catch up but I'm the star here. This is about me."

Harry gestured to the ground. "The floor is yours."

Mike gestured to his chair. Candice may have been a ghost and in no need of it but he was happy to give it up for her.

"Thank you, Mike," she said, sitting.

She looked at the others in a moment of preparedness. There was only one way to begin a discussion of this sort and what followed was typical Candice Freeman.

"I guess you're wondering why I've called you all together like this."

"Why did you hurt us so?" Miss Blunt asked.

It wasn't her intention to come straight out with it. Her emotions had gotten the better of her.

Candice felt her sorrow as she had done countless

times before and apologized. The Terror of Cloverdale St Mary wasn't hard and abrasive now. She was crying. "I'm sorry, Pru. Please don't be upset."

"I've missed you."

It was the first time anyone had heard Miss Blunt sacrifice her respect for the English language by apostrophising a word.

"And I've missed you, being able to talk to you like this, being a part of your life. I wanted to make my presence known to you. I wanted you all to know but I couldn't. The more people who knew about me the more chance there was of everyone finding out. If that had happened this village would have been swamped by reporters and paranormal investigators. You know how the press descended on the place when I died. It would have been like that all the time so I couldn't say anything."

"You felt you couldn't trust us?" Maggie asked.

"I didn't wanna put you in a position where you had to watch every word in fear of saying the wrong thing. I know I can trust you, Maggie, but it would have been unfair of me to put you under that sort of pressure. I figured it was better you didn't know. In retrospect it was a bad call. I've come to realise that we all need each other, in good times and bad. The events of the past few days is proof of that."

Martin and Janet held hands.

Sheila was less apprehensive now. She felt at ease in Candice's company. Listening to her speak had dispelled her uncertainty and she joined the conversation. "Ian told me he knew of your presence for the past year. Who else knows about you?"

"Emily and Samantha. It was just those three until today."

"Emily knew?" Miss Blunt asked.

"She didn't say anything because I asked her not to. The same goes for Ian and Sam. Don't think badly of them for keeping it from you. They would have told you if they could. Ian and Emily knew from day one. We told Sam when she moved into Meadow Cottage. She had to be informed then. If someone is gonna share their home with a couple of ghosts they have a right to know about it."

"Which brings us to you," Ron said, looking at Harry again. "How long have you been in the village?"

"I never left it. I've been here all the time. Thank you for the send off by the way. The flowers were lovely."

"You owe me £20," Ron told him.

"What?"

"You died before you settled your tab."

Harry raised his eyebrow. "I can't be held responsible for that. I would have paid you if a faulty power drill hadn't blown the lights and me with them."

"Don't give me excuses. Give me twenty quid."

"You don't want it after all this time surely?"

"Businesses have gone under for less. Maggie and I are running a pub, not a charity."

"I'll go to the cash point later."

"Make sure you do."

"Ahem," Candice sounded, clearing her throat.

"That means she wants us to be quiet," Harry said to Ron.

"Oh, she uses signals, does she? Maggie just tells me to shut up."

"Shut up," she said.

"See?"

"Does it work?"

Ron's failure to answer proved that it did.

Janet looked at Melanie. Still she paid no interest in Harry. Her attention was focused entirely on Candice.

"How did Sam react when she found out about you?" she asked. "We never saw a change in her."

"She was apprehensive to begin with. I guess that was to be expected but she got used to having us around. It troubled her that she couldn't tell you guys. You especially, Mel. She didn't want you to miss out but like I said there was no other way. I'm sorry we couldn't tell you. I really thought it was for the best."

"I wish Sam was here now," Melanie said sadly.

Candice smiled to reassure her. "She'll be home soon. Then we'll all be together again, like we were before."

Martin turned his thoughts to earlier that afternoon when he saw Samantha stagger across the green, how she fell to her hands and knees while making her escape from Brook Cottage, how she crawled and somehow got to her feet again. How he thought she had died in his arms when he reached her.

"The others said they saw you while we waited for the ambulance to arrive. Did you know what was happening in that basement?"

"No. I was there but I didn't know what was happening."

"You were there?" Mike asked.

Candice looked at their surprised faces. With Melanie present she couldn't go into details, it would have been too distressing for her, but she told them what little she could. "You'll hear the full story when the police announce their findings but Grantley had an insane notion that he could bring me back to life. He was gonna use Sam to do it.

"He'd been controlling me from the day he arrived in the village. He had some kind of power over me. When I was under his influence I didn't know where I was or what I was doing. I remembered nothing of it afterwards. This afternoon he summoned me to Brook Cottage. He was ready to proceed with his plan. I don't know how but Sam knocked him unconscious. The moment that happened the spell was broken and I came back to myself. Delia was tied up and told me to get her out. She said Sam had been drugged. She had to get away before it took effect."

"Why was she?..." Martin hesitated. He didn't want Melanie to know Samantha was naked at the time of her escape. "... The way she was?"

"Grantley said it was necessary."

The obvious question couldn't be asked. Not with his youngest daughter sitting beside him.

The police had told Martin and Janet all they could but Samantha's partial statement was private and confidential. It had to remain so until it was completed. Newton and Drysdale knew she had been raped but were not at liberty to divulge it, not even to her parents. Samantha told Martin and Janet little during their brief hospital visit. She hadn't spoken of the sexual abuse. She was tired and needed to rest. She had neither the strength or the emotional capacity to have confided something so personal.

"I called the hospital before we came out," Janet said. "They told me Sam is sleeping under sedation."

"Sedation?" Maggie asked.

Like Martin, she was guarded in her response with Melanie in attendance.

"They thought it would help."

Everyone knew the reason hidden in her reply.

"I'm glad she's in a private room and not on a ward," Candice said.

Janet looked at her curiously. It hadn't occurred to her that Candice would have seen Samantha after her escape. "You've been to the hospital?"

Candice wasn't sure how to gauge her reaction. She took the surprise in her voice to be disapproval. "I only stayed for a short time. I sat with her for a while after you guys left. I hope you don't mind."

"No. I'm glad you were there for her."

Melanie realised her mother was close to tears and held her hand. "It's all right, mummy. Sam is coming home soon."

"Of course she is, darling."

Janet embraced her. How she didn't break down amazed everyone present.

Candice thought of Samantha in hospital and Emily at home with just her misplaced feelings of guilt to keep her company. She had refused Harry's invitation to join them point blank. It would have been the best thing for her, to have been with people who understood and wouldn't have condemned a decent woman for having feelings for someone, but she couldn't bring herself to face them. Tonight she had to be on her own. She needed to talk to George's picture on the wall and beg his forgiveness.

"I hoped Emily might have come this evening. She's very upset," Candice said.

"I went to see her earlier," Miss Blunt replied. "As you say, she is finding this difficult but I am sure she will rally in a day or two."

"She will with our support," Sheila said.

Maggie was determined to help Emily in any way possible and echoed sentiments shared by all. "That we'll do everything we can goes without saying. Grantley had us all fooled. I can't imagine how she must be feeling."

Ron wasn't the kind of man who dealt in I-told-you-so's but he distanced himself from the mood of self-blame that had descended on the gathering. "He didn't have me fooled. I said there was something shifty about him from the start. People are only as nice as he appeared to be when they have something to hide."

"Well said," Harry concurred. It was like listening to himself in full cry.

"You didn't trust him either?" Ron asked.

"Didn't trust him, didn't like him, didn't have any time for him. The man is a low-life. Scum. A blot on the landscape. A cancerous growth that should be cut out and..."

"Harry, there are children present," Candice interrupted.

"Ron may be a little immature at times but I wouldn't call him a child."

"I was talking about Mel."

"What do you mean, immature?" Ron snapped.

"You are a bit of a muppet, aren't you? You only have to look at the way you hold a cricket bat to know that."

Maggie roared with laughter. "Oh Harry, I'm so glad to see you again. I've missed you as much as I've missed Candice."

Ron wasn't laughing. "That twenty quid has gone up to thirty."

"You can't do that!" Harry protested.

"Inflation. It's a bugger, isn't it?"

The others were amused by this departure into

matters less serious but the jovial mood didn't last long. It was replaced with the question of how to proceed when Miss Blunt turned the conversation back to the reason for this meeting.

"What do we do now?" she asked Candice. "The concerns you had over what might have happened if you made your presence known to us still apply. There is a possibility that we might let something slip during an unguarded moment. One word out of place could result in the whole world knowing of your existence."

Ian made his first contribution to the discussion. It wasn't sensational, nor was it profound. It was the only answer that could have been given to a question that had to be asked. "You'll have to be careful in what you say and do. It won't be as hard as you think. Emily has known of Harry's existence for seven years. I've known about Candice for a year and Harry for eighteen months. We haven't let anything slip."

Not for the first time today, Sheila failed to hide her surprise. Her husband's social circle was wider than she thought.

"How many ghosts do you know?" she asked him.

"Only Harry and Candice. And Sam Two Coats."

"Who is Sam Two Coats?"

An unexpected voice answered for him.

"He was at the Battle of the Little Bighorn but General Custer didn't like him very much so he shot him."

"Delia, what are you doing here? You should be sleeping," Candice said, greeting the new arrival.

"I woke an hour ago and couldn't get off again. My body clock is all over the place."

"That is understandable taking into account what you have been through," Miss Blunt said sympathetically. "How are you feeling, my dear?"

"I'm okay. Thank you for asking. I'm a bit hungry though. I stopped by the tearoom in the hope of buying some of that fabulous cake but it was closed."

"That's a real problem around here. It's impossible to buy a dress after eight o'clock," Candice said.

Maggie grinned and rose from her chair. "I'll make you a sandwich. Do you like ham?"

"Yes, but I don't want to put you to any trouble," Delia said.

"It's no trouble."

Ron stood up too. "It will be if you eat anything Maggie makes. I'll attend to it."

"I'm quite capable of making a sandwich," she protested.

Candice hadn't sampled Maggie's culinary delights but had heard the horror stories relating to those less fortunate. "I would go with Ron's offer," she told Delia, advising caution. "There would be three ghosts in this garden if Maggie made it."

"I make excellent sandwiches," she insisted.

Ron was having none of it. "It's been a trying day and I'm sure Delia doesn't want to end it by having her stomach pumped. Would you like mustard?"

"Please."

He went inside.

Mike fetched another chair for Delia and received thanks and an apology in return. This gathering was meant to be private and the gatecrasher in their midst explained her reasons for being there.

"I apologize for coming here uninvited but as I couldn't sleep I thought it would be beneficial if I joined you instead of counting imaginary sheep at Meadow Cottage. I may be able to answer any questions you might have regarding Candice and Mr Burgundy."

"Who?" Sheila asked.

"She means me," Harry sighed.

Delia turned to Maggie and issued a second apology. "I'm afraid I wasn't entirely honest with your staff. I told them I was expected. That's why they let me in. I do apologise for the intrusion and for being less than truthful."

"It's no intrusion, you're very welcome here," Maggie replied. "I am puzzled by something though. How do *you* know about Candice?"

"Delia is a paranormal investigator. She's been helping Candice and Mr what's-his-name," Brenda said.

Harry scowled at her.

"Is that why Grantley kidnapped you? Because you found out what was going on?" Maggie asked.

"Yes, but I didn't know about Samantha. I only knew of her abduction when he took me prisoner too. I thought he was assisting me in trying to find out what was happening to Candice. I had no idea he was the one behind it all, that he was responsible. I went to Brook Cottage to discuss the investigation with him and during the conversation he gave himself away. He realised he had let the cat out of the bag and stopped me from leaving. He knocked me out and tied me up in the basement."

Candice looked at Melanie. She hung on every word that was being said and what would follow would not have been suitable for the ears of a child. She had to find a way of distracting her.

"Hey you. Let's take a walk in the garden. We've got some catching up to do."

"Okay."

Melanie went with her willingly. Barney got to his feet and trotted off after them.

"Was Sam in the basement when you regained consciousness?" Martin asked Delia.

"Yes. She told me she had been there since Friday."

"What did Grantley do to her?"

She was reluctant to answer. She could have done so in part but rape was a personal matter and not for her to discuss.

"I think it would be better if Samantha gave you the details, Mr Copeland. I couldn't presume to speak for her."

Martin pleaded with eyes that had died. In them Delia saw Samantha's pain, the agony of a father and daughter who had suffered in a way that no one should have suffered. The torture wasn't over. It was just beginning.

"I'm sorry for putting you in a difficult position, Delia, but you were there and Janet and I don't know what happened. Candice told us how Sam escaped but she doesn't know what took place prior to that." It became too much for him and he began to cry. "Please... what did he do to our little girl?"

Ian knelt beside his chair. He was concerned for his friend and tried to persuade him not to continue. "Martin, we don't have to do this now. Samantha is safe. Draw strength from that tonight."

"I need to know, Ian. Sam was in that basement for five days... He held our daughter prisoner for five days... She was naked."

Janet squeezed his hand. His distress fuelled hers and she cried too. "Martin..."

"It's killing me, Jan... I have to know..."

A father's pain outweighed words of comfort from those trying to help. A mother's anguish demanded attention from a world that accepted brutality as a matter of course. If the guilty had a right to their day in court, the innocent had a right to know the truth.

Delia answered Martin's question. She made no attempt to wipe the tears running down *her* face.

"Sam was chained to a wall. She was in her underwear. Grantley kept her in the dark for much of the time. That was when she suffered the rat bites. When he took me prisoner he left the light on. We didn't see any rats after that.

"He came to the basement often. He beat her if she didn't answer him when he spoke. He was violent towards both of us but more so to Sam. She told me he threatened to do terrible things to her. This morning he took off her underwear. When she was naked he filmed her with a camcorder.

"He summoned Candice to the basement this afternoon. She had no will of her own. She was under his control. He made her cut Sam with a dagger. It was part of a ceremony he was going to conduct... a stupid, insane ceremony... He was going to put her in a box and drown her in chemicals he had prepared. Thank God, she managed to break free."

Delia stopped in a bid to compose herself but composure wouldn't come. It was like a father's pain and a mother's anguish. Heartbreak knew no repair.

"Did he rape her?" Martin wept.

She met those dead eyes and cried openly. "Yes... I'm sorry... I couldn't do anything to help her... I promised Sam I would... but there was nothing I could do..."

Delia's distress was such that she broke down completely.

Three inconsolable people shedding tears to fill a river.

The others sat in silence and despaired for the

"Was Sam in the basement when you regained consciousness?" Martin asked Delia.

"Yes. She told me she had been there since Friday."

"What did Grantley do to her?"

She was reluctant to answer. She could have done so in part but rape was a personal matter and not for her to discuss.

"I think it would be better if Samantha gave you the details, Mr Copeland. I couldn't presume to speak for her."

Martin pleaded with eyes that had died. In them Delia saw Samantha's pain, the agony of a father and daughter who had suffered in a way that no one should have suffered. The torture wasn't over. It was just beginning.

"I'm sorry for putting you in a difficult position, Delia, but you were there and Janet and I don't know what happened. Candice told us how Sam escaped but she doesn't know what took place prior to that." It became too much for him and he began to cry. "Please... what did he do to our little girl?"

Ian knelt beside his chair. He was concerned for his friend and tried to persuade him not to continue. "Martin, we don't have to do this now. Samantha is safe. Draw strength from that tonight."

"I need to know, Ian. Sam was in that basement for five days... He held our daughter prisoner for five days... She was naked."

Janet squeezed his hand. His distress fuelled hers and she cried too. "Martin..."

"It's killing me, Jan... I have to know..."

A father's pain outweighed words of comfort from those trying to help. A mother's anguish demanded attention from a world that accepted brutality as a matter of course. If the guilty had a right to their day in court, the innocent had a right to know the truth.

Delia answered Martin's question. She made no attempt to wipe the tears running down *her* face.

"Sam was chained to a wall. She was in her underwear. Grantley kept her in the dark for much of the time. That was when she suffered the rat bites. When he took me prisoner he left the light on. We didn't see any rats after that.

"He came to the basement often. He beat her if she didn't answer him when he spoke. He was violent towards both of us but more so to Sam. She told me he threatened to do terrible things to her. This morning he took off her underwear. When she was naked he filmed her with a camcorder.

"He summoned Candice to the basement this afternoon. She had no will of her own. She was under his control. He made her cut Sam with a dagger. It was part of a ceremony he was going to conduct... a stupid, insane ceremony... He was going to put her in a box and drown her in chemicals he had prepared. Thank God, she managed to break free."

Delia stopped in a bid to compose herself but composure wouldn't come. It was like a father's pain and a mother's anguish. Heartbreak knew no repair.

"Did he rape her?" Martin wept.

She met those dead eyes and cried openly. "Yes... I'm sorry... I couldn't do anything to help her... I promised Sam I would... but there was nothing I could do..."

Delia's distress was such that she broke down completely.

Three inconsolable people shedding tears to fill a river.

The others sat in silence and despaired for the

human race and the depths to which it had sunk.

Candice saw from a distance the agony that she had taken Melanie away from and ensured she kept the little girl's back to them in order to protect her from it. They talked about their love of horses as Martin, Janet and Delia cried in hopeless abandon. They looked forward to sleep-overs and the fun they would have as they went indoors to compose themselves in private. They played with Barney and made plans for the future as today crashed and burned.

Ron returned with Delia's sandwich and put the plate on the table in front of their chairs. He knew she wasn't there to receive it. She had passed him on the way out. "It's a mess, isn't it?" he said, sitting down.

"Now they've got Grantley behind bars they should throw away the key," Mike replied. "That bastard's got a lot to answer for."

"I wish there was something I could do. I feel so bloody useless."

Maggie reached for Ron's hand. Hearing Delia's account of what happened made her feel vulnerable. She was crying too, for Samantha, Delia and herself. For the toll it would have taken on her had she suffered a similar ordeal.

"You're not useless... You're my life."

"And you, my darling disaster in the kitchen, are mine."

He kissed her and Miss Blunt looked at them in admiration. It was like she had seen Ron and Maggie for the first time. They had once been a thorn in her side, the purveyors of alcohol who encouraged late-night revelling and drunkenness. Now she saw who they really were. Two people in love who felt the pain and suffering of others. That made them worthy of respect. The

Grantley's of this world would lie and cheat, they would use people for personal gain and think nothing of the chaos they left in their wake. Sometimes it was better to go back to basics and keep up with the Joneses.

It took time for everyone to regain their composure. Melanie knew something had happened in her absence but didn't question it. She knew her parents were upset and had been crying. She was a smart chick who knew a lot of things. She knew Candice was a ghost and couldn't high-five with her. She knew Samantha would be coming home soon. She knew her parents loved her. What she didn't know, what none of them knew, was the drama currently unfolding at the hospital.

*

Samantha had woken despite the sedative and launched forward in bed screaming. The doctors and nurses worked hard to calm her as she fought against them, desperate to get away. She was convinced Grantley would step from the shadows with the syringe. He was going to put her in the perspex coffin. He was going to fill it with the chemicals he had mixed. He was going to drown her.

The next time I come it won't be between your legs. It will be to kill you.

Grantley had come for her now, in a hospital room while she slept. The one place where she should have been safe.

The nightmare that awoke Samantha would wake her *every* night for the next five months. There would be no escape from it.

*

"As an expert in the paranormal field, perhaps you can shed some light on what happened this afternoon," Miss Blunt said to Delia. "Why were we able to see Candice today and at no time prior to that?"

Delia looked at the sandwich Ron had made for her. She was still hungry and wanted to eat but it would have been rude to have spoken with her mouth full.

"I think Candice achieved a level of human emotion. Love, fear, loss. I'm not sure what it was exactly but it was enough for her spirit to manifest itself in a mortal form. That was what allowed you to see her. Candice wasn't a ghost at that point. She was an entity caught between two worlds, neither one thing or another. She was what you saw on the village green; a friend concerned for her friends."

"I'm nice like that," Candice said.

"And you'll always be here?" Maggie asked.

"Forever and a day. Unless you want me to go."

"Why would we want that?"

Candice shrugged her shoulders. "I dunno. You could ask Ron but he's a bit immature sometimes."

"Why do I get the feeling I'm being ganged up on?" he said.

"You know I love you really," Candice told him. "It don't make no difference to me how you hold a cricket bat."

"It *doesn't* make a difference," Brenda corrected her. "Better yet, does not."

Harry laughed.

Brenda didn't take kindly to being a source of

amusement and narrowed her eyes at him. "What do you find so funny, Mr Yellow with just a hint of magnolia?"

"Your demand for exact English. And the name is Black."

"I thought it was Purple," Delia said, picking up her sandwich.

"You've called me every colour imaginable and I continue to find it irksome."

Candice was puzzled. She wished she had taken her dictionary with her. "Irksome? Is that a word?" she asked Brenda.

"It is, but no one has used it since the 18th century."

Harry scowled at Brenda again and remembered that he had never liked her. She had only known him for a matter of hours but the feeling was mutual.

"You're not really going to live here, are you?" he asked.

"I might," she replied.

"Oh joy."

In the overall scheme of things he preferred Grantley.

Candice watched a tired Melanie stifle a yawn and brought the evening to a close. "I think we should call it a night. It's getting late and it's well past Mel's bedtime."

Tired she may have been but Melanie didn't want to leave and was determined to stay out for as long as possible. She didn't have to go to bed. She was grown up now.

"Mummy and daddy said I could stay home from school again tomorrow. Let's have another drink," she said, picking up her empty lemonade glass.

She was bemused when everyone laughed.

"Candice is right. We're going to see Sam in the morning so you need to get some sleep," Janet told her.

"All right," Melanie conceded. "Can I see you again tomorrow, Candice?"

She smiled. "Of course you can. Give Sam a big hug for me. Tell her home isn't home without her."

"I will."

The assembled guests left Ron and Maggie's garden and a bad day ended on a positive note.

*

Delia had gone to bed. This time she stayed there. She slept safe and well in a village that would recover from the wounds inflicted on it. It would take time, there would be no quick fix, but normality would return and for some residents of Cloverdale St Mary their tomorrows would be better than their yesterdays.

The same was true for Candice and Harry as they relaxed in chairs on the decking in the back garden of Meadow Cottage at midnight.

"What are you thinking?" she asked, watching him stare at the moonlit sky.

"I was thinking how lucky we are. Look at what we have. That's a hell of a sky, isn't it?"

Candice looked to the heavens too. It was an awe-inspiring sight, specks of light shining against the backdrop of eternity in all its grandeur. Heavens that had the ability to mesmerise made being on earth worthwhile.

"It makes you wonder though. How something so beautiful can preside over something so ugly," she said.

"That's a bit harsh. You can be quite pretty when you put your mind to it."

Candice pulled a face at him that turned into a smile.

"Are you okay?" he asked.

"Yeah. Sam and Delia are safe, Grantley is behind bars and I'm here with you. What more could a girl ask for?"

"Next week's winning lottery numbers?"

"I've done the money thing, babe. It don't cut ice with me anymore."

"It *doesn't* cut ice with you anymore. Better yet, does not."

Candice laughed. "You don't like Brenda at all, do you?"

Harry laughed too. "No, can't stand the sight of her. Mike's all right but Brenda and I will never see eye-to-eye."

"That's a shame. She's one of the best."

"If Brenda is one of the best I would hate to see an example of the worst."

"That's not fair, Harry."

"You still have a lot to learn about being dead. The first thing you need to take on board is that nothing is fair."

"Do you think Sam will be okay?"

Harry raised his eyebrow. "You change subjects so quickly I sometimes wonder if you have them on wheels."

"It's gonna be hard for her to recover from this."

"Yes it will, but she's got a lot of good people in her corner. Skies like that and her family and friends will see her through. We came close to losing her but we didn't and life goes on. Sam would be the first to tell you how important that is."

Candice rested her head against the back of her chair and closed her eyes. Harry was right. Life and death were involved in a constant battle with each other, it went on every day, but today life had won and death took refuge in the darkness to lick its wounds.

"It went well tonight. Better than I expected," he said.

"What's your take on the others knowing about us? Are you glad about it or do you think it's a bad thing?"

Harry had given it a great deal of thought. He cast his mind back to when there was just one ghost in Cloverdale St Mary and Emily was the only person who knew. Now there were two and the number of people aware of their existence stood at thirteen. Fourteen if the ranting of a madman in police custody was to be believed. It seemed inconceivable to him that the numbers could have increased so dramatically but he wasn't concerned by it. On the contrary. He had every reason to be optimistic.

"I'm glad they know. It's better for them and better for us. I enjoyed being in their company this evening. It made me realise how I've missed talking to them, Ron and Maggie especially." A wry smile lit his face. It was one a mischievous child would have approved of. "I'd forgotten how much fun it is to wind up Ron."

"I saw you got a kick out of that."

"It's good that we can acknowledge everyone the next time we see them. No more watching from a distance. We can be involved again."

Candice nodded. "That's what I'm looking forward to. It's not just about continuing old friendships, it's about being a part of village life. That's what I've missed. It will be nice to get that back."

"We still have to be careful. It'll be a while before we can sit on any social committees. For every one who knows there are sixty who don't."

"Yeah, but it's nothing we can't handle."

Harry surprised Candice by performing the worst

Humphrey Bogart impersonation she had ever heard. "Just you and me, sweetheart. Together we can take on the world."

"I didn't know you could do Joan Crawford," she said, faking a compliment.

"It was Bogey."

"I'm sure you've got a handkerchief someplace. What do you wanna do from here? We can catch a late movie. One of mine is on at 2:00 a.m."

"Which one?"

"Killing Asia."

The thought of having to watch that film would have made Harry break out in a cold sweat but not tonight. Nothing was going to faze him tonight. Samantha and Delia were safe and he had re-established links with people who were close to him. More importantly, the threat to Candice was over. She wouldn't be controlled again by those with evil intentions. She wouldn't be taken away against her will. She would be with Harry until the light from the last star had gone out.

Forever and a day.

"Okay. You get the fizzy drinks and I'll bring the popcorn," he said.

They retreated to silence and listened to the stillness that surrounded them. A light breeze rustled the trees. In the distance they heard a dog barking. He had seen a cat sitting on the roof of a garden shed, using his elevated position in the hope of spying an unsuspecting snack that he could have dropped on. The cat looked at the dog but wasn't in the least bit concerned. Why should he have been? His species was far superior.

In Falworth Hospital the night staff busied themselves with their work. They walked with purpose in their stride, doctors, nurses and administrators tending to the needs of many, but no one hurried outside Samantha's door. She slept soundly, at peace in a pleasant dream where Grantley couldn't hurt her.

She was at home sitting on the decking with Candice and Harry. They talked and laughed, reflecting on a day that had been like any other. No crisis, no dramas, no emergencies. Just another day in a quiet village where friends enjoyed each others company and nothing bad ever happened. Soon they would retire to the lounge to watch the late movie. It was a film they had seen before but would enjoy watching again.

It was, after all, a modern-day classic.

THE GHOST OF CANDICE FREEMAN

About the Author

Dave Garty lives in the Southwest of England and writes in his spare time. He wrote for family and friends before making his work available to a wider audience by self-publishing. As well as writing he enjoys photography, travel, nights in, nights out and listening to music. He is currently working on his next novel, *The Ghosts of Cloverdale St Mary.*

Also available by Dave Garty

TO SHANNON FOSTER, A SON

EASTWICK AND BROWN

THE GHOST OF HARRY BLACK

THE KEEPERS AND THE KEPT

THE SECRET CHESTER DRAWERS FAN CLUB

STILETTOS AFTER DARK

FROM RAGS TO RICHES

THE LONG MARCH

NOWHERE TO RUN

THE ROCKS AND SANDS SERIES

EGYPT 1998

Printed in Great Britain
by Amazon